CHRONICLES OF DARTMOOR

ANNE MARSH CALDWELL

NONSUCH

To
CAROLINE MARTHA NEWMAN,
(The Limes, Witham,)
In remembrance of dear old Devon, and also in memory of those
who are gone to "the better land," from her affectionate friend
THE AUTHOR

First published 1866
Copyright © in this edition 2006
Nonsuch Publishing Ltd

Nonsuch Publishing Limited
The Mill, Brimscombe Port, Stroud, Gloucestershire, GL5 2QG
www.nonsuch-publishing.com

British Library Cataloguing in Publication Data.
A catalogue record for this book is available from the British Library.

ISBN 1-84588-071-4

Typesetting and origination by Nonsuch Publishing Limited
Printed in Great Britain by Oaklands Book Services Limited

CONTENTS

INTRODUCTION TO
THE MODERN EDITION

Anne Marsh Caldwell's literary career, stretching from 1834 to 1866, was as prolific as her work was consistently popular. Over the course of thirty-two years she was published twenty-nine times, both novels and historical works, in several countries, and in many languages. Described as part of a 'sisterhood' of writers of the age, including Jane Austen and Maria Edgeworth, she remains the 'most earnest of storytellers', a writer who could 'plunge beneath the surface, probe the mind, and the heart'.

Born on 9 January 1791 at Newcastle-under-Lyme, Anne Caldwell was schooled in the gentle arts of music, language and poetry, as befitted a young lady of means. While she wrote in her youth, it was for nothing so vulgar as publication. Her play *The Enchanted Island* was seemingly very much enjoyed by its privileged and limited audience. The financial circumstances which conspired to keep her talent hidden, however, were to change after her marriage.

In 1824, her husband Arthur's family's banking firm of Marsh, Stacey & Graham went bankrupt. The crash came as a result of a fraud perpetrated by Henry Fauntleroy, one of the partners, who was later hanged for the crime. The Marshs lost the bulk of their fortune and Arthur lost his half-brother Michael, who took his own life as a result.

It was at this point that Anne Marsh showed her novel *Two Old Men's Tales* to a friend, Harriet Martineau. So impressed was she, that she persuaded Mrs Marsh to have it published immediately. Her husband granted his permission for the enterprise on condition that she remain anonymous, lest it fail. *Two Old Men's Tales*, however, was an immediate success, which ran to a number of editions over a period of thirty years.

She continued to publish consistently, at a rate of almost a book a year. Of the work she produced at this point, including *Father Darcy* (1846), *Bella: a Tale of Vendée* (1847), and *The Protestant Reformation in France* (1847), by far the most popular was the novel *Emilia Wyndham* (1846).

In 1858, Anne's brother James Stafford Caldwell died and, being unmarried, left the family home, Linley Wood, to the two-week old Frederick Crofton Heath, a son of his niece. A stipulation of the will, however, was that Anne Marsh and her unmarried daughters should be allowed to live there for as long as they desired. A further condition James imposed was that Anne Marsh should change her name to Marsh Caldwell, which she did in 1860 by royal license of the Queen.

In September of 1860, the people of the village of Talke and the staff and tenantry of Linley Wood staged a great celebration for Mrs Marsh Caldwell's return. These festivities saw the gathered masses walk in procession to Linley House, headed by a brass band, and pass through some five triumphal arches on the way. Such was the respect in which she was held.

She continued to write for a number of years, before finally succumbing to ill health. On 5 October 1874, she died aged 83 at Linley Wood. A memorial stone commemorating Anne, Arthur, and their son Martin still stands in St Martin's Church, Talke O'Th'Hill, as does one in honour of her three unmarried daughters, the Misses Marsh Caldwell.

She is described by *The Athenaeum*, an influential London journal of the time, as a one who, while possessed of the qualities of the writers of her time, had greater power than any to charm or terrify. 'No writer had greater powers', they say, 'of compelling tears.' Her books, however, are rare and difficult to find, as she continued to publish anonymously. While some American editions credit Mrs Marsh, many others simply ascribe her works to the author of *Two Old Men's Tales*, or *Emilia Wyndham*.

Of her expansive list, *Chronicles of Dartmoor* was Anne Marsh Caldwell's final book, written at the age of seventy-five, and marking the final chapter of a distinguished life's work.

VOLUME I

WHAT HAS BEEN SAID BY MR SMILES

"WHILST the road communications of the country remained imperfect, the people of one part of England knew next to nothing of the people of the other parts. When a shower of rain had the effect of rendering the highways impassable, even horsemen were cautious in venturing far from home, and it was only a limited number who could afford to travel on horseback. The labouring people journeyed afoot, and the limited middle class used the waggon or the coach. But the amount of intercourse between the people of different districts—then exceedingly limited at all times—was in a country so wet as England necessarily suspended during the greater part of the year. This slight degree of communication consequently produced numerous distinct and strongly-marked local dialects, local prejudices, and local customs, which survive to this day, though they are rapidly disappearing, to the regret of many, under the influence of our improved facilities for travelling.

"Every village had its witches—sometimes of different sorts; and there was scarcely an old house but had its white lady, or moaning old man with the long beard. There were ghosts in the fens which walked on stilts, while the sprites of the hill country rode on flashes of fire. But those village witches and local ghosts have long since disappeared, excepting, perhaps, in a few less penetrable districts, where they still survive.

"Chagford, in the valley of the north Teign, is an ancient stannary and market-town, backed by a wide stretch of moor. The houses are built of moor-stone—grey, ancient-looking, and substantial—some with projecting porch and parvise room over, and granite mullioned windows. The ancient church, built of granite, with a stout steeple of the same material, its embattled porch and granite-groined vault springing from low columns, with Norman-looking capitals, forming the sturdy centre of this ancient town clump.

"A post-chaise is still a phenomenon in this place, the roads and lanes leading to it being so steep and rugged as to be but ill-adapted for springed vehicles of any sort. The upland road or track to Tavistock scales an almost precipitous hill, and though well enough adapted for the 'packhorse' of the last century, is quite unfitted for the cart and waggon traffic of this. Hence the horse with panniers maintains its ground in the Chagford district, and the double horse, furnished with a pillion for the lady riding behind, is still to be met with in the country roads.

"Among the patriarchs of the hills, the straight-breasted blue coat may yet be seen, with the shoe fastened with buckle and strap, as in the days when George the Third was king; and old women are still found retaining the cloak and hood of their youth. Old agricultural implements continue in use. The slide or sledge is seen in the fields; the flail, with its monotonous strokes, resounds from the barn floors; the corn is sifted by the windstow, the wind blowing away the chaff from the grain, when shaken out of sieves by the motion of the hand on some elevated spot; the old wooden plough is still at work; and the goad is still used to urge the yoke of oxen in dragging it along."[1]

WHAT THE AUTHOR HAS TO SAY

The previous pages, extracted from Mr Smiles's admirable work, "The Lives of the Engineers," will remind my readers that there are still in England localities difficult of access, and thus, in some degree, cut off from much communication with the rest of the world. Such are the towns and villages of Dartmoor[2] and its immediate neighbourhood. The steepness of the hills, combined with the terrible state of the roads, prevents a free intercourse with distant towns; thus the inhabitants necessarily retain old customs and old prejudices, curious dialects and much ignorance; and thus they remain stagnant, as it were, on their native moor, while the rest of England is advancing with rapid strides to a knowledge of the arts, science, and literature, scarcely ever surpassed in any age. It is while these manners and customs yet linger on Dartmoor that one who has lived on its borders, and known the dwellers there, would present them to the reader, ere "the horse with the iron hoof" brings civilization in its train, and the occupiers of the moor gradually learn new modes of speech, gain new ideas, and exercising their native shrewdness by greater intercourse with their fellow-mortals, suffer their own individuality to merge into that of the rest of mankind.

"The curious dialects" of the moor, excepting only in one or two instances, are avoided in the following story. They would be incomprehensible to the general reader, and encumber the work with unnecessary difficulties. "Witches" have given place to the "wise man" or "wise woman," in whom the people of remote districts have much confidence. Witches are not located on the moor now; nor are they spoken of with other feelings than those of dread or execration.

The village which will here be called "Lawsleigh-on-the-Moor," lies deeper in the moor than Chagford. It is not a "stannary town," only a village, with village lore, village customs, and village laws, handed down from father to son from time immemorial.

1. From "The Lives of the Engineers".
2. See Note A at end of this volume.

I

WHAT OCCURRED AT THE SMITHY AND THE CONSEQUENCES THEREOF

AT the southern entrance of the village of Lawsleigh-on-the-Moor stood the smithy. Isaac Watson, the occupier and owner, made the air ring with the strokes of his heavy hammer. It was a warm day in June, and from a side door which opened into the blacksmith's shed came forth an aged woman, in a dress of an ancient fashion, and bringing with her a bundle of knitting and a three-legged wooden stool.

"Now, mother, why do you not tell me when you are ready," said Isaac, meeting the old woman, and taking the stool from her hands; "and I cannot think why you will always take away the stool on a Saturday night! Do you think there is any harm in sitting down in my smithy on a Sunday? Eh, mother?"

"No, lad, no harm," said the old woman; "but what be the use to sit down in thy shed when thee art gone away?"

"Come sit down and make yourself comfortable," said Isaac, without replying to the query.

"Have you got much to do, Isaac?"

"Always my hands full, thank God," said Isaac; "for man must work—but I have plenty of spare time to do anything for you, so tell me what you want?"

"Nothing, lad; I be glad to see thee at work, and to know thee hast got work to do—for

> Satan finds some mischief still
> For idle hands to do."

"Ay, Satan has a better chance with the idle than with the industrious," said Isaac, "and so, mother, I will work."

"Ay, lad, ay; and I be a-going to knit."

This was Widow Simpson. Isaac Watson was her grandson; he followed the trade of his grandfather, for he had been brought up by his grandparents. Isaac was a tall, broad, burly-looking man, as strong a contrast as could well be to the small, fair, wiry-looking and aged woman his grandmother. Isaac was six feet two without his shoes. But this colossal height was well kept in check by the breadth across the shoulders, expansive chest, and stout limbs. His head was large and well set on; his complexion very dark, with a ruddy tinge in his cheeks; his hair black, crisp, and curly, his whiskers and beard plentiful, though there were occasions when they looked out of trim. His mouth was like his grandmother's, expressive of good humour; his eyes were grey, with black lashes and black eyebrows.

Isaac was a musician, with a well-toned bass voice—one of the choir; a ringer, indeed the head of the belfry; a reader, and, more, a thinker. He was an excellent workman at his own craft, which was beyond that of the mere blacksmith; for he was ingenious in the hanging of bells, and skilful in the construction of curious locks and keys. Isaac had much talent and many good qualities, but he had one unseemly vice. When God bestows his precious gifts so bountifully on his creatures, shall they suffer one degrading vice to nullify the whole?

Isaac's hammer, and the knitting of the old woman, were both arrested at the same time by the dull tolling of a bell.

"Isaac, it be the 'saule bell,'"[1] said the widow, sitting in the act of listening to the mournful and solemn tones of what, in some places, is yet called "the passing bell," though now in most disused, as only a relic of Roman Catholic times.

"Ay, mother," said Isaac, who had not only stopped his hammer, but walked into the street, the better to ascertain the truth, "it *is* the soul bell, but I wonder who can be dying, for I have not heard of any illness?"

"I hear it now plain and plain—it be the 'saule bell,'" said the widow in a tone of decision; and she put her knitting on the low stool, and re-entered the cottage.

"Ay, ay," said Isaac, talking to himself when left alone; "mother always prays for the dying; how good she is! I often wonder why I am so good-for-nothing. I ought to be a better man, considering that I have such a good mother. I must mend—I *must*!" added he emphatically—"I must mend my manners some day," but Isaac laughed aloud, as if he thought the "some day" was very far from the present.

"Must you indeed, Mr. Isaac?" said a young woman who had approached the shed unperceived by him; "well, goodness knows, there is plenty of room for amendment!"

Isaac looked up, but did not reply. He stopped his work, and, colouring deeply, stared at the intruder in rather a sheepish manner, as if he did not know what to do or say.

"And so you really do mean to mend your manners some day? I congratulate you on the proposed change," continued Mary Cope; "but do tell us which day?"

Mary Cope was the young schoolmistress of the village—a new importation, brought by the vicar to assist in training up the generation rising around. Mary was a good young woman in her way, and was now accompanied by her cousin, Susan Picard, fresh from London.

Susan was a shop-woman in one of the great houses there; and having fallen out of health, with, as it was surmised, too much confinement during the heart of the season, had been allowed by her employer a fortnight of holiday, to revivify her lost strength. Susan was more than pretty in the eyes of Isaac; such a vision of dress and loveliness had never been seen on Dartmoor. Before Susan's appearance Isaac had been suspected of a liking for Mary Cope, but poor Mary sank into insignificance by the side of Susan, though she had not as yet realized that fact; it is true, she had no absolute claim on the attentions of Isaac, though she was certainly gratified by the loud whispers of the neighbours, "that Isaac Watson was sweet upon Mary Cope."

"Come, tell us which day," persevered Mary.

"To-morrow," said Isaac laughing, and rallying from the confusion in which the unexpected appearance of the young women had thrown him.

"To-morrow!" said Mary Cope—"to-morrow! Ah! Mr. Isaac, you will never mend till you begin before to-morrow!" and Mary heaved a little sigh as she said, "Will he, Susan?"

If Susan was pretty and much more elegantly attired than Mary Cope, we do not mean to admit that she was one half as clever; Susan therefore did not see the point in Mary's query. But Susan, schooled in shop-life in London, knew at least when to hold her tongue, and when to speak. And this one gift was often of great value to her. It was of value now, for by remaining silent she did not betray her ignorance, and Mary Cope proceeded to say very sententiously,

"To-morrow is the fool's paradise; to-day is the wise man's resting-place. Begin to-day, Mr. Isaac, and you will have made your first step towards—towards perfection."

"Is that *all*?" said Isaac, mockingly.

"All! To begin to do well might satisfy most reasonable people, especially when they promise to themselves to mend their manners some day," said Mary.

"Then I am unreasonable, Mistress Cope, for it just does not satisfy me," said Isaac.

"I daresay, Mary," said Susan in a mincing tone and in a whisper, which whisper, as Susan intended, certainly caught Isaac's ear—"I daresay he is not bad!"

"I did not say he was," said Mary; "he accused himself, for he said, 'I must mend my manners some day.' But where is the Widow Simpson?" said she to Isaac, who did not reply.

"Ah, I know."

And after a slight pause, Mary said in a lower tone, and with some degree of awe,

"She is praying for the dead."

"No; she is not, Mistress Cope," said Isaac, sturdily.

"But she always says her prayers when the 'passing-bell'[2] is tolling." And Mary turned to Susan as she added still in an undertone, "Because here in Lawsleigh Susan, the passing-bell goes while the poor things lie dying—which, to my mind, seems so cruel, just to go telling them there is no hope left to live longer."

And then, turning to Isaac, she continued,

"But this morning it is Jim Cooke's wife, and she walked into the baker's, and sat down, and fairly died then and there."

There was a silence of a few seconds after this startling announcement, and then, with a deep sigh, Mary said,

"And that is what the bell is tolling for—the dead, not the dying."

Isaac had ceased his work, and stood listening attentively to this long speech of Mary's; and then, seeing his mother again pushing open the door that led into the shed, he went to meet her, and did not reply to Mary.

"Good morning, widow," said Mary.

"Good morning to you, Mistress Cope. Isaac, lad, fetch a chair."

"No, thank you," said Mary, "we cannot stay long."

"I heard the bell," said the old woman, "and the call of the saule bell is to prayers."

"What is the saule bell?" said Susan in a whisper to Mary, for she did not understand that the word "saule," as pronounced by the old woman, meant "soul," or the "call" of the bell.

"The saule bell is only the passing bell; but, as I have told you, Susan, here in Lawsleigh they frighten the poor dying creatures with tolling while they are yet alive; and then some good people, like the Widow Simpson, say their prayers," replied Mary.

"And what, then, is the passing bell?" said Susan, whose London education left her ignorant of rural customs.

"And you do not know what is meant by the passing bell?" said Mary, who was herself unconscious of the fact that a different kind of knowledge is rife in cities from that of the provinces; "why, Susan, you do surprise me! I have known it since I was a child, though, until I came to Lawsleigh, I had not heard it for many years."

But as Mary did not attempt to explain to Susan, the Widow Simpson said kindly,

"Maybe you havena got no bells where to you live."

"Oh! yes, indeed," said Susan, briskly, "we have plenty of bells; but I never heard any one of them called the 'saule bell' or the 'passing bell,' and so perhaps we have no such bells in London. And yet I should wonder very much at that, because there is nothing you cannot get in London, so you only go to the right place."

"Maybe you havena got no mother to tell you what the saule bell says," said the widow; "and so, when the bell calls, you don't know."

"What it says!—why, can it speak? I am sure I do not know what you mean," said Susan, a little awe-stricken.

"Then hearken to I," said the widow. "First, the saule bell goes clang, clang, clang, quite quick like—it be a saying to the passon, come, come, come. Then it settles itself steady like and goes boome, boome—it be a telling us then to pray, and then all good Christians leaves off doing their daily works and prays to the Almighty for peace to the dying saule."

"We never do such things in London," said Susan.

"London must be very different from Lawsleigh," said Mary.

"Oh! quite different—as different as light from dark," said Susan, with a little toss of her head; "and besides, we are always so busy; ours is a splendid establishment, and we go working on from morning till night. Why, when there is a grand wedding at St. George's—that's St George's, Hanover Square," explained Susan, "though it is so near our house in Regent Street, we have not time to go."

"All work and no play makes the lad a dullard, I have heard say," said the widow.

At this moment the village clock struck two, and Mary started as she said,

"Two o'clock!—oh! Susy, I must run; do not mind me," and she set off running as she called out, "Come, Susy, come, only I must run."

Mary meant to say that, though she must hasten to her duties, Susan need not put herself out of breath, but come, with more convenient leisure. But Susan either felt that there was no necessity to go at that particular time, or that there was something very attractive at the smithy, for she certainly made no attempt to follow her friend.

After running some distance, Mary turned and saw her cousin still standing by the old woman, without any intention, apparently, of coming after her. She then suddenly stopped and called lustily to Susan. Susan nodded and nodded, but only moved from one foot to the other; and poor Mary, in a bitter and angry mood, walked hastily on to the school, where, as a climax to her vexation, stood the vicar, watch in hand. He was a large man, and standing as he did on the very threshold of the door, it was utterly impossible to enter. Mary made a low curtsy. The vicar looked first at his watch then at Mary. This he did several successive times, but without speaking. Mary became hot and nervous, and felt herself colour deeply. The vicar remained in position, now examining his watch, now gazing at Mary, whose nervousness increased, and whose mind suddenly conjured up all sorts of horrors, for she knew the vicar thought want of punctuality a great defect in a person's character. Poor Mary did not attempt to justify herself, and therefore this sort of tacit reproof was more painful to bear than positive condemnation. But just as she felt her tears would burst forth in spite of her efforts to restrain them, the spell was broken by the vicar saying in a very slow and solemn way, and looking fixedly at Mary,

"Seven minutes past two."

After delivering this crushing homily, he moved from the threshold of the door, turned on his heel, and walked away.

"This is all that tiresome flirting Susan's fault," said Mary to herself, while she took off her bonnet and shawl, and then began to call her pupils to order. But in this Mary was unjust. She herself had forgotten that it was so nearly two o'clock when she and her cousin stopped at the smithy; and whether Susan chose to stay and have her chat there, or return with Mary, it would certainly have made no difference in the time of her arrival at the school, if she had remembered that her duty called her away at that time.

1. See Note B.
2. See Note C.

II

OF THE HANDSOMEST MAN IN THE VILLAGE, AND WHAT THE TWO COUSINS SAID OF HIM

WHEN the hours of school were over, Mary, to her annoyance and vexation, saw Susan Picard coming away from the smithy, where she had left her three hours ago. Mary tried hard to smother her chagrin, and not allow Susan to perceive it; and during their tea she even encouraged her to talk, almost unconsciously hoping to see into her thoughts, though she tried to conceal her own.

"Mary, I do think Isaac Watson the very handsomest man I ever did see!" said Susan, simpering; "and so pleasant—how he can talk!"

"Can he?" said Mary, chafing in spite of herself at the thought that Isaac had made himself "so pleasant."

"Yes, he can talk—oh! so well; and I quite agree with all you have said of him. But you never told me of his mother—what a queer, odd-looking old woman she is—so little, little, little; and did you ever see such a wonderful gown?—and such a cap?—or ever hear such funny words? I never did, Mary."

And Susan indulged in a hearty fit of laughter at the good Widow Simpson's expense.

"People say she is a wonderful woman," said Mary, in a tone of decision; "and Parson Hill says she knows more about Dartmoor than anyone else hereabouts."

"Why, whatever is there to know about this place?" said Susan, raising her wondering eyes to the tops of the mighty Tors;[1] never see anything here, but 'ills and bad roads."

"But this is Dartmoor," said Mary, proud of her learning, though she so modestly put aside all claim to it as she said, "and though I do not pretend to know much about Crockern Tor[2] and Wistman's Wood,[3] I have been to both places, and to many Tors also; yet, Susan, there are plenty of people who come hundreds and hundreds of miles just to go to Crockern, and see the king's chair, where he used to sit with his crown on his head, same as he does now, as I suppose—or, leastways, I should say the Queen does in the Parliament-house in London to this day."

"Well, to be sure! I should never have thought this a grand place to come to see, though I have come, just as you said, Mary, hundreds and hundreds of miles!" said Susan, simpering. "Why, Mary, it is more than three hundred, is it not?—perhaps even four hundred, from Regent Street to Lawsleigh?"

"But you do not come to see Dartmoor! You come to see me for change of air!—and—and—of course I am very glad to have you," said Mary, her better nature returning for the time being; "and I think you must be glad to get away from that dirty, smoky London!"

"Dirty! Smoky! Oh! my goodness, Mary, much you know about London!—but then, to be sure, you have never been there. Why, London is as clean as this very table, and much more sunshiny than you are here," said Susan, whose recollection of the great metropolis was as she had left it on a hot day in June, when the sun shot vividly into Regent Street; "and there are no 'ills there, except 'Olborn 'Ill and Ludgate 'Ill! But then, Mary, if you could but once see the heaps of people, all walking as fast as may be, just as opposite as can be to this place, when there are no people at all, or only one or two, and they going along so low, and so still and quiet, and so just for all the world as if they had nothing to do—and I do not believe they have much!"

After the adventures we have just recorded, Mary always avoided walking with Susan near the smithy. She knew this did not prevent her visits there during the time of her own occupation with the school; but she comforted herself with the thought that Susan's stay would not be a very long one; and then, when she returned to London, the inhabitants of the village of Lawsleigh would resume their ordinary occupations—at least such as had been in any way disturbed by the presence of Susan—and go through the daily routine of their lives free from the intrusion of a stranger.

Mary, with much prudence, tried to curb the expression of her annoyance at Susan's constant flirtations with Isaac, until one unlucky day, towards the end of the week, when certain circumstances put her off her guard, and she gave way more than she had done heretofore, or even than she was herself conscious of at the time.

The two young women were seated at dinner, when they were suddenly startled by the sound of a deep and richly-toned musical voice singing loudly snatches of an ancient Bacchanalian ditty.

'Give your toast and name the lass.'

"Who is that, Mary?" said Susan.

'Sally, Fanny, Molly, Sukey,'

roared the same voice, evidently coming nearer, while Mary had turned very pale, and did not attempt to reply to Susan.

"Goodness gracious, what a noise! Why, who can it be?" said Susan, hastening to open the door.

'Any one will please my fancy,
Molly, Betty, Kitty, Nancy,'

shouted the man, who, to Susan's astonishment, was no other than "the handsomest man in the village," even Isaac Watson!

Mary remained perfectly quiet, looking very pale, inwardly schooling herself to curb, if possible, all outward expression of her feelings; while Susan, on the contrary, looked hot and angry, and gave vent to her wrath unrestrainedly.

"Why, I thought he was tall, Mary!" said Susan, as she stood watching the antics of the man, followed by a crowd of little boys, one of whom pretended to pick his pocket, but only put in a heavy stone; and when the large man turned round upon his small tormentor, and put himself into the attitude of a pugilist, another little fellow tripped him up from behind, and Isaac fell; and there he lay at the mercy of the smallest boys in the village.

"Oh! Mary, surely he will be sadly hurt!" said Susan, now in her turn becoming pale; "he has had such a fall."

"He will take no harm from a good tumble," said Mary, with a sneer, while her cheeks suddenly resumed their colour.

"But see, those naughty little boys are actually kicking him! Why does he let them, Mary?"

"Because he cannot prevent them," said Mary; and forgetting to practise the caution she had intended, "He is very handsome now, is he not, Susan?"

And Mary laughed a little scornful laugh at Susan's annoyance.

"There! he has got one! See, Mary, he has caught one fast. Come here, Mary, and see what they are doing. He has got that one who kicked him. He—oh!—oh!—oh!—he will kill!—Mary!—kill!—oh! Ma-ary!" screamed Susan, as she turned from the door, and burst into a violent passion of tears.

Isaac, like many in his state, was too much overpowered by his plentiful potations to exert himself much even in his own defence. And the boys who annoyed him were quite as alive to the necessity of giving a kick, and running away, as Isaac was to the counterplot on his part, viz., that, to enable him to catch anyone, as he lay on the ground, and so make an example of him that should terrify the others, he must feign sleep; for one of the great punishments of the drunkard is, that he often knows what he ought to do in any particular case, but the power to do, or to act, is gone from him. Art, therefore, or cunning, rather, held watch over opportunity; and while lying on the ground, apparently unable to move—heaps of dust thrown over his thick black hair, pokes with dirty sticks given him in every part of his body, kicks, when they could be conveniently administered, and other species of torment; all of which Isaac bore as if he had neither sense nor feeling—his eyes closed, his arms listless, and seemingly unable to raise himself from the ground—while lying thus, one small boy, the youngest of the lot, uplifted his tiny foot to poke Isaac in the chest. In one instant the foot was seized, and in another the child was fast locked in Isaac's arms.

"You young rascal, I will eat you up!" roared Isaac, making grimaces at the child, who, really affrighted, screamed loudly, while Isaac, with his prisoner safe in his grasp, by dint of many efforts, at length succeeded in raising himself from the ground; and, steadying himself for a second or two, he turned round, and attempted to harangue his tormentors; but manifestly failing in his oration, his audience began to take the initiative themselves.

"Jack, lad," shouted one to the little boy in Isaac's arms, "don't thee mind. There be a lot of us gone to fetch thy mother; her be sure to come, and her will gie Isaac a good kick!"

"Oh!—oh!" said Isaac, as he held the terrified and screaming child high in the air—"oh!—she will kick me, will she! She had better not!"

"Let I go, Isaac!" said the child.

"Oh I will eat thee up!" said Isaac, opening his mouth wide.

And while the child roared the louder, he took it by both legs with one hand, and upon the open palm of the other he placed its head—which unnatural position for the poor little child, combined with Isaac's very unsteady movements, had so alarmed Susan Picard, that she foresaw nothing but certain destruction to the helpless child, as the end of all these vagaries.

"Isaac, lad!—Isaac!" said the moaning voice of a woman who came running without bonnet or shawl, "gie I the child!"

"Oh—h!—you will kick me, will you?" said Isaac laughing, but still staggering on under the weight of his burden; and as the woman raised her arms to take the child, he altered its uncomfortable position, and pressed it close to his chest, hushing it as a nurse would an infant.

"Isaac, lad, do gie I the child!" said the woman.

"You may take him if you can," said Isaac with a loud laugh, and hugging the child still closer.

And thus they went on out of sight of Susan Picard—the woman entreating, and Isaac tottering and shuffling on, still laughing loudly, as he refused to resign the child.

"I thought he was tall," reiterated Susan, as she turned to speak to Mary, when she could no longer watch Isaac.

"I cannot help that," said Mary, with the natural perversity of one woman jealous of another.

"But he really looks a fat, squat, dirty, vulgar man!" said Susan in a strange tone of dismay and inquiry; for she did not know that vice—and more especially this form of vice—not only takes away for the time being the physical strength of a man, but also so alters the expression of the figure, as to make one even of colossal size look comparatively small.

"He is all in angles about his legs and arms," continued she; "not a bit upright and straight, as I always thought he was."

"But then people are occasionally liable to make mistakes," said Mary with cruel prudence.

"Yes, mistakes," said Susan doubtfully; "but then, Mary, is he not handsome?—do tell me. Is he often ugly, and vulgar, and dirty, such as I have seen him now?"

It was very clear to Mary such a thought was painful to Susan.

"Use your own eyes, and your own understanding," said Mary in reply; for her spirits rose the higher the more she saw her cousin cast down.

"But, Susan, I must be off to my school, I cannot afford to be late twice in one week."

"What a tiresome thing school is!" said Susan. "Why, you are always going there when I most want you."

Mary, as she tied on her bonnet smiled, and felt comforted for the miseries of the three preceding days; for now, and only now, when there was no chance of her customary flirtation with Isaac, did Susan find Mary's occupation a bore, inasmuch as she herself would be left alone.

1. See Note D.
2. See Note E.
3. See Note F.

III

WHAT HAPPENED AT THE VILLAGE SCHOOL OF LAWSLEIGH, AND WHAT BEFELL SUSAN PICARD

"I'll walk with you, Mary," said Susan.

"I must go to the minute, Susy; indeed, I can't wait."

And Mary set off; but she was soon overtaken by Susan, who came running after her, and saying breathlessly,

"I am not so very long just fetching my hat that you need to walk off so sharp, Mary."

"Parson Hill is so particular," said Mary, in her own defence; "and then remember I was late on Monday."

"Good gracious, Mary, look there!—why, there is a real, right-down gentleman!—the very first I have seen in this queer place," said Susan.

"Where, where, Susan?" said Mary, in amazement.

"There, coming down the 'ill what you call Tor."

"Oh! dear, dear—am I late again?" said Mary, hurrying on.

"Well, Mary, who is it?"

"Only the parson; and he is so particular."

"Yes; I have known many gentlemen and ladies, too," said Susan, bustling on after Mary; "they are all particular, some for one thing, some for another—now, what is his 'fad'?"

"His what?" said Mary, still walking fast and looking anxious.

"Why, bless me, you need not be so cross; gentlemen have 'fads' in plenty, I can tell you. Some are 'faddy' about their gloves—my goodness, just are not they!"

"Dear me," resumed Susan, after a little pause; "why, she is actually gone into her 'orrid school and left me standing here! I wonder now if I might venture in, just to sit down a minute, and rest after my sharp run—I will try. Mary, my dear," continued she, as she timidly put her head in at the door, "may I—why, Mary, you are all by yourself!" and now Susan's tones became reproachful, "and you never once asked me to come in and sit down after running along at such a rate!"

"Do go away," said Mary, for Susan had entered the schoolroom; "I am really very busy," and she continued to arrange the room for the reception of her young flock.

Susan sat down, notwithstanding Mary's request, and felt irritable and angry with her, for, as it seemed, her churlishness.

When the village school began to fill, and there were from twenty to thirty assembled, by a second gentle hint from Mary, Susan reluctantly arose to go away. This was, however, prevented by the entrance of the very same "real right-down gentleman" whom Susan had noticed during their walk, even Parson Hill.

Mary came forward and explained that Susan Picard was her cousin, and that now that she had recovered from her fatigue she would return home.

"But perhaps this young lady would rather stay where she is," suggested Parson Hill, as he took a rapid survey of Susan from top to toe; and Susan, nothing loath, admitted that she should.

The business of the school commenced—Susan a looker-on. Parson Hill took a class of very small children, and began putting various questions; at length he selected one to spell through a column of words, upon each of which he made some remark, apparently to the edification of the child, and the amusement of Susan.

"Wig," said Parson Hill.

"W-i-g, wig" said the child.

"You know your grandfather wears a wig?"

"Yes, sir," said the child.

"Jig—perhaps you cannot dance a jig, but I daresay this young lady can," turning a bland smile on Susan, who felt greatly flattered, not only by his notice, but by his endowing her with an acquirement she certainly did not possess.

Susan did not know what was meant by a "jig," since it was not a fashionable dance in her day.

"Pig," said the parson; "now very likely this young lady never saw a pig!"

Susan's colour came brightly, and in her own mind she felt sure she never had seen one alive in London; and foolishly priding herself that she lived in London, and could not therefore be expected to know even the names of animals inhabiting the rural districts, and so far from the capital as Dartmoor, when Parson Hill ventured the suggestion a second time, she unhesitatingly said "No."

"There!" said Parson Hill, turning to his listening pupils, "you see I am right; I am sometimes. This young lady has never seen a pig. Tom Brown, fetch a pig; Jack Harris go and help him."

Meanwhile Mary Cope could not understand why Susan should say she had never seen a pig, when pigs were constantly to be seen running wild about the village, and Susan herself had complained that they were always in the way. Once or twice she was on the point of saying to Parson Hill that he must have misunderstood Susan, but oddly enough that gentlemen foiled all her attempts at explanation.

At length the two boys returned driving before them a huge pig. The doors of the school-room were placed wide open, and the inmates evidently enjoyed the introduction of so turbulent a creature to their very threshold, which constantly attempted to escape from the thraldom in which it was kept by the two boys, now dodging them on this side, now on that; while Parson Hill courteously invited the young lady to come forward and look upon the strange animal called a pig.

"That is a pig," said he.

"Dear me!" said Susan, blushing and stammering.

"Dear me!" echoed Parson Hill; "ay, indeed, you may well say 'dear me!' But don't be alarmed; huge and angry, and tormented by his present small domain, as he certainly is," for, by long poles the village boys kept the pig within a certain space, "he shall not eat you up to-day; we will all protect you. Besides, I want to explain to you some little about so rare an animal, and so fine a specimen, so that on your return to London you may be able to make others almost as wise as yourself. Tom Brown, what is that in the pig's nose?"

"A ring, sir."

"A ring—good. Now, I daresay in London young ladies wear rings on their fingers, while here, on Dartmoor, it is the fashion for pigs to wear rings in their noses. Strange—passing strange—that customs should be so different in different places! Now," continued he, addressing Susan, "can you tell why pigs wear rings in their noses?"

"No, sir," said Susan, tremblingly alive to the awkwardness of her position.

"Ah!" said he, looking at Susan, and affecting to see her ear-rings for the first time, "you, I see, wear rings in your ears. Now we shall be edified, for of course you can tell us why?"

Here there was a pause of some seconds, during which Parson Hill drew himself up to his full height, and stood in the act of listening.

"Tom Brown, listen—listen all," said he, turning round and addressing the school. "This young lady is going to tell us *why* she wears rings in her ears."

Susan at this moment heartily repented that she had not refused Parson Hill's courteous invitation to remain at the school, for again a dead silence fell on the room, and she felt her respiration increase with the nervous agitation of her position, and her cheeks flush with the consciousness that all eyes were fixed upon her. The stillness became at length almost insupportable, for seconds appeared as long as minutes; and at last, feeling the necessity of a reply, she stammered forth,

"Miss Amelia Stump had her ears pierced, and so she wanted me to have mine."

But this reason did not seem to satisfy Parson Hill, who remained standing, still in the act of listening, and the silence in the room was unbroken as before. In dread of she knew not what, and hoping to give a reason strong enough to content even Parson Hill, she said, with as much courage as she could assume,

"All the young ladies in our house have their ears pierced."

But, alas! for Susan, Parson Hill did not alter his position, and the silence was still unbroken. This torture was almost too much for her, and in despair she added falteringly,

"And—and—that's all, sir."

"Thank you," said Parson Hill urbanely; and Susan was relieved immediately by hearing the hum of the school recommence. "Little ones, thank this young lady for telling us in so clear a manner, why she had her ears *rung!*"

A loud chorus of thanks followed this, but it by no means added to Susan's equanimity.

"And now," said the parson, looking round the room, "let me inquire if you little ones understand what the young lady said. Charley," continued he, fixing his eye upon a curly-headed boy, "why had this young lady her ears rung?"

"Coz Meely Stump axed her to; and coz the t'othern done theirn—and—and—coz that's all!"

"Very well, Charley," said the vicar, approvingly; "but now we must return lore for lore. Bill Spike, tell this young lady why this pig has his nose rung?"

"Coz all the t'other pigs have theirn."

"And why have the others their noses so ornamented?" said the parson.

A dead silence fell on the school, and the parson—by signs only—repeated this question, pointing alternately to each boy without further result, until at length he came to Tom Brown, who said,

"Coz they grubs up much better."

But further information on this entirely new subject was prevented, for the time being, by the entrance of a servant, bringing a message to Parson Hill, and recalling him to his home, to Susan Picard's inexpressible relief.

No sooner was Parson Hill a tolerable distance from the school, and the pig by his orders driven back to the common, than Susan arose.

"You will wait for me, Susy dear?" said Mary.

"Wait here!" said Susan, indignantly, "when I have the power to get away? Not very likely, Mary."

And she moved towards the door.

"But, Susan, dear, I assure you"—and Mary could not control her smiles—"you may chance to meet that huge pig, and if you were alone I cannot imagine what would happen to you!"

"I do not care for any pig in creation," said Susan, angrily, "half so much as I care for being fastened up in this 'orrid school! I cannot wait, Mary."

And with ignoble haste Susan left the room, and ran all the way to Mary's cottage, inwardly resolving that nothing should ever again take her to that terrible school-room, to be so audaciously catechised by that tiresome and disagreeable Parson Hill!

IV

WHICH TREATS OF THE HANDSOMEST MAN IN THE VILLAGE AT HOME

MEANWHILE Isaac, with the child in his arms, and followed by the woman, continued his staggering walk towards the smithy, where he eventually arrived, and where as usual sat the good Widow Simpson, knitting under the shed.

"Morning, widdy, and how be you? Here's Isaac a-carrying the child," said the woman.

"I be's pratty well, Molly, thank you; and how be you?" said the Widow Simpson. "Isaac has got a kind heart, and most times takes to the leetle ones; and oftimes I wonder me he does not wed. Gie I the lad."

Isaac placed the child on his grandmother's lap, and with a keen consciousness of his small ability to walk upright, steadied himself by leaning for support on all things that were near; and by degrees he reached the door that led into the cottage, and entered it.

"Him be a fine child, Molly," said the widow. "Yes, he be a fine lad surely; two year old come the eleventh of next month."

"And sturdy limbs," said the widow, stroking the child's legs and arms.

"Ay, widdy, him be a sturdy one for a two-year old!"

"Sit you down, Molly, and rest awhile."

"No, no, I must go, thank you all the same, widdy, but I has got all the washing about, and then I has so many of 'em," pointing to the child, "four bits of things!"

"Blessings on them!" said the widow; "they'll maybe plague thee, Molly, for a two or three year, but come that time over they'll be great helps!"

And she kissed and caressed the boy, and returned him to his mother.

The Widow Simpson remained seated in the shed, watching the woman and her motherly antics with the child, and also returning the salutations that from time to time Molly made; and even for a few minutes after they were out of sight, the Widow Simpson sat quietly knitting, and apparently watching for incidents of any kind likely to occur, up or down the long village street; but though seemingly so unmoved, her heart was aching at the remembrance of her grandson Isaac, whose pitiable state she knew too well.

After a reasonable time of this decent make believe, viz., that there was nothing different from the ordinary course of things, she slowly arose, laid her knitting upon her stool, as was her wont on short absences from the shed, and re-entered the cottage.

Isaac was not in the lower room; of that she was glad. She hoped, too, that he had been able to get up stairs, and into bed. She opened the door at the foot of the stairs, and was again consoled by the fact that he was not lying there, his head resting uncomfortably on the topmost stair, as she had before seen him, and his long legs and heavy body distributed as the case might be. Slowly on tiptoe, so as to avoid all noise, the widow ascended the stairs, and pushed gently the door at the top, but found herself unable to open it. Again and again she tried, each time making some little progress, until at length she could peep into the room; and there she saw Isaac on the floor, his feet touching the door, his head close to a large wooden press that stood at the far end of the room, so near as to give her the idea that he must have had a severe blow when he fell. The poor woman stood a few seconds contemplating this wreck of early manhood, inwardly acknowledging she could do nothing for him.

All her love, and it was great—all her self-denial, and it was constant—all the anxiety she had to aid him, to restore him to his "right mind"—all these desires were of no avail. There he must lie—a log on the great ocean of the world—drifting, powerless, who shall say where? If God saw fit to require his soul on that very day, who could say him nay!

"But, oh!" thought the widow, "if Isaac was only to go to God's blessed home, why, I would bear to live here by myself for the lad's sake, though it would be cruel lonely—cruel lonely without him!—only I don't know; can the drunkard go to God's heaven? And he is so gude," continued she, as she sat upon the stair. "Oh! that the Almighty would hearken to I; he be not bad, poor lad; he be not bad in nothing but this; he likes cider—I can't say as he does not."

After a little time, she dried up her tears, and, descending the stairs, went again to the shed and resumed her knitting. On this afternoon she was not visited by Susan Picard, whose amazement at the alteration in "the handsomest man in the village," when under the influence of cider, had not yet subsided.

What, then, would have been her dismay had she seen him "at home!" And, besides this, Susan herself had not recovered from the shock of Parson Hill's wondrous catechising. The few neighbours or villagers who passed and repassed the smithy, spoke to the Widow Simpson in their customary tone and manner; none seemed to know that Isaac, the stalwart and strong, lay weaker and less powerful than a child. If any knew of the occurrences of the day, they did not condole with her, but left her in happy ignorance of their own knowledge.

About four o'clock in the afternoon, as was her wont, the widow once more left her stool in the shed and re-entered the cottage, where she busied herself by placing the kettle in such a manner as to cause the water to boil up quickly; then she ostentatiously placed the tea-things as if for two, as she said to herself,

"As suppose a neighbour was to look in, then they might think as Isaac be all right, poor lad. I wish he was."

She cut slices of thick bread and butter, such as she ordinarily prepared for Isaac; but she herself only sopped a little bread in her tea. Thus prepared, as it seemed, for any emergency, she began to fill up the teapot from the kettle, when a deep shadow came over the room, and she could not see what she was doing. She raised her eyes, and saw that the space left by the wide open casement was filled up by the fine head and shoulders of Parson Hill, who, leaning his arms inside the window, put in his head and said,

"And so, widow, Isaac's not here! I hope you will not wait for him——"

The widow replaced the kettle on the turf-fire before she replied, and then she said cautiously:

"No, yer honour, no—the lad is not here," and, after a little pause, she resumed; "but, maybe, yer honour would like to see him?"

"No, no—I can wait," said the vicar; "but since he is not here, and you have prepared so bountifully for him, what then do you say to giving me a cup of his tea?—eh, widow? Why, I am very thirsty this hot day, talking to the young ones at the school is no joke, I can tell you. Thank you—why, how quick you are! your hospitality has no doubts to deaden it. I have only to say the word, and lo! the smoking tea is in my hand."

"Will yer honour have something to eat?—I'll cut it mighty thin," and she began to cut slices of thin bread and butter.

"No, no—pray don't cut for me—thank you; I am thirsty, and your tea is very refreshing."

"Yer honor's kindly welcome," said the widow, with a curtsy and a very gratified smile.

"But I wish with all my heart I could eat one of those huge slices I see ready prepared for Isaac—that is, widow, if you would promise me not to cut any more for him; and then, you see, he would lose half his tea, and that would be a proper punishment for his negligence in keeping you waiting."

"No, yer honour, no," said she, with a shake of her head; "I don't never wait for the lad. I gets my teas most times to four o'clock, and Isaac knows it."

"Well, I am glad you don't wait; it is unseemly that the aged should wait for the young. And I am very glad I have had Isaac's tea—tell him so, will you? Tell him, if he wishes to have the pleasure of drinking his own tea, he must mind—and be in time, or it may happen that somebody will drink it for him. Here is the cup—thank you—thank you—I declare I am 'like a giant;' you know the rest," and Parson Hill walked away, while the widow finished the quotation:

"His honour means 'like a giant refreshed with wine,' I suppose; but it was only tea," continued she, as her face reflected the inward satisfaction this visit of Parson Hill's had given her. "I be fair thank-hearted," said she, as she sipped her tea; "it be plain and plain as his honour knows nothing."—

By knowing nothing she meant that he was ignorant of Isaac's state of inebriety; for though she was herself so clear-sighted as to his state, the moment she saw him, with that delusion that affection creates she hoped that others were blind. Alas! she but deceived herself—Isaac's condition was well known all over the village.— "I be not so badly off as Hannah Barker," soliloquised she, "for Peter Barker is more like to a wild beastes nor to a man. But, poor thing, I be sorry for she—poor Hannah! No, no, Isaac doesn't never do so to I—that is, never hasn't, I should say," said she, correcting herself; for she foresaw, if Isaac persisted in these bad courses, nothing could save him from becoming in the end like Peter Barker.

Hannah Barker was the Widow Simpson's opposite neighbour; her husband was a carter, sometimes employed by the farmers in the neighbourhood. He was a man of bad principle and bad habits—a lazy, cunning, cruel man. His ill-treatment of his wife was the talk of the village; seldom was Peter Barker sober, often out of work, more frequently maintained in idleness by the industry and management of his wife, than by any exertion of his own—too often wresting from her the moneys she had earned to go and sit for hours, and even days together in the cider shop, wasting his own energies, and a sore example of the consequences of such conduct to all lookers-on. And then, when he had spent his last farthing, and had also had as much upon credit as the landlady of the "Packhorse" would permit, he would manage to stagger home, sometimes stupidly heavy, and overcome by his excesses, when bed would be a refuge to which he would willingly hasten. But alas! not unfrequently he would be in an excitable and quarrelsome mood, and then his conduct would be harsh and cruel. On these occasions his poor wife would become the victim of his brutality from heavy blows, hard kicks, and horrible language. Her screams would alarm the neighbourhood, and here and there a woman, turning pale at the thought of Hannah's sufferings, would say, "Deary me! it be that Peter Barker a-thrashing poor Hannah," while the men who happened to be near would go to her assistance, rescue her from the clutches of her cruel husband, and sometimes even turn his heavy carter's whip against himself.

No; the good Widow Simpson had not yet endured the indignity of a blow from her son, though even she was conscious that there were times when Isaac's naturally fine temper was soured by the influence of the large quantities of cider he had swallowed; and when these thoughts arose in her mind, she could not but look with a trembling eye into that future which is at all times so mercifully hidden from us, and fear for the consequences of Isaac's present misconduct.

It had happened more than once that Isaac himself had gone to Hannah's assistance when her husband was ill-treating her, and at such times the jeers of Peter, who so often met Isaac at the "Packhorse," were gall and wormwood to the latter.

"Oh-h!—you doon't niver drink naw cider—yu doon't!" would Peter say, in the broadest *patois* of the moor. "Haw, haw, haw!—yu niver smokes naw pipes—yu dusn't; an' you niver hasn't wolloped naw 'oomen—coz why?—coz yu ain't got nun for to wollop! Haw, haw, haw!—yu bees a fine un, yu bees, tu set yu sen up thesen ways! Yu'm a big un, an' I's a leetle un; bu' I'll lick thee—I'll lick thee, tho' thee bees sich a big un!—coom on! coom on!"

And Peter would square his fists and try to provoke Isaac to a fight.

But here Isaac's good qualities came into play; for Peter was a small, thin man of fifty, grey-headed, and rarely in good health; and Isaac, young, tall, and strong, was obliged to swallow these taunts as best he might; conscience whispered he partly deserved them, and he could not lift his hand against a man, his neighbour, and one whose frame and health were so opposite to his own.

But the hardest stroke of all was usually left by Peter for the last; for when Isaac, satisfied with having rescued Hannah, and pertinaciously avoiding all notice of Peter's sneers, turned to re-enter his own home, Peter would call out—

"An' so yu sneaks awee, yu does—liken to a dug, as a-bunt his teale, and feared o' gettin' a gude lickin' from I. Haw, haw, haw!"

V

OF THE WIDOW SIMPSON
AND HER MANY MISTAKES

"Deary me! why, they be nine on 'em a-striking by the church, and it be most dark," said the Widow Simpson, as she went to the window with the intention of closing the casement.

While in the act of doing so, her neighbour, Hannah Barker, walked up to her cottage opposite, with an empty clothes-flasket in her hand, and as she stood unlocking her door, she turned round and nodded.

This caused the widow to linger a little before closing the casement; and as soon as Hannah had relieved herself of the flasket, she came across the road, and said,

"I be hearty glad you be not shut up yet, widdy. I be late a-getting home from the Vickridge; but Mistress Smith gave I such a lump o' figgy pudden (*plum pudding*), and I want you to have some—just gie I a knife. Here, widdy, it be cruel nice, and maybe I'll lift up the shutter. Eh, widdy?"

"Ay, lass, thank thee."

"Theere!" said Hannah, as she raised the shutter, "'tisna the first time I have give a helping hand. Gude night."

"And gude night, and thank you, Hannah, and blessings on ye, and many of them for a kind-hearted creature as you be surely," said the widow as she screwed up the window-shutter.

Outside the window of Widow Simpson's cottage—and, indeed, generally at the cottages throughout the village—hung upon hinges a large shutter of wood. There was no mechanical contrivance inside or out to assist in lifting this dead weight. For many years the widow had not attempted to raise it; and if she could have lifted it, she could not jerk it

into its position, so as to put through a hole in the shutter, and the frame
of the window, a large iron pin, which was prevented from being taken
out on the outside, or from falling back, by a bolt inside.

"Why, theere now! Him be a-coming, I do think," said the widow,
startled by some noise, and standing in the act of listening for the sound
of Isaac's feet descending the stairs. "The lad will want food—it will do
him good to eat!"

All was still, however, and the widow resumed her soliloquy.

"It be a mistake—I havna heerd him."

Then to ascertain if she had or had not heard Isaac moving in his room,
she crept softly upstairs, and, pushing the door, which now swung easily
open, she saw that Isaac had changed his position, though he still lay all
his length on the floor.

"Ay, ay, better to let him have it out," said she as she turned away and
entered another room. But the poor widow did not immediately prepare
for rest. She seated herself on the edge of her bed, and, crossing her arms
one over the other, appeared to be waiting for some event that might
happen at any moment; and while thus waiting so lonely and patient, her
thoughts reverted to her own early life.

"It's a mistake," said she; "ay, ay, many is the mistake as comes after the
first, and the mistakes of these days is only the children of that as come first!
I didna think it was a mistake to choose to be wed to he!"—the pronoun
standing in the widow's mind for the man of her early attachment. "If I
had but a-liked Jeffry Badge; but I didna—he'd a-got ways as I'd no mind
to, and he was no betterer off nor him! But the neighbours did say—they
did— 'Mind thee, Betty, Isaac Simpson's a bad un, he likes cider.' I thought
it was a mistake, cos I never seed him drink no cider; but it was not. And
then they said to I, 'Jeffry's a man well-to-do, a-baking his own bread, and
a-having folkses corn to grind;' and that was true, but I thought to myself,
'Ay, but he isna Isaac! He cannot ring the bells—the 'bob-major' and the
'grandad,' and he cannot sing with a cheery tone as Isaac does!' And then
again Jeffry was a man with a white face, and a leetle bit sort of a man, so
I didna take to Jeffry, and I did take to Isaac! It was a mistake—mistake

the first, the father and mother of all them as is now; for Isaac—rest his saule!—*was* fond of cider, and big man as he was, and red rosy cheeks, and thumping limbs, it was all no use. Only that the Almighty God in heaven knows for the bestes; else would I think as Isaac's limbs was a mistake, for why should he have such limbs, and then rollick in the cider shop, 'stead of using of 'em? Ay, ay, it be o'er now—nay, but it isna—forbye the lad is there a-doing like his grandad!" And then there was "she"—the pronoun again standing in the widow's mind for her only child. "And when the Lord Almighty gived I she and no more, and I had only got she to bring up, and no lad to be tooked off to the cider shop, and I sits a-thinking as everything is all right—why, it isna—it be a mistake, for it all goed over again. There was two of them again as comed after my pratty meeden, just the very same as they had comed after I. And one of these was uncommon fond o' cider surely; and the leetle meed wouldna have him; and I thought her was so wise, so wiser than she's mother! And so her tooked Roger Watson, and that wasna right, though it sim so; but it was a mistake; forbye Roger only lived a year, and then he leaved her with that young babby in she arms, poor thing! and she greet and greet, and then fair died outright. And so her leaved the child to I—and to Isaac. And that was another mistake; cos why, should ever the poor lad keep off from the cider shop when his grandad tooked him there! It was the grandam as gave he such a grandad as was the reason as the poor lad got into such troubles. Oh-h!—I wish as I didna make so many mistakes!" and as the tears rolled down her aged cheeks, she began to undress, and finally got into bed.

But the Widow Simpson did not attempt to sleep; she lay in bed still, in the act of listening, her countenance, if it could have been seen, expressing anxiety and eagerness. Her watch was unrewarded. Isaac slept on.

"Four of 'em," said she, as the church clock struck the hour; "and if he cannot ring they bells, mercy on us! but I am afeared as this time the passen'll turn he adrift—adrift—ay, drift—drifting on—down—down—"

But by this time the poor woman, overcome by drowsiness, lost the thread of her thoughts, and fell into an uneasy slumber. When she awoke, the sun was shining full upon her as she lay, and though on first awaking she had only a sensation as of some heavy care on her mind, in a few seconds full consciousness returned, and she remembered the events of the preceding day.

"Six of 'em," said she, as she started up in bed when the clock struck the hour, "and this a *Saintses morn*![1] Oh! my lad, my lad, and art thee not awaked up?"

She partially clothed herself, and went to Isaac's room. To her astonishment he was not there. The bed had not been slept in; the window was wide open. Isaac's cap lay just where it had fallen the night before, and there were drops of blood on the floor, close by the press where his head had lain in heavy sleep when the poor woman saw him last. Overcome by her night of anxiety and watching, her nerves gave way; she sat down and made no effort to restrain the tears that now flowed freely.

"Oh—h! him be gone again," said she; "him be off again to that 'Old Packhorse!'—what shall I do? It be a saintses morn, and him such a good un to they bells."

Some slight unusual sound arrested her attention, and she sat straining her ears to understand the noise. She heard a step, combined with the removal of some piece of furniture in the lower room.

"I have made another mistake," said she almost joyfully; "I do think as that the lad be a-settling the chairs a bit."

She returned to her own room, and while she continued to dress herself she listened occasionally to the sounds from below.

"Ay, ay, it be the lad," said she, peering through the scanty window curtain, which had not yet been undrawn, "and it will do him gude," continued she, as she saw Isaac with his head under the natural spring of water that flowed from a rock at the back of the cottage.

Cheerily now the widow attended to her personal appearance, though she did not venture to draw aside the curtain or open the window while Isaac was so near; for few things in this good woman's conduct were more to be valued than the absence of reproaches to him for his misdeeds.

It was well-known in the village that Hannah Barker, when her husband was sober, taunted him with his mal-practices, and, to use the phrase often applied to her, "Hannah Barker couldna keep a ceevil tongue in she's head."

While the contrary was the case with the Widow Simpson, we must do Isaac the justice to say that this forbearance on the part of his kind old relative made him often determine to be steady, to leave off drinking cider, and not pain her by his misdoings. But Isaac's resolution was not equal to the temptation, and the widow had still to mourn over his folly.

Only, therefore, when Isaac left the spring, did she venture to undraw the curtains and open the window. Always an early riser, there was nothing unusual in her being up soon after six on a summer's morn. But on this especial morn, the kind old soul tarried about her room longer than usual, and busied herself with little nothings to give Isaac time to put away from his clothes or his own appearance any remains of the previous night's debauch.

When she at length ventured down, Isaac was not there, but the heavy window-shutter had been put back, and again the casement stood wide open. The room had evidently been "tidied" by hands accustomed to it. The turf fire blazed brightly, the kettle was singing loudly, the breakfast-things were on the small three-legged table, the loaf and a jar of butter.

"Ay, ay, and I be thankful—I do say as I be thankful; and I do thank the great God in heaven as a-hearkened to my prayers. And the lad's better the morn—and I *do* think as they Saintses will have they bells—I *do*!"

Her reverie was interrupted by the entrance of Isaac, tall, upright, and manly-looking. On the previous day Susan Picard had seen him "all angles in his arms and legs," but this appearance had vanished, and Isaac was himself again.

On this occasion there was rather more shyness in his manner than usual, consequent on his self conviction of his culpability; and perhaps there was also a little more haste and eagerness in his attentions to the widow, as if by this he could atone for his misdeeds. He kissed her, as was his custom morning and evening, and they began breakfast.

Conversation was now a difficult matter, for none of the incidents of the previous afternoon could have been ventured upon by the widow without fear of reminding Isaac of, and thus covertly reproaching him for, his sin; and as Isaac himself had no ideas at all on that same afternoon, there was little to marvel at in the present dearth of a subject. The widow, however, as is too often said of the female sex, "found her tongue first."

"I feared I was just a bit late the morn, Isaac."

"Oh! no matter, mother, I shall be in time."

"Ay, lad, so as you have got time to get up into the belfry, it be all right, eh? And how be the new one getting on?"

"Very well," said Isaac; "they are trying to raise a full set of men, who shall practise twice a week, and so get their hands in."

"Ay, but they will be many a year afore they'll ring as you do, Isaac!"

"They do very well now," said Isaac; "two or three tried their hands a month ago, and made a very good beginning."

"When they does the 'bob-major' and the 'gran——"

"There's the quarter," said Isaac, interrupting; "I must go."

And away he went, his head unconsciously held up, for he was proud of his position as head of the belfry, and glad that the previous day's debauch had not entirely unfitted him for this day's duties; he was thankful in his own way that he had escaped a great mortification, but not so humbled in heart as he ought to have been, after such misconduct. For on one occasion Parson Hill had told him, if he ever again entered the belfry in a state of intoxication, it should be the last time he would permit him to ring. Parson Hill was well known to keep his word; but Isaac, instead of feeling humiliated at the recollection of his intemperance, rather rejoiced that his sin would be unknown to Parson Hill, and that he himself was still head of the belfry.

1. See Note G.

VI

OF PARSON HILL'S METHOD
OF GROWING TURNIPS

"Why, the bells are ringing!—somebody is married this morning, eh, Mary?" said Susan Picard to Mary Cope.

"No, Susy; it is a saint's day."

"A what, Mary?" said Susan in surprise.

"A saint's day. Did you never hear of a saint, Susy?—St. Matthew, St. Mark, and many more?"

"Yes, to be sure I have," said Susan. "I know all about the saints and the apostles too, but I never heard the bells rung for a saint's day."

"That is because you live in London, where, if I may judge from what you say, they do nothing as they ought to do."

"Bless me, Mary! why, then do you think we have time enough on our hands to remember such things as saints' days? Birthdays, I suppose you mean—a saint's birthday. What should we in London care for St. Matthew's birthday?—why, sometimes we even forget our own!"

"But here, Susy, we do all things just as they have always been done," said Mary, "from the time——"

"From the time when Adam and Eve and all the saints and the apostles lived together in Paradise, I suppose," said Susan, interrupting.

"How can you talk such nonsense?" said Mary.

"Nonsense!—I don't call it nonsense to know one's bible; but you always did think you knew better than other people, and you think so still," said Susan, with a little sneer.

"When you talk of the saints and the apostles living with Adam and Eve in Paradise, I cannot think you better informed than myself on such subjects."

"And pray why not? You are so conceited, Mary. I have read all about Adam and Eve living in Paradise; and if the saints and the apostles did not live there with them, can you tell me where they did live? Why, there was no other place on the earth then," said Susan, triumphantly.

"Hush! Susan," said Mary, putting her hands to her ears, as if to shut out further argument, and going to the open door. She stood for a few seconds in the act of listening, and the sound of the bells came merrily on the wind. She heard enough to satisfy herself that Isaac was in the belfry, and then returned to her breakfast.

"Well, you have a colour, Mary!" said Susan in amazement; for the fact that Isaac was once more saved from the disgrace of being expelled from the ringing had sent the hot blood thankfully and hopefully into Mary's cheeks.

Mary, up to the time of Susan's arrival in Lawsleigh, had affected not to care for Isaac's attentions; but the daily flirtations at the smithy had awakened in her a better knowledge of her own heart. She had discovered her jealousy of Susan, and she now felt that humiliation to Isaac would be sorrow to herself; and yet poor Mary remembered, with a shudder of disgust, Isaac's inebriety of the preceding day.

"Yes; I generally have rosy cheeks," said Mary quietly.

"But not so red as now. I am sure you are thinking about something, with your eyes so sparkling and your mouth so trying not to laugh, and something pleasant too!"

Mary no longer tried to conceal her laughter, as she said,

"I am sure, Susy, you would make any one laugh with your queer remarks; but come, let us have some breakfast."

"Breakfast indeed!—so you gobble up your food as fast as you can that you may rush off to that 'orrid school," said Susan. "I am glad I have nothing to do with such a place."

"I am not going to the school to-day; I don't go on a Saturday; and it is not a horrid school."

"And you are not going? My what good news!"

"I wish you would remember the school is bread to me, and a very decent and very respectable way of getting one's bread," said Mary, rather grandly.

"It's him as makes the place so 'orrid," said Susan, "that Parson Hill! I am sure if he looks like a gentleman, he does not behave like one. He's so very tormenting."

"You should not tell falsehoods," said Mary, laughing, "or affect ignorance of well-known things. If you had not been affected, Parson Hill would have been very kind to you."

"Goodness gracious, Mary! Me affected! do you call me affected! Why, what will you say next? And as for telling a falsehood, you know very well, Mary, I never had been in this empty, slow, and 'illy place in all my life before; and I am very sure I never did see a live pig in London, so it was no falsehood after all."

"You have not lived in London all your life. But, Susy, pray don't be cross, for I can assure you the parson is very kind. Oh! Mr. Marvel, you are just come right; now do tell Susan, is not Parson Hill very kind?"

"Vary, vary indeed, Mistress Cope," replied a tall thin man, who stood looking in at the open window.

Susan thought she never had seen so ugly a man; the thick, curly, sandy hair, light blue eyes, and gaunt-looking features of the sturdy James Marvel did not suit the taste of the fastidious Susan.

"He's very queer in his school, I can tell you," said Susan.

"Is he?" said the cautious Scotchman.

"No, he is not," said Mary, in a decided tone; "and, Susan, it is better not to speak at all than to say evil of the absent."

"Gude advice, miss," said James to Susan; "I am a-thinking as 'tis very gude advice. Mistress Cope's a sensible little body, as weel as a learned."

"Do you know Parson Hill?" said Susan, pettishly.

"Know him! If twenty years' time enough to know a body, perhaps I do know him, miss."

"Twenty years! dear me, have you lived in this queer, odd, silent place for so long a time? Why, a month of it would kill me," said Susan.

"You are very soon killed, then, it's my belief. But why shouldna I live here these twenty years? I was a lad rising close upon twenty when

I come first, and I may say I certainly do know something about the minister; and there's one thing I know, he's made a mon o' me!"

And James brought his fist so heavily on the window-sill as to make Susan start.

"Perhaps he sometimes takes extraordinary means to convey information," said Mary, rather grandly, and in a decided tone; for James Marvel was much looked up to in the village, and Mary was a great favourite with him. His occasional bits of flattery to her intellect and personal appearance were gratifying to her, and at this moment, and in Susan's presence, she tried to keep up her character for wisdom.

"He takes queer ways," said Susan, scornfully.

"People has difference in opinions, miss," said James. "Maybe, now, if you knowed how the minister made a mon o' me you'd say 'tis vary queer—but I be no to that mind."

"Come in and have a cup of tea," said Mary.

"Na, na, thank ye kindly," said James; "I's a-watching for auld Jacob as is gone to the ringing, so I'll just stand here till th' peal's out."

"Then, James, do tell Susan about the turnips and the strawberries when you came here first."

"Maybe, miss, ye wouldna like a lang story?" said James, as he lifted his cap from his head, and pushed his fingers through his hair.

"Indeed there's nothing I like better," said Susan, joyfully, her mind reverting to the cheap literature, in a serial form, with which not only London, but all England, is inundated, excepting only places so difficult of access as Dartmoor, and little imagining it was the history of some part of his own life that he would relate.

"Vary weel. Then I must tell you I wasna twenty years auld, and I come here to the minister, and grandfather's his head mon then, and got me in. And so I was a-standing to the back of the master's chair, while he was a-eating of his dinner, and he said, 'Some turnips,' said he. That means, miss," said James, explaining to Susan, "as I was to hand they turnips, and as he would help hisself. But there was none; so I goes up to him, and says I, 'There's no turnips.'

"'And why not?' said he.

"'Coz they has not growed yet,' says I; for I was a-gardening then, miss, though I was a-doing hosses, and a-driving, and a-cleaning the carriage, and everything else to that time o' day!"

"Goodness gracious me! how dreadfully tired you must have been!" said Susan.

"And when, pray, would you have a mon tire hisself," said James, staring at Susan, "if not at twenty years auld?"

Susan did not reply, and James continued:

"Weel, miss, in a few minutes more, 'Some turnips,' said the master. So I thought he'd maybe forgotten, and I goes up to him as bould as bould could be, and says I, 'There's no turnips!'

"'And for why is there no turnips?' says he.

"'I have a-telled yer honour why,' says I.

"'You have told me, sir,' says he, mighty angry; 'then, sir, tell me again.'

"'Coz they has not growed yet,' says I, most mazed.

"'And why have they not growed yet?' says he.

"'Coz it's mighty early yet, and coz there's no rain,' says I.

"'Rain or no rain,' says he, 'I mean to have turnips. Turnips grows by nights as well as by days; there's plenty time to grow turnips; now you know my mind!'

"And, miss, I can tell you," said James, as he pushed his cap back from his forehead, "I was uncommon glad when the dinner was over; I was fair flabbergasted out o' my very wits!"

"What a 'orrid man, Mary! He really is, whatever you may say," said Susan.

"I take leave to differ with you, miss," said James, in a serious tone. "The minister's a very gude mon; and if I didna take care to grow turnips enough, I was a big fule for my pains!"

"I can't see the good of going on at you in that way," said Susan.

"Maybe you can't, miss, but I could, and most 'specially with grandfather's help. And it was not only turnips, but peas, and beans, and carrots, and parsnips, and sparrowgrass—everything to its turn; and he was always a-worriting me to give him something as I hadna got."

"That's just what I say," said Susan; "he is such a worry—in such a cool and contented sort of a way—and all about nothing!"

"Begging your pardon, miss, but I thought it was all about something! Howsomdiver, there comed a time when the master began a-axing for strawberries; so I up and told him there was none, and wasn't going to be none for a long whiles; and I thought then I had fairly stopped his speechifying. But no such thing, for just after I had leaved the dining-room, I hears the bell ring, so when I goes in, says he:

"'Some strawberries, James.'

"I stood stock-still and stared at him.

"'Some strawberries, James,' says he again.

"But I was that feared I could not speak, and I stood stock-still a-staring my eyes out; and he leaved me standing there a-staring at he for most ten minutes, as it seemed to me; and I got so much worse feared, I was fain to take hold of the table, coz I trembled that much."

"And that is just as he does," said Susan, "puts every body in a tremble, and I am sure he made me quite ill. How I do pity you, poor man; but do go on."

"Peety! oh! I don't desarve no peety. But when he had let me stand long enough in that there ague-fit, says he:

"'If I said to you a glass of water, James, would you stand staring in that way?'

"'But there isn't none,' says I, a-thinking of the strawberries.

"'Do you mean to tell me there's no water?' says he.

"'Oh! yes—yes, there's plenty water,' says I.

"'Then,' says he again quite slow-like, 'how durst you to say there's no water.'

"And he bringed his fist slap down on to the table with such a noise, I fair roared out; for I thought my head was gone clean aff my shoulders."

"Oh! gracious me! I knew I was right, Mary. It is the most miserable way of treating a fellow-creature."

"Oh!" said James, laughing, "it was all moonshine. And presently after says he, that was when I had comed a bit to my senses, miss, says he,

"'Do you happen to know my riding-whip?'

"'Yes, sir,' says I.

"'Then fetch it,' says he."

"Abominable, quite abominable, Mary! I can't bear to hear of such cruelty to a fellow-creature."

"But the bells is down, miss, and auld Jacob's a-coming. Morning, miss; morning, Mistress Cope!" and, with a nod of his head, James Marvel walked away, leaving Susan in a state of excitement as to the probable termination of the scene between him and his master.

"Gracious goodness!—what a pity he can't stop and finish his story! I suppose he was very much hurt—very cruelly used," said Susan. "I can quite credit it from my own knowledge of the man. So hard-hearted, Mary, and especially to a lady!"

For Susan was thinking more of herself than of James Marvel.

"Why, Mr. Marvel is not a lady," said Mary.

"Never mind that," said Susan; "the ill-treatment can be proved."

VII

OF ISAAC WATSON'S HAMMER, AND MARY COPE'S FOREHEAD

"And, Mary," continued Susan, "this cruel treatment is just the same sort of thing as we read of in 'Uncle Tom's Cabin.' The wicked master taking advantage of his position to use his poor servant ill."

"What nonsense you do talk, Susan; you seem to have read very queer books, and gained very foolish ideas."

"And you seem to live in a queer place, and get foolish ideas in that fashion. Anyhow, my ideas are as good as yours, inasmuch as they come from something real; for let me tell you, Mary, I have read 'Uncle Tom's Cabin.' You, I daresay, have never heard of the book; as, indeed, how should you, living in such a 'orrid place as this, and with such queer people about you."

Mary did not reply, and, after a little pause, Susan resumed.

"But since you have no school to-day, what then shall we do? Where shall we go?"

"I mostly do up my sewing Saturdays," said Mary; "and after that we can walk where you like."

"Then we'll go to the smithy—shall we?" said Susan, eagerly, "and see how the old lady is getting on."

Susan stopped in the middle of her speech, for she saw Mary's countenance change, and altered her words. It was on the tip of her tongue to say "And have a talk with Isaac;" but instead of this she made the Widow Simpson the cause of her wish to go there.

Mary—though she was vexed at Susan's eagerness to see Isaac, for she was not deceived by the fashion of her speech—inwardly acknowledged she herself was nothing loth. Quietly, therefore, she acquiesced in Susan's proposal, and after their early dinner, the two young women set off for the smithy.

When within a short distance of Widow Simpson's cottage, they were alarmed by loud and piercing shrieks from a woman, accompanied by horrible oaths in a man's voice, and the sound of heavy blows. While for the moment arrested in their walk by these unusual sounds, to their astonishment they saw Isaac Watson, with his great hammer in his hand, rush excitedly from the smithy to the opposite cottage. He tried to enter, calling out as he did so—

"Peter!—Peter!—I'll break the door down if you don't either open it or stop your blows!" The sound of the blows ceased, but the woman's wailing voice continued, and a man's rough head appeared at the open window. It was Peter Barker, who, after prefacing his speech with curses and foul oaths, said—

"Isaac, haw!—haw! I dun thee this time. The doore's fast. Comin' an' a-separatin' man an' wife won't du by no manner o' means! Them as God's a-jinded——"

"Hold your tongue!" roared Isaac; "how dare you use such words? Open the door, or I tell you I'll break it open," and he uplifted his huge hammer as in the act of striking.

"Goo on—goo on; brak en oppen, an' I'll hae yer afore t' justices for knocken a man's door down—haw!—haw!—haw!—goo on!"

All this time the two young women distinctly heard Hannah's moans, but, to their surprise, in a few seconds the door of Peter's cottage was opened, and she, with her hair in a tangled mass, no cap on, her gown sleeves nearly off, her arms bleeding, and faint and terrified, rushed out.

"Thou p'isonous ferret, where't going?—cum back!" said Peter, and he turned from the window and came forth, cracking his whip as he said, and seemingly with much enjoyment, "I'll wollop yer hide!"

"Stand back!" said Isaac, trying to prevent Peter from putting his threat into execution; and Hannah crossed the road safely, and took refuge in the smithy.

"I dar' yer to tich my wife," said Peter, cracking his whip.

"I'll touch you, you coward!" said Isaac, "if you don't let the poor thing alone!"

"Oh! you'll tich I, wull yer; an' I'll tich ye," and Peter again cracked his whip and made a feint at Isaac's legs.

"Keep off!" said Isaac, uplifting his hammer; "I shan't stand any nonsense."

"You been't a-gooin' to stan' noo nonsense; then here's some sense," and Peter now used his whip smartly about Isaac's legs.

Peter had had just enough cider to make him what he called merry—in other words, he was not so completely under its power as that his bodily strength succumbed to its influence; and, moreover it had had the effect of making him enjoy his own agility, and the horror that his uplifted hand inspired. He was, as we have said before, a small, wiry man; when sober, capable of great activity. In this instance the pleasure of lashing Isaac seemed so great, that though the latter made repeated attempts to strike with his hammer, Peter, with delighted nimbleness, always evaded the blows of the tall strong man. Isaac grew eager and angry, but Peter laughed.

"Oh, heavens!—mercy me! how frightful!" said Susan; "why, they'll kill each other!"

"Hush, Susan, hush! Let us try to get into the smithy cottage," said Mary.

They kept close to the wall, creeping by its side as well as they could, but a heap of stones, accidentally placed by Isaac's shed, stopped their further progress, and they were obliged to wait a better opportunity to enable them to pass the two men without harm. It so happened while Peter was flourishing his whip in the air, and making occasional feints at Isaac, and the latter repeatedly uplifting his hammer in the act of attempting to strike, that the lash of the whip accidentally curled round the head of the hammer and knotted itself. Isaac took immediate advantage of this by seizing hold of the lash, and Peter, tugging at the handle of the whip, was dragged here and there at the mercy of Isaac, until the latter suddenly let go the lash, and the jerk brought Peter to the ground.

During the early part of this extraordinary fight Isaac stood with his back to the young women, and Peter had taken no notice of them; but this last turn of events had caused the men to change places, and as Isaac, in passionate fury, sprang upon the prostrate man, uplifting his hammer, Mary and Susan rushed simultaneously forward to try and gain the shelter of the cottage.

Isaac's extended arm fell powerless and unnerved at the unexpected sight of the two young women; while Mary Cope, in her haste to escape from her uncomfortable position, set her foot on a rolling stone and fell on her face, her head coming in contact with Isaac's lowered hammer. The Widow Simpson and Hannah Barker, at sight of this catastrophe, came from the smithy to Mary's assistance, and, with Isaac's help, lifted her senseless into the cottage.

Thus Peter escaped from Isaac's vengeance, and went grumbling away; while Isaac, dismayed at the sight of Mary Cope with a deep gash in her forehead, bleeding profusely and insensible, could only lament over the evil, blame himself, and ask his mother what was to be done.

"Run and fetch the doctor, Isaac, lad," said she; and without another word, Isaac set off to find the nearest medical man.

Three miles Isaac walked, or rather ran, on that hot summer's day, and on reaching Mr. Smith's house, was told "he was out on his rounds, but if he returned in any reasonable time, he would certainly ride over to Lawsleigh." This was not satisfactory, and Isaac trudged on two miles more to the next nearest professional man; and there met with the same reply. He now turned to retrace his steps, and felt that he must trust to Mr. Smith being able to reach the moor at some period of the day; and up to this time he had allowed his thoughts to dwell more upon the hurt Mary Cope had received, than of his own ill-treatment by Peter.

Isaac was not an ill-tempered or a revengeful man. Having succeeded in rescuing Hannah, he would have returned to his shed in spite of Peter's taunts, had not the little man attempted to strike him; and then when he actually made good his intention, and lashed Isaac most painfully, independent of his suffering, the indignity was enough to make him wish to revenge himself when the opportunity offered. It might have fared ill with Peter if the two young women had not arrested Isaac's attention, but this fact was not uppermost in his mind as he journeyed to fetch assistance; indeed, he was unconscious of the great escape he had had from the sin of taking the life of a fellow-creature. All that haunted him, besides the fact of Mary Cope's illness, was the humiliating position in which he had been seen by the two belles of the village. They had looked on while he was ignominiously lashed with the carter's whip! And so Isaac's heart was embittered, for the time being, against Peter—against Hannah, whom he had so willingly rescued—and even against himself, for, as he said,

"Being such a fool as to help another man's wife. It's clear to me that pretty Miss Susan will never come near the smithy again after this; and as for Mistress Cope, why, it is quite true that, until I saw her lying so white and still and quiet, I did not know that I *do* like her—like her very much; and for them two to be looking on."

But we must leave Isaac to his weary walk and sad reflections, while we return to Mary Cope.

The Widow Simpson and Hannah quickly applied the necessary means to restore Mary to consciousness, and then they bathed and dressed the wound, while Susan stood helplessly wringing her hands and bemoaning her cousin's fate.

"Goodness gracious! what a face she has got, poor thing!" said Susan. "Why, she was so nice-looking, and now she is all swelled up and half blind, and—and——"

"Prythee don't fash about good looks," said the widow; "think how great the mercy that the poor saule is alive."

"Alive, why, goodness me!" said Susan; "how could just a little tumble like that kill a body?"

"Knocking yer head on a hammer's like enough to kill a bigger and a thicker head than that," said Hannah, as she stood by Mary's side.

When Mary had sufficiently recovered to understand the nature of the accident, and to know that, though she felt ill from the loss of blood, and shaken by the heavy fall, the result would probably be only a temporary inconvenience to herself, she, like the Widow Simpson, felt deeply grateful that the Almighty had mercifully prevented any more terrible mischance. And, in the course of an hour from the time of Isaac's departure, Susan and she left the smithy for their own home; the widow promising, if medical assistance should arrive, to direct the gentleman to Mary's cottage.

"And so all our pleasure is destroyed by that tiresome Peter Barker—to think that there should be such heaps of tipsy men in this place!" said Susan; "and they always stopping other people's comfort."

"I am sure, Susy, I am very sorry," said Mary; "but you can have a nice walk without me; we are just at home, and I shall not wish to deprive you of——"

"Oh! nonsense, Mary! I shall stay with you. Indeed, I am not quite sure that you are in a fit state to be left alone," said Susan, with great magnanimity as she entered the cottage with Mary.

VIII

WHICH CONVICTS PARSON HILL
OF FAVOURITISM

"Now, Mary, dear, put up your feet," said Susan, "and lay your head back on this nice soft pillow I have fetched downstairs for you; you must not work or read—you must be content to be idle."

"It's all very well to say such things, Susy, but what am I to do for to-morrow if I am not better?"

"Why, what is to-morrow so particular?" said Susan.

"It's nothing particular, only it is Sunday," said Mary.

"Oh! yes; but then let us hope you will be well enough to have a nice walk; and you must keep your veil down, and hide that horrid patch," said Susan.

"I don't wear veils, Susan; and it is not about missing the nice walk that I mind—it's the singing, for I lead the choir."

"You'll be better, Mary, dear."

"But if I am not better?—if I should feel as I do now?—that is what I'm thinking, and that is what troubles me."

"Why, somebody must lead for you, that is all; I can sing beautifully—suppose I try?"

"Yes; but you don't sing Gregorians," said Mary.

"Glorians!" said Susan, staring and opening her mouth wide—"what do you mean?"

"Why, chants called Gregorians. I have got all the volumes of the 'Parish Choir'—Parson Hill gave them to me—and there is a great deal about chants, and many good psalm tunes that we sing in church; and, indeed, Susan, there is much in them that is amusing as well as instructive."

"Yes; but what do you call them?—Up-roarians? Why, Mary, I never heard the name."

"Perhaps not; but, fortunately for me, I have been well taught, and Parson Hill has always been so kind to me; so I know all the Gregorians, Susy, not uproars, as you miscall them, and we sing the fourth to-morrow."

"I have such an ear, Mary, and learn everything in such a little minute, that if you will just tune one, you will see how soon I catch it up."

"My head is like a lump of lead, Susy; I can hardly lift it from the pillow, and I do feel so faint and tired, I could not sing a note; but then, if you will get me the book, I will find you the right chant, and you can learn it from the notes."

"Thank you, dear Mary, but I shall not trouble about it now. I know I can sing anything I please in a minute, so why should I hurry?"

Mary wearily closed her eyes, and gave up the point.

Isaac Watson had many enemies even in the small village of Lawsleigh, though he was himself so little quarrelsome, censorious, and ill-natured. But great talents too often excite the envy of those less brilliantly gifted; and these, coupled with his well-known failing, conjured up bitter thoughts in the minds of more steady-going men. Then, again, Parson Hill's evident liking both for Isaac and the aged widow excited jealousy in many.

"The Passon's very keen after poor Peter Barker. Why cannot he look after Isaac a leetle more?" said they.

But this was a wrong reading of Parson Hill's actions. Isaac's more gifted, as well as more educated mind, combined with his kind heart and general good temper, rendered him less disagreeable when in a state of intoxication than Peter, and, therefore, less prominently offensive. The women were apt to say of him, "Poor Isaac! he's the worst to hisself!" For even when overpowered by his excesses, he was still good-humoured, and rarely irascible and quarrelsome like Peter.

It may be said of Parson Hill that he was a man of few words. If there was absolute necessity to speak, he did not flinch; but if there was little or no good to be gained, he waited a better opportunity.

Peter was caught in his sin almost daily—this could not be overlooked. Isaac's transgressions were much less frequent, and he was always ashamed of his folly, which was not the case with Peter; indeed, the latter rather gloried in his misdeeds. It is true, Isaac did not on all occasions manfully resist the temptation to inebriety; and the women said, "Poor Isaac, & c., but the men said, "And why can't the Passon see Isaac?—'tis the Passon's own fault as Isaac's such a drunkard!"—whereas the only instance of favouritism towards Isaac that weighed upon the parson's conscience was that, on hearing of his being in a state of inebriety on one occasion when ringing, he had said, "Only men who are sober should be allowed for the future to enter the belfry." It had been his intention to say, "Only men of strictly sober habits should be permitted to ring."

But the too evident gratification expressed on the countenances of the listeners, on the anticipation of Isaac's expulsion from the belfry, caused him to make a less absolute law, and thus give the sinner not only a chance to escape, but also an opportunity to reform. Nevertheless, he was not the man to punish one and let another escape; although he took into consideration that the misconduct of each man was different in degree, the consequences different, the men themselves different in their example to the village, men of different mind, different manner, and even of different behaviour under the influence of cider—the balance largely in Isaac's favour.

The sins of Peter always brought evil upon others, and his language and conduct were low and brutalized. But the women were right in their remarks about Isaac; his vice, sad and demoralizing as it was, did not render him a terror to women, and a hard and cruel master to his nearest relative; and thus Parson Hill said to himself, "Give him time—spare him yet awhile—if not for his own sake, at least for the sake of his aged relative, the good Widow Simpson. Who shall say but that he may yet amend?—He, possessed of so many gifts—so good of heart—so cultivated in mind?"

But let not anyone suppose Isaac was not an object to be pitied the more, the more his great talents, handsome person, and good temper were rendered useless by his infirmity. It was because the loss was so great to Isaac personally, and to the world at large generally, that the vicar pitied so compassionately, and so mercifully gave him yet time to repent and amend. He was not blind to the envy of this man or the hatred of that to Isaac; but until some more serious case than had hitherto happened should occur, it did not seem to him wise to interfere more publicly than he had already done.

IX

HOW PARSON HILL'S STEADY LITTLE SCHOOL-MISTRESS, MARY COPE, WAS CONVICTED OF RECEIVING VISITS FROM A TOPER

IT was on Friday afternoon that Parson Hill had called on the Widow Simpson, and cheered her by affecting ignorance of Isaac's unseemly state, and by asking her for a cup of tea; and on Saturday, as he was returning home to dinner, he was overtaken by Mr. Smith, the medical man who had been sent for to Mary Cope.

"Good morning. Why, what brings you this way?—no sickness near us, I hope?" said the parson.

"Rather nearer than you will guess; for by your question you are still in ignorance of what has happened."

"And pray, then, what has happened?" said Parson Hill, as he let the entrance gate fall to, and walked quickly up to Mr. Smith.

"I am told that Mary Cope and her young friend have been sadly hurt," said Mr. Smith.

"Mary Cope!—pray speak out!" said the parson, sharply. "What can have happened to Mary?"

"It appears," said Mr. Smith, "that Isaac and Peter were fighting—both of course the worse for the cider they had consumed—and Mary and her young friend, in attempting to separate the two men, were knocked down."

"Good heavens! this cannot be true!" said the parson impetuously.

"I can only say I met two men from Lawsleigh, going to spend Sunday on the other side of the moor; they told me exactly what I have repeated to you, adding that Hannah, Peter's wife, had her clothes torn off her back; that Mary Cope had a great gash on her head and face, and her friend was hurt and bruised in no slight degree. I have been sent for—this proves there is something serious in the case."

Parson Hill remained silent for a second or two—the communication seemed beyond credibility.

"Can I see you again after your visit to the school cottage?" said the vicar.

"Certainly—I will call," said Mr. Smith, as he went away.

The parson re-entered his grounds, and crossing the lawn to his house, he came upon James Marvel at his work there.

"Have you heard that Mary Cope has met with an accident?" said Parson Hill, hoping by this means to prove that Mr. Smith's statement was exaggerated.

"No, yer honour," said James.

"Do you know what took place at the smithy this afternoon?"

"Du yer honour call that a accident?" said James, resting on his spade. "I *did* hear tell as Mistress Cope bringed they blows down on herself, and as Isaac wasna to blame. My boy Alic has ha telled me, yer honour, as 'tis said in the village as Peter Barker was a-horse-whipping Isaac with his big carter's whip, and as Isaac was a-hammering Peter wi' his big hammer. And as Mistress Cope and the young leddy was a-going to the smithy cottage to see the widdy, and as they just comed up in time, and so runned up to part Isaac and Peter, and thereby Isaac hammered Mistress Cope 'stead o' Peter, an' hurted her amazing! But then, yer honour, the most peoples says as he didna mean to hurt her, and as he's vary sorry."

Parson Hill did not venture to make a remark on the strange account given him by James Marvel. He walked quietly on, wondering in his own mind what could have so upset the mind of his hitherto steady little Mistress Mary Cope, as to cause her to try to separate two drunken men.

On Mr. Smith's return, his report was not so satisfactory as Parson Hill had hoped. It is true he gave an account of Mary's present state, and added that fortunately her friend had escaped without injury. And further, his opinion was that if Mary would keep herself quiet until Monday morning, she would then be equal to her duties at the school. She had a wound on her forehead, which luckily might not prove of more harm than the disfigurement of a large scar for some weeks. She was a good deal shaken by her fall, but he thought there was not any serious damage to fear.

Mr. Smith offered no further information as to the original cause of Mary's fall, and Parson Hill was left in a state of great vexation and annoyance, inasmuch as he refused to credit the accounts he had heard, and yet almost feared, by a stricter investigation, to prove that they were but too true.

In the cool of the evening he once more strolled on his lawn; but the mighty Tors, tipped by the silvery beams of the moon, here and there, or stretching their huge forms in shadow, no longer attracted his notice. His mind was full of Mary Cope and her illness. He longed to ask her what the facts really were, but his dread that she had been in fault prevented him. "For," said he, to himself, "I must rebuke and reproach her; but not now, while she is ill and suffering."

Inadvertently the parson walked to the entrance gate; from thence he could see Mary's cottage. The moon shone full on that side of the village, leaving the vicarage and its grounds in the shade. To his amazement and additional vexation, he saw Isaac Watson come away from Mary Cope's cottage. He saw him come reeling unsteadily down the street, his head hanging down, his appearance forlorn and uncared for, as was the case when Isaac had visited the "Packhorse."

"Can it be? Is it so?" said the parson. "Isaac Watson a visitor to Mary Cope, and when his sad state is so plainly to be seen! Poor Mary! poor Mary!" groaned he, as he returned home even a sadder man than he had gone forth. "It's my own fault," mourned he. "Have I not wilfully shut my eyes to Isaac's intemperance? Have I not pleased myself with the hope that in time he would do better things than visit the cider-shop? This must not, nay, it shall not be. I will prevent their future intimacy. Could I not foresee that Isaac's manly appearance and handsome person would naturally attract such a girl as Mary Cope? Did I not know that Isaac was well read beyond his station? And is not Mary well read also? Has not Isaac the most magnificent voice in the whole parish, or in parishes for twenty miles round?—and has not Mary a splendid voice? Are they not both thorough musicians?—both leaders in the choir? Is not he the most well-to-do man of his class for many and many miles round?— and is not Mary well-to-do? Dolt that I have been, to let these two come together under my very eyes, almost, as it may seem, with my very sanction! And now what can I do in the matter? for put a stop to their intimacy I will!"

X

OF WIDOW MASON AND HER CUSTOMERS AT THE "PACKHORSE"

IT will be remembered that Isaac Watson set off to fetch help as soon as Mary Cope's wound was discovered; and that he went five miles without bringing back assistance. It was not much after two o'clock when Isaac started; it was between five and six when he returned.

"Isaac, lad, come in and sit down," said the widow, as she saw him stand moodily in the shed, doing nothing. "Here's a dish o' tea—come in, lad!"

"Mother," said Isaac in a hoarse voice, "is young Mistress Cope much hurt?"

"I think not, lad; but anyhow she have a-walked safe home with the t'other young meeden."

"I'll go and see how she is," said he; "and as you say Dr. Smith has gone through the village, perhaps I shall hear his opinion of her."

"But have a dish of tea first, Isaac, lad."

"No, thank you, I can't stay."

And Isaac set off to inquire after Mary Cope. It so happened that, as Isaac neared the school cottage, Mr. Smith came out, and stood talking to some one within. To avoid meeting him, Isaac turned down an opening to the right; and as this led direct to the "Packhorse," he went in and called for a pint of cider, just to give time for Mr. Smith to finish his conversation, before he intruded himself into Mary Cope's presence.

"And I have heerd say as you have been a-hammering Peter Barker," said one of the frequenters of the "Packhorse" to Isaac.

"No, I have not," said Isaac.

"You have smashed young Mistress Cope," said the Widow Mason, who was the landlady of the "Packhorse."

Isaac looked angry, for the woman had touched a tender string, and with a woman's insight into character she quickly saw that her shaft had struck home; and then with a woman's jealousy of another, younger and fairer than herself, she added, with too evident pleasure at the fact,

"Anyhow, you have spoiled she's beauty, Isaac."

"Maybe, I can't spoil yours!" said Isaac, angrily.

"Heyday!—Massy me!—Here's grander!" said the widow, rising from her chair, and confronting Isaac. "Maybe ye ca-an't spoil mine!" said she angrily, and mimicking Isaac. "Maybe ye sha-ant, ye lazy, hulking feller!— a-coming and a-drinking your fill, and a-never paying yer dues!"

"What!" said Isaac, in a voice of thunder, as he set down the empty tankard with a bang. "Do you say, widow, that I don't pay!"

"Yes, yes! I do say as you never pays!" And the widow tossed her head, and rushed out of the room.

"I do pay every time I come here," said Isaac in a tone of decision.

"Theere be a mighty lang score up to thy name, lad," said one of the old men sitting there.

"Widow, come here!" said Isaac, opening the door that led to an inner room. "Come here, face to face. I say I do pay every time I come here."

The widow came forward with a red and shameless face, and a bold, unquailing eye, and dared Isaac to prove his words.

"I know that I pay," persisted Isaac.

"Yes, yes; in course you pays at first; and then you goes on and on, till you canna pay no longer. You be not in a fit state, you bean't, Mr. Isaac, and there be plenty knows it, let alone I; and you be one to cheat the poor widdy, be you? Why there be your score!

And she pointed triumphantly to a long array of chalks on the back of the settle.

"Then tell me the amount, and I will pay it now," said Isaac, instinctively recollecting his late debauch, and feeling himself in the power of the enemy.

"Sit you down, Mister Isaac. It will take I a lang whiles to count up that lang row," said the widow. "Sit down, Mister Isaac, another time will do as well." For now that the widow had gained her point in making Isaac pay for his uncourteous speech, she was willing to retain him as a customer.

"No, no. I am going," said Isaac. "But pray let me know as soon as you can what I owe you." And he turned to go away, but the widow stopped him as she said,

"And must I chalk up this pint, Mr. Isaac?"

"Ah! I beg your pardon, widow, I forgot," said Isaac, as he fumbled first in one pocket, then in another; but, after some time of vain search, he was obliged to confess he had come out without money.

"And it be not the first time as you've a-done that, Mister Isaac, only you just please to remember, as in coorse I don't mind—coz why? I knows you'll pay sometime, only when you says hard words to I, why, I gets a bit put out, I does—not as I'm such a very bad temper, most times."

And the widow looked round and laughed, expecting that the listeners would support her view of the case; and as those present were much indebted to her on certain occasions happening now and then, if they did not agree with, they did not venture to contradict her.

"I'll call to-morrow—Monday I mean," said Isaac, correcting himself— for he did not frequent the "Packhorse" on a Sunday, "and pay your bill."

"All right, all right, Mister Isaac," laughed the widow as Isaac departed.

And she inwardly congratulated herself on her foresight with regard to Isaac's score, and on the profit she had gained by taking offence at his words. She knew well his debt was a mere trifle, for Isaac was strict in his payments, but sometimes negligent in seeing the score obliterated.

And here we must state that Isaac Watson was a man with a healthful appetite generally speaking, and whose means allowed of a comfortable daily supply of animal food. His work was heavy and fatiguing, and he required suitable support during his hours of labour. At mid-day he was accustomed to restore exhausted nature by a plentiful meal; but on this day, so immediately after the intemperance of the previous night, his desire for nourishment had not returned, and the twelve o'clock meal was sent away untouched by him.

After the affray with Peter he set off on his long walk, and, as we have seen, on his return his mind was too anxious for the fate of Mary Cope to suffer him to bestow a thought on himself, and being accidentally prevented entering her cottage, he had gone to the "Packhorse."

He had made but a poor breakfast, and that before seven o'clock, and since then the pint of cider was the only restorative that had passed his lips. He would now have been glad of food, for the walk and the anxiety of his mind began to tell upon him. The Widow Mason's ill-treatment had prevented him from asking for bread and cheese there, as he might have done under other circumstances, and, as he walked on, he said to himself,

"I'll just stop at the school-cottage and inquire after Mistress Cope, and then go home and have some supper."

Poor Isaac! how one false step rapidly brings on another!—how sin in any form must meet with its punishment, be the sinner ever so wary! Isaac thought his yesterday's folly hushed up in the all-absorbing past— forgotten by all. He thought he had nothing to dread from the effects of it, the more so as that he had been well enough in the morning to return to his duties. But the consequences of his sin tracked him by the heel, and followed him in his future life more than he was then capable of foreseeing.

XI

ON THE DIFFERENCE BETWEEN "WHERE THE BEE SUCKS" AND "SWEET HONEY-SUCKING BEES"

ISAAC knocked gently at Mary Cope's door. Susan Picard opened it, and in a glad tone of surprise said,

"Mr. Isaac! pray come in, pray do come in."

"I called to ask after Mistress Cope," said Isaac, humbly, and not daring to accept Susan's invitation.

"Come in, sir," said Susan.

But as Isaac still hesitated, she turned to Mary and said,

"Here is Mr. Isaac come to see how you are, Mary; must not he come in?"

"Yes, certainly, Susan; tell him I shall be glad to see him," said Mary.

Now, on any other occasion the prudent young mistress of the school assuredly would not have invited Isaac in. But several feelings combined in this instance to cause her glad acquiescence. One was that Susan might suppose there was a greater intimacy between Isaac and herself than there actually was, hoping by this means to lessen Susan's flirtations with him. But as this only proves Mary's little knowledge of human nature, it will not avail her much; for there are few things more pleasurable to a vain and foolish flirt like Susan Picard, than to attract the notice of men already supposed to be engaged.

Again, Mary was glad at the real interest in herself Isaac's call made prominent; and, moreover, the interior of her cottage was such a little paradise in comparison with Widow Simpson's, or indeed with most of the dwelling-houses in the village, that she gratified a very pardonable vanity in her desire that Isaac should see it. And so Isaac came forward; the tall, strong man, subdued in spirit, bending his head, and speaking in gentle tones to Mary Cope.

Susan was astonished at this change in Isaac—thus quiet in speech and humble in manner; she could hardly think he was the same hearty, shouting, laughing, and joking Isaac with whom she had flirted so comfortably only three days ago. Susan was not more learned in human nature than her cousin Mary, or she would have known that powerful emotion takes away the eloquence of the tongue; and by Isaac's deference to, and subdued manner in the presence of Mary Cope, she would have read that her own pretty face and gay attire had made no impression on Isaac Watson's heart.

"I am sorry indeed to see you look so pale," said Isaac, addressing Mary. "I can never forgive myself, though indeed I had not the least intention of hurting you—I did not know you were there—shall you ever forgive me, Mistress Cope?" and Isaac stood, cap in hand, before Mary.

"But do sit down, sir," said Susan, placing a chair.

"Sit down, Isaac," said Mary.

And thus spoken to, he at last seated himself very uneasily on the edge of a chair, and listened attentively to Mary Cope's statement of Mr. Smith's opinion.

"But," continued she, "there's only one thing that much troubles me, Mr. Isaac, and that is the singing to-morrow."

Isaac shook his head as he said,

"There is not any one in the village that can supply your place."

"But, Mary, I can sing beautifully," said Susan.

"At all events you must not fret yourself, Mistress Cope," said Isaac.

"I can sing, I tell you," said Susan once more, and in a tone that showed her great desire to attract attention.

"Perhaps, then, you would be so kind as to lead the trebles for Mistress Cope," said Isaac.

"To be sure I would. Only tell me the tune, and I'll do it most beautifully. I can assure you I sing like Miss Louisa Pyne," said Susan.

But as this last piece of information was not at all understood by Isaac or Mary, the former proceeded with the important matter in hand.

"It is Purcell in A for the 'Venite,'" said Isaac; "and the 'Te Deum' will be——"

"It is the 'Benedicite' to-morrow," said Mary, interrupting, "and to the fourth Gregorian. Will you get me the 'Parish Choir,' Susan; it is on the top shelf," said Mary.

But Isaac, anticipating Susan's movements, and, moreover, being taller and stronger, arose so hastily as to upset the chair which had hitherto served him for an uneasy resting-place; and in his eagerness to get the book, pulled from the row half a dozen others, which toppled one over another and fell to the ground. Then Isaac had to try to hide his confusion at this *contretemps* by picking up the books and replacing them, which, by some unlucky process or other, always tumbled down again the moment Isaac thought he had them all right. This made Susan titter, Isaac more sheepish than ever, and Mary Cope very grave.

"Will you give me the book you have in your hand!" said Mary rather crossly, and shaking her head at Susan; and when the "Parish Choir" was at length given to her, she busied herself so successfully in finding the chants that would be required for the morrow, that Isaac had time to recover from the effects of his awkwardness.

"Would you just sing over the 'Venite' with Susan?" said Mary to Isaac, as she pointed out the chant to Susan and gave her the book.

"Yes, certainly," said Isaac, proud to find himself of use, and, taking his pitchpipe from his waistcoat pocket, he sounded the keynote.

"But what is this book for?" said Susan.

"Why, these are the notes of 'Purcell in A,' the chant for the 'Venite,' and Isaac will give you the keynote."

"La—a—a—" said Isaac, holding the note for Susan's better comprehension.

"But I don't know what you mean, Mary."

"You said you could sing!" said Mary, reproachfully.

"So I can!" said Susan proudly. "You should just hear me sing 'Where the bee sucks;' everybody says I do it most beautifully."

"The bee sucks?" said Isaac. "Don't you mean, 'Miss, Sweet honey-sucking Bees,' a charming madrigal," for Isaac's musical lore and Susan's were strangely different; and though "Where the Bee sucks" was a widely-known melody, he had never heard of it.

"No, no," said Susan, pettishly; "I mean 'Where the Bee sucks there lurk I,' Ariel's song from the 'Tempest;' it has nothing to do with 'Honeysuckles'—"

"But we don't want such stuff," said Mary, now becoming a little irritable.

"Stuff indeed!—why, it is lovely!—Mr. Isaac, I'll sing it to you—I am sure you will appreciate it." Isaac felt flattered by the compliment, and Susan sang without Mary making any attempt to prevent her.

She had, as she had said, a charming voice. She was accustomed to go frequently to public places of amusement in London, where she heard good music well sung. And though Susan was no musician, for she did not know a note of music, she had a good ear, and her companions in the shop in which she served being all more or less musical, it came to pass that Susan could sing many operatic songs.

There was no denying that Isaac Watson's closest attention was given to Susan the moment she opened her lips. Mary Cope instinctively hid her face, as she read Isaac's astonishment and delight.

Susan carolled away to her heart's content. The clear bell-like notes rose and fell on the ear, evidently entrancing the strong man. And when at length Susan's song ceased, Isaac heaved a deep sigh as he said enthusiastically,

"I never heard anything like that in my whole life!"

"I should think not," said Susan; "such, songs cannot very well find their way to Lawsleigh; and if they did, there would be no voices to sing them!"

"Ah! you are right, you are right," said Isaac, "there is no voice like yours in these parts;" and, for the first time since his entrance into the cottage, he seated himself comfortably; and, forgetting Mary Cope, sat steadily gazing on Susan.

"You see, there is nothing about 'honeysuckles' in it," said Susan.

"Honeysuckles! no; but I spoke of the madrigal—'Sweet honey-sucking Bees,' said Isaac; 'honey-sucking' not 'honeysuckles.'"

"Oh, yes; and what is a madrigal?"

"But Isaac, about to-morrow?" interrupted Mary Cope, whose eyes were wide open to the flirtation going on in her very presence; and poor Mary felt very sad-hearted, in addition to her other troubles.

XII

OF THE DIFFERENCE BETWEEN SUSAN PICARD'S LEARNING AND MARY COPE'S

"I THINK we need not have any fear for to-morrow, Mistress Cope," said Isaac, replying to Mary's query. "What a splendid voice Miss Susan has!"

"Yes," said Mary; vexed though she was at Isaac's praise of Susan, she could not but acknowledge the truth. "But then, Isaac, had not Susan better try over 'Purcell in A'?"

"Certainly," said Isaac; "now then, miss," continued he, and addressing Susan, as he once again gave the key-note, lengthened out for her edification—"La—a—a"

"But what is that to do?" said Susan, staring.

"That is the key-note, and you see 'Purcell in A' begins on the third—'O come let us sing unto the Lord,'" sang Mary, "only I must not sing; I feel my head quite painful when I make the exertion."

Isaac's countenance now expressed the deepest compassion, and his voice sank into a low key as he said,

"No, no, don't sing; don't do anything that can cause you pain."

And then Susan, with a woman's quick eye, observing that Isaac's attention was gone from herself to Mary, immediately sang the very words and tune Mary had just given for her instruction, "O come let us sing unto the Lord," and Isaac's educated ear at once turned to the attraction of her charming voice.

"Go on, miss—do go on," said Isaac, eagerly and heartily.

"Go on!—yes, you keep saying 'go on,' but go on with what, pray?" said Susan.

"With the 'Venite,' to be sure," said Isaac, standing up and holding the music of Purcell's chant before Susan's astonished eyes.

"But what *is* the 'Venite,' Mr. Isaac?—I never heard of the song in all my life," said Susan, rather pettishly; "I know I can sing it, if you will but just tune it."

"Goodness me! Susan, dear, don't talk such nonsense," said Mary, looking vexed. "I know you are in the habit of going to church—that 'pig' affair was not so successful that you need to try another of the same kind."

"Mary, how can you say such things?" said Susan, now in her turn becoming excited. "Whether you believe me or not, I never did hear the 'Venite' song in my whole life, either at church—though of course they don't sing songs in churches—or anywhere else. I have often helped to sing 'O come let us sing unto the Lord,' just to some tune like that you did just now—often in church I have done that; but indeed I don't know the 'Venite' song."

Mary Cope saw in an instant that Isaac was surprised at Susan's ignorance, and she could not help feeling some gratification at her downfall in his good opinion. While Isaac, with true tact for the feelings of another, did not officiously point out to Susan what was meant by the word 'Venite;' but after a moment or two of silence, broke the spell that seemed to have fallen upon them, by saying,

"Then, miss, if you will have the goodness to sing that psalm now to this chant," pointing out Purcell in A, "I'll take up my part."

"That psalm?—what psalm?" said Susan.

"'O come let us sing unto the Lord,'" said Isaac; "but perhaps if you had a prayer-book you would sing more easily."

"Yes; of course. If you'll give me a prayer-book, and tell me all the tune, I can sing that psalm."

"Here is the chant," said Isaac; "that is the 'tune,' as you call it," continued he, as he once more held open a music-book before Susan.

"Do take away that great book," said she, pettishly.

Isaac looked dismayed, and Mary Cope smiled. She was quite woman enough to feel gladdened by the shortcomings of her rival.

"I think Susan wants to hear the whole of the chant, Isaac—will you sing it? I am afraid to attempt a note, my head aches so."

"Of course I will," said Isaac, kindly.

And in a high falsetto he sang through two or three verses of the "Venite."

Susan, who did not in the least comprehend the trouble Isaac and Mary were taking to render her superb voice useful on the morrow, and not possessing Isaac's fine intuitive tact for the feeling of others, Susan, on hearing the first notes, looked up in surprise, then began to titter; and this, checked, became a loud laugh by the time the tune was finished.

"Susan! Susan! what is there to laugh at?" said Mary, angrily; while Isaac, understanding he had made himself ridiculous in Susan's eyes, closed his mouth, and stood silent, and shy, and awkward.

"I can't help it," said Susan, still laughing rudely; "why, he sings like a woman!"

"He has done that to oblige you, Susan, or——"

"To oblige *you*, Mistress Cope," said Isaac, chafing; for he could not conceal the irritation he felt at the ridicule Susan so unsparingly bestowed upon him.

"Thank, you, Isaac," said Mary, much gratified, and not sorry at heart that Susan's conduct was gradually lowering her in Isaac's good opinion. "I can tell you, Susan," continued she, "Isaac has a very fine bass voice, and he only sang up there to help you, and to teach you Purcell's chant, because it makes me ill to sing."

"And that is just what I expected to hear, a fine manly voice; and then when those queer topsy-turvy pipes sounded, how could I help laughing?"

And again Susan did not attempt to restrain the expression of her mirth.

"I shall not be of much more use, eh, Mistress Cope?" said Isaac, feeling angry as well as crestfallen; "and therefore I will say good night."

"There, Susan," said Mary, sorrowfully, clasping her hands, "now you have offended Isaac, and what am I to do for to-morrow."

"Bless your heart, Mistress Cope!" said Isaac, heartily, "but I will not be the least bit offended if I can be of any service to *you*!"

With a slight accent on the pronoun; for he had been touched by her evident distress when he attempted to go, and now felt proud at the implied compliment to himself. And Isaac reseated himself, and, after a little pause, said to Mary,

"I am quite willing to help Miss Susan, just for your sake, Mistress Cope."

And now that Susan's mirth had subsided a little, she saw she was in danger of losing her admirer, and in an instant made an attempt to recall him to herself, as she said,

"You are really very kind; and indeed, Mr. Isaac, I am quite ashamed of being so naughty; but I don't mean it,"—and she smiled a languishing smile as she continued—"and I'll try not to give you any more trouble; I think I know what you want me to do—that is, to sing this from beginning to end, to the same tune you did?"

And she pointed to the "Venite" in the prayer-book.

"Yes—yes, Susan; now do try," said Mary.

And then Susan began; and, to do her justice, she sang the psalm admirably, if we except an occasional trip at the end of the verses, which Isaac quickly corrected; and now joining his rich bass voice with hers, even though the harmonies were not filled in, it was easy for Mary Cope, as she listened, to foretell that "to-morrow"—the "to-morrow" that weighed so heavily on her spirits—would be a day of triumph to Susan.

When the last notes of the "Gloria" died away, Isaac and Susan looked at each other.

"What a voice you have, Mr. Isaac," said Susan, glowing with the feeling of delight she had had in the two voices blended so well. "You really *do* sing beautifully!"

"It was most enjoyable, was it not, Mistress Cope?" said Isaac, much gratified, both with Susan's praise, and with the sound of his own voice combined with hers.

"Yes, Isaac," said Mary, again feeling as if the ground were receding from under her feet; "but it is getting late, would you just try the 'Benedicite'?"

"Certainly I will," said Isaac, eagerly. "Now, miss," continued he, holding the open music-book once more before Susan, and giving the key-note, "fa—a—a," lengthened out as he had done before.

"Now you are teazing me again with that, tiresome book; I tell you I hate the sight of it!" said Susan, tossing it aside.

Isaac shrunk back, feeling himself snubbed; and Mary Cope smiled, as she felt her footing a little more secure for the time being.

"Remember, Isaac, Susan does not sing from notes, therefore the music is of no use to her," explained Mary, and yet half ashamed of the satisfaction she felt in exposing Susan's ignorance to Isaac. "But will you be so kind as to sing the first verse of the 'Benedicite,' she will learn it by ear?"

"By ear!" said Isaac, in a loud voice of contempt, which, as truthful chroniclers, we must admit was gratifying to Mary. "And you want me to sing the fourth 'Gregorian'" continued he, rather crossly, for he did not much like the thought of singing falsetto to be laughed at by Susan.

But Susan, with her woman's penetration ever on the watch, and understanding in a moment the reason of this change in Isaac, turned all to her own account, as she said, in a most flattering manner,

"Sing in your beautiful voice, Mr. Isaac. I shall know the tune just the same."

"Shall you, indeed," said he, staring at her, and greatly relieved by this announcement; for, in dealing with young untrained voices in the choir, Isaac had always been accustomed to give the exact note. Now, however, at Susan's request, he ran through the first verse of the "Benedicite" in his natural voice, and she took it up immediately, and chanted—"O all ye works of the Lord, bless ye the Lord, praise him and magnify Him for ever!" so exactly with Isaac's right appreciation and expression, as fully to content him, and make him quite forget he had looked ridiculous in her eyes only a few minutes previously.

And so Susan succeeded in the "Benedicite," and then there was only the "Jubilate" to be attended to; and as by this time her peculiarities were better understood by Isaac and Mary, they were not long in teaching her a third chant, when, to the surprise of all three, the church clock struck nine. Isaac started up as he said—

"I did not know it was so late."

"I am sure I did not," said Susan, "it is so pleasant to be singing together, Mr. Isaac. I quite forgot the time, and I have so much enjoyed the music."

Isaac looked at her: not a particle of uncomfortable feeling at her former misbehaviour remained to take away from the pleasure he felt at his society being prized by so pretty a girl, and one who possessed so charming a voice as Susan Picard; for though Isaac was well known to be a great admirer of the fair sex, he was diffident of his own power of pleasing or attracting women.

"I am sure I am pleased, miss," said he heartily. "I never heard such a voice as yours; the notes are as clear and as round as the treble bell. It is a fine gift!—a fine gift! is it not, Mistress Cope?"

"Yes. Susan has a magnificent voice," said Mary; "but I must thank you for so kindly coming to inquire for me, and for helping me so nicely out of my trouble for to-morrow. And please tell the widow I am doing very well, and Susan I am sure will thank you."

"'Tis nothing—nothing," said Isaac. "You are welcome to anything I can do. Good night." And he moved towards the door.

Susan followed him, and could not resist the pleasure of a little flirtation there while the moon shone full upon Isaac, and he stood with admiring looks, listening to her little nothings. At length the last good night was said, the door shut, and Isaac walked away.

And now it was that he felt the full effect of having eaten nothing since twelve o'clock the day before. He reeled as he went along, but he knew it was from exhaustion. He had had a day of fatigue and anxiety, winding it up by two hours of singing.

"If I can but get home, and have some supper," thought he, "I shall be all right to-morrow."

It was at this moment that Parson Hill was gazing upon him with surprise and vexation: it was then that Parson Hill recorded the fact— "That he had seen Isaac Watson go from Mary Cope's cottage between nine and ten o'clock at night, and in a state of inebriety that rendered him almost unable to walk home."

XIII

WHY PARSON HILL READ THE "VENITE," AND WHY THE CHOIR DID NOT SING

AND the morrow came bright, and clear, and sunny, and the bells pealed forth through the rarefied air; but their pleasant sound did not as beforetime bring pleasurable emotions to the heart of Parson Hill.

"He is ringing, I can hear," sighed he, as he thought of Isaac. "But this affair shall go on. I will make a public example of that man the first convenient opportunity. Mary shall feel ashamed of him and his deeds." And then as he recollected the aged widow, he continued—"I am grieved to my heart for the poor mother; but in this matter it will not do to let the grass grow under my feet. I wonder how the choir will manage to-day? They are not accustomed to sing without Mary; and of course she cannot make her appearance. At all events, I can read the 'Venite' and 'Jubilate,' and, fortunately for me, the congregation can respond." And thus soliloquising, Parson Hill went forth to his duty at the usual hour.

Meanwhile, the children belonging to the choir had assembled at Mary's cottage-door, and she gave them in charge of Susan, admonishing them to be good girls and sing their best—the more so as she herself would not be there to guide them. But on the way to church, and while what Widow Simpson, in the language of former days, called "the bidding bell," was ringing, Isaac Watson came forth from the belfry, and joined Susan and her bevy of girls.

"Good morning, miss; and how is Mistress Cope?" said he.

"She is quite well, thank you, sir," said Susan, forgetting, in the delight she felt at being noticed by Isaac, that Mary Cope was ill.

"Quite well!" said Isaac, in surprise.

"Oh! of course, I mean she is better; but, Mr. Isaac, shall you sit next to me?" simpered Susan.

"Sit next to you, miss! Why, what do you mean? I must sit in my proper place in the choir, and you in Mistress Cope's place."

"Why, I hope you will sit next to me, because you will have to give me the note to begin."

"Give you the note!—no such thing; the treble voices lead—you must find the proper pitch yourself."

"But I don't know how, Mr. Isaac," said Susan in much distress.

"I thought you understood what you had to do," said Isaac, looking troubled, and not the less so when Parson Hill passed hastily, and took no notice either of him or his pretty companion.

"So the parson knows I was at the 'Packhorse,'" said Isaac's conscience, for he thus interpreted the neglect with which he was treated.

"Yes, I do perfectly understand," replied Susan; "but you gave me the note—you put it up to your ear, and then sung out."

"Put it up to my ear!" said Isaac, becoming more and more uneasy the nearer they approached the church.

"Yes, the what-do-you-call-it—you had it in your waistcoat pocket."

Isaac instinctively felt in his pocket, and drew forth a pitch-pipe.

"It is the 'pipe' you are meaning, miss," said he, greatly relieved.

"Yes, that is it; and so you see you must give me the note to begin with."

"No, I must not do that. But if Mistress Cope has forgotten to give you hers, if you please, miss, I will lend you mine," said he, gallantly offering the tiny instrument to Susan, "and then you will be able to begin—to lead off, I mean."

"Thank you, Mr. Isaac, how very kind you are; now I shall do wonders—of course I shall."

"Of a certainty you will," said Isaac confidently, and in a whisper, for they were just entering the church.

The service was intoned, and after listening and finding out for herself what others were doing, Susan took up the note, and joined the congregation in reading the responses, her mellifluous bell-like voice ringing through the whole building, to Isaac Watson's intense satisfaction and delight, to Parson Hill's great surprise, and to the ill-concealed astonishment of the inhabitants of Lawsleigh.

At length it was time to commence the "Venite." The choir stood ready with their open books, the parson occasionally resting his eyes inquiringly upon them, the congregation looking on, and mutely marvelling at the sudden stop in the service; and Isaac Watson bending his large and tall person forward, looking at Susan, and straining his ears to catch her first note; while Susan, hot and uncomfortable, stood up holding Isaac's pitch-pipe to her ear. As the fork emitted no sound, she untied her bonnet, and put it closer to her ear. But as all this had taken more time than it was customary to waste in a church between one part of the reading and another, Parson Hill surmised that something was going wrong, and commenced reading the "Venite," to which the congregation responded; and in due time it came to an end.

Poor Isaac Watson was ready to sink into the earth at the thought of the choir being disgraced in that public way—by seemingly its own neglect; and Susan Picard, as she afterwards said, "could not for the life of her find out what was the matter."

During the reading of the first lesson, Isaac sent a message to Susan, passed from one to another through the choir, to the purport that "she would be pleased to send his pipe."

"Tell him I shall not," replied Susan.

Isaac sent a second message, more peremptory than the first, and Susan returned the same answer. But then Isaac, though well-known in Lawsleigh to be a "shamefaced" man, screwed up his courage, left his place in the choir, and went, in the eyes of the whole congregation, to speak to Susan. He was determined, at any personal sacrifice, to prevent a second mishap.

Wise Isaac Watson!

"I must have my pipe, miss," said Isaac, whispering.

"What a useless, senseless thing it is," said she, angrily; "it cannot give out a sound."

"Give it me back."

"Here, then," said she, offering it to him, and then mischievously withdrawing it, as Isaac attempted to take it.

"This is no place for tom-fool-eries, miss," said Isaac, brusquely; "and if you don't give it me, I will walk out of the church."

"Oh! pray, Mr. Isaac, don't do that. But indeed I can't hear it emit a sound."

"Give it me back," said Isaac.

"But why can't I make it useful?—it guided you."

"Perhaps you don't pinch it."

"Pinch it!" said Susan, trying the effects of one. This she now discovered was the secret—she heard the note, and delightedly exclaimed, "Thank you!—oh! thank you, Mr. Isaac. Now you must leave it with me—well, I never thought to find such good in a pinch!"

"Hush!" said Isaac; "and I think I had better have——"

"When you know I can sing so well," said Susan, reproachfully; "you must leave it with me."

Isaac stood for a second or two irresolute; but Susan again pleaded, and he at length allowed her to keep it, reminding her, as he turned away, that she must begin the fourth Gregorian.

And the strong man, with all his wisdom, was once again bound helpless by the words and looks of the pretty woman.

XIV

HOW SUSAN PICARD TRIUMPHED OVER ALL DIFFICULTIES AND HOW ISAAC WATSON LONGED FOR HIS PIPE

"I DON'T care a bit what you call it," thought Susan; "Glorian or Uproarian, all the same to me—I know I can do it,"

But Susan had still another difficulty to conquer, of which she was in perfect ignorance. It is true she now knew how to obtain a note from the pitch-fork, or pitch-pipe; but she did not know that from that she should take the key-note of anything she wished to sing. It was sufficient for her that the pipe distinctly gave a note on which she could begin. And when the long lesson was over, she pinched the fork, heard the note, and immediately commenced the "Benedicite" to the fourth Gregorian upon C in the space, the note the fork had given her.

For an instant, as was but natural, the choir wavered; but Isaac, feeling instantaneously what Susan had done, and foreseeing a terrible breakdown if she was not supported, dashed in with his bass, roaring like a bull, rather than singing like a man. It was evident to all who saw or heard Isaac, that he was very much excited and very angry. Only one or two others ventured to join, and this compelled Isaac, as it seemed, to sing the louder, and thus try to make up for the absence of many voices.

After the first few verses, Parson Hill, who was an excellent musician, recovered from the shock of hearing the "Benedicite" led off four notes higher than it ought to be; and he, also, like Isaac, having the vision of a crash floating in his imagination, joined in the chant, and assisted in keeping the choir together.

Parson Hill's example—for he did not usually sing during the service—was not lost; and soon the trebles, tenors, and basses one by one began to sing; so that by the time the "Benedicite" drew near the end, the entire choir was singing its loudest, Susan Picard attaining a great triumph, and Isaac Watson heartily lamenting the unlucky moment that he had yielded to Susan's entreaties, and left his pitch-pipe in her hands.

When at length the overtaxed choir ceased, and reseated themselves, Isaac busied himself in wiping away the heavy drops of perspiration that accumulated rapidly, in spite of his efforts to stop them. His mind was running on the "Jubilate," for he foresaw that Susan would lead off again upon C—the note given her by the pipe—and, to his additional vexation, he remembered the chant he had selected for the "Jubilate" was in the key of C, and began on the dominant, so that it would again be raised four notes higher. He dared not again venture to Susan, for, besides the discomfort to himself of going to her in the face of the whole congregation, he intuitively felt that he should gain nothing by it. He felt that, by some means or other, she would manage to retain the pipe, and send him back as he came.

Wise Isaac Watson!

While Isaac was thus uncomfortably summing up his past miseries, and looking forward to more, Parson Hill also was recalling the past, and looking into the future. He was conscious he had in his own mind accused Isaac of making visits to Mary Cope; but now he must change his opinion, for he had seen Isaac walking to church with Susan Picard, and seen, also, that little episode of his attention to her in the church.

"It is the London belle that attracts the handsome smith," said Parson Hill to himself. "I have misjudged him—I thought he had more taste."

And he was so comforted by this turn of events, and so satisfied with Isaac's efforts to keep the choir from a break-down, that he magnanimously determined once more to forgive him all his past offences, and help him in his present dilemma. The fact that Isaac Watson did not wish to appropriate Mary Cope, made his mind easy; and when he again joined his rich voice in the chant, there was not in the whole congregation a voice more hilarious or jubilant than Parson Hill's. A great weight had been taken from his mind. He enjoyed this freedom from perplexity, and revelled in his own happiness.

Wise Parson Hill!

But to return. Exactly as Isaac had anticipated, so it happened. Susan raised the chant four notes, and though he was prepared for this dilemma, he was so completely unstrung by the extraordinary slips of the morning, that when he made the attempt as before to bellow forth a hearty bass, his notes came out wavering, unsteady, and jerking, very unlike Isaac's usually clear, sonorous, and excellent singing. By degrees the choir took up their parts, but as the "Jubilate" is much shorter than the "Benedicite," Susan sang the greater part without any assistance from the trebles, much to her own great delight.

At length the service came to an end, and no one was more relieved by this fact than Isaac Watson, who almost made up his mind that he would never enter the choir again. It must be taken into consideration that Isaac was a shy man, and to be thus publicly lowered in the opinion of the entire inhabitants of Lawsleigh, and from no fault of his own, was almost more than he could bear.

Susan, on the contrary, quite unconscious of all the misery she had occasioned, or of all the trouble she had given, plumed herself on her own performance, held her head high, and felt, as was really the case, that she had acquired a great success. She did not know that she must except from her admirers Parson Hill and Isaac Watson. On returning from church, the villagers complimented her. Hannah Barker knew Susan, and joined her as she said,

"Yours be a sweet voice, surely, miss—you sing like to a bird," and then she turned to speak to another, and said, "Gude morning, Widdy Mason, and how be you?—I have a-been telling miss as her sings like to a bird."

"Like to a bird!" said the Widow Mason. "Moore like to a angel, I say; and Hannah, she's a-gotten the angel's face, anyhow. And pray, miss, and how bees Mistress Cope? I be a-told as she's a-had she's face spoiled."

"Mary's better this morning, thank you," said Susan, much charmed with the notice she attracted, though, upon examining the Widow Mason, she did think her a great fat, red-faced woman, and very vulgarly dressed. But Susan was fond of praise, and even from this woman it was welcome.

"Her's better, is her? Her's a pert minx anyhow," said the widow, turning to her friend; "and I shouldna care much if she's face be a-spoiled out and out; not that it was ever so much of a face, only to have a gude big sore on she's cheek, and all a-swelled, and she's eyes bunged up a bit, must put she down. And most times 'tis that as she wants, Hannah, to be put down—coz, you see, th' passon makes such a fuss of she."

Susan did not hear all the Widow Mason said, or understand even what she did hear, but thinking the widow and Hannah Barker would be glad to know Mary was doing well, she said,

"Mary quite means to go to the school to-morrow—it was Dr. Smith said she had better not sing to-day," and Susan simpered, and looked conscious of her own good voice.

"Ay, miss. And it be a gude thing as her didna sing the morn," said the widow; "and such a angel's voice to sing for she! And sure, miss, you be a-going to sing again the afternoon? And yours be a bonny face! Now, if you had spoiled your face—but you havena—I should have been sorry; but that minx, Molly Cope—and for why is her to be called Mistress, pray?—such a stuck up thing! I can't bide she—no, I can't."

Susan, though delighted with the flattery to herself, did not understand why evil must be said of Mary; but as Hannah was going one way to her home, and the widow another, Susan turned to meet Isaac and his mother, who she saw were coming slowly from the church.

"Good morning, Mrs. Simpson—how do you do?" said Susan, quite unconscious that she had bestowed an unusual epithet on the old woman.

The dwellers on the moor were all called by their Christian names, except in cases of widowhood, when the distinctive word "widow" belonged to the bereaved woman. This in part accounts for the Widow Mason's jealousy of Mary Cope's claim to the title of "Mistress;" but Mary herself was unaware that this was an offence in the eyes of the inhabitants of the moor, and Parson Hill had not foreseen that to call her "Mistress

Cope" would cause any misunderstanding or ill-will, especially as no one thought of disputing her claim to the title of "schoolmistress."

"Thank you, miss—I be cheery," said the widow.

"Didn't the singing go well, Mr. Isaac?" said Susan.

"Well!" said Isaac, in such a tone of astonishment and annoyance as to make Susan start; and then he added, in a tone of entreaty, "Oh! miss, do give me my pipe!"

"But I shall want it for the afternoon, Mr Isaac; and you know you promised Mary you would come between the services and teach me the tunes you want me to sing."

"No—no; I tell you—no. Just please to give me my fork," said Isaac.

"No. I shall certainly want it again, so I shall not give it up; and I shall do my very best this afternoon—I shall astonish even you," and Susan looked at Isaac with a smile that she intended should say, "How can you refuse me!" But Isaac either did not understand the language of the eyes, or he was intent on having his own way, for all the reply he made was,

"Give me my pipe."

"Everybody says I sing beautifully—quite like an angel, Mr. Isaac—they do really," added she emphatically, as she caught an incredulous expression creeping over Isaac's face. And after a pause, as Isaac said nothing, she continued in a tone of reproach,

"And you yourself said the very same thing last night, Mr. Isaac."

"Ay, ay! Mercy me!" said Isaac, shaking his head in a comfortless way. "But now I want my fork."

"Well, then, you have given up thinking I have a charming voice?" said Susan, paying no attention to Isaac's reiterated query. "Why, how strange and fickle you are! for say whatever you will, it positively rang through the church."

"Yes, miss, you have an excellent voice," said Isaac, thinking to satisfy Susan and his own conscience at the same time; and then he added afterwards, as if he would not be cajoled out of his rights, "but I want my pipe."

"Yes, miss; yours be a 'stonishing voice," said the widow; "a-piping up to the top so cheery and clear."

"Then you will come to Mary's cottage, Mr. Isaac?" pleaded Susan, taking no notice of the widow's complimentary speech, in her anxiety to secure Isaac.

"Ay, miss, in course he'll come," said the widow. And then turning to Susan, and speaking in a whisper, she added—"He is that shy as is 'stonishing; but maybe he'll come in spite of that."

"If you please, miss, do give me my pipe," said Isaac humbly, as they arrived at that part of the road where their routes diverged.

Susan held up the coveted pipe, and laughed, as she walked away, saying,

"You must come, Mr. Isaac, if only to fetch this."

And with a sigh, that almost amounted to a groan, Isaac walked home with his grandmother.

XV

HOW SUSAN PICARD BECAME MISTRESS OF LAWSLEIGH SCHOOL, *VICE* MARY COPE, DISMISSED ON ACCOUNT OF ILL HEALTH

SEVERAL of the choir went to Isaac's house, as soon as they had despatched their early dinners, but they all failed in their attempts to induce him to go with them to Mary Cope's, and so to try and put Susan Picard under some sort of restraint, and thus prevent her from destroying the beauty of the music. Isaac seemed to think—"The better part of valour was discretion." He foresaw all his pains and trouble would be thrown away. Susan's entire ignorance of the science of music, or even of musical notes, would render all his exertion useless, and he should again, in all probability, be humiliated.

The choir, therefore, eventually agreed amongst themselves that Susan should be kept in ignorance of the chants they intended to use; that one of the boys who sang treble should be taken to sit with the men, and by them be made to lead, so that they would be independent of Susan Picard's fine voice.

"Necessity is the mother of invention," saith the proverb; for Isaac had not thought of this very simple arrangement until he had been made so uncomfortable by Susan's errors.

And so the Sunday came to an end, and the afternoon services at the church were much more enjoyable to Isaac Watson than those of the morning, and the chants were sung in the keys intended by the writers of them; but still there was no denying that Susan Picard's voice was charming in the ears of all who appreciated sweet sounds.

In the evening "the School Cottage," as Mary's house was called, was beset by all who strolled forth for their Sunday's walk; and amongst others came

Parson Hill himself. A few words of explanation from Mary satisfied him that she had not been to blame at the time when the accident happened; and having, as we have seen, settled in his own mind that it was Susan Picard, and not Mary Cope, to whom Isaac was a visitor on the preceding Saturday night: and also having made himself happy by coming to this conclusion, he was able to make amends to Susan for any imaginary insult she had received from him on the morning she had visited the school, by heartily praising her magnificent voice, and thanking her, in the presence of all assembled there, for the service she had rendered the Lawsleigh choir during the absence of Mary Cope. And Parson Hill left Susan Picard convinced that she had made a great mistake—viz., that he was not a "'orrid man;" for at all events he understood music, and appreciated her voice.

And when the long day was fairly over, Isaac's anxiety as regarded the choir at an end, Parson Hill doubly happy in the thought that Mary was not in fault, as had been represented to him, and that Isaac's visit was to Susan—and the inhabitants of the village of Lawsleigh gradually sinking into repose—there were two who were unable to sleep: Susan, because she could not cease to think of her great triumph, and of the admiration she had excited; and Mary, from a creeping dread of the entire annihilation of her hopes in the future.

As a rule Mary was not of an envious or jealous disposition, but the large amount of worship given to her cousin in her presence, joined to Susan's exaggerated account of her own doings, almost made Mary wish she had taken the services upon herself, although she by no means felt equal to the exertion.

On Saturday she had disquieted herself in anxiety for the Sunday; and yet her place had been filled up, and she herself left to the rest she required. When she recalled this fact, she felt ashamed of her jealousy of Susan. And now she troubled herself with thoughts of the morrow—Monday. Poor Mary, she was like many others, swayed by human feebleness; and so her mind was full of "how she should manage with the school tomorrow." She knew she was disfigured that she looked weary, and felt ill. At another time she would hardly have cared for this change in her personal appearance;

but as her strength of body had succumbed, so her mind was less steadfast; and foreseeing from instinct that the young villagers were much more likely to laugh at the great patch on her forehead, and at her swollen face, than to sympathize with her sufferings; and having had plenty of proof that the villagers, with the vicar at their head, were Susan's most devoted admirers, and concluding, therefore, that Isaac Watson must be completely charmed, she suffered these things together to render her unhappy and dissatisfied in the present, and to crush her hopes in the future.

When she at length slept, she was pursued in her dreams by failure in all she undertook, and by the vision of Susan triumphantly resident in the village, as schoolmistress and leader of the choir!

But the morrow came. On Monday morning at nine o'clock the village schoolroom was prepared for the reception of the scholars by its young mistress, Mary Cope.

As Susan's dislike to Parson Hill had quite melted away after his complimentary speeches, she consented to go with Mary and try to help her; and as the latter was very reluctant, in the present state of her health, to be left alone, Susan remained at the school. She thought her magnificent voice had captivated the parson as well as his flock; and she was not unwilling to add to her former triumph by giving him a chance of bestowing his praises in the presence of the school. And in due time Parson Hill made his appearance. He told Mary "he was glad to see she was able to resume her duties, and by the following Sunday he hoped she would be well enough to lead the choir, and thus preserve the voice he had heard so mellifluous in the Church from wasting its sweetness on the hoary Tors of Dartmoor, and allow it to return in its pristine freshness to entrance the cognoscenti of the metropolis."

The business of the school commenced. At length a ragged and dirty-looking little girl went up to Parson Hill with her spelling. He started back, apparently in extreme surprise, and after surveying the child steadily for a second or two, he said,

"Turn round—back this way."

The child turned and stood with its back to him, and after a few seconds more of deliberate survey, he said,

"Turn again—this way;" and when the child obeyed, he continued, "and pray has your mother hands?—has she two hands like these?" exhibiting his own to the child.

"Yes, sir," said she.

"Then she has not any water?—she has not any soap!"

"Don't know, sir."

"Has she no thread?—no needles?"

"Don't know, sir," again said the child, now showing symptoms of agitation.

"Mary Cope, is the school full of work?" said he.

"No, sir; there was but little to do last week; now there is no sewing left."

"Then mend this child; and there is another and another," said he, as he pointed out those children whose garments were in rags and disorder.

"The old story," muttered he to himself—"all things, substances, people, want mending on this earth. What a marvellous place heaven must be, where all things are perfect—perfect," thought he. "And, Mary," continued he aloud, "I do think this kind young lady will help you—she looks good-natured, and—and wishful to oblige. I should like to ask you a favour," said he to Susan, in the most deferential tone; and she, radiant with the inward satisfaction his flattery had excited, said,

"I am sure I shall be very happy if I can do anything to oblige you."

"Thank you," said he, bowing; "you can oblige me. I see that Mary is already tired with the exertion she has made, and I shall indeed be indebted to you," added he, courteously, "if you will supply her place here as well as you did at church yesterday—just for this one morning. The repose will do Mary good; and I trust the exercise of mind do you no harm," and again the parson bowed. "If you will become the head of this large establishment," and here he drew himself up to his full height, and spread out his hands as if he were indicating an extensive domain, instead of a simple village school filled with ragged and dirty children, "and allow Mary Cope to return home."

After a few seconds of ineffectual thought on Susan's part, to make a proper reply to Parson Hill's speech, she was saved the trouble, for he turned to Mary and said,

"I see your friend grants my request, Mary; go you therefore to the repose you so much need. And, children," continued he, thus calling the attention of the school, "here is your new mistress for the time being—Mistress Susan Picard, *vice* Mistress Mary Cope, on sick leave."

Mary left the school; but Susan felt a strange, disagreeable feeling come over her as she heard her new title from the lips of Parson Hill; she did not like to be called "Mistress."

XVI

HOW PARSON HILL INSTRUCTED MISTRESS SUSAN PICARD IN HER NEW DUTIES; AND HOW THE NEW BOY, JOE SANDS, ENJOYED HIS FIRST DAY AT SCHOOL

SUSAN was promoted to Mary's chair.

"Now, ragged and dirty little child," said Parson Hill, "go to Mistress Susan Picard," and it seemed to Susan he singled out the dirtiest and most untidy child in the school. As Susan did not know what was required of her, Parson Hill went to her assistance.

"You see these holes in this child's frock?"

Susan assented.

"It is now your duty, as representing Mistress Mary Cope, to take this garment from the child—in other words, to unfrock her, and teach her to mend it."

And Susan fancied the parson's voice was already less suave than it had previously been.

"But she is *so* dirty!" stammered Susan, in dismay.

"True, O young lady—that is, Mistress Susan Picard, she is dirty; but bring her this way, we will mend even that—come, come, come, dirty child—come, Mistress Susan Picard."

And Parson Hill led the way to a natural spring, flowing from a rock at a few paces from the entrance to the school.

"Now, if you please, Mistress Susan Picard," and the parson bowed and spoke in his most courteous tones, "make clean the dirty child—oh-h! we will mend, mend—we will mend!"

For one moment Susan hesitated; but thought is rapid, and she feared, if she resisted this, some worse scrape would happen to her. She therefore began to untie the child's frock, while the vicar called out lustily,

"Jane Hanmer, bring soap and towels."

And Susan now set herself to work in earnest, washed the dirty child, and returned to the schoolroom sore at heart and sadly discomfited.

Her next task was, *not* to mend the soiled garment of the child, for that would have been comparatively easy, but to teach the little thing to do it. As the child could not sew well or darn at all, it happened, naturally enough, that Susan had a great deal of trouble; and Parson Hill amused himself, unknown to her, by watching and observing that every time Susan took the frock in her own hand, ostensibly to show the child what to do, she herself darned several rows up and down; by which means the long tear progressed very quickly; and whenever Susan thought Parson Hill's attention was entirely withdrawn from herself—though, in point of fact, this never happened—her nimble fingers stitched away at their topmost speed, in the hope of the sooner getting rid of the nasty, dirty, smelling frock, and very stupid and dull little child.

Susan expected to find the acute and painful sharpness, or knowingness, of a London child; she met only the stolid obtuseness of unawakened intellect in the Dartmoor born.

"I should not care one bit hearing them say their lessons," thought she to herself; "but this 'orrid, dirty, ragged, stupid child to be washed and darned—it is quite abominable!"

If Susan had set herself to work with alacrity and apparent good humour, to a task altogether at variance with her former habits or her present desires, no one would more have appreciated such self-sacrifice than Parson Hill, or have more highly rewarded it on a fitting opportunity; but as it was, few could have had more pleasure than he in thus humbling pretensions to fine ladyism, and affectations in dress he thought unbecoming to one in Susan's position. When Susan's labour was drawing to a close, she took opportunities occasionally of watching what

Parson Hill was doing, and his actions and conversation only the more convinced her that, after all, her original opinion was the right one.

It happened, soon after the opening of the school, and before the arrival of Parson Hill, that one of the boys, a new comer, had been unruly, and Mary Cope had placed him in the middle of the room standing on a stool, the customary punishment for some kinds of insubordination.

When Parson Hill entered, he did not apparently bestow any notice on this boy; but during the exercises of a class of boys, in which they were called upon to explain what was meant by being "at ease," and to which one replied, "To sit us down when us is tired," and another, "When us has got no hurts," and to which one brisk boy answered, "To sit, or to stand, or to lie down, just where us likes;" and to him Parson Hill said, "Then I conclude the boy standing on the stool in the middle of the room is a friend of yours, and that he agrees with you in opinion; I conclude he has pleased himself in occupying that conspicuous position, but I humbly confess I should not be 'at ease' so placed. It is true there is no accounting for taste," added he in a conciliatory tone. "Perhaps that boy likes to be looked at, therefore he is 'at ease.'"

The boy coloured and held his head down.

"If he enjoys things in a different form from others, I do not wish to dispute his right to do so. He has my permission to continue to stand there, since we may infer it adds to his happiness; but I do not enjoy standing on a stool—do you, Jack?" addressing a great boy.

"No, sir."

"Tastes differ, as I said before," said Parson Hill, blandly. "But why do not you, Jack?"

"Coz folks stares so."

"Exactly," said the parson with a smile; "well, new boy," continued he, addressing the culprit, "what is your name?"

"Joe Sands, sir."

"The clock is about to strike twelve. Do you know, Joe Sands, we are going to leave this room?"

"Yes, sir," said the boy, now roaring loudly.

"Would you like to stand there until we return at two?"

"No, no, NO!" bawled the boy.

"Pray do not distress yourself," said the parson kindly; "if you had wished to remain here longer, standing at your 'ease,' I would have given you permission."

"Please, sir, I don't."

"Very well; I quite understand. What then, new boy, Joe Sands—what would you wish to do?"

"Please sir, to goo hoome."

"Go—go home, new boy, Joe Sands."

But by this time the boy had left the school, and Parson Hill, speaking to those remaining, said,

"The new boy is evidently impatient to tell of his first day's experience of our school. It may be different in some things from his previously-formed opinion, and his friends may wonder when they learn that, of his own free will, he placed himself above every boy here."

Parson Hill bowed to Susan, and told her when the clock struck twelve she might dismiss the school.

When Susan returned home she was very angry.

She never had been so treated in all her life; she never would go near to that abominable school again. And as for Parson Hill, Mary might say what she pleased, but he was, without exception, the most disagreeable, the most tormenting, and the most 'orrid man she had ever met with. He treated those poor children most shamefully; and if he treated Mary as he had done herself, she could only say that Mary deserved it for putting up with it. In point of fact, he ought to be "shewn up" in the *Times*; and when she got back to town—which, she was happy to say, would be in a few days—she would just see after "a leader" on the subject of Dartmoor parsons, and so let the world know of their cruelties.

"And then again," resumed she, "even Dartmoor itself was a very much over-rated place! If people knew exactly what it really was, instead of what it was supposed to be—something grand and glorious, she imagined—if only they knew it as she had seen it, they would never come near it. There were no omnibuses, no cabs, no theatres, no great

singers, no public gardens, no parks, no shops, no churches—only one—
and almost no people. And it was so still and quiet, it made her quite
nervous; and as for the heaps of tipsy men, they were a disgrace to Old
England."

When Susan ceased speaking, Mary ventured to ask what she meant
by a "leader."

"A leader! Don't you know what I mean by a leader? Why, how very
ignorant you must be! Everybody reads the "leading article" on this or
that question, and everybody talks of it, and not only one day, Mary, but
every day in the year. And you don't know what I mean! Well, you are
ignorant!"

"Then tell me, Susy, what is it about?" said Mary, simply, "and where is
it to be found?"

"It is about everything," said Susan, with enthusiasm, "and it is to be
found everywhere! Give me to-day's *Times*, and I'll soon show you a
leading article."

"Oh—h! if it is in a newspaper," said Mary, "of course I am not likely
to know, because I never see newspapers."

"No, you have no newspapers, actually no *Times*!" and Susan lifted up
her arms in the greatness of her astonishment—"no *Punch*! no *Fun*!" and
then Susan laughed uncontrollably as she reiterated, "no fun, no fun—I am
quite sure you have no fun, you are so solemn and steady." And here she
tried to pull her features into an expression of demureness, but failing in
this, she made the room ring with her hearty peals of laughter as she said,
"No *Punch*, no 'Punch and Judy,'—they are quite different, Mary, though
you don't know even that. No *Cassell*, no *Leisure Hour*—oh—h! what a
mistake, why, all your hours are leisure! But, indeed and in truth, you have
no anything that civilized people have! Mary, you may believe me or not,
but this is the most dreadfully dull and disagreeable place on the face of
the earth; and I cannot help saying, though it may seem ungrateful, that I
shall be most thankful to get back to Regent Street and to life."

Susan clasped her hands joyfully as she finished her speech, and
Mary looked grave. Mary had often had the best of the argument in

conversations with Susan. She had often marvelled at her ignorance of things generally well-known; and sometimes she had prided herself that her cousin fell in the opinion of others for the want of knowledge such as she herself possessed. But now Susan had fairly turned the tables, for Mary had never heard of a "leading article" or seen a "leader," or even knew what either was, or the difference, if any, between them. And then, too, Susan had hinted something about the harm that one or both could do to Dartmoor parsons; which at first struck Mary with a little awe, for, though she was not born on the moor, she had never known anybody in the whole world so powerful as Parson Hill.

But Mary's reverie on this important subject was brought to a close by the appearance at the cottage of a third person.

XVII

WHICH TREATS OF SUSAN PICARD'S OPINION OF PARSON HILL

WHILE Susan's anger was at its height, and Mary Cope engaged in clearing away the remains of dinner, James Marvel put his head in at the open window, as he had done on the previous Saturday morning, and said,

"Aweel, aweel!—so you are mighty busy, Mistress Cope?"

"Oh! Mr. Marvel, do come in!" said Susan; "you never finished telling me of Parson Hill's abominable treatment of you."

"Eh, lassie! what be that yer saying?"

"You were telling me, when you were here last, how very ill the parson behaved to you."

"No, no," said James, shaking his head—"I never said any ill of the minister."

"Yes, you did—you said he horsewhipped you."

"I said as the minister told me to fetch his whip."

"To be sure you did; and now, Mary," said Susan, "did you ever hear in all your life of any one behaving so disgracefully? In London no person would bear it—that is, no one who had ever read 'Uncle Tom's Cabin,' and that is everybody. It is even worse treatment than the poor slaves have in America! Why, Mr. Marvel, why don't you show him up in the *Times*?"

"Show—him—in the *Times*!" said James, slowly. "I have never seen a picture of the minister, but that is a gude idea, miss. I am thinking the *Times* Noos would look very well with a pictur of the minister to its head."

"Dear me!" said Susan, "how ignorant people are! Surely, Mr. Marvel, you have never been in London, and perhaps never seen the *Times*!—there are no pictures in the *Times*. *Punch* has very good ones, and *Fun* is excellent; there is *Diogenes*, too, and there are many illustrated papers quite wonderful to see, but the *Times* is not illustrated."

"Mercy me, miss!—never seed the *Times* Noos?—aw, aw, aw!—and Lon'on Ceety I have seed afore you was born."

"Well, never mind that," said Susan, seeing her error, and therefore willing to change the subject; "just finish your own story."

"There is no much to tell," said James.

"You have told me quite enough to raise my resentment," said Susan, smarting under the fancied indignities she herself had suffered. "To think that any one should dare to treat a fellow creature as you have been treated, Mr. Marvel!—and when we know we are all equal!—you have just as good a right to horsewhip him as——"

"Law, massy me!—horsewhip the master!—and what for, then?"

"Because he horsewhipped you."

"He didna, I tell you!" said James, bringing his fist heavily down on the window-sill. "It be true as he worrited about them there strawberries, and I goed off to grandfather, and axed him to lend me a hand-glass to cover up some roots, and so force them to come early, and grandfather lended me a glass; and then the weather come fine, and I watered my strawberries, and taked such care on them, as my master had a-got them a whole fortnight afore the rest of the neighbourhood."

"I am sorry for it," said Susan—"heartily sorry! I wish he had never seen another strawberry as long as ever he had lived!"

"But then, miss, don't you see the minister did me much gude. He made a mon of me whiles I was but a lad—I grew so sharp after everything, and set myself a-doing everything. At first I did these ways only to keep off such worrits for ever and ever; but then I soon found the gude of it and soon got to have a great pride in doing everything the bestest way, and a-having everything the first of anybody in the whole country round. It was a fine plan—a fine plan!"

"Well, I never!" said Susan— "a fine thing to be horsewhipped!"

"Massy me, miss!—aw, aw, aw!—why, that there was all gammon."

"Gammon! I am sure you said he horsewhipped you!"

"Susan," said Mary, "you forget what you are saying."

"I don't, Mary. I have quite the conviction, clear on my mind, that Mr. Marvel said his master horsewhipped him."

"Bless your pratty face!" said James, much to Susan's delight—"no no, he never didn't touch a hair of my head!"

"You said he told you to fetch the whip, and——"

"I know—I know; and most times when my master mounted his horse he would say, 'Now, James, my whip-if-you-please,' so slow and solemn-like."

"'Orrid man!" said Susan, angrily—"why did not you tell him to fetch his whip himself, and so then run away?"

"Weel, miss, you see I had been brought up to mind and be obedient; and then I had not nowhere's to run to, so I always fetched the whip, and——"

"There now, that is what I say; every time, if you don't say it, you make me feel quite sure that that 'orrid Parson Hill did horsewhip you unmercifully."

"And it be pratty much as I felt myself, miss," said James, laughing. "Every time it sim to me as I had had a gude licking—but I hadna. The master never touched me—never; and there is not a kinder master the whole country through, nor a betterer!"

"Why, I thought all the time you meant quite the contrary," said Susan, in a tone of disappointment. "I am sure I quite mean what I say—that I have never known so disagreeable, or ungentlemanly, or hardhearted a person."

"Perhaps, miss, when you know him betterer, you will maybe think betterer of him."

"No, I shall not," said Susan in a decided tone, as James Marvel turned away. "I shall always detest and despise him, as a man who takes every mean advantage. He is enormously fond of making other people work— it would be more becoming to him to work. He is very desirous other people should give reasons for everything—had he not better give his own reasons? I despise him!"

XVIII

OF THE WIDOW MASON AND THE DOINGS AT THE "PACKHORSE"

Isaac Watson had not forgotten the taunt of the Widow Mason, *viz.*, that he did not pay his score; and on the evening of this same Monday he determined to go and take his name out of her books. And after having made his mind easy on that subject, he thought he would call at the School Cottage and see Mary Cope once more; for though, as we have seen, Susan's voice had power to charm him each time he heard it, her want of science not only troubled him, by putting everything wrong, but left a feeling of uneasiness on his mind whenever he thought of the humiliation of the choir through her misdeeds. Neither Susan nor her charming voice had any share in the attraction that drew Isaac to inquire after Mary Cope. And so Isaac went first to the "Packhorse," but did not as usual seat himself or call for cider.

"Now, Mister Isaac, I'll bring your cup, eh?" said the Widow Mason.

"No, thank you," said Isaac, hesitating, and stroking his cap round and round; for though he had made up his mind, as he walked to the "Packhorse," that he would not touch a drop of cider until after he had paid his score, on being actually there he found it more difficult to resist than he had anticipated.

His old companions were looking on. He felt awkward thus standing aloof, and half ashamed of what now appeared to him deserting those with whom he had formerly been so friendly.

"No cider, Mr. Isaac!" said the widow, tossing her head. "In course, then, I be obliged to you for your gude company—been't I, Mister Peter?"

"In course, Widdy—in course you be."

"But," said Isaac, hesitating, "I want to pay off my score."

"Oh—h!" said the widow; "that be a very differenter tune—coz why? when people pays their scores, then the landlady stands treat. So just you toss off that there cup the whiles I reckon up."

We have said Isaac was good-natured and good-tempered. The widow's disagreeable manner had not made him angry, but her kindness in standing treat subdued him. He was naturally shy, and he felt painfully the awkwardness of his present position—all his old companions staring at him, and wondering why he kept aloof. Isaac, as he analyzed his feelings, felt that he marvelled at himself. He saw them whispering and elbowing each other. This combination of circumstances caused him to accept the widow's treat with more alacrity than he would otherwise have done. At length Peter Barker said aloud, in a jeering tone, and pointing his thumb over his shoulder to indicate Isaac:

"Don't you know? He can't never noo moore come and sit along of us, and smoke his pipe, and drink his cider—coz why!—eh!—don't you know?"

"Know!" said another, in a still louder tone, "to be sure I knows. He be a-going and a-sweet-hearting to that theere pratty young meeden as singed to the church."

"Ay, lad," said Peter; "*and* to Mistress Cope."

"What, both of them to one time?"

"Ay, lad. First the one, then the t'other," and the men who were listening to this dialogue chorused it with,

"Both of them to one time?—both!"

"Mistress Cope, did you say?" said the Widow Mason—"Mistress Cope! Here, Mister Isaac, here be your score a-added up—five shelling and nine pennies."

"Five shillings, widow!" said Isaac in amazement.

"Five shelling, Mister Isaac. Here, Ann, lass, fill up Mister Isaac's cup. In course you will have a gude treat; it never shall be said as Widdy Mason does not treat well. Now, Mister Isaac, take another pull."

"But, widow," stammered Isaac, "I think——"

"Why for, pray, is that young minx, Molly Cope, to be called mistress?" said the widow, interrupting Isaac; "can you tell I that?" continued she, as she snapped her fingers at the men who were drinking.

"Meedens is called mistress, I have heard tell," said one, "when they haves schools."

"No," said the widow, sturdily, "meedens is not never called mistress."

"It be the passon as calls she mistress, I be a-thinking," said another.

"Ay!—it be the passon—and for why?" said Peter.

"And what does you think, Mister Isaac" said the widow.

"Why, I must say I think five shillings a large sum, and——"

"An-an," said the widow, interrupting him, sneeringly, "and pray now, Mister Isaac, what would you please to be a-saying?" and then, before he could speak, she added, in a good-humoured tone, and with a hearty manner, "come, come, mop up your drink—I be a-standing treat—what! thee art not a-going to be a milk-sop 'cause thee hast gotten a score?"

"He would like to have a score of such treats!" laughed one of the men.

"And he *shall* have so much treat as he likes. Come, Mister Isaac," added the widow, coaxingly, "don't stand there in the doorway, there be somebody as wants to come in, and I be a-wanting to sit down, my legs be tired of standing; and most times I do stand when a genelman be a-going to pay his score—ho! ho! ho!" laughed she, holding her fat sides; "coz why?—in politeness I must make my curtsy."

"Here, widow—here is the money," said Isaac, crossly; "six shillings—give me the change."

"And give you the change—here, Mister Isaac, one, two, three pennies," and the widow, after making her curtsy, seated herself heavily on a wooden chair, as Isaac slowly took up the pence.

"And, Mister Isaac, you did not tell us your 'pinion about Molly Cope, as I calls she," said the widow, tossing her head.

"Molly Cope," repeated Isaac, staring and jingling the pence in his hand.

"For-bye you call she Mistress Cope; but us have a-been saying," said the widow, thus craftily drawing in all who were present, though she alone had uttered the slur, "as meedens has not no right to be called mistress."

As this reading of Mary Cope's title was quite new to Isaac, he began to feel irritable; and clever though he was, his intellect was more solid than brilliant, and in such a case as the present, required time to look round and see his position.

"Isaac, lad, come, come, I knows you be not too grand to sit you down and have a pipe," said an old man, a great crony of Isaac's; "don't you mind that saucy widdy—come, come and sit you down," and the old man made room for him on the same settle.

"Oh-h!" said the widow again, jeeringly, "you need not ax Mister Isaac—Jacob Smerdon, you need not ax he—coz why?—him be a-going a sweet-hearting!"

This sally made the men laugh; but Jacob Smerdon continued to make signs to Isaac to come and sit by him; and Isaac, uncomfortable at standing thus aloof from his former friends, as well as disturbed by what the Widow Mason had said about Mary Cope, at length yielded.

"What was said about Mistress Cope?" said Isaac, in a low voice to Jacob.

"Don't thee mind what that saucy widdy says; her hitted Mistress Cope a slap; but her's always gotten a slap for somebody."

"And does you happen to know if Molly Cope's face be a-mended yet?" said the widow, who had not heard what Isaac and Jacob had said.

"It be that spoiled as be 'stonishing," said Peter.

"Massy me!" said the widow, laughing; "quite spoiled outright—I never didn't think it was so much of a face—I have knowed many betterer. Now, Mister Jacob, there be your grandchild, Phœbe her have a-gotten rosy cheeks, and face is a long way afore Molly Cope's."

"'Pinionses differs, widdy," said Jacob; "Mistress Cope's be a more delicater face, and Mistress Cope's a-gotten a more delicater speech. Most times I thinks Mistress Cope be so white, and so still, and so smiling—just like to they grand ladies as be to the vickridge."

"Queer notions yours be, Jacob," said the widow; "Mistress Cope's skin be not no more delicater nor she's neighbours, only she be mighty stuck up—she holds up she's head as if she was somebody—she be not—she be nobody; leastways, she be only Molly Cope. Why for should Molly Cope hold up she's head higher nor mine? I gets my living, she gets she's—I be just so 'spectable as she. And you be quite right, Jacob, after all, for 'pinionses does differ,'" and the widow went and looked at herself in the small cracked glass that hung up by the side of the clock, and tossed her head as she continued, "I have knowed the time when there was plenty 'pinionses as—as—" the widow hesitated, but one of the men, seeing her meaning, said,

"As admired your face widdy; and there be plenty of them 'pinionses leaved yet—aw! Aw! aw!"

All this time Isaac sat drinking, quite unconscious that he was becoming gradually unfit for the visit he contemplated to Mary Cope; but he continued to sit on and on and to drink pint after pint, until at length Jacob Smerdon arose to go.

"Come, lad," said he, to Isaac, "don't thee stop no longer; I be a-going to pay my score."

"Very well," said Isaac, rather glad to go, though he had been unwilling to make the first move, "and I will pay for what I have had."

But when the widow demanded "one shelling and four pennies," as due from him, Isaac again found to his dismay that he had not so much with him.

"Never you mind, Mister Isaac, I'll score you up again," said the widow.

"But I cannot have had all that," said Isaac, remonstrating.

Cider was fourpence a quart, and he thought he could not have had so much.

"Maybe as you have a-given it away," said she, sneeringly.

Isaac remembered that the score he had paid off was much larger than he had anticipated, and now he knew that he had not had so much as amounted to one shilling and fourpence. But he also knew his thoughts had been pre-occupied; and once again he felt he had put himself in the power of Widow Mason, and that for the present there was nothing left but to submit to have a score.

He left the "Packhorse" with Jacob Smerdon, none the better for the cider he had had, though not actually overcome by it; vexed with himself that he had not resisted more manfully, and troubled with the Widow Mason's disparaging mention of Mary Cope.

XIX

WHAT JANE SANDS SAID TO MARY COPE

WHEN the old man Jacob Smerdon turned off to his home, Isaac walked slowly on towards Mary Cope's cottage; and while pondering on the kind of reception she might vouchsafe to him, he heard quick steps following him, and turning round, saw Jane Sands, the wife of a labourer in the village.

"Mister Isaac!" said the woman. "And how be you?"

"And how are you, Jane?" said Isaac, shaking hands with the woman. "And where are you going at this time of night?"

"I be a-going to the school-mistress."

And Jane, who was somewhat of a virago, clenched her fist and nodded her head, as if she meditated something terrible.

"To see Mistress Cope? Why, Jenny, woman, we can go together, for I am going there!"

"I'll gie't her!" said the woman, as she quickened her pace, and clenched her fist the tighter.

"Why, what can she have done?" said Isaac, in astonishment at the ill-feeling he again saw manifested towards one of whom he had always thought so well.

"Done! rabbit her! I'll let she know what she have a-done. She be a fine mistress to a school, Isaac, she be!"

And the woman strode hastily on, and, as she neared the cottage, left Isaac, ran forward, and knocked at the door with a loud and startling knock. Susan came to the door, and Isaac quickened his pace as he heard Jane Sands's loud voice, and saw her uncourteous manner.

"I wants the school-mistress—where be she?"

"How do you do, Mr. Isaac?" said Susan, in joyful tones.

But the woman pushed her aside and entered the cottage.

"I be come for the penny as my boy Joe gied you the morn," said she, addressing Mary.

"I don't understand you," said Mary, gently.

"I be a-going to make you understand," said the woman, clenching her fist and menacing Mary. "My boy Joe goed to your school the morn, to be larned his letters, and you never larned he no thing, for you set he a-top on a stool, when all the tothers in the school was a-sitting theyselves down quite comfortable. Be I to pay a penny for that? So you'll just gie I back the penny!"

"If you have anything to say of any child belonging to the school," said Mary, "you must have the goodness to go to the school-room to-morrow morning at nine o'clock and state your case."

"Aw-w-w! And you thinks as I be a-going to that there school, does you? And you would set I a-top of a stool, would you? Oh-h-h my!" said the woman, shaking her head, and holding up her fist at Mary. "But you be a very fine school mistress, you be! And I sha-a-an't go to your school, I sha-an't. Be I to go an be pointed at by you, and by the passon, and by all the leetle lads in the village? Be I?—no, I been't; and you will just gie I the penny!"

And the woman went nearer to Mary, and looked more threatening.

"It is against the rules to——"

"Gie I the penny!" interrupted the woman.

"I tell you," said Mary, "it is not in my power to——"

"Gie I the penny!" again interrupted Jane Sands.

"Jane Sands," said Mary, stepping back as the woman approached nearer.

"Gie I the penny, or I'll make you repent—you white-faced——"

"You have no business here," said Mary.

"Gie I the penny!" reiterated the woman, bringing her heavy fist down on the little table, upon which stood supper for Mary and Susan, and making the crockery fly in all directions.

"Oh! good gracious, woman!" said Susan.

"Gie I the penny!" said Jane, now turning on Susan. "My boy sha-an't be set a-top on a stool and be pointed at, and laughed at! And be I to pay a penny for he to be so ill-used?—no, I been't. And gie I the penny!"

Though Isaac had not enough money in his pocket to pay the Widow Mason, he had some; and at this crisis he gallantly stepped forward, and laid a penny on the table, as he said,

"Here, Jenny, woman, take your penny."

But Mary Cope had seized it before Jane could touch it.

"Thank you, Isaac," said she in her quiet, mild tones. "I should return the penny to Jane Sands, if it were right; but it is not."

"I shall make you gie it to I, you spotted-faced hussy!" said Jane, again interrupting.

"Go out of this cottage, Jane, or I shall ask Isaac to turn you out."

"Isaac Watson a-turn I out at your bidding! He better not. Gie I the penny!"

"Come—come Jenny," said Isaac, coaxingly.

"And I sha-nt 'come, come' till I has a-gotten the penny, as my boy Joe gived to that there school."

"Susan, shall you be afraid to fetch the constable?" said Mary.

"Oh, Mary, how can you ask me? I am sure I am terrified till I can scarcely stand." And Susan sank into a chair, and covered her face with her hands.

"Shall I go, Mistress Cope?" said Isaac.

"Thank you. Do go, Isaac—I shall be much obliged."

"And *you* may fetch the constable," said Jane, jeeringly; "and *I* will have my penny." And she again thumped her fist upon the table.

"You will break every bit of the China," said Isaac, as he turned to leave the cottage.

While Susan exclaimed—

"Oh, gracious goodness!—how very frightful!"

And Mary said,

"And she will have it to pay for." The woman's language now became much worse, and it need not be repeated here. Isaac, seeing her thus excited, did not like to leave Mary exposed to her fury, until she again said,

"Pray, Mr. Isaac, don't mind the woman's turbulent and ungovernable manner; leave us and fetch the constable."

Thus desired by Mary, he set off at a good pace, and the woman turned to heap fresh insults on Mary; but calculating shrewdly the time it would take ere Isaac would bring help, she took care eventually to leave the cottage before the arrival of the constable.

When Isaac returned, and the little cottage was restored to some degree of order, he ventured to say,

"He had come to ask how Mary was; and he hoped she was getting better."

And he was then much gratified by Mary mingling with her thanks for his kind inquiries an acknowledgment that she was glad of his very opportune arrival; for though she did not in the presence of Jane Sands show any signs of fear, yet she could not deny that she expected every instant the excited woman would strike her.

"But, Mary, if to give the woman the penny would quiet her, and send her off, why did not you?" said Susan.

"Because the money belongs to the school, and I am answerable for it," said Mary.

"Well, but, Mary, a penny is such a little! I would much rather pay the penny than be frightened out of my wits in that way, and have my nice china broken, and myself made ill and all of a tremble."

"It is not right to give it back," said Mary. "I allow it would have been easy to have returned the penny, and so have saved myself much annoyance this evening; and here is yours, Mr. Isaac, and thank you much for wishing to help me," continued she as she blushed at her own deed; "but if I were to give way in one instance, I should only add to my trouble in the future."

"I cannot see, Mary, how to give back the penny to the woman, and so lose it yourself, could add to your future torment—such a little thing as that!" said Susan, laughing.

"It is the small things neglected that bring on the large ones to our destruction, miss," said Isaac, sententiously; but in the matter of visiting the "Packhorse," or counting his cups of cider, we rather fear he did not apply this wisdom to himself.

"If I suffer myself to be stormed out of a penny, because this woman chooses to interfere with the rules of the school, or from cowardice on my own part, another may come to-morrow and demand the very same!—and after her another!—and another! So that if I once were to give way, I should make a precedent upon which all who came afterwards would found their claims, and each would be more difficult to withstand than the former. So it would not be one penny, but many pennies—it would not be one false step, but the many consequent on it; and these might bring on not only my own ruin, but in all probability the ruin of the school!"

Isaac all this time had looked on with wonder and amazement at this fair and delicate-looking little woman, shaken as she was by her fall from her usual health, who first battled it out so bravely, yet so gently and firmly, with the large, coarse, and angry woman, and then who so wisely reasoned upon her own course of action. He looked at her with a very visible admiration; but he was himself unconscious how strongly his feelings were expressed in his countenance.

XX

WHICH TREATS OF THE EFFECTS OF STALE TOBACCO AND CIDER ON MISTRESS COPE

"Come, Mr. Isaac, do have some supper," said Susan, who had been helping Mary to clear away the broken china and replace it with other.

"Thank you, miss, I must go," said Isaac, humbly.

"No, you must stay," persisted Susan; "indeed, Mr. Isaac must not go, must he, Mary? And, besides, after supper we can have such nice singing—eh, Mary?"

"Why, I feel so much obliged to you for so kindly coming to inquire for me," said Mary to Isaac, "and then for standing by me while Jane Sands was so rude, as well as for fetching the constable, that I should be most ungrateful if I did not wish you to stay. But, Susan, we must not forget that Mr. Isaac is accustomed to much better things than I have to offer—" and her eyes fell upon the little table, where a loaf, butter, and two or three lettuces, with a jug of water, comprised the whole of the fare!

"Better things, Mistress Cope!" said Isaac, in a tone of reproach, "I come to see how you are; and I shall go away glad to find you are getting better. But I assure you, Mistress Cope, I am proud to sit down at your table, so don't mention 'better things.' And when I look round and see all the beautiful furniture in your cottage—your bright tables and pretty chairs, your carpet, your sofa, your pictures on the walls, and many other things, I am fairly amazed at your condescension in asking me to sit down with you!"

Mary blushed at Isaac's long speech, and Susan gazed round the room with a supercilious air. But we feel we ought to explain that Mary Cope was of a different class from the hardy denizens of the moor. She required warmer clothing, more fire in her cottage, more indulgences. Her physique was too delicate to rough it, as most did there, and thus what appeared luxury to Isaac was in fact only necessary comfort to her.

And now Isaac, with his customary shyness and humility, seated himself on the edge of a chair, and kept as far from the table and the two young women as it was possible, consistently with eating his supper.

But when supper was over, and they began to sing he also began to feel more at his ease. He drew his chair close to the table, and telling Mary he knew his part by heart, placed the open book before her, sounded his pitch-pipe, gave the key note, and they sang a trio for two soprani and bass.

Isaac was so intent on the singing, and so charmed with Susan's voice, that, unintentionally, he sang with great heartiness, staring at Susan all the time; and as Susan, as well as Isaac, did not require notes, for she did not understand them, this attention from Isaac was not only seen by her, but greatly valued. While poor Mary Cope had only sung a few bars, before she became conscious of a highly disagreeable odour of cider and stale tobacco; and the more they advanced in the glee, and the more heartily Isaac sang, the more faint and ill she became, with this, to her, offensive scent.

Isaac, when the glee was over, quite unconscious that anything was the matter with Mary, continued his attention to Susan, who, absorbed in her own conquest over Isaac, and in his undoubted attentions to herself, was equally blind to Mary's illness.

"I never heard such a voice," said Isaac, earnestly. "Every time I hear it I like it better, and this music suits you so well; your upper notes are very clear, and the lower so round and full. I really never did hear so charming a voice!"

"I know; you never have heard one like it," said Susan, complacently. "I myself never heard one—no, not one, except, perhaps, Jenny Lind's; and there are those of my companions and admirers in London," minced she, affectedly, "who even doubt if Jenny's equals mine."

And then, looking round, she started as she said,

"My dear Mary, what is the matter?"

For Mary Cope, while Isaac and Susan were so absorbed in each other, had slowly left her chair and gone to the cottage door, which, with some difficulty, she opened; and then seating herself within the current of fresh air, she gradually recovered.

"I think the room is rather close to-night," said she, looking very white.

"And you are not strong, dear," said Susan, kindly; while Isaac, the moment he saw Mary's pale face, was ashamed of his attentions to Susan. Not that he had the vanity to think Mary's pallid countenance expressed an inward pain on her part, caused by his notice of her cousin, but that he marvelled at himself for being drawn away for one instant from such purity and goodness, and even beauty, as Mary's.

"Perhaps you have tired yourself with singing, Mistress Cope?" said he, in a very gentle voice.

And in his good-nature and solicitude for her comfort he stooped his tall person down to her as he spoke. But as the nearer he approached the more offensive became the odour of stale tobacco and cider, so Mary only felt his presence a serious inconvenience.

"She is very delicate, Mr. Isaac," said Susan, hoping to draw his attention to herself.

"I think I am too tired to sing any more," said Mary, in the hope that Isaac would see the necessity of leaving them; but Susan prevented this by saying,

"Yes, dear, you don't look well. But Mr. Isaac and I can sing some duets, and that will amuse you."

"Oh! no miss," said Isaac, "I am afraid I do not know any duet that will suit your voice and mine."

Soprano and bass, Isaac meant; but Susan, not understanding this, said,

"How very modest you are, Mr. Isaac! Why, there is 'Sweet sister Fay,' and 'What are the wild waves saying?' and 'The Fairies' Call,' and many others that are very enjoyable."

"They are all for two trebles," said Mary.

"Well, that is of no consequence," said Susan; "bass will do just as well, Mr. Isaac."

Isaac shook his head, and after a moment's pause he said,

"But if you know that very charming duet for soprano and bass, 'Haste, my Nannette,' I shall be most delighted to sing with you."

It was now Susan's turn to shake her head in the negative, for that classical *morceau* was unknown to her. But speedily recovering from this disappointment,

"I will sing you a song," said she, unwilling to allow any opportunity for display to pass without attempting still to charm the strong man by her sweet voice. "It is a lovely thing from Bennett's 'May Queen:'—'With the Carol on the Tree.'"

And without more ado Susan began.

Mary Cope had anxiously hoped Isaac would, when he saw her so ill, go without more singing; but now, though she was in part relieved from the annoyance he had been to her by his attention becoming entirely absorbed in Susan's song, she found another cause for inquietude. Sitting apart she could the better look on. She could not be mistaken in Susan's eager desire to make a conquest of Isaac; and she felt also she could not be mistaken in reading, distinctly expressed on Isaac's features, his intense admiration of Susan.

The large, strong man sat still:—in one position, like a statue:—immoveable:—scarcely daring to respire:—intently absorbed in Susan's song—a very charming one, and, we need hardly add, entirely unknown to Isaac.

When the last note died away, he did not move for a second or two, and then with a deep sigh he said,

"Is that all?"

"All! Why, yes, Mr. Isaac. Did you like it?" said Susan. "It is quite new—from the 'May Queen.'"

"I don't care what it is from. It is the most entrancing song I ever heard in my life! I never did hear anything like it!" said Isaac, enthusiastically. "Did you, Mistress Cope?"

"I have heard Susan sing it before to-night; and I have always liked it. But I am afraid I am rather tired, and——"

"Tired! Of course you are, Mistress Cope, and I ought not to be stopping here in this way; but we don't hear such music every day, or so fine a voice." And Isaac turned and looked at Susan. "But I cannot go away without saying I am very anxious you should get better, Mistress Cope. I cannot forgive myself for the share I had in——"

"Say no more—pray say no more on that subject," said Mary, rising, and offering her hand to Isaac. "I have no doubt I shall soon be better. Good night, and many thanks for all your kindness."

"I assure you, Mistress Cope," said Isaac, deferentially, as he retained Mary's small hand in his own, with a hearty grasp, "there is nothing I would not do for you!"

"Good night, Mr. Isaac. When shall you come again?" said Susan, impatient to recall his attention to herself.

"Good night, miss," said Isaac, as he hastily left the cottage without replying to her query.

"People on Dartmoor cannot help being vulgar!" said Susan, tossing her head, as she heard him walk away. "He might have given a civil answer to a civil question!"

XXI

PARSON HILL'S COMMENT ON THE BEHAVIOUR OF JANE SANDS

AT the school-room the next morning, Mary Cope gave an account to Parson Hill of the visit she had had from Jane Sands. He heard her patiently to the end, then standing up, he called the attention of the school; and at his bidding employment was laid aside for the time being.

"Does any one here remember the introduction of the new boy, Joe Sands, to our school yesterday?"

Chorus of many voices—

"Yes, sir."

"One stand forth—you, Tom Brown."

And the boy came forward immediately.

"Do you know if Mistress Cope compelled the new boy, Joe Sands, to come to our school? Did she fetch him, or did he come of his own accord?"

"Please, sir, the mistress didna fetch him. He comed by hisself."

"He came himself? Then how did he find the way?"

"Please, sir, he comed with his brother Bill and his sister Bess. They shewed he the way."

"Brother Bill and Sister Bess to Joe Sands, stand forth," said Parson Hill. And when they obeyed his order he asked—"Did you show the new boy, Joe Sands, the way to this school?"

"Yes, sir."

"Why did you so?"

"Please, sir, coz mother told us to bring him; and gave us the penny to gie to Mistress Cope."

"Your mother, Jane Sands, sent him here? Does she know that there are rules at this school that cannot be infringed upon?"

"Don't know, sir."

"Do you, Bill and Bess, know these rules?"

"Please, sir, us knows; and us told mother as——"

"Stop," said Parson Hill authoritatively. "Answer my question—Do you know the rules of the school?"

"Please, sir, us does know."

"Did the new boy seat himself on his entrance into the school?"

"No, sir; he wasn't 'bedient."

"He was disobedient?" said the parson; "tell me what he did."

"He runned up and down the school, and laughed and made a noise, and us couldna learn us lessons."

"What happened then?"

"The mistress told him he must sit down; but he wouldna."

"What happened then?"

"The mistress told him she would put he a-top of that there stool."

"Then he was forewarned that punishment would follow his disobedience?"

"Yes, sir."

"And because he persisted in disobeying, he was placed by Mistress Cope on a stool in the middle of the room?"

"Yes, sir."

"Mistress Cope was quite right; all who come here shall obey the mistress, and none shall break the rules without suffering the punishment due to his or her fault," said Parson Hill. Then speaking in a more gentle tone to the two children, he continued, "Bill and Bess Sands, it has pleased your mother, Jane Sands, to go to Mistress Cope's cottage, and make a furious attack upon her, demanding back again the penny you paid when you brought the new boy; now mind what I say," and the parson held up his finger to attract the notice of the school, "moneys paid into this school are never returned—your mother cannot have her money back." And then, gazing round the school, he continued in a louder tone, "And pray, may I ask, why is the new boy, Joe Sands, not here?"

"Please, sir, mother said as Joe shouldna come to be put a-top of a stool, and pointed at."

"Who wants to set him on a stool?" said Parson Hill; "not I—not Mistress Cope. The young ne'er-do-weel himself wished to stand there; inasmuch as that he did the very thing that caused him to be raised to that honour—therefore he wished to stand there did he not?"

"No, sir, he didna."

"I say he did," said Parson Hill, authoritatively. "Mistress Cope told him he must stand if he continued disobedient, did she not?"

"Yes, sir."

"Then why did he continue disobedient, if he had no desire to stand on the stool?"

"Please, sir, Joe thought as Mistress Cope wouldna stick he a-top on a stool."

"Boy!" said Parson Hill, in a tone of great astonishment, "she told him she would."

"Yes, sir; but Joe thought she wouldna do it."

"Not do as she said she would!" said the parson, starting back with an angry look; "not do as she said!—then why should she say it? Boy, does the new boy, Joe Sands, think Mistress Cope tells falsehoods?"

"Don't know, sir."

"Does the new boy know what is meant by a falsehood?—Do you, Bill Sands?—Do you, Bess?"

"Yes, sir."

"Can you tell me why the new boy accused Mistress Cope of telling falsehoods?"

"Please, sir, coz why—mother says to Joe as her'll wollop he; and, please, sir, her never doesn't."

"Hump!—Jane Sands says she will, and she does not; well, what has that to do with Mistress Cope?"

"Please, sir, Joe thought as Mistress Cope was like to mother, and when her said as her would stick he a-top on a stool, as her never would."

"Then the new boy, Joe Sands, pays Mistress Cope a great compliment," said Parson Hill, bowing to Mary; "and she must feel much inward gratification at being compared with so tall, and strong, and rapid-tongued a woman as Jane Sands; but I humbly beg to differ with the new boy—I see no similitude between the two—do you, Bill and Bess?"

"No, sir."

"And your mother wanted him at home this morning? Is he coming to-morrow?"

"No, sir—never no more."

"Oh-h!—oh-h!—I now begin to understand the meaning of all this. And we are never again to have the happiness of seeing the new boy, Joe Sands, in our school again, and that because *he* behaved ill, and received the punishment due to his disobedience," and after a pause, Parson Hill added, speaking slowly and impressively, "Then, Bill Sands and Bess Sands, it becomes my painful duty to send you two away from this school. If Joe Sands, whose name is entered in our book, is to stay away because his mother pleases, you, Bill and Bess, must remain away because I please. Go, therefore, to your mother, and tell her we have no desire for the company of her cherub child, Joe, the disobedient; but we are sorry that her behaviour compels us to send you away—in other words, dismiss you from the school."

"Please, sir—uh! uh! uh!—please, sir, us doesna want to go!" said they crying bitterly.

"Very likely not," said the parson; "but the innocent often suffer for the guilty, and you are in that dilemma at this time." And then turning to Mary Cope, he added—"Of the woman, Jane Sands, so careful of her cherubian Joe, we must make an example to all other mothers. Mothers must be taught that when their children are sent here, they are under my control, until they are finally removed from the school; and that without my permission a mother has no power to take her child away; neither can she interfere with our rules, rewards or punishments, or have her money returned. If mothers choose to threaten to 'wollop' their cherubs, and then let their kind hearts interfere with their stern duties, that is nothing to us. If we threaten, upon sufficient cause, we put the threat in execution." And then again turning to the weeping children, he added—"And so, Bill and Bess Sands, if your mother chooses to take home the new boy, Joe Sands, whose name is on our books, to please her own fancy, she will also take back you two, to please me. Go, Bills Sands!—Go, Bess Sands!"

And weeping and humiliated, the children left the school.

XXII

OF PARSON HILL'S NEW CURATE, AND OF PARSON HILL'S OLD CLOTHES

AND have you heard the news, widdy?"

The Widow Simpson looked up from her knitting, and saw Jacob Smerdon and his wife, Nanny, standing in the shed.

"Jacob and Nanny! I be very glad you be come. Isaac, lad, bring the chairs," said the widow.

But Isaac had already gone into the cottage, and now returned with two chairs, which he placed comfortably in the front of his shed. The three old people seated themselves, and Isaac returned to his work.

"And have you heard the news, widdy?" said old Jacob, as he rested both hands on the top of his stick and gazed at the widow.

"No, Jacob, nobody has never told I no news."

"The passon be going to have a coorit, widdy!" said Nanny Smerdon, eagerly.

"A coorit, Nanny! And what be a coorit?"

"A coorit be a kind of 'prentice to the passon," said Jacob. "He learns to do passon's work."

"'Prentice to the passon! Massy me! It be very queer times when passons have 'prentices," said the Widow Simpson.

"The coorit comed to the Vickridge may be a month agone, widdy," said Nanny Smerdon, "and he gived us that there fine sermon in the church."

"He be called Mister Gray," said Jacob.

"And he goed back again, and didna 'prentice hisself, then. But it be all right now, forbye Mister Gray be the passon's new coorit," said Nanny.

"But if the coorit preaches the sermons for the passon, Nanny, then what be the passon to do?" said the Widow Simpson, laying down her knitting as she became more interested in the news.

"The passon be a-going to rest hisself, and he have got this young one to do his work. And, widdy," said Nanny, "I mind as that there coorit, Mister Gray, gived us a fine sermon about a month agone."

"Fine sermon!" said Jacob. "Yes, the new coorit doth preach mighty fine sermons. It be a peety as he be such a leetle one."

"A little one!" chimed in Isaac. "Why, what has big or little to do with preaching fine sermons?"

"Nothing, Isaac, lad, nothing at all," said Nanny, in a tone of decision. "A coorit may preach just so well if he be a leetle one or if he be a big one."

"The passon be a big man," said Jacob, striking his stick on the floor of the shed, "and I be a-thinking us would miss he."

"Miss the passon, Jacob!" said the widow, "in course us would; but then us mustna go again Mister Gray 'cause he be a leetle one. Gude stuff be in a leetle space most-times."

"I knows it, widdy," said Jacob; "and I be not again' the coorit. But I be a-thinking as I shall not be so well off for breeches."

"Maybe the passon have been a gude friend to thee, Jacob," said the widow.

"Maybe he have, widdy," said Jacob, with a shrewd nod of the head. "And may be many folk will like the coorit's sermons, but I be a-going to stick to the passon." And again he struck his stick against the floor.

"The coorit speaks up fine!" said Nanny, in great admiration; "and he says such long words and such a many of them!"

"You are quite right, Nanny," said Isaac. "Mr. Gray gave us a learned discourse."

"Ay, it be true," said Jacob, shaking his head; "and it be a peety as he be such a leetle one."

"His sermons be not leetle ones," said Nanny. And then she added, as it seemed in a tone of defiance to Jacob, and tossing her head, "Gie I the coorit for a sermon!"

"And gie I the passon for a pair of breeches," said Jacob, slapping his thigh with great vigour.

"You be most so big as the passon be, Jacob," said the widow.

"I be, widdy," said Jacob, stretching his legs out, "the passon's breeches be very gude ones."

"And the coorit's sermons be very gude ones," said Nanny.

"The parson is a good friend to the parish, Nanny," said Isaac, "and the parson always preaches excellent sermons; I don't see how any curate can ever do better than the parson has done; and he has always had a free hand, a kind heart, and a gentle word."

Isaac spoke feelingly, for he felt that the vicar had been very merciful to him in his transgressions.

"And there will be some as will live to miss him," said the widow, "though maybe I shall not."

"Ay, widdy, ay; but don't you see," said Jacob, knocking his stick on the floor to attract attention, "now as the passon have a-got this new coorit, him might go clean off hisself somewhere! And then what be I to do for breeches? Can you tell I that?" said he in a loud voice.

"Jacob, I be a-thinking as I must look up the old ones, and mend them up a bit betterer, and then these here will last the longer!" said Nanny.

"The passon has got a many pair of breeches," said the widow. "I have a-seed him with white ones, and gray ones, and black ones, and brown ones; he have a many pair, surely!"

"Ay, widdy, you be right," said Jacob; "and the passon, God bless him, gives his breeches to many folk. There be that Peter Barker, I have knowed he have the passon's breeches, and then I have knowed he to misbehave hisself!"

"Yes, Jacob, and I have known Peter Barker tell the parson he could not go to church because he had not clothes fit to go in. And then the kind parson has sent him what he required," said Isaac.

"And after that, lad," said the widow, "Peter did not go to church."

"He went twice," said Isaac.

"Did Peter Barker go to church two times, lad?" said Nanny. "I have never seed he there."

"Yes, he went twice, and then several Sundays passed and he was not seen at church again. Then the parson asked why he did not go, because now he had clothes, so that could not longer be an excuse."

Isaac paused for a second or two and then proceeded.

"And then Peter said, 'If your honour thinks as I have not been to church often enough for the clothes you sent me, I don't care if I do go once more!'"

"Shame on him!" said Jacob, tapping his stick on the floor. "I say as Peter might ha' been proud to walk up the church in the passon's clothes. I be."

"Him always was a bad one, Isaac, lad," said Nanny.

"It be said as Peter goes a methodying," said Jacob.

"They methody churches be new things—be not they, Jacob?" said the widow.

"For-bye that I have not never seen them in my young days," said Jacob; "I be a-thinking as you be right, widdy."

"What be they like to? Can you tell, Isaac, lad?" said Nanny Smerdon.

"Methodist chapels have a strange appearance on the outside," said Isaac; "something like a large square cottage, with big windows."

Dissent was unknown on Dartmoor, and the chapels that were erected in the towns near were small.

"I have no curiosity about them," said Isaac. "I never was inside any one of them."

"And how be your leetle grandchild, Phoebe?" said the widow. "Isaac says her has gotten very gude looks."

"Her be a very pratty meeden," said Nanny. "I be a-thinking as her will come to be like to Mistress Cope, delicater and more trim than moor meedens be!"

"And do she like she's place?" said the widow.

"Ay, widdy, there be two young mistresses as she 'tends to, and they be pleased with she," said Nanny.

"Jacob!" said Isaac, coming forward, and speaking in a low voice, "what did the widow Mason mean about Mistress Cope?"

"Isaac, lad, don't thee take no 'count of that there widdy; her be too sharp with her tongue, and her be too sharp with her score! And—and if there was but another 'Packhorse' in the village of Lawsleigh, I would never let she see I inside her door again!—I would not!" said Jacob, striking his stick loudly.

"But what did she mean—can you tell?" said Isaac.

"Her meaned to pull she down: coz why, old widdies like Widdy Mason—her be a bad widdy—be always jealous of the young meedens as be pratty, and got rosy cheeks—and—and it be a-said, lad, down in the village, as you be a sweet-hearting with Mistress Cope, and so the Widdy Mason wanted to run she down while you was there."

"She has no business to call her 'Molly Cope,'" said Isaac, angrily.

"She be a very bad widdy, us all knows that, and what be the use to say any more? Us cannot take hold of she—her be a slippery widdy—and her be jealous—widdies be most times, when they be bad and the young meedens pratty."

"I wish there was another 'Packhorse' in the village," said Isaac—"What! are you going, Nanny?"

"Us be a-going to the mill, lad."

"Be you, Nanny?" said the widow; "then may be you will come in as you pass by this afternoon, and have a dish of tea?"

"And thank you kindly, widdy—us will. Eh, Jacob?"

"Ay, woman, ay, and thank you, widdy."

And the two old people set off to the mill.

XXIII

WHICH INTRODUCES THE NEW CURATE TO THE READER

Mr. Gray was an eager and hopeful aspirant after all things good. He had only just taken his degree at Oxford; he was therefore young, and to a certain extent inexperienced. He was a man of studious habits, but of practical knowledge he had none. He had been brought up by an uncle—a hard man—who was in a high position, and possessing much of this world's wealth.

This hardness of temperament was excruciating to Mr. Gray, whose heart was kind and generous. Before he went to college, his uncle had given him a tutor as harsh by nature as himself, who had kept his pupil in great restraint, and who did not attempt to find the way to his heart. When Mr. Gray at last left home, and found himself able to do as he pleased, he joined a set of young men, whose marked eagerness for most things in extremes gave a sort of charm to his hitherto cramped and pent-up desires.

Mr. Gray had read of the miseries of the poor and the oppressions of the rich; the latter he thought he knew from experience, because his uncle was too crabbed by temperament to be charitable, and too careless and selfish to devote his time or give his money to the poor. These things combined made him unconsciously to himself a severe judge of all wealthy people, but more especially of the clergy, who possessed, as he thought, good livings. He did not himself desire to benefit by the riches of the Church, but he earnestly wished to distribute some part of her wealth amongst the poor and suffering.

He had accepted Mr. Hill's curacy because of the far-off—and, as it seemed to him—dreary locality, in which he would have a large sphere for usefulness. He was not either attracted by or astonished at the magnificent grandeur of the Tors rising here and there around, for he had not a poetical mind; neither was he daunted by bad roads, precipitous hills, or miry bogs, for he was not of a cowardly nature. But he brought his peculiarly nurtured ideas with him, and when he saw the small cluster of cottages that comprised the "village of Lawsleigh" seated in desolation in the heart of the moor, he felt convinced that the inmates of each home must be ill fed and ill clothed. Because he thought that the poor ought to have the same food, wear the same clothes, and have their dwelling places as comfortable as the rich! He forgot, in his great zeal for their well-being, that one precept of holy writ, that there shall always be "rich and poor— master and servant." How then can all things be equal? And he could not, on his first arrival on the moor, be made to comprehend that the cottages he thought so wretched were in reality homes of much comfort to the hardy dwellers on the moor, with their turf fires in great plenty, and, if coarse, substantial fare, and such as they had always been accustomed to. If their clothing appeared rough and scanty to one from a distant county, it was more in appearance than reality, for they had all they required.

Mr. Gray, it will be observed, was educated in the manners and customs of the Church, as observed in the present day. He was ignorant of her ancient forms and ceremonies, even as they were in use all over England up to the end of the reign of Charles II.; and when he met with some few still lingering on Dartmoor, he displayed more zeal than prudence. Nevertheless, Mr. Gray was a hard-working, pains-taking, humble-minded, zealous clergyman; perhaps a little too zealous over trifles, whose very nature would in time correct themselves.

As we have said, he wanted experience. Mr. Gray had been but little more than a week at the village of Lawsleigh, but he had strolled day by day to the more distant parts of the parish, and, to use his own expression, had "looked up" the people here and there; and now he was going to the vicarage, for the third time, to dine with Parson Hill. On his way thither, he used many arguments, the better to convince himself he was acting rightly, when he determined not to let even the vicar himself continue longer in such total ignorance of many things conformable to the ways of the Church, or the customs of her priesthood, without a word or two of advice or sturdy remonstrance.

And now Mr. Gray is seated at the vicar's table. During dinner he introduced his intended expostulation by first staring rudely at Parson Hill's coat, and then saying,

"I have not seen a blue coat and gilt buttons for so long a time, yours quite attracts my attention. We clergy always wear black."

"I am glad that I wear my blue coat and glittering buttons, inasmuch as they must recall to you many happy days of your youth," said Parson Hill.

"Indeed, I don't remember that I ever wore a blue coat," said Mr. Gray; "I should rather say such a colour has not been used in my day—not even in my boyhood."

Mr. Gray thought, by pushing the blue coat into the days of the past, he should the better prove it had no business to be used in the present day; but Parson Hill stared at Mr. Gray for a second or two without speaking, and then said, courteously,

"Probably I misunderstood, for I thought you said, 'I have not seen a blue coat or gilt buttons for so long a time,' from which I should naturally infer that, at some period of your life, you had seen one, though I daresay they are rare now."

This quiet nonchalance from Parson Hill irritated Mr. Gray; he discovered, too, that, in his eagerness to introduce the subject, he had inadvertently committed himself to the fact of having seen a blue coat at some time or other—he could not remember that he ever had seen gentlemen wear blue coats and gilt buttons; but this only vexed him the more, and he said in an irritable tone,

"You must allow me to say, I never saw a clergyman, and especially the vicar of a parish, wearing anything but black."

"Did you not, indeed?" said Parson Hill, in a tone of surprise; "I have often. I seldom have a new coat; and as this happens to be blue, and to fit me comfortably, and I like it, indeed much better than either of my black coats—for I have black," added he, bowing to Mr. Gray; "why, it goes on and on from one year to another—dress coats last so long, if you happen to have more than one, as I have."

"I don't see why blue should last longer than black," said Mr. Gray, testily.

"Nor do I," said Parson Hill, sipping his wine.

"But, may I ask, why do you wear blue, since you say you have black, and black is so much more becoming to the clergy?" said Mr. Gray.

"Yes, you may ask," said Parson Hill, slowly, and staring at Mr. Gray.

"And perhaps you will give me a reply?" persevered Mr. Gray.

"Certainly," said Parson Hill, bowing; and then drawing himself up and speaking in most suave tones, he said, "I wear blue because I happen to have blue; and I do not study the becoming, as I may infer, from the information you have just given me, that the clergy do. When a man gets to my time of life, he rarely studies the becoming."

"I do not mean personally becoming, I mean becoming to your cloth," said Mr. Gray.

"I think, as a rule, blue is a more becoming colour than black," said Parson Hill; "though, as I have said, I do not study the becoming." And then, turning round, and speaking to his attendant, he said, "Wine, George," and addressing Mr. Gray, he added, "Will you have sherry or Madeira?"

"Thank you—no wine, I never drink wine," said Mr. Gray.

"Ah! I beg your pardon," said the parson, courteously. "You have told me that before. George, never take the wine to Mr. Gray; bring it to me. Madeira!"

And Parson Hill, before sipping his wine, bowed in the old-fashioned way to Mr. Gray.

"You will excuse my resuming the subject of dress?" said Mr. Gray.

"I will excuse you," said Parson Hill, complacently eating his cutlet.

"You should not wear top-boots and knee-breeches. Such things are never seen now-a-days."

"I beg to differ with you; top-boots and white corduroys are seen every day on this moor. Would you have me ride to the meet without them? You might as well ask me not to ride in pink! Why, sir, if you happen to stick in a bog, your beautifully bright pink gleams out in the midst of the slush; and if you required help, your friends would see you, and come and give you a helping hand! And don't you think the corduroys keep out the wet? Ah! you have never tried them!"

And Parson Hill, having finished his cutlet, put down his knife and fork, leaned back in his chair, and met Mr. Gray's ruffled look with one of kind inquiry.

"No," said Mr. Gray, sternly, "I never have tried such garments, and I trust I never shall."

"Have you ever seen an up-country horse flounder in a bog?" said Parson Hill, eagerly, and leaning forward.

Mr. Gray did not reply.

"A moor-horse will struggle through a bog, or, if down, flop out of it, but your up-country thorough-bred has not been bred to it, and can neither understand nor get through a morass. I hope you have moor-horses, Mr. Gray."

"I have no horse," said he, in rather an irritable tone. "But you, sir, allow me to observe," continued he, "you, sir, as a dignitary of the Church, do you ride across country in pink? And——"

"As a dignitary of the Church!" said Parson Hill, drawing himself up proudly.

"But, sir, I assure you," said Mr. Gray, eagerly, "the dignitaries of the Church do not ride!"

"And I assure you, you are mistaken," said Parson Hill, blandly. "And not only do they ride, but they are welcomed. And why not, pray? And not only are they welcomed, but, sir, they would be missed. I rather mean, if they were to absent themselves from the meet, &c., &c., their absence would be regretted!"

Mr. Gray shook his head deprecatingly, and Parson Hill continued.

"Did you ever read 'Collyn's Chase of the Red Deer?'"

"No, I have not time for such reading."

"Now, there; you will excuse me if I quote a passage that dwells on my memory. The writer says, 'Without wishing to see the dignitaries of the

Church again maintaining their kennels of hounds, I should feel regret if I were to miss from the field the familiar faces of some of those members of the clergy who now join in the sport in our country, and whose presence is always welcomed at the covert-side.' I have no kennels of hounds—I never had—but I ride, of course I ride! And I don't see what else one has to do at particular seasons of the year, on this moor, away from the world and society in general. I don't see that one can do anything but ride!"

And now Parson Hill leaned back in his chair, and looked at Mr. Gray with a smile of inquiry.

"I suppose you could attend to your parish?" said Mr. Gray.

The smile faded from Parson Hill's face, and for a few seconds he continued to gaze fixedly on Mr. Gray, who, to do him justice, met the parson's eye unflinchingly. At length the smile returned to the vicar's expressive countenance, and he said,

"When I dined with Archdeacon L., at Oakhampton, I met a young clergyman who had had a good deal of pernicious reading, 'Essays and Reviews' for instance; though I must admit in my time I have read some hundreds of sterling 'Essays '—Pope's 'Essay on Man' occurs to me at the present moment as an example—and some thousands of excellent 'Reviews,'—the review of 'Collyn's Chase of the Red Deer' in the *Atheæum* was admirable—I have read such 'Essays and Reviews' without ever finding any harm, and I could not but think of the old proverb, 'What is one man's meat is another's poison!' *I* do not meet with—poison. Even bygone things called 'Oxford Tracts'——"

"Oxford tracts, pernicious things!" interrupted Mr. Gray.

"Pardon me," said Parson Hill, "I have never read them. But as the gentleman of whom I spoke backed up much that he had to say with Tract 000, and as much that he said was not worth the saying, I took upon myself to blame the 'Tracts' from which it appeared to me he had gleaned his worthless remarks."

"They were the finest things of their day," said Mr. Gray.

"Were they indeed!" said the vicar, in a tone of surprise. "If they at all resembled the sort of 'Tract' I have seen in my people's cottages within the last week, I can only say they are great trash!"

"Pray, did you notice the titles of the tracts you so easily condemn?" said Mr. Gray, colouring deeply.

"'Happy Jack,' 'The Good Old Woman,' 'The Two Boys who went Different Ways,'" said Parson Hill.

"No, these are not at all like the 'Oxford Tracts.' I gave them to the poor ignorant people," said Mr. Gray.

"If the 'Oxford Tracts' were the finest things of their day, I should think they must be superior to 'Happy Jack,'" said Parson Hill, courteously.

"Give the 'Oxford Tracts' to such benighted heathens as are to be found on this moor? It is clear you don't understand them. I will explain."

"Excuse me, sir," said Parson Hill, bowing low, "they may be as fine as you say they are, but I do not desire to know more of them than I do at this moment."

"How strange!" said Mr. Gray.

"Strange!" said Parson Hill, smiling. "And yet I must assure you, strange though it may seem, I do not wish to read the 'Oxford Tracts;' but then I do *not* wish to give up my top-boots, my corduroys, my pink coat, or even my blue one; they are all satisfactorily suitable for the purposes to which they are applied."

"Consider your cloth, sir," said Mr. Gray, angrily.

"No, no; I shall not spare it, after all these years of wear," said the parson.

"*Your* cloth, sir; your cloth," reiterated Mr. Gray.

"It is my cloth," said Parson Hill, mildly.

"But, sir, the clergy are called 'the cloth,'" said Mr. Gray, in his desire to explain, only mystifying the more.

"In the 'Oxford Tracts?'" said the incorrigible parson. "Now, Mr. Gray, since you don't drink wine, perhaps you eat fruit?"

"In London—indeed I may say in all places—the clergy always dress in black," said Mr. Gray.

"There is no class of men who ought to cultivate coolness of temper more than the clergy," said Parson Hill. "Black is very heating, it attracts the sun. How glad the London clergy must be of a trip to the country!

and you, Mr. Gray," continued Parson Hill, blandly, "you, fresh from Town, pray wear your blue coat, or your pink if you prefer it. Fortunately, we are free as air on Dartmoor, and may wear any colour we please. For my part, I always wear my comfortable blue at dinner; and when I have had my wine, I go to my snuggery, take off my blue, pop it into its hiding-place, put on my loose wrap, and have my agreeable pipe!—that is the way to enjoy your pipe; and then George serves me with coffee there; that is, when I am alone—and I hope to make you, Mr. Gray, quite at home with me," said Parson Hill, bowing; "and if you don't drink wine which I confess is an extraordinary thing, perhaps you can enjoy a pipe or a cigar? I have both. I wish to meet your taste, and make you—"

"No, sir, thank you—the clergy don't smoke!"

"Oh—h—the 'Oxford Tract' clergy—they must be rather a—a—marvellous class of men," said Parson Hill, musingly, "for it seems to me that they don't smoke, they don't drink wine, nor wear blue or pink coats, nor ride to cover—perhaps they can't ride at all—nor wear top-boots, nor corduroys. Well, well, they miss many pleasures; but let us not grudge them their own way; let them have their day while it lasts! and we, Mr. Gray, will have our day in our way! And now, since I see you don't even care for fruit, suppose we go to the drawing-room—but—" and he hesitated— "I am sorry there are no ladies to receive us. Perhaps now the 'Oxford Tract' clergy would think me a very barbarous host, if they were by any chance to visit me? Or—must I add to their long catalogue of dislikes, that they don't like ladies? Come, come—I see I weary you—perhaps you like music—I have a capital Broadwood, you shall try it."

"I don't play," said Mr. Gray.

"I do," said the parson, as he opened the instrument and seated himself.

XXIV

WHICH INTRODUCES THE FUTURE "QUEEN OF DARTMOOR"

AND now we must transfer our readers from Dartmoor and its solitudes, and small population, to London, the busy mart of the world; and in one of the large squares, though not one of the most fashionable, we will follow the postman with his loud *rat-tat*, until he stops to deliver a letter from Parson Hill; and over the shoulders of the lady to whom the letter is written we will look at the parson's clear caligraphy, and read for ourselves:

"DEAR MRS. HARCOURT,

"I do not intend this as a proper answer to your last, kind, *long* letter; but I heard promiscuously you had been at Tihidy in your way to Penzance; and I can hardly understand what that means, as I thought your stay at Tremissic was to be a long one. You will see above 'long'; well, so it was, but I rejoiced thereat; and pray do not think for one moment that such an epistle does not give me much pleasure. I tell you it does; and I acknowledge I am very selfish to send you such short replies—pray do not grumble at my shortcomings.

"But this is not what I intended to write about. I have been thinking that, as I have promised myself the pleasure of visiting Cornwall early in August, I should meet you in my rambles, and that then I would say, 'that I hoped you would not leave Tremissic for the East—if that be your destination, though I don't mean Bagdad—without coming to pay the old vicarage—I now call it hermitage—a visit.' That was what I meant to say to you in Cornwall; but as you appear to me 'shifty,' as we say of the wind on Dartmoor, I think it safer to tell you now, since I fear I have lost the chance of seeing you.

"By the way, you are fond of 'something new.' I have freshly imported a curate, whom I hope to present to you. He is clever, zealous, well-read, gentlemanly, and marvellously well-dressed. Black, from head to foot! You will be charmed; and I am thinking of astonishing, and probably alarming, our next 'meet' by imitating my curate, fresh from the world of parsons who only wear black, and personating for the time being the character of the worthy 'gentleman in black.' And if you will only come in time, you may canter by my side on the pretty grey mare, and take upon yourself, also for the time being, the spotless character of 'the woman in white.' And then I can answer for it 'the moor' and 'our meet' will have seen something extraordinary, and have something unusual to say, though the remainder of the huge world lies slumbering in ignorance of our dress, our words, or our deeds.

"Of Mr. Gray, my excellent curate, I may say he has the 'Oxford Tracts' at his fingers' ends, and the 'Essays and Reviews' in his head.

"And now of Charlie, and his sweet wife, I can tell you but little. They have taken up their abode at 'Paul Tavey,' about ten miles from hence. But forest trees, shrubs, plants, and exotics don't come to their full height, blossom, and show their richly coloured flowers so quickly as madame could wish. You don't know her yet. All the better for both. Your happiness in each other lies in the future. You will dovetail *á merveille*!

"Now pray, my dear Mrs. Harcourt, if you are not better engaged, fix your own time, and let me know when I may have the pleasure of meeting you at the station at N——within a week or two?

"But now, I have more wonders to speak of. For, fancy me, from my hermitage in the heart of the classical Dartmoor, with the heavenly ambitious Tors rising round my domain—fancy me within a drive of a station—a railway station! I give it up! I see, in my mind's eye, the curling smoke from the nostrils of the iron horse; I hear the clatter of the multitude in his train! The world is coming to dislodge me from my wilderness—me! almost the last of the old moorland parsons! Make haste, dear Mrs. Harcourt, and come and take a last look at the hermitage, and at

"Yours as ever sincerely,
"WILLIAM HILL."

Mrs. Harcourt sat thoughtfully looking out of the open window into the square below, with the letter in her hand, when her reverie was broken in upon by the hasty entrance of a lady, who said, as she went up to her,

"I saw the postmark, dear Mary! You have another letter from Mr Hill?"

"Yes," said Mrs. Harcourt, musingly.

"Yes—is that all?" said Mrs. Curzon, in a tone of disappointment.

Mrs. Harcourt started perceptibly as she offered the letter to Mrs. Curzon, and said,

"You may read it, dear Sophia—there is nothing in it."

"Then do you mean if there was something in it, something desirable, and very much to be hoped for—do you mean that then you would not let me see it?" said Mrs. Curzon, as she took the letter.

"Oh, no! Indeed I do not mean that, dear Sophia. I only mean your suspicions with regard to Mr. Hill and myself have no foundation."

Mrs. Curzon was by this time too much absorbed in the letter to reply. When she came to the end she arose with *empressement*, and throwing her arms round her sister said,

"You always say there is nothing. Call you this nothing—this charming letter? True, he does not actually ask you to have him, but he is always writing, and keeping watch and ward over you, and always asking you to go to him."

Mrs. Harcourt made no remark, and Mrs. Curzen continued:

"Does he not write very often?"

"No," said Mrs. Harcourt.

"Nonsense! He wrote to you only last week?"

"No. Six weeks, perhaps two months ago."

"I am sure you are wrong, Mary. And he asks you to forgive him, that is, he tells you not to grumble, which is a proof he thinks you have cause to grumble. And he says how much he likes your letters; and I am sure I don't marvel at that, for you have indeed the pen of a ready writer. And then he asks you to fix your own time to go and see him! Oh! Oh!" continued she, "you seek to throw dust in my eyes! You can't, Mary. I will not shut my eyes to your prospect in the future. You know well, none would rejoice more than I to see you once more in a suitable and luxurious home of your own. And you shall not take from me the conviction that I shall soon have the pleasure and delight of saluting you Mistress Hill, Queen of Dartmoor!"

"Hush, Sophia, hush!" said Mrs. Harcourt. "Indeed you are mistaken. You do not know Mr. Hill. He would as soon think of having a world's fair, like our present Great Exhibition, on the top of one of the Tors of Dartmoor, as of marrying again! He has been a widower eighteen years."

"Yes; but now that his only son is married, and Mr. Hill left 'alone in his glory,' the case is altered. You will accept this invitation?"

"I must think a little. It may be better to go," said Mrs. Harcourt, musingly; "but I confess I do not see my way. It is true that if I go I shall be able to silence for the future all this disagreeable gossip. It has its foundation only in the fact that Mr. Hill and Mr. Harcourt were such warm friends; and that since my dear husband's death Mr. Hill has shown a kind desire not to lose sight of me in my altered fortunes—that is all."

"How can you be so hypocritical, Mary?" said Mrs. Curzon with a sneer. "You cannot blind me to your future, unless you wilfully put aside what lies within your grasp. And then his sister, Mrs. Russell, pray what did she say?"

"I do not remember," said Mrs. Harcourt wearily.

"Did she not say—'You will never be allowed to live alone. Only wait quietly a few months longer, and see what next year will produce; for you know you are a pattern woman in the eyes of those arbiters of our fate, men.'"

"Mere talk—mere kind-hearted flattery!"

"Has she not always told you, you are the only lady on whom Mr. Hill ever bestows a word of praise. Does she not say he is constantly instancing you, and saying—'Mrs. Harcourt would do so and so. Mrs. Harcourt understands this and that.'"

"All nonsense," said Mrs Harcourt quietly.

"And when you wrote to Mr. Hill in reply to a former invitation from him, and said you did not intend to visit, and must decline his kind proposal, what did he reply?—'You say you will not visit me. I say you shall.' I saw the letter!"

Mrs. Harcourt smiled as she said,

"And still, dear Sophia, I cannot hope that the end will be as you say. I rather mean I have no just grounds for such a hope."

"But tell me this—Should you be surprised if he asked you to have him?"

"Nothing surprises me!" said Mrs. Harcourt as she turned away to avoid Mrs. Curzon's searching look.

And here we had better explain, that Mrs. Harcourt is the widow of the late Rev. John Harcourt, Rector of Mooraven. Through the death of her husband she had passed from affluence to comparative poverty; inasmuch as that now she had no settled home, nor income sufficient to allow of her taking and furnishing a residence, and hiring servants of her own.

Mrs. Harcourt's relatives and friends all "harped on the same string," her probable marriage with Mr. Hill, her husband's great friend.

Mrs. Curzon is Mrs. Harcourt's sister, living with her husband and family, in all the luxury and ease belonging to the position of a London merchant of high standing. She and others have prevailed on Mrs. Harcourt not to take measures for some permanent home in one of the many boarding houses in London—houses of refuge for ladies so situated—but to wait amongst her connexions the expiration of the two years of her widowhood, and the not very remote chance of proposals from Mr. Hill.

The two years have passed by, the crisis has arrived, and Mrs. Harcourt, as we have seen, is asked to fix her own time for a visit to Parson Hill.

XXV

HOW THE NEW CURATE STOPPED THE BELLS, AND WHAT THE RINGERS HAD TO SAY

In the course of a few days Mary Cope felt sufficiently recovered to take her customary walks with Susan, and permitted herself to be taken, as her cousin said, "just to see how the old lady at the smithy was getting on; and if they did happen to see Isaac, why, she could say goodbye to him," for her fortnight of absence had expired.

Mary did not look upon Isaac's evident admiration of Susan with other than a troubled mind. She was vexed to see her so attractive in his eyes; and yet, with a strange perversity, she felt that she would not accept him, even if he were to ask her to have him. She had been flattered by his coming to inquire for her after her fall, much gratified by his evident sorrow at her indisposition, and softened by his humble and gentle manner. But when, on his last visit, Isaac's well-known vice was made so clear to her understanding, and so offensive to her own personal sensitiveness, Mary resigned all thought of him as being connected with herself in the future. But still, like the dog in the manger, she felt equally averse to seeing him the husband of Susan Picard.

As it happened on this visit to the smithy by the two young women, the Widow Simpson was alone. She explained that there was a funeral, and that, according to custom, Isaac had gone to ring.

While the three sat talking, the mournful peal of the village bells broke upon the stillness of the air, and Mary and Susan paid the old woman some compliments on her grandson's skill in ringing.

"Mr. Isaac is so very clever," said Susan, admiringly.

"I am told he takes after his grandfather," said Mary. "I remember hearing, when I came first to Lawsleigh, that Isaac Simpson was by far the cleverest man in these parts."

"There be no mistake about that," said the widow. "Isaac was larned in most things—rest his saule."

The bells at this instant, instead of continuing their mellifluous sound, appeared to come to a sudden halt in the middle of a peal, and excepting the unmeaning tang of a bell now and then, and as if rung accidentally, the peal was heard no more. In the course of the next ten minutes Isaac and the ringers came up to the shed in a state of great excitement.

"I tell you it be not lawful by no means," said one.

"Him be a fine coorit, to not to know the rights about bells!" said another.

"What be amiss? Be the bells broked?" said the Widow Simpson.

"Why, widdy, here be a coorit as must have come from some outland-isher place, wheere men knows nothing, coz why, he be ignorant about church bells!"

"Not know about church bells!" said the widow. "Havena they got no bells in his village, where he have a-been living?"

"Oh! they have bells enough!" said Isaac, angrily. "How can the parson give us such a curate?—he is more ignorant than any little child in Lawsleigh village, for he does not know when the church bells ought to be rung!"

"Do not say nothing against the passon, Isaac," said the widow; "him be a kindly, gude man, and him knows when the bells must be ringed and him can ring his own self—the passon can."

"But what has been the matter?" ventured Susan, to a young man standing by her side.

"Why, miss, in course us was ringing the peal after the burial—as us be in duty bound to do—and the new coorit—forbye he be called Mister Gray—comes up and stops the peal. Isaac, theere, spoke up to the coorit, and told him us was a-doing us duties; and then the coorit spoke up to Isaac, and us was obliged to come away."

Susan, who was no wiser for this explanation, held her peace. She had a great dislike to exposing her own ignorance, the consequence of which was that she shut up from herself many sources of information and improvement.

"What!" said one, "be us to die, and have no peal?"

"The coorit be larned in sermons—I have heard Nanny Smerdon say as his sermons be fine," said the widow; "and mayhap him does not know about bells."

"Maybe as the passon will larn he betterer, widdy," said one.

"But gude save us, Isaac, lad, be us to have no bells? What be they poor dying creatures to do when there be no 'saule bell' to call the passon?" said the widow; "and us gude Christians can't say no prayers if us doesna have the 'saule bell.'" And the old woman wiped away her tears with the corner of her apron.

"But the curate seems a very gentlemanly person," said Susan. "You are speaking of Mr. Gray?"

"Yes, miss; it be Mister Gray, the coorit— him be uncommon ignorant about bells, surely."

"The new coorit must come from long ways off," said old Jacob Smerdon; "and it be my thinking, widdy, as theere must be places as got no bells—coz why?" continued he, drawing himself up to his full height, and looking round upon the ringers, "where theere be bells, theere be them as knows how to ring them, and what for they be ringed; us have had bells from *generashion* to *generashion*; and us knows how to ring them from *generashion* to *generashion*; and us knows what for they be ringed from *generashion* to *generashion*."

And Jacob struck his stick on the stone floor of the shed to give force to his words.

"Yes, us knows how to ring them, Jacob, and us knows what for they be ringed," chorussed the men.

"Maybe the new coorit never heard no bells," said one.

"Oh! nonsense," said Isaac, impatiently, "he has heard bells enough; but it seems to me he does not know the times and seasons when they are appointed to be rung. He said we must not ring after a funeral—what does he mean? Can we go against the rules of the Church at his command? We are the ringers—what then is our duty?"

"Go to the passon, Isaac, lad, and ax him?" said old Jacob Smerdon.

"Here be James Marvel a-coming up the village," said one; "him will know what us be to do."

"What be you about, you ringers?—what a mess you have made of the peal!" said James, "stopping short in the middle that ways—what be you about?"

"It be the new coorit, James—him has a-been and stopped the bells; us thinks as him must be a outlandisher—coz why? him be uncommon ignorant about bells."

"Him stopped us from ringing after a funeral."

"Lor' bless you!—the new coorit!" said James.

"James, lad, can you tell whereto the new coorit was born?" said the widow.

"What, the new coorit!" said James, looking very dignified; "it be true, widdy, as I have a-heard the master and the coorit a-talking together, and I have a-heard the coorit say, 'Us in Oxford do a-this fashions;'" thereby, widdy, us would *na*turally think as the new coorit was born in Oxford."

"Be there no bells there?" said the widow.

"Can't say, widdy," said James; "in course and the new coorit so ignorant about bells, us would *na*turally think not."

"Be Oxford a outlandlisher place, James?" said Jacob Smerdon.

"Can't say, Jacob," said James; "coz why, I have not never been there."

"Theere be law about bells, I have heard say," said the widow. "The new coorit cannot go against the law, can he?"

"The passon will larn he the law, widdy," said Jacob. "Coorits comes to passons to be learned to do passon's work, and then they be passons theyselves afterwards."

"The coorit said as us hadna no right to ring a peal after a burial, James," said one. "Him be a fine coorit, and I sim as he'll make a fine passon, to not to know about they bells!"

"It is a rule of the Church," said Isaac, sternly. "I cannot understand how Mr. Gray can put aside such rules."

"Young ones be young ones, Isaac," said James; "and us as be older must allowance accordingly. But," continued he, as he shook his head gravely, "it be a uncommon queer thing to take a-top of his young shoulders a-stopping a peal after a burial."

"Him said as us hadna no right to ring the peal afore the burial, same as us always has done from generashion to generashion," said Jacob. "And if us be not to ring they bells afore a burial, and if us be not to ring they bells after a burial, when be us to ring they bells? Can you tell I that?" And again he tapped his stick on the floor.

"The bells have not been 'falled,' James," said Isaac.

"Massy me! Isaac, lad, be they bells expected to 'fall' theyselves?" said James.

"As the new coorit doesna know nothing about hells," said the widow, "in course he thinks as they would 'fall' theyselves."

"Oh! but him be ignorant, widow."

"Suppose," said Isaac, putting up his finger, and arresting the attention of the men—"suppose when a curate, who is ignorant on the subject of bells, takes upon himself to stop a peal in the middle, and so leaves the bells out of place—suppose it was the law that the curate should 'fall' the bells himself!"

The shout that greeted this supposition of Isaac's made the walls of the old shed ring.

"He would have something to do, would he not?" said Isaac, with a sneer.

"Ay, lad, ay," said old Jacob. "But as him be so ignorant about bells, it sim to I as he might fall they bells down on his own self."

"It be all right, Jacob," clamoured the men, as they surrounded him. "When coorits be such ignorant folk they must expect as something will happen out of the common."

"Isaac, lad," said Jacob, "shall us go to the new coorit, and tell he, as he have a-stopped they bells when he hadna no business to, as us won't never 'fall' they, but as him must do it his own self?"

Again the men shouted, and filled the air with their boisterous mirth.

Isaac smiled a grim sort of satisfactory smile, but he made no reply. The men thumped him on the back, and asked him to lead the way; but though Isaac was both angry and indignant at this uncalled-for interference on the part of Mr. Gray, he declined to accede to Jacob's proposal.

But the men went away in great good humour. The idea of the new curate being called upon to perform the impossible feat of "falling the bells" himself tickled their fancy; and they told the Widow Simpson "not to be feared, for they feeled sure that Isaac would still be 'cock of the walk,' in spite of that uncommon ignorant coorit."

XXVI

WHICH INTRODUCES TWO NEW CHARACTERS, AND TELLS OF PARSON HILL'S TROUBLES

AT the time the bells of Lawsleigh were so unceremoniously stopped, Parson Hill was riding across the moor, and after a second or two of doubt and listening, he checked his horse, and sat quietly waiting to hear the peal resume its broken strain. When he was convinced the ringing would not be resumed, he let his horse walk slowly on as he said to himself,

"What can be the matter?—umph!—a bell-rope broken; and yet that is not to be expected, for there is no stint of new ropes, for the men take good care to apply to me the holder of 'the bell-rope pightel,' and keep their gear in good order;"and, after a pause, he resumed,"Now, if this has happened through any misconduct on the part of Isaac Watson, I will—I really do think I will show him no mercy!"

And he put his horse into a trot, and pressed his lips firmly together, as he recalled the fact that Isaac had actually visited at Mary Cope's cottage when in a state of intoxication; and even granting that his visit was to Susan Picard—which he did not doubt—he still objected to such companionship for Mary.

Parson Hill eventually went on at a quicker pace. As a rule, he was extremely well-informed of all things happening in his parish, yet he rarely, if ever, searched into causes for this or that, but patiently waited until by ordinary means the subject was brought before him. And in this case, though he did not dismiss from his mind the fact of the bells coming thus suddenly to a stop, he lost no time in conjecture, but, to use his own expression, allowed his mind "to steady itself," by remembering it was best to let occurrences unfold, or settle themselves without interference on his part. But when he arrived at Paul Tavey, Mrs. Hill, the wife of his only son, accused him of having a brow more overclouded with care than usual.

"And I have more cares on my shoulders," said he.

"Then pray let us share them," said the lady.

"Bear ye one another's burdens," quoted the parson; and then he added, "but it would not be fair that you should share mine."

"Why not?"

"Because I suffered myself to have them thrust upon me, and ought therefore patiently to endure them."

"That is a very ingenious way of preventing one from loving one's neighbour."

"I deny that. I give you permission to love me as much as you please."

"I do so—I indulge myself womanfully. And now, by the thraldom of that love, dear sir, I ask you to let me share your trouble?"

"Trouble!—oh! you quite mistake me—I have no heartache, but I will tell you all my other aches and pains."

"Gout and rheumatism!" laughed the lady.

"Madame, no!" said the parson, with a stately bow; "you shall hear—first, an elegantly dressed and very pretty London miss, with a voice like Malibran and whom I permitted my schoolmistress to invite for change of air; and next," here the parson gave a slight but perceptible groan, "the new curate, who, you, madame, and you, Charlie, would insist, was required, because—because of my increasing infirmities."

"Gray is a capital fellow," said Mr. Charles Hill.

"Humph" said the parson, putting his hat on the carpet, and laying his whip across it.

"Here, Charlie, take away this hat and whip, and these gloves," which Parson Hill threw carelessly into his hat, "for you must stay and see all we have done," said the lady.

"Must I?" said the parson, doubtfully.

"You will stay all night ?"" said she, eagerly. "Say yes?"

"Indeed I must return home," said Parson Hill, shaking his head, "as soon as I have had a good look at you both."

"Why so?—why must you go?" said Charlie.

"Gray will send the crier after me."

"I did not know you possessed so wonderful a personage at Lawsleigh," said the lady.

"No; you do not know half as much about us as you ought," said Parson Hill.

"What can you mean?" said the lady.

"Gray says, 'I must look after my parish,' while I have not the most remote idea that it will attempt to run away. He says, too, 'I must not ride across country'—where then am I to ride? Perhaps he will ask me to walk—and over such roads. I dare say he will try to put a veto on my going to the Exhibition, whereas I made a point of having him three months earlier than I intended, on purpose that I might feel myself unhampered, and so enjoy the 'world's fair,' like a sober-minded parson as I am." And after a little pause, he continued, "Therefore, all things considered, you will understand I cannot stay and sleep here."

"You are laughing at us," said the lady; "you shall stay—I decree that."

"In spite of Mr. Gray—or to spite him," said the parson.

"Both," said she.

"Well, well, I give it up," laughed the parson; "I will lunch with you, but I would rather return home for dinner."

"And now that we have managed to agree thus far," said Mrs. Hill, "tell us what makes Mr. Gray such a bugbear?"

"Indeed, he is not at all a bugbear; on the contrary, he is a handsome man," said Parson Hill.

"We know that—but why is he a thorn in your side?"

"He is so active and zealous; I have hardly time to eat my meals, or saunter about my grounds, or even to muse over the past and ponder on the present. And then he is so well-read, and well-bred, and well-dressed."

"Ah! you are jealous," said the lady.

"Just so," said the parson with a smile.

"Because you are all three, and have hitherto——"

"I thank those angel lips for thus so kindly restoring me to my self-love," said Parson Hill energetically. "Gray does not admire my style of dress; he says I must wear black—so I do on proper occasions—but at all times and seasons, hot or cold, wet or dry, at home and abroad, I must wear black, because 'the clergy always wear black.'"

Mrs. Hill looked surprised, but did not speak, and Charlie laughed aloud.

"He says," resumed Parson Hill, "I must not wear top-boots, or blue coats, or other garments not necessary to mention—would he like me to go without? He would make me very uncomfortable indeed, and—but you think I may still continue to wear what I please?—and still pride myself on keeping up one of the requirements of my college when I matriculated—to be *bene vestito*."

And the parson drew himself up to his full height, and gazed from one to the other as they sat eagerly listening to this account of himself. At length Charlie said laughingly,

"Gray is one of the 'high and dry,' and you are——"

"High and dry! Nay, Charlie, Gray is not tall, and I have not had a ducking since I was ten years old, therefore, I may add, I am as 'dry' as Gray—what do you mean?"

"And so Gray bothers you?"

"Wrong again, sir—I disdain to allow myself to be what you call 'bothered.' I tell you he says, 'I must take care of my parish!' Now, speaking with all humility," said the parson, bowing, "I thought he was paid to do that. But in even justice, I must add that he says of himself, 'he has looked it up, and walked it over; he finds it in a state of abominable pools, sloughs, bogs and fogs' —what will he say in the winter?—'and hills, and stones, and water-courses, some wet, some dry; and the people so ignorant, they cannot speak their own language'. Does he find them speak French, or German, or Greek, or Latin?"

Parson Hill paused; but, as no remark was made, he resumed enthusiastically,

"Does Mr. Gray know what is their own language? Does he know that these people have spoken this patois from century to century?—ay, and they would still go on from century to century, ignorant of the wonders outside their beloved moor, if it were not for the arrival of the great iron horse! That famous horse, which, in the last thirty years, has brought about more changes, and been the cause of more innovations than have taken place in hundreds of years previously—that horse will, at length, link this moor to the rest of the world; the people will mix with others, civilization will come to them here, and then they may, in the course of a few generations, learn to speak English! But at this time they do speak their own language—the vernacular of the moor; and also—as if I had not told you enough—and also, Mr. Gray has kindly fed the poor ignorant minds of these poor ignorant people with a few trashy tracts."

"Tracts!" said Mrs. Hill.

"Tracts," said the parson. "But let me do him justice—not 'the Oxford tracts,' I ascertained that."

"He must be 'low and slow' if he goes about with tracts," said Charlie.

"He is neither, I assure you," said Parson Hill; "his motions are all rapid; his words come out with great velocity; I expect he was born in an express train, poor fellow! And, although he is by no means large and tall as I am, he is very nearly your own height, Charlie. So pray find some other epithet, for clearly Gray is neither low nor slow."

"But the pretty girl from London," said Mrs. Hill, "tell us how she managed to torment you. I thought you were quite beyond the reach of even the prettiest girl in the world!"

"And I humbly trust I am," said the parson, with a low bow. "And, again, if there is any tormenting in the case, it is I who have tormented her."

"That is impossible," laughed the lady.

"You then have a good opinion of me," said Parson Hill; "I wish Gray had," and he affected to sigh.

"And he will not let you go to the Exhibition?" said Charlie.

"If I ask him, he will surely say no; he is so good himself, he likes to make others as good through the virtue of self-denial. I candidly confess it would be a piece of most heroic self-denial on my part not to go to this 'World's Fair'—my heart is so full of vanity!"

"And now your care-clouded brow is accounted for," said Mrs. Hill; "your spirit is full of vexation."

"Unquestionably," said the parson, with a bland smile.

"We go to town next week," said Charlie.

"No doubt you intend to take me with you?" said the parson.

"Yes; all our plans include you," said Mrs. Hill.

"Then I cannot help myself—I must go; and I will tell Gray I could not find in my heart to spoil your plots; in point of fact, I was a party to them."

"Then you promise to go with us?"

"I promise. So now I have fairly outwitted Gray, for he cannot ask me to break my promise—he is too good for that. But will you credit me? He actually wants to take the school children, breed and born on Dartmoor, with their steady little mistress, to see this Great Exhibition! Did you ever listen to so mad an idea?"

"It is quite the custom, I assure you, sir," said Charles, "not only to take schools, but choirs, and, in some cases, whole villages!"

"Houses as well as inmates?—to the Exhibition? Is the whole world gone mad?" said Parson Hill.

"To the Exhibition—the people, not the cottages," said Charlie, laughing.

"And are these schools, choirs, and villages, sent to be exhibited?" said Parson Hill; "and if so, pray how are they shewn off?—and under what auspices?"

"They shew themselves off to the keen-eyed and awe-stricken Londoners, under the auspices of their own barbaric pomp and singularities," said Mrs. Hill.

"And pray is the vicar of the parish—unhappy wretch!—expected to exhibit himself at the same time?" said Parson Hill.

"Many are proud of such a distinction," said Charlie; "but there are good men and true among the magnates of the Church, who put aside their own selfish craving for the pomps and vanities of this world, and allow them to culminate in clustering glory round the aspiring brows of their curates!"

"Is it possible!" said Parson Hill; "their abnegation of self is a bright example. I will follow in their steps. I will let all the glory and all the honour fall on the shoulders of Gray, on condition that he marches with the parish and the schools, and the choir. And I will take all the expense of the journey on my own shoulders, on condition that I may be allowed to stay at home, and—and—'take care of my parish.'"

"You incorrigible creature! Why, there will not be any one left to care for!" said Mrs. Hill.

"Except myself, who am of no value," said the parson.

"You shall come to us," said Charlie.

"Or you to me, and so try to enliven the parish in the absence of its customary inhabitants."

"Have you heard from Mrs. Harcourt?" said the lady.

"Yes; she replied by return of post. She refuses me. She says the Exhibition has more attractions than my Hermitage, and——"

"I cannot credit that," said Mrs. Hill.

"She hints as much, I assure you—for she says, 'After you have seen the "World's Fair" will suit me better than at present, if equally convenient to you.' It seems she did not know we should go to town so early. How should she indeed? I did not know myself."

"Wise—wise Mrs. Harcourt!" said Mrs. Hill; "for when you once return from that holiday trip, you will ensconce yourself safely on your dear moor for many months to come."

"Well, what then?" said Parson Hill.

"Then there will be nothing to disturb or cut short her very agreeable visit, to a charmingly situated Hermitage, or her very pleasant conversations with a very dignified and very fascinating host."

"Ah!—you women!—you women!" said Parson Hill, shaking his head. "But while I think of it, let me say, you and Charlie had better pack up for London, as soon as may be, and come to me. And for this reason, you are so far from civilization, I should not marvel much if you had never seen a railway station. Now I——"

"Living in the world as you do," interrupted the lady.

"I am within ten miles of a station," continued Parson Hill, laughing and shaking his head at Mrs. Hill.

"And, on Monday, we can travel express, for we can reach N——in time for that train. What say you? Will you come?"

"Thank you. I says yes," said the lady. "What do you say, Charlie?"

"Your slightest wish is my law," said Charles, demurely.

"And now it is my turn to say, 'Oh, you men!——you men!'" said Mrs. Hill, shaking her head at Charlie.

XXVII

WHICH ACCOUNTS FOR THE BROKEN PEAL AND LOOKS INTO PARSON HILL'S THOUGHTS

On his return home, Parson Hill overtook Mr. Gray about a mile from the Parsonage; on seeing whom the polite parson dismounted, and, hanging the bridle rein over his arm, walked by Mr. Gray's side. It was now that the stopping of the bells was accounted for, as Mr. Gray of his own accord commenced the subject with,

"The men rang a peal after the funeral this morning—or rather began to ring, for I thought it my duty to prevent such conduct."

"To prevent the men ringing?" said the parson.

"Certainly; could anything be more distressing to the feelings of the surviving relatives and friends?"

"Distressing!—nay, sir, consolatory," said the parson.

"Consolatory!—uproarious bells clanging forth after a funeral consolatory?"

"Uproariously clanging!—nay, then, that is unpardonable—how could it have happened?—were the men our own ringers?—the usual set?"

"The leader is, I should think, the ringleader of all the evils that infest this poor parish," said Mr. Gray.

"Ringleader!—of—of evils?—who, sir?"

"Isaac Walton."

"Umph!—I thought that man died many years ago. How can he encroach upon my parish now?"

"The blacksmith at the entrance to the village, Isaac Walton—or—or Waller."

"Ah!—he who wrote verses to my lady Dorothy Sidney," said the parson; "and is he alive now?"

"The blacksmith!—a big man, with a red face and a rough tongue," said Mr. Gray; for the confusion he had made in names irritated him.

"Perhaps you mean Isaac Watson?" said the parson in a suave tone; "he is tall, and his face has a florid hue; but the man talks well, sir, extremely well; he is in fact a wonder—a perfect wonder, on this moor, for from his earliest years he has been a reader; and of what do you accuse him?"

The parson was now, in his own mind, taking Isaac's part against Mr. Gray. He had for the time being quite forgotten his intention of "making an example of him" on the very first opportunity, for Parson Hill did not feel pleased with Mr. Gray for taking the liberty of stopping the peal.

"Was he tipsy?" continued the vicar, after a slight pause.

"They were all drunk, you may be very sure."

"All drunk!" said the parson, standing still, and thereby checking his horse.

"Yes, I repeat it, all drunk!—you seem astonished—do you think that sober men would ring a peal after a funeral?"

After a pause of some slight duration, Parson Hill said, in a softened tone,

"Yes."

"Yes!—you think men who were sober would ring a peal after a funeral!—you do?"

"Of course they would," said Parson Hill, in a decided tone; "and pray, sir, why not?" and the parson resumed his walk.

"Why not!—gracious Heaven, Mr. Hill! excuse me. Do you not think that the husband of the poor woman I buried will be groaning in spirit over his heavy loss!—then why should the bells peal forth as if for joy?"

"The spirit of the man may yearn for his lost wife," said Parson Hill, in a gentle tone, "but his spirit hopes to rejoin her spirit, and it is a custom in our Church, probably obsolete in many places now, that the bells shall be rung in peal, to tell him 'not to sorrow as those who have no hope,' for that 'the soul of her who has gone hence is now in joy and happiness.'"

"How can he tell that? It is surely presumptuous to suppose it."

"Our Church commands," said Parson Hill, impressively, "that the bells shall ring out in solemn cheerfulness after a funeral. And we may all humbly hope to be one of those whom our Saviour died to save; or, in other words, that she whom you buried is now in peace and joy. Will you dine with me?"

"Thank you, not to-day," said Mr. Gray.

"When shall I see you?—I go to town on Monday, and must therefore first make some arrangements with you."

"You are going to the Exhibition!" said Mr. Gray, in a tone of great surprise.

"I am," said the vicar, with a smile.

"And have you thought over my proposal of taking the school, and perhaps some others, to see this grand 'World's Fair?'" said Mr. Gray.

"Yes, yes. I want to talk it over with you. Since you cannot come to-day, are you engaged on Friday?"

"No; I shall have much pleasure——"

"At six, if you please," said Parson Hill.

"I thank you, yes. Good morning," said Mr. Gray; and he muttered to himself, as Mr. Hill mounted his horse and rode away, "And there he rides off to his own good dinner, in much fear that the trout will be spoiled, or the soup cold, or—in short, he is a veritable type of a clergyman of the old school—full of himself, forgetful of the rest of the world!"

While Parson Hill also muttered to himself, "And as you take the liberty of always coming half an hour late, I shall take the precaution to order dinner accordingly."

And now Parson Hill has dined. He has not, however, left the dining-room, for, comfortably seated in an easy chair, he is indulging in a reverie on the subject of "Isaac Watson, the ringleader of all the evils of this poor parish;" of the bells, and Mr. Gray's strange ignorance; of the ringers, and Mr. Gray's extraordinary accusation, "All drunk!" Even Parson Hill, who considered himself a person of some experience, had never known, either in his own parish or any other, "all the ringers, drunk at one time;"—and of the poor ignorant people who could not speak their own language.

"That language that is dead or unknown to Mr. Gray, though a living one on Dartmoor," said the parson to himself, "and the current tongue of its inhabitants. They may be uneducated," mused he, "but they understand all the ancient customs of our Church; they may be ignorant, but they live in the knowledge of God, and the blessing of a Saviour; they may be heathens in speech, in looks, and in manners, but they are Christians in their kindliness and charity to each other; they speak the language of their ancestors and the locality, and they look like what they are—dwellers on Dartmoor, far from the haunts of fashion and her ever-changing gewgaws, and they have the manners of their class; and if these manners are somewhat odd and strange in the eyes of better educated people, they are at least free from affectation, and, if unpolished, sincere. Now it seems to me," said the parson, speaking to himself, "that if the 'cloth,' as he called the clergy," and the parson elevated his eyebrows, "understood more of the ancient customs of our Church, and thought less of their own 'black' coats, the world might benefit thereby. He prides himself"—by *he* the parson meant Mr. Gray—"on his 'black coat,' and stops the bells from 'ringing out in solemn cheerfulness' after a funeral! He opens his eyes wide at the sight of my small-clothes and top-boots—a convenient costume to ride in—and I open mine wider at his unpardonable ignorance! For, though I grant that many of the ancient customs of our Church are obsolete in cities, towns, or thickly-peopled places, that is no excuse for his want of knowledge. As an educated man, and, above all, as a clergyman, he should be well 'up' in the Church from her earliest times. But he stopped the bells after a funeral! Why, the moor people will not understand him!—how should they? And as to the men being 'all drunk,' I do not believe it. I know as a rule ringers are a sad lot; but these men are better than most others. Isaac and Jacob are the two worst; but I do not believe either of them would go to ring a funeral peal in a state of intoxication—I cannot! No, no, it is all wrong. I had no business with a curate, for a curate fresh from Oxford and London, and 'black coats'"—here the parson shrugged his shoulders—"and patent leather boots, cannot so well manage to balk a bog of its prey as I who have lived here the best part of my life. But

I managed to mystify him charmingly," and the parson chuckled at the thought. And then, resuming his soliloquy, he said,

"It is true I rode in 'pink' when I first came to this moor; but not of late years—no, no. And it is also true that the other day, when I put in to Culmstor in the dreadful storm, wet to the skin, my kind old friend lent me a faded old pink to ride home in—a 'pink,' because it was the only one in the house sufficiently large for me, ha! ha! ha! I scarcely knew myself when I entered my dressing-room; even now I cannot help laughing at my strange appearance. The pink did me right good service then; it has done me a better *now*, since the recollection of it helped me to make that 'wonderful young gentleman in black' elevate his eyebrows.

"And then again Gray says, 'The moor people have been standing still for centuries,' and I say, 'Stand on, good friends, stand on! The ancient formula of our Church, if obsolete elsewhere, will do us no harm on Dartmoor.' We—I include myself with you, my people—we shall not go over to Rome, for we seldom roam from home," and the parson chuckled in his easy chair. "Gray may have an inkling that way, though I do not wish to accuse him, and so deems it necessary to keep temptation from his eyes and his ears.

"'I must take care of my parish.'" The parson felt rather sore on this point. "I wish I could kick Gray out of it! What an egregious ass I must have been to give him a title!—a title to preach to me! A young, hot-headed, black——"

But here the parson's reverie was interrupted, and we lost for ever the concluding word, by the announcement that Isaac Watson wished to see him.

"This is an unusual hour," said Parson Hill; "Isaac knows it is against my rule to see any one after dinner."

"Yes, sir; but Isaac asked me to tell you that he would not have intruded upon you now but for something of importance."

Parson Hill remembered the stopping of the bells, and, connecting Isaac's untimely visit with this unusual occurrence, he said,

"I will see him in the library."

XXVIII

WHICH TREATS OF THE LIVING AND THE DEAD—THE PAST AND THE PRESENT

Isaac's business with Parson Hill was to tell him that, in consequence of Mr. Gray stopping the peal, the bells were not "falled." Mr. Gray had taken Isaac's keys, to prevent the ringers having the power to re-enter the belfry; but Isaac, understanding bells as he did, knew that they ought not to be left in that position, and now came to the vicar for advice.

We need only add that, as Mr. Hill was as learned on the subject of bells as Isaac, he saw immediately what ought to be done, gave Isaac his own keys, and told him to collect the men and "fall" the bells.

When Isaac went away, Parson Hill did as he had previously informed Mr. Gray he was accustomed to do. He took off his blue coat, opened the door of a closet, and hung it up on a peg; then he put on his comfortable wrap, and then he lighted his agreeable pipe. When the fingers of the clock on the mantelpiece pointed to ten minutes past nine, George brought coffee.

George had lived with Parson Hill for nearly twenty years, and on this occasion, while handing coffee to his master, he said,

"They say, sir, that Parson Melson is very ill."

"Melson of Tiddycombe?" said Mr. Hill; "I am sorry to hear it."

"Yes, sir—old Mr. Melson—he was so ill at Totnes great market on Wednesday, that he could not ride home. Mrs. Taylor was obliged to drive him home in the dog-cart."

"Bless me! George; when did you hear this?"

"I heard it several days ago. Totnes great market was last week, but the postman said this morning that Mr. Melson was much worse."

"Worse, George! You should have told me this before now," and the parson turned to look at the clock.

"Dr Beanie from Ashburton has attended him all along, but yesterday they sent to the station at N——, to telegraph for Dr. Leader from Plymouth, and Dr. Shapgood from Exeter."

"You should have told me this before, George."

"I thought you knew, sir. They say he won't recover!"

"I did not know!" said the parson, in a reproachful tone. "Who was to tell me of Melson's illness? Order the carriage to come round in half an hour."

"Yes, sir," and George turned to look at the clock. "At twenty minutes to ten, sir?"

"In half an hour," said the vicar, sipping his coffee.

"Yes, sir," and George turned to leave the room. "The carriage, sir?"

Parson Hill did not reply immediately. Thought is rapid, and he thought—"Ah! I suppose it is a good deal of trouble to get the carriage ready at so late an hour, and so I do not mind if I ride." And then, speaking to George, he said:

"You may order 'Sir Harry,' George. I can ride."

"Yes, sir; in half an hour?"

"In half an hour."

"'Sir Harry,' sir?"

"'Sir Harry!' yes, 'Sir Harry!'"

And now the vicar spoke in a tone of command, and yet he condescended to add:

"The bay mare has had her gallop to-day, and 'Butterfly' does not like the moon, and——"

"There is no moon, sir," said George, closing the door, and coming up to Parson Hill as if the conversation interested him.

"'Sir Harry' will not mind that," said the vicar, quietly.

"Won't he, sir. But, sir, you'll excuse me, sir?"

The parson sipped his coffee, and did not raise his head.

"You will excuse me, sir?"

"That depends upon circumstances, George," said Parson Hill, leaning back in his chair, and looking fixedly at him.

"Yes, sir, of course, sir," said George, with a smile. "But if you must go all across the country at this time of night——"

The man paused, and the parson again sipped his coffee.

"If you must sir: and no moon, sir: and Parson Melson quite dead by this time, sir——"

The parson raised his head and looked sternly at George.

"Mr. Melson must have died by this time, sir," said the man.

"Then I will close his eyes, George," said the parson, as he returned the empty coffee-cup; and he added to himself, "the man is trying to prevent me from going."

"And now, George, no delay," said the vicar, as he rose from his chair. "In five minutes bring 'Sir Harry,' round."

"Yes, sir, 'Sir Harry!'"

And the man left the room.

Parson Hill's thoughts were pre-occupied with the news of Mr. Melson's illness, but he continued to make the necessary preparations for his ride across the moor.

At length George re-entered the library.

"Who is to go with you, sir?" said George.

As Parson Hill always rode unattended, he did not condescend to reply to this query.

"It is a dark night, sir; it will rain before morning."

"Rain is much wanted, George," said the parson, as he buttoned his coat.

"Yes, sir, but not tonight, when you will ride across country in spite of everything!"

"I do not feel spiteful, George," said the vicar, with a smile.

"No, sir, of course not. But who is to go with you, sir?"

"You, George," said Parson Hill, in a tone of command.

But George was an indoor servant—a sort of factotum—and did not ride.

"I am sure, sir, you ought not to go alone all across country, and such numbers of bogs!"

"I shall not be alone if you go with me, George."

"True, sir; but how am I to go?"

"You may ride 'Butterfly,'" said the parson, turning round to hide his laughter.

"Oh—h! yes, sir; but I know that won't do, sir; and so, sir, who is to take care of you?"

"You, George," said the imperturbable parson.

"I have been thinking, sir, had you not better have the carriage, and let Marvel drive you?"

"I asked you for the carriage at first, George, and you seemed unwilling to let me have it; but just give me that good thick walking-stick, and as it seems to me that you do not mean to let me have either the carriage, or 'Sir Harry,' or 'Butterfly,' or the moon, or the rain, or even yourself, George, to take care of me, I think I will set off and walk to Tiddycombe Vicarage alone."

"Yes, sir; but I hope you will excuse me, sir,"—and the reader will surely say that George is as imperturbable as his master—"but I *did* take the liberty, sir, to order the carriage, and Marvel to drive you, for it is not safe to go across this moor,"—at this instant the hall door bell rang—"and that must be the carriage now, sir, if you will excuse me?"

"I have not time to excuse you now, George, but on my return we can go into the subject; and if I find such a proceeding impracticable, you will——"

"Yes, sir, of course."

"Of course what, George?" said the vicar, as he was getting into the carriage.

"I am sure, sir, I do not know," said George as he closed the carriage door. And then turning to Marvel, who held the reins, he continued,

"Mind how you drive, James. It is a shameful country to go across on a dark——"

"Drive on, Marvel," said the vicar. And George's last words were not heard.

"Now if I were as young and inexperienced as Mr. Gray, I daresay I should think George an impertinent and meddling old fool!" said the vicar to himself. "He is to a certain extent like all servants who have lived many years with one master, he takes an interest in everything; and because he takes an interest, he gives an opinion, and sometimes thinks he knows better than his master. Perhaps he does; it is not a difficult matter to know more than I."

And here it is necessary to say a few words to introduce Mr. Melson, though he will not take any part in our story.

Mr. Melson was one of that class of the clergy who farmed his own glebe—it may be said many do that; true, they do. But Mr. Melson, in the dress of a farmer, worked with his men as a farmer on Dartmoor would work, and carried on every operation of a large farm in full work, under his own eye. He bought and sold; bred horses, and made money thereby; rode to market two or three times a week, and to all fairs of note within the counties of Devon and Cornwall, and at such times he gave himself to the farmers, and seated himself at the tables provided for them.

Until late years there was no school in his parish; no educated choir even now; no visiting of the sick at anytime, that is as the clergyman of the parish, and comforter of the dying, though there was abundance of kind-hearted private charity. He spoke what is called "broad Devonshire," and in his farmer's dress under his gown, he has taken the Sunday duty in the church year by year; but for the remaining days in the week, he was to all intents and purposes a farmer.

In the latter days of his life, when the moor has been invaded by troops of tourists, curious little notes have been taken of Mr. Melson's sermons but to use his own words "You might as well attempt to wash the blackamoor white"—as to change the Rev. Mr. Melson.

Mr. Melson was a well-known character in Devon and Cornwall. He was very learned in the localities and the history of Dartmoor, and trusted as an authority, and his name is mentioned with honour in several sterling works on that subject. He was a bold rider, and certainly in his day followed the hounds with the best of them—both he and his niece who lived with him, for Mr. Melson was a bachelor.

At the time that Parson Hill crossed the moor to visit him in his illness, Mr. Melson was in his eighty-third year.

Perhaps my readers wonder why, if the Rev. Mr. Melson has nothing to do with my story, he should be spoken of at all? If Parson Hill was such an anomaly to Mr. Gray, what would he have thought of the Rev. Mr. Melson? There was a much greater difference between him and Parson Hill, and greatly in favour of the latter, than between Parson Hill and the orthodox clergy of the present day. And yet they were contemporaries, and both had livings on Dartmoor. Mr. Melson died soon after Parson Hill's visit. There are but a few of the clergy now left on Dartmoor, if any, who were contemporaries with Parson Hill.

XXIX

IN WHICH WE HEAR THE "JOY-BELLS," AND INTRODUCE MR. GRAY TO THE RINGERS

AT the close of the week, and just as Parson Hill had entered his dressing-room to make his toilette before dinner, he was gratified by the sight of a travelling carriage driving up to his door.

"Charlie and his sweet wife, I do really think," said he, as he hastened down to receive them.

"Now this is truly kind," continued he, as he gave his hand to Mrs. Hill, and assisted her to alight.

"Too late for dinner, I fear?" said Charlie.

"No; by great good fortune," here the parson shrugged his shoulders, "Gray dines with me, and as, from experience, I know his engagements are numerous, and his time much occupied in this enormous parish," spreading out his hands and affecting to sigh, "I usually give him a little law, and dine at seven instead of six. And so you are indebted to him for a hot dinner, and to me for a hearty welcome."

"We give our choicest smiles to the last, and make our best curtsy for the first," said Mrs. Hill, curtsying; "and we are so glad to come."

"And I am so glad to have you," said Parson Hill.

"What a charming drive it is from Paul Tavey to Lawsleigh!" said Mrs. Hill; "the Tors are magnificent, and they seem to be never ending; and what a sweet spot you have—this Hermitage of yours!"

"She has been in raptures all the drive," said Charlie.

"Charlie, dear," said Mrs. Hill, turning to speak to him before she entered the house, leaning on the vicar's arm—"Charlie dear, will you hasten—the—the—I must make my toilet."

"There, get away," said Charlie, impatiently—"as if I did not know."

At dinner, and while the soup was going round, the bells of Lawsleigh pealed forth a joyous sound.

"What fine bells!" said the lady.

"The men have evidently got scent of your arrival," said the parson. "There is a clash!—all in honour of yourself, fair madam."

Meanwhile, at the first attempt at raising the bells, Mr. Gray started, and, with evident surprise, appeared to be listening attentively.

When the eight bells were all raised and the musical peal came cheerily on the ear, he fidgeted on his chair, did not join in the conversation, did not hear if he were spoken to—or, at least, made no reply—did not touch his soup, and seemed annoyed and disturbed.

"George," said Parson Hill in a low voice, "change Mr. Gray's plate."

And the cold soup vanished, and was replaced by a hot cutlet of salmon. This arrested Mr. Gray's momentary attention, inasmuch as he mechanically helped himself to sauce when it was handed; but his mind still seemed absent from the present scene and company.

"What a magnificent peal!—do listen, Charlie!" said the lady; "these are indeed 'joy-bells.'"

"Clash, clash, and race, race, one after the other! They are a capital set of ringers—do not you think so, Gray?" said Charlie, who was quite unaware of Mr. Gray's delinquency in the matter of bells.

"Where could they get the keys?" said Mr. Gray, in an irritable tone.

"Change Mr. Gray's plate," said the parson; and the untouched cutlet was replaced by a *pâté*.

"The men have their own keys," said Charlie.

"This is my son's first visit to Lawsleigh since his marriage," explained the parson; "and our good old ringers, many of whom have known him from childhood, delight to testify their joy at his return home," and then, turning to George, he said in a lower tone, "remove Mr. Gray's plate."

But Mr. Gray prevented this order from being obeyed, by attacking the *pâté*—though he again relapsed into silence as he marvelled to himself,

"Where did they get the keys?"

And here we should explain that when, on the day the peal had been stopped, Mr. Gray parted from Parson Hill, he did not return to his own lodgings, but walked some miles across the moor to dine with a friend in the next parish. Consequently, the fact of the bells having been touched since he stopped them on the morning of that day was unknown to him.

And thus it was that he sat ruminating on the probable or improbable means by which the ringers had contrived to repossess themselves of the keys of the belfry; and thus he lost his fish and soup while conjecturing on things past, instead of compelling his mind to amuse itself by the contemplation of things present.

And the party had assembled in the drawing-room, and the fumes of fragrant coffee and delicious tea scented the air. The windows were wide open; the moon was about ten days old, and not at a very high altitude, but her light was bright and clear.

Mrs. Hill stepped out of the window on to the lawn, enthusiastically pointing out now this Tor tipped with silver, now that in mighty shadow, when she suddenly grasped the arm of Parson Hill as she said,

"What have you there? Something moving amongst the shrubs?"

"The 'dimpse' (twilight) deceives you," said the parson, "no one will venture to intrude into my grounds."

"I saw the moon just light up for a moment the head of a tall man—a giant! he seemed to me!" said Mrs. Hill, "and even now I can see in the distance—"

"Yes, so do I," said Parson Hill, leaving the lady, and walking forward to meet the intruders, whom he evidently joined and conversed with; soon, however, he returned and explained,

"That the ringers had brought their hand-bells, to know if Master Charlie's Missus would like to hear them?"

Mrs. Hill looked puzzled and made no answer, but Charlie dashed across the lawn, and was seen, as the party drew nearer, coming round by the path, to be shaking hands with each man, and apparently bringing them all up to the drawing-room windows.

"Now, Jacob," said Charlie, as the men stood bowing to the parson and his party, and putting his hand on the shoulder of a tall old man, "that is my Missus leaning on my father's arm!—Isaac," turning to another, "what do you think of her?"

"I hope you will make the lady a good husband, Master Charlie," said Isaac Watson.

"But you do not tell me what you think of her?" said Charlie, as he gave Isaac a friendly thump on the back.

Isaac looked shy, and tanged his bells; the men formed in a semicircle; and Parson Hill and the lady seated themselves on the garden chairs; while Mr. Gray came to the open window, and stood there sipping his coffee. At first, the sounds were only the soft and silvery imitations of the grand peal that had so recently been heard from the tower; but after a few minutes the peal stopped, and the men played, or rather rung, a well-known air with much precision and effect. When this was over, Charlie was enthusiastic in their praise, adding that "they had much improved since he had heard them last."

While Mrs. Hill said to the parson,

"Independent of the sweet tones of the bells, and the skill with which they are managed, I am very much struck with the perfect ease and even grace of movement displayed by the ringers."

"Yes," said the parson, "and perhaps I shall surprise you when I say that the men try to acquire that graceful ease from the time they commence learning to ring, and think as much of managing their bells in an elegant unlaboured manner as you would of your superb curtsy."

Mrs. Hill laughed, and the men re-formed and played another tune. When they again stopped, Parson Hill said in a low voice to the lady,

"Now, if I take the liberty of presenting these men to you, do you think you can imagine yourself 'Queen of Dartmoor,' since I have no lawful Queen, and offer your hand for a Moorland salute?"

"What! to each of those men! For what do you take me? Marble!"

Parson Hill laughed.

"You are incorrigible!" said Mrs. Hill, shaking her head.

"Oh! no, no," said the parson, "only playful," and he once again drew her arm within his own, and approached the men.

"You play charmingly," said he—"you know you do; and I must have a turn with you one of these days; I do not like to forget my accomplishments—do I, Jacob?"

"Your honour was always skilled in they bells," said Jacob, looking much gratified.

"And now I wish to present you to Mrs. Hill, my Charlie's wife:— Jacob Smerdon, Isaac Watson, John Mead, John Crocker, Thomas Lear, Peter Jones, Matthew Skinner, and James Harden."

The men all bobbed their heads as they were named, and Charlie joined the group, and said,

"Now, Jacob, tell me what you think of my Missus?"

"You be uncommon full of tricks, Master Charlie," said Jacob.

"That is what you think of me. I know your opinion of me. Can't you tell me if my Missus 'be a bowerly woman?'" said Charlie, in the patois of the moor.

"Why do they call him *Master Charlie?*" said Mrs. Hill, in a low voice, to the parson, who laughed, and made no reply.

Cups of ale were now brought, and handed to the men. Jacob Smerdon, as the oldest man present, stepped into the centre of the semicircle, and said,

"Us be cruel glad as Master Charlie's ha gotten a Missus. Us sees you bees a bowerly woman. Ees fè—Fags!—us be cruel glad!—An' us tell 't the ton tu the tother; eef in course as Master Charlie's ha gotten a Missus, us hops her bees gude and kind like tu Master Charlie, an' tu th' passon's own sen, an' us hops her bees bowerly. Here's tu yu, muman' us wissen ye mony yearn o' happiness."

And Jacob and the men then drank their ale, the men chorusing "us wissen ye mony yearn o' happiness."

"Now for your speech," said Charlie to his wife. But as Mrs. Hill was in much the same predicament as the reader at this present moment, and as she had understood but few words of Jacob Smerdon's speech, we think that for her sake, as well as the reader's, we had better translate it into a readable tongue, viz.—

"We are very glad Master Charlie has a wife. We see you are a handsome woman; yes, faith! and we are very glad. And we said one to another, if Master Charlie has a wife, we hope she will be good and kind like Master Charlie, and the parson himself, and we hope she is handsome. Here is your health, Madam, and we wish you many years of happiness."

And, as we have said, Mrs. Hill was called upon to reply.

"Oh no! indeed you must speak for me," said she.

"No," said Parson Hill, coming to her side, "give the men a word yourself."

Thus encouraged, and though she had not understood many words of Jacob Smerdon's speech, Mrs. Hill thanked the men for their kind wishes, and told them how much pleased she had been with the "joy-bells" from the tower, as well as with the beautiful tunes she had heard them ring on the small bells.

"I will ring with you to-morrow," said Charlie, "and we will have a 'grandsire triple.'"

"Yes, Master Charlie, if you please."

"What is a grandsire triple?" said Mrs. Hill.

"Every change is alternately in and out of course," said Parson Hill, smiling; "the hand changes of the treble lead being 'out,' and the back stroke 'in.'"

"I do not know at all what you mean," said the lady.

"Back stroke changes," said Charlie, laughing, "and rounds cannot be brought at hand without turning the 'course' of the bell."

As Mrs. Hill looked only the more puzzled, Parson Hill joined Charlie in his laugh, and took up his explanation by saying,

"Courses, on account of the bell in the hunt, cannot be had complete; but this method is held in great estimation," added he, nonchalantly, "and a greater variety of 'touches' are introduced."

"We can 'bob' every fourth lead, or each time five, six, seven, come home," said Charlie. "And," continued he, "I should think, with so decidedly clear an explanation, you must quite understand what is meant by 'a grandsire triple.'"

Mrs. Hill and Charlie now stood and talked with the men, and delighted them by their affability and the interest they took in their ringing; while Parson Hill stepped back and talked with Mr. Gray. In a short time the two latter gentlemen came forward, and Parson Hill said,

"And now you must allow me to introduce you all to my very good friend and representative, Mr. Gray." (Here he again mentioned the name of each man.) "He has kindly consented to come and live on our moor, and help me in my old age. At present our local customs, though themselves handed down from time immemorial, are new to him." (here Mr. Gray looked uncomfortable.) "Nor can he know and appreciate you all so well as I who have lived the best part of my life amongst you; but we may reasonably hope that each day will bring him nearer to that kind of lore best suited for his position; and I am very sure that any friend or companion of mine, even though at present a stranger, you will all treat as kindly, and obey, where needful, as promptly as you do myself. I ask no more."

"Of course, your honour; yes, certainly," chorused the men, as they bobbed their heads to Mr. Gray, who stepped forward and cordially shook hands with each man, as he said:

"I am very glad to know you all; and I hope and trust we shall soon understand each other." And to Mr. Gray's credit be it recorded that he courageously walked up to Isaac, and restored the keys of the belfry, simply observing:

"I take this opportunity of restoring your keys."

NOTES

NOTE A

"'DARTMOOR,' so named from the Dart, to which it gives rise, as it does to most of the rivers in Devon, constitutes the south-west part of the county on the north of the 'South Hams.' On approaching this tract from the south and south-east, the eye is bewildered by an extensive waste, exhibiting gigantic Tors, large surfaces covered with vast masses of scattered granite and immense rocks, which seem to have been precipitated from deep declivities into valleys. These huge fragments, spread in wild confusion over the ground, have been compared to the ponderous masses ejected by volcanoes, to the enormous ruins of formidable castles, and to the wrecks of mountains torn piecemeal by the raging elements.

"'Dartmoor,' and the waste called the 'Forest of Dartmoor,' include between two and three hundred thousand acres of open and uncultivated land. Of these, Dartmoor alone is supposed to comprise upwards of eighty thousand. Swampy declivities, unfit for cultivation, also abound in many parts of this district."—*From "The History of Devonshire," by the Rev. Thomas Moore.*

"Dartmoor is hallowed by the most interesting associations; and forms of beauty and of grandeur everywhere meet the eye of a close observer of nature. The purple heathbell springs up beneath his feet—the variegated lichen encrusts the shivered rock—the creeping moss sheds a loveliness over the moist hill-side—the fern waves gracefully in the passing wind—the spiral foxglove displays its sparkled bosom—the tall reed, and the glossy plumes of the cotton rush, nod in the same breeze that wafts along the delicate thistle-down—the torrent fills the glen with romantic music—the mountain bee hums his soothing lullaby, and the song of many a melodious bird echoes sweetly amid the frowning crags. He, however, who wishes to behold the moorland in its utmost magnificence should visit it when the wintry gale is fiercely howling around—when the Tors are clothed in the majesty of the tempest—when the murmur of every little brook is swollen into a voice of power—when the lightnings have unbound their 'blue and arrowy pinions,' and he who dares, at that fearful hour, to confront the angry spirits of the storm in this their hereditary and undisputed stronghold, will be amply rewarded for his perils by the feelings of grandeur and sublimity which will then steal into his mind.

"Dartmoor, both above and below the surface, abounds in enormous blocks of granite; and those which are scattered on its mighty slopes, exposed to the influence of the elements, and the ravages of time, are mouldered into the wildest and most impressible forms imaginable. In some places they are piled on each other with a regularity which seems almost the effect of art, and it requires but very slight aid from fancy to make them resume the most interesting resemblances. The poet will picture to himself the remains of sublunary grandeur—will muse amid fallen columns and shattered arches, and sigh over the bygone renown of fabrics which have passed away from the face of the earth, even as a flower withereth;—the antiquary will image ruined castles lifting high their tottering turrets, and crumbling abbeys, with their wind-swept aisles and mouldering cloisters; or he will recognize the relics of a remoter age in the semblance of moss-grown cromlechs and druidical monuments;—the moralist, in contemplating the rude scene, will be reminded of the awful wrecks of human ambition; and the misanthrope will exult in the solitude of spots where he may indulge his gloomy imaginings undisturbed."— *"Dartmoor, a Descriptive Poem," by N.J. Carrington.*

The notes are taken from the preface to the second edition by H.E Carrington.

NOTE B

"SOULE BELL."—"And when any is passing out of this life, a bell shall be tolled, and the minister shall not then slack to do his last duty. And after the party's death, if it so fall out, there shall be rung no more than one short peal, and one other before the burial, and one other after the burial."—*Canon* 67 (1603), 4.

NOTE C

"PASSING-BELL."—"Passing from life, sometimes called the "soul-bell," rung that others might pray for the person then dying. The passing-bell continued in this use all over England until the reign of Charles the Second. Now, it means, generally in the rural districts, some person is dead."

NOTE D

"TOR."—"The Rev. J.H. Mason, the worthy incumbent of Widdi-coombe on-the Moor, and Mr. Shillibear, of Walkhampton, persons better acquainted with Dartmoor than, perhaps, any other men living, state the most remarkable Tors to be, in the north, Cosdon, Little Hound, Great Hound, Stuperton, Wild, Watern, Kit, Far, Brat, Hamster, South Lynx, North Lynx, Dunnagoat, Stenger, Rough, High Willow, The Three Mill, Yes, Arm, and Belston Tors. In the east sixteen Tors, among which is Crockern, or Tinner's Parliament. In the south six; and in the west thirteen. Colonel Mudge, in his Trigonometrical Survey of Devon, enumerates many more; but of the whole it has been found impracticable to gather particulars; although, in the language of Lucan, 'Nullum est sine nomine saxum;' but, as to the larger proportion, that is all. They have braved the elements and ruthless Time ever since the deluge; but their frames and the adamantine materials of which they are composed alone survive. In strictness, but comparatively few of them, and those mostly the Tors named by Mr. Mason and Mr. Shillibear, are on the moor; the others lie at a greater or less distance all round it.

"The Rev. Mr. Jones, in his interesting observations on Moreton-hampstead and Dartmoor, eloquently describes Hound Tor as 'a magnificent group of rocks, like the remains of some ruined castle, rising in the horizon with its beetling front from the dreary plain; its toppling crags having the appearance of pinnacles which the hand of time had loosened; and, as it throws its dark shade across the heath, it increases the natural wildness of the desolate downs, in the midst of which it is situated.'

"'Fox Tor' has been connected by tradition with 'Child the Hunter.' Some of the Tors, as Hey or High Tor, South Brent Tor, were formerly beacons or 'fire towers,' which the word 'Tor' itself, in the Celtic and other languages implies; and anciently there were watchings and wardings of the beacons. The Rev. Mr. Polwhele imagines some of them to be extinct volcanoes; but this is not supported by facts, although there are, certainly, a few Tors of a conical shape. With much more probability certain of them, as Lynx, Bear, and Hound Tors, are so called from the respective animals of those names."—*From Carrington's "Dartmoor."*

NOTE E

"CROCKERN TOR."—"This Tor, so well known to antiquaries, though few of them, perhaps, have seen it, stands at the back of a cottage and estate belonging to the Rev. J.H. Mason, about a mile distant from "Two Bridges," in the east quarter of the moor, of which it is reputed by some to be the centre. The president, or judge's chair, part of the bench for the jurors, and three irregular steps for ascending, are still partially visible; but, either by the course of time or spoliation, it has become dilapidated, and report affirms the latter.

"Crockern Tor must always command respect as an interesting relic of old British manners, and as a memorial of the Saxon 'Witena-gemote,' or early parliament of the realm, which, like the Stannary parliament, as it is most commonly styled, was held in the open air."

NOTE F

"WISTMAN'S WOOD."—"Tradition relates that Wistman's, otherwise Welshman's Wood, was planted by the renowned Isabella de Fostibus, Countess of Devon."—*From Carrington's "Dartmoor."*

"This solitary relic, as it is supposed to be by many, of the woods formerly existing on the moor, stands on a slope near the West Dart, on the north Crockern Tor, a mile or more above Two Bridges, and consists of scrub, or dwarf trees, chiefly oak, whose stunted roots, finding scarcely a covering in the thin granite soil, or being entirely exposed on the bare surface of the rocks, obtain in such a situation little nutriment for their support. There are several patches of wood near each other, covering an extent of several acres. The trees seldom exceed ten feet in height; the branches are long and straggling, nor are their trunks large, although, from the vast accumulation of moss, together with thorns, brambles, and other parasites, they have assumed a bulky appearance. Unpropitious, however, as the situation of the wood unquestionably is, it has withstood the tempests of the moor and the disasters of its climate many centuries:—it is supposed to be a thousand years old."—*From the "History of Devonshire," by the Rev. Thomas Moore.*

NOTE G

"Saint Days."—"Bells wake the heart to gladness on all the Holy Feast days of the Church, loudly calling upon us to 'rejoice in the Lord.'"—*Blunt, "On the Use and Abuse of Church Bells."*

THE END

VOLUME II

I

OF MRS. HARCOURT'S WISDOM, AND OF MRS. CURZON'S FOLLY

AT her sister's house in —— Square, London, Mrs. Harcourt—already introduced to the reader—once again opened a letter that excited Mrs. Curzon's curiosity. It did not seem to affect Mrs. Harcourt herself, but the former lady evidently wished to know its contents.

"From Devon, Mary?" said she, after a few minutes' quiet surveillance of her sister.

"No, Sophia," said Mrs. Harcourt, cheerfully; "the letter is from Mrs. Russell."

The two ladies were silent for a short time; Mrs. Curzon apparently at work, but really watching Mrs. Harcourt, who continued to read the letter to herself.

"Have you disagreeable news?" said Mrs. Curzon, allowing her curiosity to conquer her reticence.

"No," said Mrs. Harcourt, looking up, while the colour came brightly into her cheeks. "Read," continued she, offering the letter, "and you will see it is mere chit-chat, rather pleasant than otherwise."

When Mrs. Curzon had read the letter, she said:

"I do not wonder at the expression I saw flit across your face!"

"You often fancy you see more than really exists," said Mrs. Harcourt with a smile.

"We will not argue, dear," said Mrs. Curzon; "but I remember Mrs. Russell's letter to you, in which she said, 'Keep up your spirits, do not fret and so lose your good looks,' or words to that effect. 'You will not be suffered to live alone! Wait and see what the year 18— will produce. You know you are a pattern woman, and I feel sure of your future being a bright one!" While here," continued she, turning to the letter in her hand, "she says, 'Am I not a true prophetess? You are living with your sister! I said you would never be suffered to live alone.'"

Mrs. Harcourt occupied herself with the embroidery in her hand, and did not reply.

"But she says," resumed Mrs. Curzon, "that Mr. Hill is in town! Surely he will call and see you?"

"I do not know; perhaps he may," said Mrs. Harcourt.

"I hope he will," said Mrs. Curzon; "indeed, he ought to call. I should not marvel much, all things considered, if he were to offer to take you back with him!"

"Oh! I do not know, dear Sopia;" said Mrs. Harcourt, hurriedly; and then, recovering herself, she added, "but I do not see much difference in Mrs. Russell's letters last year and this. It is true, I am only on a visit with you; and she surmises I am to live with you; that is only a trifling misunderstanding."

Mrs. Curzon put down her work, and, raising her head, looked full at her sister, as she said:

"Of late, Mary, you have become the most barefaced hypocrite! You may laugh," continued she, playfully holding up her finger, "but you cannot deny your hypocrisy!"

"Nonsense, Sophia; I have nothing to conceal, therefore I cannot be a hypocrite," said Mrs. Harcourt.

"You try to blind your best friends to your future prospects."

"Indeed, you are mistaken! I have no future; that is—I——"

"Yes, we know; you live in the past!—and if a good offer came, from a good man, in a good position, and of a suitable age, you would refuse!—of course you would!"

"But that is an impossibility," said Mrs. Harcourt.

"What is impossible?" said Mrs. Curzon, with a little sneer; "the offer or the refusal?"

"The offer, certainly."

"There speaks the hypocrite!"

"Hush, Sophia dear, do not deceive yourself—indeed, there is no happy future for me."

"Did you not understand, by Mrs. Russell's former letter, that she affected to foresee you would marry again?" said Mrs. Curzon, with a little satire in her tone.

"If I did put so foolish a construction upon it, you see I was wrong, and I am very sorry that my foolishness should have misled you."

"If you did! Ah! Mary, you cannot deceive me!" And then, after a pause, Mrs. Curzon resumed, "But I shall not give up the hope that, with your elegant manners, and still very charming appearance, with your excellent sense and numerous accomplishments, your happy temper and marvellous adaptability to circumstances, *I* shall not give up the hope that some worthy gentleman will see, appreciate, and long to possess, and to place you in the position to which, by birth, nature, and education, you are so well fitted."

Mrs. Harcourt leaned back in her chair, and laughed as she hid her face from the penetrating eyes of her sister; but, recovering herself, she said,

"My dear Sophia, I assure you I could not accept any gentleman to whom I am now a stranger, however much this 'stranger to me' might be struck with the many perfections with which you have so kindly endowed me."

"Nobody asks you," said Mrs. Curzon; "but some one to whom you *are not* a stranger," continued she, playfully holding up her finger, "and who is no stranger to you, and to your good qualities—such a one——"

"Will not ask me," interrupted Mrs. Harcourt, as she turned away to hide the expression of her countenance from her sister.

"Then it will be your own fault—you will lead him to see 'no' written on your lips, and so spoil your own fortune."

"I shall neither take steps to induce him to whom you allude——"

"Oh! do not be afraid of his name—I mean Mr. Hill!"

"To induce Mr. Hill to like or to dislike me," said Mrs Harcourt, a little angrily; "in such matters I am always a cipher."

"It is well to be a cipher, if, by taking its place, you will take also its value; in that case you may make all that is offered of ten times its original value."

Mrs. Harcourt did not reply, and the conversation was put an end to.

But in about ten days came another letter from Mrs. Russell to Mrs. Harcourt, in which she said, "Mr. Hill had returned to Devon, leaving Mr. and Mrs. Charles Hill in town; and that he had asked her to make his excuses to Mrs. Harcourt when she wrote again, and say he was sorry he had not had an opportunity of calling upon her."

There could be no denial to the alteration in Mrs. Harcourt after this news. She affected neither headache nor nervous illness of any kind, nor did she complain that Mr. Hill's neglect had vexed her. She pursued the apparently even tenor of her way, just as before; she was always employed, and very rarely disturbed in manner, or changeable in temper. But her cheek looked paler, and her voice had an occasional melancholy cadence, in which, though there was not an atom of affectation, there was an expression of sadness to which her manner seemed to give the lie, for her smiles were as frequent as usual, and her appearance as cheerful.

Mrs. Curzon—with, as she fancied, a deep insight into her character—Mrs. Curzon saw and understood these signs.

"No," said she to herself, "Mary will not complain; but there is a something on her mind that robs her step of its elasticity, and her tongue of its eloquence for the time being."

"I am greatly vexed for poor Mary," said Mrs. Curzon on one occasion to her husband.

"What, about Hill? Nonsense, Sophia, she does not care a straw. Indeed, between ourselves, I think she would rather not marry again."

"If she had a sufficiency of income, that might be all very well; but now, with her poor pittance, she ought not to be so unwise as to fling away the chances that fall to her share. Yet she does not encourage even one of her admirers, and I begin to fear Mr. Hill will not propose."

"You are right—she does not look favourably upon any one; and yet she has a certain regard for Hill, because he is connected with the past, and had so great a friendship for her husband."

"But what is to become of her? She has not so much as one hundred and fifty pounds a year! It is clear she cannot live on that paltry sum."

"That is her concern; if she likes to live alone upon a crust, instead of marrying a man for his wealth, I, for one, honour her."

"What nonsense you talk!—it is not marrying for wealth; you men put such hard constructions upon the actions of women. She is the widow of a man who possessed an income of near two thousand a year—accustomed all her life to her carriages and attendants, position and influence, wealth and the luxuries it can command;—what is to become of her now, with scarcely bread to eat? I tell you 'Barbarossa'—as we have christened him—would be a very good match, if she were not so taken up with Mr. Hill, who evidently does not care for her; to say nothing of Mr.——"

"To say nothing of likes and dislikes, Sophia—for which you women are famous."

"Nonsense! she could like Barbarossa if she would try."

"It is just one of the things she will not 'try,'" said Mr. Curzon, laughing.

"Then she is more foolish than she ought to be—and you, my dear husband, should try to reason her out of such folly."

"My dear Sophia, you a woman, and put away the choicest feelings of a woman so easily!"

"I know this—that one brought up as Mary has been, cannot live on her little mite of one hundred and fifty pounds a year."

"She has contrived to do so for these two last years," said Mr. Curzon, "which is pretty good proof not only that it can be done, but that she means to do it."

"You blind creature! Just like you men, who think we women may be crammed into nut-shells and kept out of sight! I do not deny that for these two years she has managed very well; and perhaps even for another year she would put up with, to her, strange and uncouth customs, in the bright hope of emancipation from such thraldom at the end of that time."

"Then you mean to tell me that ever since her husband's death she has had another man in her head for her next—eh, Sophia?"

"How can you shock me so?" said Mrs. Curzon; "why, Mary would expire at the very thought."

"That is the plain reading of the information you honour me with."

"Then it is wrong. As I have said, you men are so hard. To do Mary but the simplest justice, I never heard her mention any one with favour as regards herself and the future. But then, she never attempts to hide that she likes Mr. Hill."

"Quite right. I know she never conceals her liking for Hill as a friend, but then the regard goes no further."

"Then do you in your wisdom think she would say 'No' if Mr. Hill made proposals?"

"That is another thing. All we have to remember is that he has not proposed; and, if I may judge from appearances, he has no intention."

"I begin to fear so," said Mrs. Curzon dejectedly; "his coming to town and not calling on her looks so very slow."

"That she, like a wise woman, puts aside all idea of a query of consequence from his lips."

"You are Job's comforter, indeed!" said she.

"But why should you so trouble yourself about Mary? If she likes to remain as she is, though poor, instead of becoming rich by marriage with a man for whom she does not care a straw—what is that to us?"

"She cannot live on her income, I have told you that before. She will die. She will pine away for lack of food and clothes."

"We will feed and clothe her; give her the shelter of our roof, a warm, seat at our hearth, and a cosy place in our hearts. Will that do, Sophia?"

"She is too proud for that!"

"Poor Mary! too poor to live, too wise to marry, and too proud to benefit!"

In a day or two after these conversations, Mrs. Harcourt had a letter from Mr. Hill, apologizing for his apparent neglect, and telling her—"That he was so much exhausted by the great heat of London, accustomed as he was to the fresh moor air, that in self-defence he was compelled to return to Devon. That he had left Charlie and his wife with only half an hour's notice, and that he would write again shortly."

If this letter did not revive the supposed-to-be-extinguished hopes of Mrs. Harcourt, it certainly had a pleasant effect on Mrs. Curzon, inasmuch as that she again settled it in her own mind—

"That Mr. Hill was an eccentric man, who had a way peculiar to himself in most things; and that when the right time came, he would surely indemnify her for all her anxiety, by making proposals to—Mrs. Harcourt."

II

HOW THE VILLAGE OF LAWSLEIGH FARED IN THE ABSENCE OF PARSON HILL

PARSON Hill was not absent from Lawsleigh for more than a fortnight; and during that time Mr. Gray had the parish in his own hands. He was indefatigable in his attempts to bring it into what he called "order." But as each day, and week passed, he was obliged to acknowledge that he was no nearer that great desideratum, "a perfect parish," than when he began.

Peter Barker was the same drunken, cruel, and worthless character. His wife the same painstaking, hardworking woman; but, alas! also with the same indiscreet tongue.

The scenes at the "Packhorse" had not improved. The Widow Mason's guests were just as uproarious, and she herself as bitter and sarcastic as ever.

In Mr. Gray's visits to the smithy, we are sorry to say, he still continued to allow his zeal to outrun his discretion. He had but one subject upon which to exercise his eloquence—the evils of gin-palaces, public-houses, and beershops. But as none of these were known at Lawsleigh—for apples are grown plentifully in the county, and cider is the common beverage—so in proportion as Mr. Gray's conversation was not understood by the aged Widow Simpson, did she think it "a very larned discourse."

Not so Isaac, in whose heart Mr. Gray contrived to stir up more bitter feelings than he was accustomed to cherish towards any one. His covert attacks wounded Isaac's self-love, made him feel indignant, and fancy himself treated like a child.

"If he would but speak out," thought Isaac, "instead of talking about such heaps of wickedness and misery as I do not believe possible to exist anywhere."

The dwellers in rural districts happily have no idea of the amount of sin and wickedness to be found in large cities; neither are the temptations to immorality so numerous, or the facilities so great; and undoubtedly, as a class, the inhabitants of the provinces are more pure than those of cities.

Even Isaac, with all his relish for cider, was not a bad man. He had no other vice, nor was he at all to be put in comparison with the habitual frequenters of gin-palaces in large cities, or even of public-houses in towns.

The cider-shop was a lesser evil than either of these, and its frequenters less morally vicious than those. Still it was an evil, and Isaac felt it to be so; acknowledged it daily; prayed against the temptation; and yet, like an erring mortal, was overcome of it.

All this Isaac admitted to himself, with sorrow of heart and contrition of spirit. But to a certain extent he was incredulous as to the enormity of the evils arising from drunkenness. He thought Mr. Gray purposely exaggerated them, to try by that means to deter him from indulging in cider. And so Isaac became sullen in manner to Mr. Gray, and irritable in temper to his aged relative; for his mind was always full of the hideous scenes so powerfully portrayed by Mr. Gray, in which Isaac felt sure he never had been, and never could become an actor.

And then Isaac went again to the "Packhorse." He went because he would not be deterred by Mr. Gray! He indemnified himself for the annoyance of Mr. Gray's visits by a dogged determination to oppose him in all things as far as he could.

Poor Isaac! The opinion of the women was still, even in this case, true, for "Isaac was the worst to himself!" He knew very well Parson Hill had committed the parish to Mr. Gray during his own absence; he remembered the parson's speech when he introduced the ringers to his curate, and he acknowledged in his heart that Parson Hill had asked them to obey Mr. Gray as they would himself. But Isaac put away all responsibility by saying to himself, "The parson would never talk at me in this way. And Mr. Gray has no business to come here day after day and talk at me as he does. I cannot stand it, and I will not!"

Isaac forgot it was his own conscience that brought Mr. Gray's words so powerfully home to him. And so, as we have said, he went again to the "Packhorse."

If Mr. Gray succeeded so little to his satisfaction in the village generally, he thought his efforts in the school were rewarded by some improvement. And, on the vicar's return, he expatiated, with much pleasure, and some pride, on the success that attended his labours there; to which Parson Hill listened with complacency.

"But suppose you come with me this morning," said Mr. Gray, "and just hear me question the first class of boys?"

Parson Hill assented, and they went forth together. After putting a few queries, which the boys answered with great readiness, Mr. Gray said:

"Who was Julius Cæsar?"

A long pause—all the faces expressive of being puzzled.

"Who was Julius Cæsar?" reiterated Mr. Gray, indicating by his finger first one boy then another of the class, until he had pointed to each without gaining an answer.

"Who was Julius Cæsar?" again said Mr. Gray, in an angry tone. "Tom Brown, I am sure you know. Speak out; a—a—Roman——"

"A Roman Catholic, sir!" said Tom Brown, looking up brightly and the whole class looked, as it felt, easy and happy in an instant! The knotty query had been answered by that clever boy, Tom Brown!

"Bless me!" said Mr. Gray, rubbing his hands through his hair.

"I say the hot weather accounts for many things," said Parson Hill, kindly, and as it were apologetically. "But nevertheless I am quite willing to allow this boy"—pointing to Tom Brown—"is much more learned than when I left Lawsleigh; for I do not think he had ever heard of a Roman Catholic, or knew"

"It is astonishing how nervous the boys seem this morning!" said Mr. Gray.

"No doubt! no doubt!" said Parson Hill; "the temperature is very high—it was ninety-eight in the shade when I left London, or something enormously high," added he, correcting himself.

And having thus tried to soften Mr. Gray's disappointment, he turned to speak to Mary Cope, and, in so doing, saw, to his intense astonishment, the banished trio, Bill, Bess, and Joe Sands, seated very cosily together.

"How is this?" said he to Mary. "How came these children to re-enter the school without my permission?"

"Mr. Gray brought them soon after you went away, sir," said Mary.

"Umph!" said the parson, knitting his brows.

But the fact of his noticing these children attracted Mr. Gray's attention, and he came forward and said appealingly to Mr. Hill:

"That boy Joe Sands is, for his age, the cleverest boy in the school."

"Umph!" said the vicar, once more. Then, as a smile rippled over his countenance, he turned to Mr. Gray, and said, "Can he count twenty?"

"Undoubtedly," said Mr. Gray. "I see you don't credit me, but I will prove my words. Come here, Joe Sands—let me hear you count twenty."

No answer from the "Cherubian Joe," who stood with his mouth wide open, and his fingers pulling and twisting at the only button left on his jacket.

"Now, Joe," said Mr. Gray, in a very kind and coaxing tone, "tell me—do not be afraid—can you count twenty?"

"Noo, sir."

"Do you know how many fingers you have?" said Parson Hill.

"Noo, sir."

"Can you tell me the days in the week? mouths in the year?—or can you spell your own name, Joe?" reiterated the parson.

"I don't know, sir."

Parson Hill recollected that he had an engagement, and could not therefore remain any longer; and Mr. Gray, we are sorry to add, felt rather disappointed in his school that morning.

Parson Hill's practical measures for awakening the slumbering intellects of children born of ignorant parents, were not appreciated by Mr. Gray.

He aimed at better instruction and higher information. We are bound to add, he thought all children knew how many fingers they had—the right hand from the left—the days of the week—to count twenty; ay, and many more things of which the children born on Dartmoor were profoundly ignorant.

Mr. Gray had not, until now, been in contact either with such young children, or on so remote a locality, where, for many ages, learning had necessarily been restricted to "things generally known," and where, even in Mr. Gray's time, the excellent work on "Things not generally known," had not then penetrated. But Mr. Gray lived to know that the further a people are from civilization, the more simple must be the means employed to civilize them; and that the children of unlettered parents require the utmost tenderness and forbearance from any difficult mental process, until they have first exercised their minds upon the most simple things; and this even for some considerable time. The mind requires time to awake from its torpor, and if rudely awakened by subjects too hard for its comprehension, may chance to remain always dull.

Mr. Gray is himself a fair example of the many kind, good, and zealous young men who enter the Church, and who intend to devote their time and talents to the amelioration of the state, and the emendation of the education of the poorer classes. But these good young men, in their zeal for well-doing and entire abnegation of self, forget that others who have lived before them, have, from their years of experience, amassed an amount of parochial knowledge, and an insight into the minds of their people—and, by consequence, a successful method of instruction—which the untrained cannot be supposed to know.

Experience, the great teacher, comes slowly; but we are far from thinking that the admission of our young clergy fresh from Oxford into the wilds of the—at present—uncultivated Dartmoor is an evil. We know that what is called "new blood," re-invigorates and amalgamates with the sterling though inactive "old blood;" and from its youth and purity germinates for succeeding years better and stronger minds.

As has been so ably described by Mr. Smiles, the introduction of railways alone has done much towards placing the whole world on a level; and thus, figuratively speaking, the introduction of railways on Dartmoor may eventually bring its Tors and valleys on a par with the metropolis. Then, again, the alteration of postal dues by Sir Rowland Hill brought within the means of all the power to have tidings from their distant relatives. To this succeeded the desire on the part of the lower classes to learn to write—for we must admit that in the remote parts of the West of England, and up to a comparatively recent period, very few of the people on the moor could read—still fewer write.

The author received a bill from a wealthy farmer living in a hamlet on the borders of Dartmoor, and near to a large and flourishing borough town, written thus—"Tu 3 beags o' potites," which, duly translated, means, "To three bags of potatoes."

But now all is fast changing. Thanks to the scientific skill of the present century, which, by levelling roads, brings townships together, and causes man to see his fellow-man. Thanks to our Exhibitions, which, now that we have railways, are seen and appreciated by millions. And soon it will be the old nursery story over again,

> And the fire will begin to burn the stick,
> And the stick will begin to beat the pig,
> And the old woman will get home.

For the roads are improved, and so the post can travel. The post goes to remote districts; and so they who read, wish to learn to write; and they who can both read and write, in these days, are not content with Dartmoor, mighty though it be, grand and sublime as are the Tors, picturesque and beautiful as are the valleys, rushing, rapid, and ever-flowing as are its rivers. And so the people go to the "World's Fair," and return home wiser.

III

OF THE LOSS TO THE GREAT EXHIBITION OF A GLASS CASE FROM LAWSLEIGH

THE school, the choir, the ringers, and a good many of the villagers from Lawsleigh, were, by Mr. Gray's good management, to go by an excursion train to the "World's Great Fair." It need scarcely be told that none of the inhabitants of this part of the moor, except James Marvel, when he was a boy, had ever seen London; but few had seen the city of Exeter; and those who had seen Brent, Chagford, Denbury, Newton-Abbots, and other fairs more immediately within reach of Lawsleigh, were but a small portion of the population.

At first the wondering villagers could not understand why they must, at Mr. Gray's desire, leave their native soil and go to an unknown world, as it seemed to them, to see what they had never heard of, and what, when seen, very few would comprehend. Some had a wondering sort of awe at the vastness of the undertaking; some an indefinite sort of fear that they should never see Lawsleigh again. The aged wept at parting with the young; and some even of those who ventured to go, and who had suffered themselves to be persuaded against their own judgment, passed the long journey in sighs, and trembling doubt as to the results. But Mr. Gray's courage rose the higher, the more he met with opposition.

"What be London like to?" said one of the village boys to James Marvel.

"It be like to a great big ceety, the biggest in the whole world."

"What be a ceety, James?"

"A ceety be a town like to Ashburton or Exeter, and London be a big town."

"Be it the very biggest?—surely, then, James, just you tell I, be the houses all ditched (*fastened*) together, like as they be to Bovey Tracey?"

"The vary same," said James; "rows and rows of houses all fast together."

This alone was a sufficient marvel to a Lawsleigh boy, for the cottages all stood separately, with little palings before the doors.

"I sim it must look very queer, James," said the boy. "Have they gotten a church like to Lawsleigh church?"

"There be a many churches, lad—a great many; and there be Paul's, as I have a-heard tell, the biggest of all."

"What be Paul's, James?—and what for have they such a many churches?"

"Can't say," said James.

"Be one for Sunday, and one for Monday, and one for Tuesday, and so on?"

"No, lad, they be all for Sunday."

"All for Sundays, James! My!—then have they a-gotten a many Passon Hills there?"

"No," said James, with a shrewd smile; "my belief they have not got one Passon Hill."

"Lor', James, not a-got one Passon Hill! My!—then they be vary badly off. What, then, be the passons there all coorits?—be there a many Mister Grays?"

"I think as you be right this time, lad. Mayhap there be a plenty of they coorits."

"Oh-h! And why havena they got no Passon Hill, James?"

"Coz why, lad—coz Passon Hills isna plenty to be had. Us has a-got to be thankful as us have a-got a Passon Hill here to Lawsleigh."

"Oh-h!" said the lad whistling, as he walked away.

On the arrival in town of the party from Lawsleigh, Mary Cope, with Mr. Gray's permission, went to see Susan Picard. When the greeting of the cousins was over, Susan said,

"Mary, dear, two of the men in our shop will take their day for the Exhibition on the same day as I do mine. You see we shall then make a nice party."

"Yes," said Mary; "and when can this be?"

"One day next week. You stay a fortnight in town, and I will let you know when the day is fixed. John Green and Fred Owen, Mary. And oh, Mary, you will like Fred Owen; he is so handsome; and has such taste in dress."

"Is he handsomer than Isaac Watson?" said Mary, simply, for her jealousy seemed to have died a natural death when Susan left Lawsleigh.

"He is quite different," said Susan blushing. "Isaac is to my mind wondrously handsome, for I like large men; but then his dress is so common, quite unfit for London."

"I am afraid mine is not much better," said Mary, looking at her own; "but, like Isaac's, it does very well for Dartmoor."

"Oh! you will do, of course—you are different. We do not expect to see country people so well dressed as we are. Indeed, they can't, for they have no shops, and no materials; no millinery, no dressmakers, and no taste such as we have. But you will do, Mary," added Susan, with a little patronizing pat. "Everybody will see at a glance you are from the country."

Mary did not reply, and Susan proceeded:

"And about Fred Owen. Why, he is not tall, and he has light hair and blue eyes; quite the contrary to Mr. Isaac, who is so dark. And then Fred Owen has such a soft voice. And, Mary, dear, put off your bonnet. Here, give it to me! What a thing it is!" continued she, superciliously, as she held it at arm's length.

"It will do very well for me, Susan," said Mary, quietly; "please to give it to me?"

"And what do you think of London?" said Susan, as she returned the bonnet.

"It seems to me to be all houses and people, and——"

"Is it not different from your queer Dartmoor?" said Susan, enthusiastically. "There's no 'ills, and there's plenty of people, and, as you say, Mary, heaps of houses, and always something to do, and somewhere to go, and everything to see; while on Dartmoor there's nothing to do, and nothing to see!"

Susan thought of theatres, concerts, museums, panoramas, or exhibitions as being rife in London. The Tors and valleys of Devon, "Crockern Tor," and "Wistman's Wood," "Lustleigh Cleave," and "Becky Fall," the great lions of Dartmoor and its neighbourhood, were of no value in her eyes.

"And you have no houses," resumed she, "only little bits of cottages, and no people; but you have 'ills enough, and to spare, that nobody can deny. But you are so lazy; everybody going along so slow. I wonder they don't all die of mere slowness, only that would be too much trouble!" and Susan laughed aloud.

"I am sorry Dartmoor did not please you, Susan. I know many think it a very grand place, and come long distances to see it. But, then, Susy, I am sure I don't understand it, though I live there, and perhaps I never shall."

"No, Mary, take my word you never will understand that queer place. And, pray, may I now enquire after that abominable parson? What is he doing?—standing looking on while young ladies wash those filthy moor children?"

"I shall not let you talk against Parson Hill, Susan," said Mary, rising to take her leave. "If there was anything strange, or not kind, in his treatment of you, you brought it on yourself. He is always kind to me."

"Yes; I was told in the village of Lawsleigh that Parson Hill makes a great favourite of you, Mary, and the people don't like that; slow as they are, they are wise enough not to like to see one favoured more than another. Is the parson in London now?"

"No; he came to London last month, and saw the Exhibition and everything he wished; and now he is at Lawsleigh, and Mr. Gray with us."

"If you Lawsleigh people had had your wits about you," said Susan, eagerly, "but you have not, you are so slow I should think you were born without wits," added she laughing—"but if, as I have said, you had had your wits about you, you would have packed up your great big parson in a glass case, and sent him to the Exhibition; for indeed, Mary, much as you, coming from that queer place Dartmoor, may expect to see there, you may take my word for it, you will see nothing more strange, more curious, more wonderful, or better worth looking at, at a distance, than Parson Hill."

"I am sure I do not know what you mean, Susan," said Mary, chafing; "I know you do not like the parson, but that is your own fault."

"Of course you do not know what I mean," said Susan triumphantly; "how should you, dear? Come, kiss me. Are you sure you can find your way to your lodgings, or—"

"Thank you, I know my way quite well. And you will let me know, Susy, which day will suit you?"

"I will write when my holiday is fixed; and, Mary, mind and tell Mr. Isaac to go to the Exhibition on that day."

"Oh of course," said Mary, with a little twinge of jealousy.

IV

WHICH TREATS OF "WORKS OF ART,"
AND "MINDS" UNEDUCATED

Isaac Watson and Jacob Smerdon were in the habit of strolling together about the streets of London. Their astonishment at the crowds of people always on the move, at the great numbers of vehicles of all kinds and sizes, at the vastness and beauty of the parks, and at the public buildings was ever increasing. Sometimes they mounted upon the outside of an omnibus in the front, and went as far as the conveyance went, making their own remarks on everything they saw, to the great amusement of the other passengers, or asking questions of the driver of what they did not understand.

Nevertheless, these occasional excursions did not prevent their going to the Exhibition; and on the day that Susan Picard intended to be there, they also went, with an intention of meeting her.

Susan and her party arrived just as the rush of eager waiters on the opening door had been admitted, and they now went in with the ever-flowing stream of visitors. They entered at the east dome. The scene was not new to any of the four; to Mary its vastness and extreme novelty had not faded, but, as her companions were more experienced in sight-seeing, and more accustomed to see extraordinary sights, they were better able to understand what they saw, and more willing to give an opinion.

Susan began immediately to talk to Mary about the Majolica Fountain as a work of art. This was incomprehensible to poor, simple Mary, who, if we may be allowed to express her real thoughts, felt sure:

"That it was a queer thing, to say the least of it—and she could not see it was of much use; the water gushing from the rock at the back of her cottage was much brighter-looking, and there was much more of it, and it was of a great deal of value to her. But as for this being made of 'clome'(china), she did not believe a word of it; and she could not think that such a queer thing could be of any use." But then Mary was too discreet to express this opinion; and thus, early in the day, she escaped from falling in the estimation of Fred Owen.

They were descending the steps into the nave, when Susan, with an exclamation of delight, seized Mary by the arm as she said,

"There is Mr. Isaac! Mary, Mary, do look! Is not that Mr. Isaac?"

Mary acknowledged Isaac was there, with old Jacob leaning on his arm.

"And, Fred, we had better go to them directly," said Susan, "for they will never find the 'Reading Girl' unless we show them where to go. Mary has been here three times, and she does not know what I mean by the 'Reading Girl.'"

The party moved on and soon came up with Isaac and Jacob. The two men were very much pleased to meet once more with the "young lady," who, on her visit to the moor, had fascinated the inhabitants of the village of Lawsleigh by her wonderful voice! To do Isaac justice, he had not regretted Susan's departure, though now that he met her again he could not fail of admiring her really pretty face and figure, and even in some degree contrasting, to Susan's advantage, her stylish-looking attire with Mary's more unassuming costume.

"We want to show you 'the Reading Girl,'" said Susan, "quite the gem of the Exhibition, I assure you; and fortunately we are so early, we can see her to advantage, before the great crowds intrude upon our pleasure;" for Susan, like many another in that vast building, forgot that she herself was one of "the great crowd."

Isaac explained to Jacob Susan's kind intention of piloting them to see "the Reading Girl;" but as Jacob was quietly enjoying each sight as it came before him, and, moreover, as he was selfishly wrapt up in the pleasure of Isaac's companionship, he did not like either to be separated from him or carried away to some distant object; and though he did not venture to dissent from a wish that seemed congenial to the whole party, he turned to Susan and said,

"Be she a live meeden?"

Susan, whose short residence on the moor had made her conversant, in some degree, with the peculiar phraseology used there, replied,

"Alive!—oh dear, no! It is a marble statue of a 'Girl Reading,' by Pietro Magni, said to be the daughter of the great patriot Garibaldi; she has an open book before her—and—"

"Oh-h—then I have a-seed she," said Jacob, giving Susan a patronizing little pat on the back; "you be a kind young meeden, miss, and thank you, but us have a-seed the other meeden."

And then, turning to Isaac, he added,

"And so Isaac, lad, us will go on just the same, slow and sure; why should us hurry skurry to theere, when there be such a many things to here?"

Susan's lip curled as she heard the words "slow and sure," and Mary turned away in dread of what Susan might say. But Susan, always great in emergencies, placed her arm within Isaac's, as she said,

"If you have seen her, you can see her again, can't you, Mr. Isaac?"

"Certainly," said Isaac, rather absently, as he saw Fred Owen offer his arm to Mary Cope. But Isaac had not the least recollection of the statue Jacob persisted he had seen; and yet the two men had never been separated.

"Where did we see 'the Reading Girl?'" said Isaac to Jacob.

"Come this way, lad; here, never thee mind what her says," indicating Susan by a back jerk of his hand, "come with I."

Jacob took firm hold of Isaac, and compelled him to retrace his steps, Susan still clinging to his arm. A few paces backward down the nave, Jacob stopped, and, pointing triumphantly to a statue said,

"There she bees, with a book in she's hand!"

"That is the statue of King Edward the Sixth," said Isaac.

"And will not him do all the same?" said Jacob, not liking to be disturbed in his cosy walk with Isaac. Susan tittered and held her head down; while Fred Owen and John Green said to Mary,

"The man must be a simpleton to take that for 'the Reading Girl,' or to suppose one statue would do as well as another!"

But as Mary was not more learned in works of art than old Jacob Smerdon, she thought their opinion a very hard one.

After some few slight interruptions, the party eventually arrived at the court in which the "Reading Girl" was placed. At first, Mary opened her eyes wide with astonishment, then she turned away blushing deeply. But John Green entreated her to take a good look at this unique gem, while Fred Owen expatiated on the hands and feet, the beautiful forehead, the repose of the mouth, the contemplative expression, &c., &c.

"Now, Mr. Isaac, what do you say?" said Susan.

"I am not prepared to give an opinion at once," said Isaac, evasively.

"But you must admire her," persisted Susan; "and the chair—oh! don't you admire the chair?"

"Has her got no clothes to she's back?" said Jacob.

No one replied to this query, and he continued,

"If her was my daughter, her shouldna be a-sitting and a-reading there. I would just make she put she's clothes on, and I wouldna let she sit stark naked before folk—shame on her!"

Fred Owen was shocked at Jacob's vulgarity and odd language, and tried to induce Susan to leave Isaac and go with him; but Susan was not to be persuaded. She would take Mr. Isaac to the Roman Court, and shew him "the Cleopatra," "the Sibyl," and "the Fortune-teller."

"Oh! Mr. Isaac, that sweet, sweet fortune-teller; I could wish she was alive—could not you?"

But as Isaac did not see much to admire in an old woman, he wisely made no reply. He did not care much for Susan's talk at any time—but less than ever did it please him now, where he would have been glad to have been left to himself, with his own thoughts undisturbed. He was certainly the only one of the very large party from Lawsleigh, who could appreciate statuary at all. Mary could not bear to look at the nude figures so plentifully displayed; and Jacob liked other things much better. But once, while they were in the Roman Court, Isaac turned to speak to Mary, and caught her with a face rippling over with smiles. She stood looking at the infant asleep under a veil of lace, the only piece of statuary in the whole Exhibition that gave any pleasure to Mary Cope.

"Because, you see," said Mary to Susan, "that is just as if it was alive. I could quite expect to see it open its eyes; and then it is not horrid in a little baby to be naked—the little darling!"

Our party had a push at the jewels; Susan expatiating on their brilliancy and beauty, John Green on their value, while Mary wondered what could be the difference between green glass and emeralds.

In the picture gallery, Susan would insist on seeing the two "Christian Martyrs." Fred Owen told the story of each—from the youth so peacefully sleeping in his small cell, and who, on awaking, was to meet so dreadful a death. Mary turned away with horror, entreating to be left in ignorance of such terrible details.

But Isaac had read of Rome, and of her doings in her days of splendour. He understood but too well that small glimpse of the interior of the Coliseum, as seen through the half-open door of the cell, and he listened with a fixed attention to an explanation that he knew must be historically true. When they stood gazing on the female thrown from the rock into the lake or river, old Jacob said to Fred Owen,

"What be the matter with she, sir?"

"Why, she is drowning, to be sure," said Susan.

"No; she *is* drowned and come up to the top of the water with the glory on her head," said Fred Owen.

"Then be she's head light?" said Jacob.

"I do not know what you mean, good man," said Fred Owen, condescendingly.

"He means," said Isaac, still looking at the picture with straining eyes— "and I rather agree with his idea—he means, why is the lady's head so high out of the water?—because the head being heavy would naturally sink, unless we admit it is raised up by a miracle!"

"Oh! it is a most beautiful picture, Mr. Isaac! What is the use of asking anything about the head, when you see it before your very eyes floating so silently down the stream?"

And Fred Owen said Mr. Isaac's remark was hypercritical.

Isaac turned to Mary, and said,

"I am afraid you do not much enjoy these pictures; tell me—is there anything you would like to see?—any other part of the Exhibition?"

"They say, Mr. Isaac," said Mary, modestly, "that there is somewhere to be seen, a small machine that can sew like a woman—now that would be curious to see, would it not? But perhaps it is too much trouble to go—or perhaps I am mistaken, and there is not such a thing."

"Oh! yes, there is," said Isaac; "and you shall certainly see the machinery!"

And later in the day, in spite of all Susan's manœuvres to the contrary, Isaac offered his arm to Mary, and took her himself to see what would please her so much. The whole party followed where Isaac led, not without some little grumbling on the part of the London trio, who, as they had no taste for machinery, thought it a waste of time. Their taste lay in the French courts, among silks and satins, lace and jewelry, among elegant glass and costly china.

Mary was fortunate in seeing the sewing-machine used in perfection by the hands of the skilful *artiste* employed in the building. It was totally different from her preconceived idea, which was that of an actual figure sitting sewing like a woman. The simple beauty and delicacy of the machine came out in strong contrast in her eyes to the huge pieces of machinery she had previously seen.

Isaac watched her; he saw that her whole soul enjoyed it; her eyes strained themselves in attempting to follow the intricacy of the motion— her attention was riveted. In short, all that eager and impulsive devotion that the mind gives to a new and very desirable object was present in Mary's manner; and Isaac's pleasure was little less than hers.

Isaac had never till now wished for riches, but now he wanted to carry back with him to Dartmoor such a treasure of art, such a proof of mechanical skill, and so useful a machine, to give to Mary Cope.

Mary was quite unaware of this desire on Isaac's part; and Isaac took an opportunity, unknown to her, to inquire the price; and he was both surprised and pleased to find, at what comparatively moderate prices the machines could be had.

"Mistress Cope, do you think you could learn to work with that sewing-machine?" said Isaac.

"Dear me, yes!" said Mary, enthusiastically; "why, nothing could be easier. I watched how the lady put the thread when she began her work; and I saw how she used her feet. Ah! Mr. Isaac, if I had that sewing-machine in my cottage, trust me but I would soon find out how to do it. But they must cost a great deal of money—a hundred guineas a-piece, or perhaps even more," continued she, looking a little awe-struck.

"Not so much as that," said Isaac, with a smile; "though I am sure I wonder they do not demand a fabulous price. It is a marvellous invention."

"It is such nonsense to waste your time and trouble about sewing-machines," said Susan, disdainfully; "why, they are used every day in our work-room—I am sure I hate the sight of the things!"

"Oh! Susy, dear, to have them in the house in which you live!—how I do wish I lived there! And yet you have never shown them to me," added she, reproachfully.

"I can take you into the work-room, miss," said John Green, "if you will like to go; though, I must tell you, it is not easy at first to use a machine skilfully—you must have lessons, if you would really know how to manage it well; and then you must practise daily if you would arrive at perfection."

"I would not mind any pains and trouble, sir," said Mary. "I feel sure I could soon learn; but I need not think about it as it is not the least likely, after my return to Lawsleigh, that I should ever see another machine;" and Mary sighed, and Isaac heard her.

"If you like to take employment in our house, miss, I can ensure it to you," said the persevering and practical John Green; "just now we are greatly in want of hands. If you like to learn machine work, I can promise you plenty of occupation."

At first Mary almost ceased to respire at what appeared to her the magnificence of John Green's offer; but happening to catch Isaac's eye resting upon her, she saw there, in one second of time, what she had never before seen. And Mary's colour came brightly into her cheeks, and she instantly felt that her destiny was not for London and sewing-machines. And for the moment she also felt quite sure that she preferred Dartmoor and its magnificent Tors, her small school in the village, the village choir—especially when Susan was absent; but that remark is a mischievous addition of our own—the village church, Parson Hill, and, though last not least, that picturesque old smithy, built of grey granite, with the quaint-looking and kindly-hearted old woman sitting knitting in the shed, to all the London employment or machine work that could be offered to her.

Thought is always rapid—we doubt if it ever surpassed the fleetness of Mary's thoughts at this time.

Nevertheless, John Green, steady and practical as he was, contrived that Mary should see the sewing-machines so constantly at work in Regent Street; and he also put the means of having lessons so easily before her, that for some days Mary devoted herself to this task, and in the end became so tolerable a work-woman, as to make her sigh deeply as she reflected she never could possess a sewing-machine of her own.

V

OF MR. GRAY'S ADVICE TO MARY COPE—"NEVER SEE HIM AGAIN"

We have not before explained that the women and young girls from Lawsleigh were all lodged under the same roof with Mr. Gray. The men got accommodation were they could.

On returning from the Exhibition on this day, Susan went away with her two companions, and the two men from the moor took charge of Mary Cope to see her safe home. Perhaps it was not unnatural that Isaac and Jacob should enter the house with Mary, or that they should seat themselves and talk over the events of the day. The substance of this conversation is not of importance, but the fact that Mary Cope allowed her mind to be occupied with Isaac, and his sayings and doings, is worth recording.

It happened that Mr. Gray returned from visiting some distant part of London, with several of the women and young girls, before the men's conference with Mary Cope was at an end. This, combined with Mary's unusually playful and happy manner, excited in him the suspicion that she and Isaac were more friendly than they ought to be.

Mr. Gray, during his residence in Lawsleigh, had been totally oblivious of any admiration on the part of Isaac Watson for Mary Cope; but here, isolated as it seemed from the rest of the world, the parting between the two struck him as rather more protracted than was necessary. He was sure Isaac held Mary's hand in his own much longer than was needful for a mere "good night." He was sure Mary blushed very deeply, and that the blush lingered a long time after Isaac and Jacob were gone!

"This will not do," said Mr. Gray to himself. "I will not let that drunkard, Isaac Watson, marry Mary Cope, if any effort on my part can prevent it! I have taken a great deal of pains and trouble with him, and, at present, all to no purpose; for I know that he still goes to the 'Packhorse!' Perhaps he thinks because he is in London he can do as he pleases, without any interference from me, but I will let him see that nothing escapes my watchfulness. I consider it my duty to guard the young women under my care from harm, and I am sure they will get no good in the company of Isaac Watson!"

Mr. Gray determined that he would not let the grass grow under his feet; and later in the evening he sent for Mistress Cope, to come to him in his sitting-room. After a few trifling questions as to how she had passed the day, &c., he said:

"I think it my duty to warn you, Mistress Cope, against becoming intimate with men of bad character!"

Mary started, and her colour came indignantly into her cheeks. She did not understand what Mr. Gray meant, for Mary Cope did not look upon Isaac Watson and Jacob Smerdon as men of bad character.

"Of all vices drunkenness is the worst!" continued Mr. Gray. "A man is not himself while under its influence; he therefore commits deeds, of which, in his sane moments, he would be ashamed."

Mr. Gray paused, and Mary covered her face with her hands, as she said to herself,

"Can he be meaning Isaac Watson? Can he be a bad man?"

"I regret much," resumed he, "to infer, from what I have witnessed here, that you are upon very familiar terms with these men in Lawsleigh."

Again Mary's colour came indignantly into her cheeks, as she heard his words, "familiar with these men!" But still she hid her face, for she thought she must surely misunderstand him.

"Let me warn you against them," said Mr. Gray, in a kind tone, for Mary's silence and evident annoyance made him hope that he should succeed in his desire to make her think ill of Isaac. "Fly from them as you would from murderers! What are they other than murderers who destroy body and soul? You think their example will have no evil effect upon yourself! Alas! but too well I know all evil example corrupts, and the most innocent are in the greatest danger!"

Mary did not reply; she felt stunned and helpless.

"Sit down," said Mr. Gray, kindly compassionating her mute sorrow, and feeling sure his words would have a salutary effect upon her future conduct; and then, resuming the subject, he added, "Let me warn you, let me tell you, this well-looking young man—this Isaac Watson, with all his intelligence and superior manners, when free from the influence of the destroyer, will never be other than a bad neighbour and a worthless friend; if married, he would be an unkind husband—an unworthy father! I make no doubt he has always been an undutiful son."

"Oh! no, no, sir!" said Mary, clasping her hands together, as the tears streamed down her cheeks. "Mr. Isaac is the best of sons; he has always been so—everybody says so."

Mr. Gray was not prepared for so energetic a defence, and there was a short pause before he again spoke.

"His parents are not living, are they?"

"No, sir; he lives with his grandmother."

"To be sure; I know it," said Mr. Gray—"with the old Widow Simpson. How can you then know that this Isaac Watson was the best of sons?"

Mr. Gray alluded to his parents.

"All grandmothers are foolish old women, who spoil their grandchildren with indulgence, and——"

"No, no, sir!" said Mary, interrupting him in her eagerness; "the Widow Simpson is the best and kindest person in all Lawsleigh!"

"You seem to know a great deal about these Watsons and Simpsons," said Mr. Gray, rather angrily. "I am afraid you see more of them than will be altogether good for yourself."

Mary did not reply, and Mr. Gray, after a little pause, again spoke:

"The old woman may be 'kind,' as you call it, by which I conclude you mean 'indulgent,'" said he, with a satirical smile; "but that is all the worse for her grandson."

"No, sir, no!" said Mary, more quietly; "I do not mean indulgent—I mean good. She would never give Mr. Isaac cider; she laments his folly as much as we all do. I thought you would know that, sir, since you know the Widow Simpson so well," and Mary spoke half reproachfully.

"No; now that the evil is done, she wishes it undone—all old women do that. She must have been indulgent in the young man's boyhood," said he, in a decided tone, "or he would not have had so much of his own way then, and so persevere against her wish in this pernicious habit now."

"I have been told, sir, Isaac Simpson, his grandfather, took the lad with him to the 'Packhorse,' and that is how Mr. Isaac came to be so fond of cider."

"You seem to know all about him," said Mr. Gray, in a sharp tone; and Mary once more hid her face in her hands.

But again Mr. Gray's stern manner, and sometimes harsh expressions, were softened by Mary's evident distress. And yet he would not give up his point.

"It is my duty," said he to himself—"I must do my duty." But if his manner continued serious, his tones became more gentle as he said, "You will excuse me pursuing a subject that is painful to you, but I think it my duty to say a few words, and I wish to say them with kindness, and of course with a view to your future welfare. Have nothing to do with Isaac Watson!—give him up!"

"Give him up!" said Mary, innocently; she thought Mr. Gray meant "give up thinking of him," for she knew he had occupied much of her thoughts of late—"give him up?"

"Do your friends approve of this intimacy?" said he.

"What friends, sir?"

"Your own family—your relations."

"I am quite alone, sir—that is why I am the 'schoolmistress of Lawsleigh;' the clergyman who wrote for me to Parson Hill told him I had no friends, and so it was such a good thing for me to get the situation of 'schoolmistress.'"

"Yes, that clergyman, Mr. —— what is his name?"

"Talbot, sir—Mr. Talbot, of Wearsley."

"Would Mr. Talbot approve of this Isaac Watson, do you think?"

"Oh! sir, he does not know him at all," said Mary, not understanding the drift of Mr. Gray's question.

"No, he does not know him; but if he did know him, do you think he would approve of your intimacy with him?"

"I am sure I do not know, sir," said Mary.

She was turning over in her own mind what Mr. Gray meant by her intimacy with Isaac Watson.

"Pray, does Mr. Hill approve of such goings on? As the schoolmistress of Lawsleigh, your conduct and your example should be free from suspicion."

Mary sat silent. She did not understand Mr. Gray. She inwardly accused herself of allowing Isaac to occupy her thoughts; but this she knew was her only sin as regarded Isaac Watson.

"Does Mr. Hill know that you and Isaac Watson speak to each other, and are upon——"

"Oh! yes, sir," said Mary, timidly interrupting him; for she had an intuitive dread of being asked some question she did not understand, though she felt quite willing to reply when Mr. Gray's meaning was clear. "Everybody knows that I know Mr. Isaac—of course, sir, I know all the people that live in Lawsleigh," and somehow connecting Mr. Gray's query with her present locality, she added, "you know, sir, our village of Lawsleigh is not a bit like London. I know all the people that live there, and they all know me."

"Yes, yes," said Mr. Gray, slowly shaking his head, "of course you know everybody, and everybody knows you. But does Mr. Hill know that you are engaged to Isaac Watson?"

Mr. Gray, in his eagerness to understand all the knotty points of the case, and in his great dislike to Isaac personally, and disgust at his habit of intemperance, had ventured to assert that as a fact, that he had only suspected about an hour previously, and of which he had not yet had any confirmation.

But the term was new to Mary. Again Mr. Gray had puzzled her, and she could only repeat the words in a tone of surprise.

"Engaged, sir!—not that I know of!" and she raised her eyes fearlessly to his.

Mr. Gray's countenance settled into a stern expression, as a faint doubt of Mary's truthfulness attempted to creep into his mind, and he remained silent a few minutes. Upon consideration, he thought he would not press for an absolute reply at this moment, but he would take another opportunity of talking to Mary and learn all he could before their return to Lawsleigh. Meanwhile, he determined that he would not have that man Isaac Watson enter that house again, as long as he remained in it.

"I never allow any one known to be in the habit of inebriety to enter my doors," said he.

Mary—who had been trying to understand what Mr. Gray's last speech meant—was not at all prepared for this, or able to infer that it was meant to point out any particular person, said simply, "No, sir."—She had not the most remote idea that Mr. Gray had told her, "Isaac Watson must not come to that house."

"I consider my home is my home for the time being—I consider it polluted by the presence of such men. I should be extremely offended by any one, having the privilege of my protection, permitting such characters to darken my doors."

"Of course, sir," said Mary, for she felt perfectly innocent on her own part of any intention to introduce such people to Mr. Gray's presence. Mr. Gray now thought Mary's manner so quiet, and at the same time so frank, that he at once jumped to the conclusion he had made a mistake, and that she was not engaged to Isaac Watson. And this idea gratified him so much, he said with a smile:

"I fancied you were engaged to be married to the man Isaac Watson; but I am glad to see——"

Mary's start of surprise and bright blush of innocence strengthened her words as she said,

"No, sir!—no, sir! Mr. Isaac has never 'kept company' with me!"

"And I am wrong, truly wrong in my conjecture?" said Mr. Gray, now feeling the greatest desire to befriend Mary, and the greatest wish to encourage her to remain as she was—or, at least, to prevent her engaging herself to Isaac Watson; and, under the influence of these feelings, he extended his hand to her, and shook hers heartily, as she said,

"Sir," and Mary wept, "there may be people in our village who say—" Poor thing! how often had she been told that Isaac Watson was sweet upon Mary Cope! "That is, sir," resumed she, "who have given Mr. Isaac to me; but indeed, sir, it is all talk—we have never 'kept company.'"

And Mary heaved a deep sigh, which did not escape Mr. Gray's penetration.

"I am very glad to hear it; and as a true friend I say, shun the society of that man. He has gifts of a dazzling nature to a young woman. He is manly-looking and handsome, to some extent educated, and—for I do not wish to be unjust—he has some superior qualities."

"Yes, sir," said Mary, feeling gratified, in spite of herself, with this catalogue of Isaac's perfections, and softened towards Mr. Gray by his very kind and friendly manner, and the interest he took in her welfare. "Yes, sir, and I am sure I thank you, sir, for I know you wish to be kind."

"To be sure I do," said Mr. Gray, heartily, as he rose from his chair, and thus gave Mary a hint that she was at liberty to go. "To be sure I wish to be kind to you, and I hope and trust I am. And pray remember, if he were ten times as handsome, as manly, or as gifted, all would be valueless—all would be destroyed by that one vice. It is the arch-enemy's strongest weapon. Because the man who is drunk is not himself, is not a man; he is a demon. You have seen this man in that miserable condition?"

"Yes, sir," said Mary, still weeping and hiding her face.

"Take my advice—drunk or sober, never see him again."

Mary turned to leave the room.

"Never see him again," said he, as Mary curtsied at the door. "Never see him again," said he. And Mary closed the door, and went to her own room.

VI

WHAT ISAAC WATSON SAID TO MARY COPE, AND OF MR. GRAY'S UNEXPECTED RETURN

"NEVER see him again!" repeated Mary to herself. And still she comforted herself with the thought that she could not avoid seeing him again—that without the smallest effort on her part, she must see him again! Isaac and herself would certainly travel down to Lawsleigh together, even if she did not meet with him again in London. And when once there, what could prevent their almost daily meeting?

And then again, she could not but have many misgivings as to the future. She felt it was not right for him to occupy so much of her thoughts but she also felt Mr. Gray had been very severe in his judgment of him. Isaac was bad enough, but not so bad as Mr. Gray seemed to think; and yet, with a strange inconsistence, she thought, in all Mr. Gray had said against intoxication, and the evils arising from it, he had not gone too far.

Mary lay awake the greater part of the night, occasionally recalling the scenes that had occurred in the day, and then again returning to the conversation she had had with Mr. Gray.

"If I could but do Mr. Isaac any good!" thought she. "Mr. Gray says how clever and sensible he is; and sometimes I think if I was but to talk to him, and tell him what a pity it is to go on so—for it always seems to me that he minds what I say."

And now she confessed to herself that Isaac drunk, and Isaac sober, were two distinct men; and that the latter must be heartily ashamed of the conduct of the former. And yet she could not promise to herself to break off all intimacy with him, although she acknowledged she did feel a great horror of this particular vice; and she repeatedly said to herself through that wakeful night—

"No, of course I must not 'keep company' with him, even if he asks me—that is unless, suppose I could do him any good, because Mr. Isaac always minds what I say."

As a rule, women, when they are attached, think they have power to change the nature or the temper of the men they love. Mary was no exception to this rule. But how many of these charming women have lived to find themselves powerless!

It is true that men are for the most part humble and submissive during the thraldom of passion; and woman, in her credulity, endows this state of things with perpetuity, But when the hour has passed, man resumes his energy of will, gives the customary flow to his temper, rough or smooth, as the case may be; and woman looks on, helpless and in much wonder!

When the morning dawned, Mary fell into a troubled slumber; and when she rose for the day she felt unhappy and spiritless. Her faithful memory conjured up the expression she had seen flit across Isaac's face at the time when John Green had offered her employment in London.

She then took herself to task, and wondered if she had read that look wrongly.

"But it did not matter—rightly or wrongly read, that look could never be anything to her. She must not keep company with Isaac Watson, unless he would give up cider and tobacco!"

Impossible hope! and Mary heaved a deep sigh as she came to this conclusion.

The long day passed, and Mary was sitting alone in a little back parlour appropriated to the use of the women from Lawsleigh. She heard the door open, and instinctively turned to see who was about to enter.

"Mistress Cope," said a voice she knew.

"Mr. Isaac," said she, rising hastily; "how glad I am to see you!"

"That is very kind of you, Mistress Cope," said Isaac, as he held her hand in his powerful grasp, and did not seem inclined to relinquish it; "then I am very glad that I made up my mind to come and see you, for—"and Isaac hesitated a little, "considering all things, and considering—considering—why, Mistress Cope, if you had said you did not want to see me, and more than that, that you would not see me, I should only have had myself to thank."

Mary stood there listening to Isaac, quite unconscious that her cheeks were suffused with blushes, and that her hand trembled in his; but she replied—

"I am always glad to see you;" and then she thought of Mr. Gray, and a spasm of dread convulsed her features, as she said rather hastily,

"But Mr. Gray—Mr.——"

"I have just seen Mr. Gray," said Isaac, relinquishing her hand; "I told him I was coming here, for I have a letter for John Lear's wife; and Mr. Gray said if the woman was not at home as he thought there was a party gone to the Crystal Palace that I should leave the note with you; and here it is, for Kitty Lear is not to be found."

Mary took the note, and now very gladly gave Isaac a hearty welcome. She placed a chair for him, and said once again,

"Indeed I am very glad to see you."

"God bless you, Mistress Cope; and I will make myself worthy of your goodness."

Mary did not reply; the conclusion of Isaac's speech startled her a little, and Isaac proceeded,

"Jacob wanted to come with me—for you see, Mistress Cope, we have been everywhere together, and it has been a great pleasure to me to have him always for my companion—and I daresay he thinks it a little hard that I would not let him come with me tonight; but, in truth, I wanted to come alone."

Isaac had been speaking loud; and when he suddenly stopped and looked at Mary, without exactly knowing why she felt confused and unable to reply.

And here it may be remarked, that, in this meeting of Isaac and Mary, the two characters seemed to have changed places. Isaac's habitual shyness had given place to an eager and a hearty manner—he did not seem afraid to speak, and he appeared to have plenty to say; while Mary, usually so calm and collected, was now nervously timid in manner—she did not venture to raise her eyes to Isaac's; and she spoke not a single word.

After a little pause, Isaac proceeded, leaning eagerly forward, stooping his head, and lowering the loud tone of his voice, as he said,

"You see, Mistress Cope, in Lawsleigh I said there was nobody like you—I never had seen anybody like you in my life." Mary leaned her head upon her hand, and partially shaded her face. "Now, here in London it is the same—there is not one like you—not one. But," said Isaac, again hesitating, "that was not what I was going to say. I wanted to tell you, Mistress Cope, that—that I am ashamed of myself—fairly I *am*," continued he, holding up his head and letting his fist fall more heavily on the table than Mary liked. "Now I am come to tell you this, that you may know I am not going to the 'Packhorse' any more—when I get back to Lawsleigh, I mean to be a better man!"

Like a true woman, born credulous, and which credulity no after-teaching or experience can ever entirely eradicate, it never entered into Mary's mind to doubt his words. She clasped her hands together enthusiastically, and said:

"Oh! I am so glad!—I am so glad! Why, Mr. Isaac, how very happy everybody will be!"

"But shall *you* be happy, Mistress Cope?" inquired Isaac, as once again he stooped his manly form and lowered the loud tone of his voice.

"I!" said Mary, looking up brightly, and quite unconscious how much her words would confess of the nature of her feelings towards Isaac. "Why, Mr. Isaac, that is the only thing I want to make me happy!"

"Then you have got it to the full!" said Isaac, heartily, as he jumped up and suddenly seized her hand. This action awoke in Mary Cope some idea of her unintentional error; and when Isaac continued to retain and caress her hand, as he said, "God bless you, Mistress Cope!—you have saved me, you have!" all she could do was to try to withdraw her hand from his powerful grasp, and try to hide the expression of her face from his scrutiny. She only succeeded in the latter—in the former Isaac had the mastery; and he continued:

"I assure you, on my word, you have saved me! I care only for you, and if I can have you, I am saved!"

Mary trembled with the suddenness and strength of her emotion; down plump to the very bottom of her heart went Isaac's words, "You have saved me!" Had she—she, Mary Cope!—had she saved Isaac Watson? What a joy!—what a blessing upon her head!—what a happiness in her heart for the rest of her life!

And pray, why should not woman credit what man, supposed to be the more intelligent of the two, says to her? And pray, why may she not hope and trust that she is of some small use in this mighty world, and that the purity of her example may have a beneficial effect on her companion, man? And pray, why is she to be ridiculed for her credulity? She is born credulous! Disappointment, and a knowledge of evil, come soon enough; and when a woman is not credulous, she has had her full share of both!

Poor Mary Cope! she is in the age of her credulity.

"But, Mistress Cope," resumed Isaac, "you see I should never have had the courage to tell you how much I love you if we had not come up to London."

Mary now ceased that useless struggle of trying to free her hand from his grasp.

"I have seen more of you since I have been in London, and—and I have always seen you the same, that is—somehow I have thought once or twice——"

Isaac was going to say "I thought you seemed glad to see me," but, upon consideration, he dared not venture to say so much, and commenting instead on his own suspicion, he added fervently,

"It was your goodness, Mistress Cope; God bless you for ever!" as again he raised her hand to his lips. "You might have thought I was not worth the trouble to save, seeing me as you have at Lawsleigh. But now, if it please the Almighty, Mistress Cope, to let us get safe back to the old shed, and the church, and the bells, and the good Parson Hill—he has always been very good to me, Mistress Cope—and to the kind old mother, you will just see that I shall never see the inside of that 'Packhorse' again!"

In point of fact, it never entered into Mary's mind to doubt Isaac's words. He had always had a character for straightforward honesty, and was known to be a man of integrity in his business dealings. No one ever accused Isaac Watson of more than one vice; and now that he came voluntarily to tell Mary he had done with it, and, as his words seemed to her to imply, that he would smoke and drink no more, with all that charming credulity to which we have before referred, and that lingers even late in life with some of our most excellent women, Mary Cope readily credited every word!

And now Mary, like a true woman, by this time feeling her own position very secure, and willing to hide her embarrassment as much as possible from Isaac, glided from the subject in hand to another, by saying, as she raised her eyes timidly to his:

"And, Mr. Isaac, what a joyful day for your good mother! I cannot help thinking of her."

"To be sure, Mistress Cope, that is because you have such a kind heart, and are always thinking to make everybody happy," and Isaac pressed the hand he still retained. "And so do I think of her, for now will I never again cause her one moment's pain."

And now he seated himself on the sofa by her side as he said,

"I want to tell you all about everything I have been thinking."

Mary turned her eyes inquiringly upon Isaac, and he proceeded in softened tones,

"You must know, Mistress Cope, Jacob and I have been together a great deal, and seen many things that you would never see—and, indeed, they are not fit for you to see, or hardly to know about."

Mary perceptibly winced at these words, and cast down her eyes, for she inwardly dreaded a confession of some outrageous scene of inebriety. But Isaac, with a strong desire to let Mary Cope know the worst of him, so that nothing in the future should arise from his past misconduct to mar their present good understanding with each other—Isaac referred to a day in which he and Jacob had entered one of the numerous gin-palaces—a day in which they had been silent witnesses of many drinking to excess, but also a day in which they themselves had refrained.

He expressed his horror and amazement at the sight of the crowds flocking there for stimulants of kinds such as he had never even heard the names; and he described the thin and squalid looks of the young girls and women of all ages, whom he had seen intoxicated with drinking "Old Tom."

"A drink ten times over stronger than cider, Mistress Cope."

He did more; he told her the impression made upon him that night by the sight of so many human beings brought to the same destitution, disgrace, and misery by the daily use of stimulants, so disgusted him, not only with them and their wretched condition, but also with himself at the thought that he had ever been seen in a like disgraceful state—that he inwardly vowed, before leaving the gin-palace he would sin no more in that way.

He had there—by witnessing these sights—been convinced of the awful punishment that, sooner or later, must overtake the drunkard. And he would now pray with all his might to be preserved from committing himself in future.

"And so you see, Mistress Cope, though I don't wish to deny one atom of the truth—that is, that I have been a sad disgrace to my name, and to my native village—why, 'it is never too late to mend.'"

In her own mind Mary quite agreed with the concluding phrase, but she remained silent, and Isaac continued,

"And that is why I am so grateful to you, Mistress Cope—because you do know how bad I have been, and yet you quite believe me that I am not going to that 'Packhorse' again; and I feel this minute, while I am telling you this, happier than I ever did in my whole life before."

And now Isaac ventured to put his arm round Mary's waist.

But we do not intend to tell our courteous readers how Isaac Watson made love, or how Mary Cope listened. We only permit ourselves to acknowledge that Mary was not prepared for the stealthy approach of Isaac's arm round her waist. But, as all of the female sex will know how easily she managed to withdraw from the snare, it is unnecessary for us to dilate upon it. And if the male sex are not as wise as the female in this instance, we advise any one, conscious of his ignorance, to place himself in a like position with any charming young woman he may be permitted to select, and thus learn by experience a fact that we do not think necessary to describe. But in the fear that my readers should fail of understanding whether Isaac Watson made Mary Cope comprehend that he was making her an offer of his hand and heart; or whether, if she did comprehend, she said "yes" or "no"—in the fear that my readers might be misled at this critical time, I permit myself also to state that, later in the evening, the parlour door was opened hastily with a sharp jerk, and Isaac Watson was seen with his arm round Mary Cope's neck, and his lips so suspiciously close to hers as to leave no doubt on the mind of that intrusive looker-on of the fate of Mary's lips.

That looker-on was—Mr. Gray!

VII

OF MR. GRAY'S ANGER,
AND OF MARY COPE'S DISTRESS

Now, Mr. Gray had been so perfectly satisfied with the conversation he had had with Mary Cope on the previous evening, and so gratified with the fact that Mary and Isaac, according to Mary's statement, did not "keep company," that, to say the least, he was but ill prepared for the scene upon which he intruded.

When Mary went away, he paced his room backwards and forwards very contentedly for the next half hour, thinking the matter over, a little elated with his own penetration, and certainly proud of his success. For he did not doubt, for one moment, that the gentle-spirited and thankful-hearted little woman, so thanking him for his kindness to her, would obey him to the very letter. He repeated to himself, as he walked from one end of the room to the other,

"Never see him again!"

So mild, and tearful, and sorrowful a little woman, and, moreover, "the schoolmistress of the village of Lawsleigh," would be grateful for his kind notice and consideration of her, and, as a matter of course, would never dream of disobeying him.

"Never see him again!"

And, rejoicing over the phrase, and glad that he had given Mary such good counsel—and, moreover, succeeded so well—unlike the "little woman," who had a restless and wakeful night, Mr. Gray slept!

"And is this the way you abuse the trust I have reposed in you? Is this the way you repay my kindness?" were his first words to the happy pair so unceremoniously and uncomfortably interrupted in their enjoyment of that "first kiss."

Oh! Mr. Gray, Mr. Gray, if ever, during the course of your life, unwelcome intruders should, on any interesting occasion, present themselves to you, may your memory faithfully recall your own vexatious appearance on this occasion; and may you inwardly acknowledge, with all due contrition of spirit, the retributive justice of the event!

Mary stood speechless in the presence of the angry Mr. Gray, and up rose vividly and instantaneously before her the scene of the preceding evening. Mr. Gray's accusations and queries—her own innocence, and her sturdy denial—his reiterated command, which sent her in sadness and sorrow to her own room, "Never see him again!" And now, here she stood, convicted!

Yes, she felt she was convicted of something; but convicted of what?

"I beg your pardon, sir," said Isaac, humbly, and drawing Mary's arm within his own; "I did not mean any offence by coming here; I came to give—to give Kitty Lear's letter to Mistress Cope, because Kitty is gone to the Crystal Palace; and—and—I wanted to thank Mistress Cope for——"

"Thank her!—is that the way you thank people?"

Both Isaac and Mary looked a little "foolish" at this query, and Mr. Gray proceeded still angrily——

"A pretty way of thanking people, upon my word!"

Mary blushed deeply, and cast down her eyes; and Isaac to confess the truth, Isaac thought it was a "very pretty way" of thanking Mary Cope on that special occasion.

"Did Mistress Cope tell you I had prohibited your entrance into this house?"

"No, sir," said Isaac, as he still would not allow Mary to withdraw her arm; "I told Mistress Cope you sent me to her."

"I sent you to her?—how dare you say such a thing?"

Isaac explained that he had met him, and reminded him of the letter for Lear's wife, which he had delivered to Mistress Cope.

It appeared almost as if Mr. Gray had forgotten he had seen Isaac, and sent him with the Mary, for he turned to her and said,

"You can receive this man here after my strict orders to the contrary!—and you can allow yourself to be polluted by his touch! Young woman, I have done with you—never more expect me to befriend you!"

At this moment Mr. Gray stepped forward and rang the bell violently.

Mary had struggled to free herself from Isaac, and he had vigorously detained her. She now attempted to speak, but Isaac raised his voice above hers, as he said,

"Sir, Mistress Cope is innocent. I came here unknown to her."

The room door opened, and a servant appeared to answer the bell.

"Leave my house!" said Mr. Gray, imperiously.

"Sir," said Isaac, more humbly, "will you allow me to assure you Mistress Cope did not know I was coming, until I was in her very presence."

"Answer me this, Isaac Watson—yes or no. Don't waste your eloquence on me, it will not do; but answer me this—Did Mistress Cope, on your arrival here, tell you that I had forbidden her to receive you?"

"No, sir; I told her you had——"

"That will do—that will do," said Mr. Gray, impatiently.

"I did not know, sir," said Mary, unable to restrain a passionate outburst of tears.

Mary remembered but too well the words, "Never see him again!" but she did not know that Mr. Gray had forbidden her to receive Isaac there. She had not understood him when he spoke on that subject.

"Did not know it!" said Mr. Gray, with a look of contempt. "And you can stand there and deny that I told you I would not allow a drunkard to enter my doors? And pray is not this man a drunkard?"

And then he turned to Isaac, and said, "Leave my house!"

"But it is not Mistress Cope's fault, sir," said Isaac, unwilling to leave Mary to bear the brunt of his anger alone. "And, sir, I am not a drunkard."

"Mr. Isaac means never to go to the 'Packhorse' again, sir—never!" said Mary, looking up with some sort of undefined hope that this must arrest Mr. Gray's anger; but she was mistaken.

"Oh-h—upon my word!" And now Mr. Gray rang the bell again, for the attendant on the former summons had wisely retired almost as soon as he appeared. "Leave my house, or I will send for a policeman."

This threat made Isaac raise his head the higher, with a proud almost disdainful air, as he said,

"I will go, sir." But he looked at Mary, as if unwilling to leave her.

"Go, Isaac—pray go!" said Mary. And he left the room, followed by Mr. Gray. When Mr. Gray returned, he found Mary abandoning herself to her sorrow. She sat sobbing and weeping unrestrainedly.

"And so you have thought it right, Mistress Cope, to impose upon my kindness and good-nature!"

Mary was silent.

"You told me last night you were not engaged to be married to Isaac Watson; and now—and now I actually enter this room, and see him with——"

Mary now blushed crimson, and tried to hide her confusion by covering her face with her hands. She could not prevent her tears from streaming down her cheeks, or restrain her loud and convulsive sobs.

"All that I can say is, if you are not to be married to Isaac Watson, your conduct is most indelicate and most reprehensible; and if you are—for I cannot acquit you of having told me a falsehood—if you are, you will be a most wretched and miserable woman for the rest of your life!"

For a few moments Mary did not speak. She dreaded to have to confess to Mr. Gray, that Isaac and she had agreed to "keep company;" but she could not remain silent under the stigma of falsehood.

"I told you—you—I told you the truth, sir," said she, between her sobs.

"You told me last night you were not going to marry this man, or to let him marry you; then how dare you let him take such a shameful liberty—and you, the schoolmistress of Lawsleigh—how dare you, I say!"

Mr. Gray's tones were anything but suave.

"I could not help it, sir." And Mary covered her face with her hands, and turned her back rather abruptly on him, as she felt her neck and ears glow; but, in spite of these signs of sensitiveness, Mr. Gray continued—

"Could not help it! What do I hear? Why, this fact will stamp your own character for ever. To let a man, who is not to be your husband"—Mary started, and turned half-round—"a drunken, disorderly reprobate—to let him pull you about with his polluted hands; to let——"

"Oh, no, sir!—oh, oh, no, sir! I am sure it is all wrong. I never meant——"

"All wrong! I should think it is all wrong—"

The conversation was interrupted by a servant, who told Mr. Gray a gentleman waited to see him.

"Go to your own room, Mary Cope," he said sternly; "and remember, at my desire you are a prisoner there for the remainder of your stay in London."

And very gladly did Mary Cope avail herself of the permission to retire to her own room, and nurse her sorrow unwitnessed or unquestioned by Mr. Gray. In her solitude there, by degrees, she recalled the events and conversations of the preceding day; but she could not unravel several things that appeared mysterious to her. She did not remember that Mr. Gray had forbidden her to receive Isaac Watson there; and she felt sure she had never said, "she would not let him marry her;" but in spite of this strange entanglement and apparent misunderstanding, and in spite of the disgrace in which she knew she must stand in Mr. Gray's opinion, and of her own anxiety on these accounts in spite of all this, she could not help acknowledging to herself that, in her heart of hearts, she had a comfort that almost nullified her pain; a balm, as it seemed, for all the ills by which she was surrounded—Isaac Watson loved her! He had promised her never again to go to the "Packhorse;" and as his visits there, and his consequent intoxication, made the only blot in his otherwise estimable character, she had nothing to reproach herself with in the fact that she had accepted him.

Mary's faith in Isaac was that of a pure-minded young woman, who suspects no ill of any one, but who trusts, with her whole heart and soul, the man she loves; for he is in her eyes the best, the truest, the sincerest, and the most worthy of men. That sort of faith—independent of intellect—is common to all women. Women deify men, and endow them with perfections that, in too many instances, they do not possess.

VIII

HOW MARY COPE TRAVELS
EXPRESS TO LAWSLEIGH

On the platform of the Great Western, at Paddington, two ladies were sauntering together while the train was preparing to depart for the west of England. Their conversation was interrupted by the arrival of a gentleman, who said,

"I am going to give you a companion in the form of a pretty young woman—what do you say to that?"

"What do you mean, Charlie?" said Mrs. Hill, for she and Mrs. Harcourt were the two ladies before mentioned.

"I have just seen Gray, and he wants you to take charge of a young woman—one of the wicked ones of this very wicked earth," said he, turning to Mrs. Harcourt.

"A wicked one!" said she, not attempting to hide her surprise.

"Why, I suppose she is wicked—indeed," added he, turning to his wife, "I think she must be desperately wicked, for she was caught by Gray with her lover."

Mrs. Harcourt walked up to the book-stall, and affected to occupy herself there, while Mrs. Hill said reproachfully.

"You should not say such things in the presence of Mrs. Harcourt."

"And why not?—Mrs. Harcourt would not be sorry to be in a like position with her lover; for my part, I believe she would be glad."

And Charlie placed his hands in his pockets, and nonchalantly walked away; while Mrs. Harcourt's enjoyment of the book-stall being satiated, the two ladies again promenaded together.

"Suppose we get into a carriage—the train seems nearly ready to start," said Mrs. Hill.

They did so; and from the windows thereof saw Charlie and Mr. Gray, accompanied by a young woman, whom neither of the ladies knew as the schoolmistress of Lawsleigh. After the usual greeting, Mrs. Hill ventured to ask Mr. Gray—

"If that pretty-looking young woman had been convicted of picking and stealing, since she was to be put under the care of two such steady matrons as herself and her friend!"

She spoke in French, so that Mary could not understand a word she said.

"Her lover was stealing a kiss—he was the thief, not she. I returned home unexpectedly, and caught them in the very act!"

As Mr. Gray was not given to hyperbole, or even to jesting, this sentence sounded more strange from him than it would have done from another. Mrs. Hill did not reply, and he continued, "Her lover is—that is, the man is, for I cannot allow him to become her lover—the man is a drunken reprobate; and she, the supposed-to-be-steady schoolmistress of Lawsleigh. You will easily comprehend, therefore, that such thefts cannot be permitted with impunity."

"Poor thing!" said Mrs. Hill, compassionately. "And is that all?"

"Why, is not that enough?" said Mr. Gray, in extreme surprise. "Consider the man—a drunkard!—and then the young woman, a schoolmistress—the thing speaks for itself! Is not that enough?"

"No," said Charlie, who was standing by; "women don't thank you for only one kiss at a time; and a man will always thank a woman for more."

The shrill whistle now arrested their attention. Charlie entered the carriage, and Mr. Gray moved hastily away.

"And so, Charlie, the poor thing was just letting her lover kiss her!" said Mrs. Hill, still speaking in French. "Is that such a crime?"

"Was that all?" said Mrs. Harcourt, feelingly.

"That all!" said Charlie, laughing; "the query does honour to your sense of justice!"

"I really thought she had committed some high crime or misdemeanour, by being classed among 'the wicked ones of the earth!'" said Mrs. Hill.

"And I can tell you it is both a high crime and a great misdemeanour, in the judgment of the Bishop of Lawsleigh, to have permitted such a well-known drunkard as Isaac Watson to pollute her sacred schoolmistress-ship by even a touch, to say nothing of the man having been seen stealing a kiss by the very eyes of the very bishop himself! I do not see, for my own part, how the little mistress could be in a worse scrape!"

"Poor thing!" said Mrs. Harcourt, again, sympathisingly; "and she is so pretty, and looks so modest."

"That is just it," said Charlie, laughing; "you will always find a modest woman gets lots more kisses than defiant-looking, impudent women. A man has not the courage to approach women who are always on their guard; but modest young women, who have no sort of idea that men would like to steal kisses from them, are sometimes besieged, and not unfrequently won. I conceive, now, that the modesty of that pretty little woman was at least half the reason why that great big Isaac Watson fancied her more than the fat red-faced woman, the landlady of the 'Packhorse;' for undoubtedly it would be very convenient for Isaac to become landlord there—he would be just in his element!"

Meanwhile the unconscious object of all this talk sat gazing out of the carriage windows, and wondering why she was separated from her companions. She had only been a prisoner in her own room two entire days; for on the second morning Mr. Gray sent her word that she should leave for Dartmoor by an early train the next day, and that she must hold herself in readiness for his summons."

Her heart leaped for joy. She should see Isaac. He would go down to Devon in the same train with her. He would seek her out; he would talk to her; he would comfort her. But when, on being taken to the station, she found herself consigned to the care of two ladies who were strangers to her, and kept entirely from her own people, even from the women from Lawsleigh, Mary's disappointment and mortification were great; and she could not smother a feeling of indignation against Mr. Gray, for, as she thought, such undeserved harshness.

Mary knew Mr. Charles Hill by sight, but she did not know either of the ladies. They did not speak to her; and so poor Mary sat sad and silent, wondering when she should come to the end of her troubles, and why she was to be with the ladies, and Isaac Watson never came to speak to her before the train started.

"By-the-way, I have forgotten to tell you," said Charlie, "you are forbidden to hold any conversation with that young woman! Bishop Lawsleigh"—it was thus he designated Mr. Gray—"will not permit it. You may give her something to eat, if you like, at Swindon, when we stop there—or at Exeter, before we start for the moor—but it is forbidden to put her into an interesting state of talk."

"What will be the penalty of disregarding these orders?" said Mrs. Hill.

"Nothing short of excommunication! The pains and penalties of the bishop's indignation would not suffice for the occasion! His lordship has a plan of his own; he means to convict the young woman from her own mouth, in the presence of his excellent curate, my trusty and right well-beloved father, William Hill!"

"Charlie, how absurd you are!" said Mrs. Hill, in English, and the unconscious object of so much care turned her pale face and looked at the speaker.

"I am sure she is innocent," said Mrs. Hill.

"So am I," said Mrs. Harcourt.

Both ladies spoke in French.

"So am I," said Charlie. "All modest women receive the first kiss innocently; and, as far as I am a judge, I do not think they become corrupted even by the first half-dozen!"

"Charlie, how foolish you are!"

The ladies left the train for a short time at Swindon, and took Mary with them into the refreshment-room. In crossing the platform some gentleman set his foot on Mrs. Hill's dress, and tore off a large piece of the trimming.

"How very tiresome!" said she, gathering her dress round her.

"I have my work-roll in my pocket," said Mary; "I can easily stitch the trimming on again, if you will allow me."

"You are very kind—thank you," said Mrs. Hill; "but come and eat some luncheon—do not mind my dress."

"I cannot eat, thank you," said Mary, disconsolately, for she had not seen a symptom of Isaac, even now that, by the stopping of the train, he had an opportunity of finding her out and comforting her.

But Mary had not discovered that she was travelling express, and would therefore reach her destination many hours before the excursion train, which would bring Isaac and the remainder of the people from Lawsleigh.

"You cannot eat!—but you must try," said Mrs. Hill kindly, as she saw Mary's eyes filling with tears.

She placed some sandwiches and buns before her, and turned to talk to Mrs. Harcourt while Mary, regardless of Mrs. Hill's "Never mind my dress," wiped away her tears, took out her work-roll, threaded her needle, and, stooping down, unperceived by Mrs. Hill, began to repair the fractured trimming.

Charlie came up to the ladies while Mary was thus employed; and after watching her steadily for a short time, he said, in a low voice,

"I do not marvel that Isaac Watson should admire that little woman; he has always been a man of taste, barring his taste for cider; and do look at her—she sews as deftly as a lady!"

The two ladies, turning, saw Mary on her knees, employed on Mrs. Hill's dress.

"Indeed you must try to eat some luncheon," said Mrs. Hill, attempting to withdraw her robe; "I cannot allow you to be so troubled."

"Employment is pleasureable to me," said Mary, as she raised her eyes to Mrs. Hill, "and I am not hungry."

"But you must eat—why are you not hungry?" said Mrs. Harcourt.

"Thank you, madam, I—I cannot eat," and again Mary's eyes filled with tears.

"But pray do not mind my dress; I am quite ashamed to give you so much trouble," said Mrs. Hill kindly, and again trying to pull the robe from Mary.

"But you may quite spoil your beautiful dress," said Mary, as she held it fast, "if I do not finish sewing on the trimming; and"—and she raised her eyes to Mrs. Hill—"I do so like to do it for you, if you will let me," added she, blushing deeply as she saw the notice she had attracted from the two ladies and Mr. Hill.

"I declare, Kate, I could kiss her myself," whispered Charlie to his wife, as he put his hands in his pockets, and carelessly sauntered away.

"Tell us what it is that troubles you," said Mrs. Harcourt.

"We shall wish to befriend you, if we can," said Mrs. Hill.

"Thank you," said Mary, as her tears pattered quickly down; "I have not done anything—I mean I could not help it."

Mary was thinking of that first stealthy kiss, which took her as much by surprise as Mr. Gray himself. The two ladies turned away for a second or two to hide their smiles. They both intuitively understood "that Mary could not help it."

"And who blames you, then," said Mrs. Hill, "if you 'could not help it,' whatever it was?" and she tried to look unconscious of any knowledge of the actual event. "If you 'could not help it,' you can hardly be to blame."

"Mr. Gray thinks it was all my fault."

"Thank you. How very nicely you have stitched up the trimming!" said Mrs. Hill, as Mary arose from her knees, and rolled up her working materials.

"And now you must eat some sandwiches," said Mrs. Harcourt, "and drink this glass of wine; I shall not let you refuse me—I see you are out of spirits, and this will do you good."

"And Mr. Gray, then, accuses you?" said Mrs. Hill.

"Yes; but, indeed, madam, I did not know of it."

Then Mary blushed, and cast her eyes down, as she felt she could not tell the ladies what she meant by "it." And as the ladies were much better informed on the subject than Mary was aware of, of course it followed that they were too well-bred to ask her to explain more fully.

"I did not know till it was all over," said Mary.

So short, so sweet a dream, to prove such a bitter reality on awaking!

"Now you must have some buns to take into the carriage," said Mrs. Hill, "for you have eaten nothing."

The bell rang, Mr. Charles Hill reappeared, and the ladies and Mary reseated themselves in the train.

IX

WHAT WAS SAID AT THE VICARAGE ABOUT MARY COPE AND ISAAC WATSON

In due course of time our travellers arrived at Lawsleigh; and Mary was not sorry to find herself safe in the interior of her own cottage, and free from the surveillance of any one.

She felt that the two ladies had a friendly feeling towards her, but she felt also how utterly impossible it had been to explain her position to them, and to tell them that, as she expressed it to herself, "it was all in such a little minute—Isaac's arm round her neck, and his great lips close to hers, quite before she knew; for she had only just time to shut her eyes, and then the door opened, all at the same time, and Mr. Gray stood there looking at them."

Mary lamented that she had not had the courage to tell them this. She felt sure they would then have understood that it was not her fault. Though whether Mary Cope had any intuitive notion that other females had been taken by surprise just as she herself had been, at some time or other of their simple lives, the author does not think it necessary to declare.

"And what is all this hubbub about Mary Cope and Isaac Watson?" said Parson Hill, as the party from town were cozily seated at their fruit and wine after dinner, and the domestics had left the room.

"Isaac was surprised in the act of——"

"Do not let us have any more nonsense, Charlie," said Mrs. Hill interrupting; "and," continued she, turning to Mr. Hill, "if my opinion is of any value, that young woman will clear herself from all accusations against her."

"But what has she done?—of what is she accused?—and what has Isaac done? Surprised in some act! In what, pray?" said Mr. Hill.

The two ladies looked at each other. Mrs. Harcourt blushed, and Mrs. Hill smiled, as they both recalled the magnitude of Isaac's sin.

"You ask too many questions at once," said Charlie. "Put them singly, and you will get the whole truth."

"What has Mary Cope done?" said the vicar.

No one attempted to reply. Mrs. Harcourt felt the colour come brightly into her cheeks; she also felt Parson Hill was looking at her.

"Ah! the ladies know all about it, I see," said Parson Hill. "May I ask of you," addressing Mrs. Harcourt in very courteous tones, "what has Mary Cope done?"

"She told me she had not done anything," said Mrs. Harcourt; "and she also said 'she could not help it.'"

Parson Hill stared; and Mrs. Hill took the opportunity of attesting the truth of Mrs. Harcourt's statement.

"Humph!" said the parson. "Poor Mary has 'done nothing'—hard to blame her for that—and she 'could not help it!'—worse still to blame her in that case—and what has Isaac done?"

"That was not your second question," said Charlie, with a mischievous look at Mrs. Harcourt.

"Oh! never mind asking such numberless questions," said Mrs. Hill, "for I assure you I quite think the young woman will get through her troubles with credit to herself."

"At all events, all womankind is kindly interested in her favour," said Parson Hill.

"It would be hard if we could not be kind and charitable to each other," said Mrs. Harcourt.

"And you believe Mary 'could not help it?'" said Parson Hill. And, after a few moments of silence, he looked very much surprised at the change in Mrs. Harcourt's countenance—who so well understood the meaning of the little word "it,"—at Mrs. Hill's attempts to hide her smiles, and at Charlie's suppressed laughter.

"Am I to be kept in the dark?" said the parson, looking from one to another. "I know you," addressing Mrs. Harcourt, "always stand up for your sex—but then I rely upon your words, for I am sure you would not deceive me," added he courteously.

"I have used the young woman's own words," said Mrs. Harcourt, so demurely as to cause an additional burst of laughter from Charlie.

"Poor Mary!" said the parson; "I should be sorry if she were to get into any scrape with Isaac Watson. And Gray seemed to hint at some love-making. Now, Isaac Watson was taken up with that silly little milliner woman who came to visit Mary. I thought he had more sense, and more taste. But love-making, or making love with Mary Cope, would be a very different thing."

"But what of that?" said Mrs. Harcourt; "so pretty and so modest a young woman must attract admirers."

"Quite unconstitutional," said Charlie.

"True, O queen!" said the parson; "but we opine, to be without a lover is better than to have an unworthy one. Unworthy—well, I rather mean unsteady. I must admit, in all truth, Isaac is not so unworthy as he is unsteady—it is a hard matter to give an honest opinion of the man. Sometimes I almost fear he is more than unsteady, that is, wavering—he is positively—positively——"

carried away by his subject, and having a great horror of any attention from Isaac to Mary Cope, the good vicar for the moment felt that he deserved the epithet 'drunken;' and yet, his natural kindliness towards Isaac, made him hesitate before pronouncing a word of such powerful significance; and he at length stopped, without finishing the sentence.

"Did Gray make any complaint of Mary to you, Charlie?" said the parson.

"He told Mary not to receive visits from Isaac Watson; in point of fact, he forbade Isaac to go to the house."

"Well, what then?"

"He came home unexpectedly—Gray, I mean, came home, and found Isaac and Mary together."

"You don't say so!" said the vicar in a tone of surprise.

"Yes; the grand scrape between the pretty schoolmistress and Isaac Watson," said Charlie, "is——"

"Don't, Charlie!" said Mrs. Hill.

"Is that Gray surprised Isaac Watson in the very act of kissing Mary Cope," said Charlie, unmoved by Mrs. Hill's words, or by her look of entreaty.

"Heavens and earth!" said the parson, pushing his chair back; "what do you mean, Charlie?"

"That is all," said Charlie, listlessly sipping his wine.

"That is all, indeed! I hope it is enough!" said the parson, now replacing his chair. "Isaac Watson!—umph—and Mary Cope! Now you see, Charlie, all this comes of the Exhibition! I never did approve of it; and I am happy to remember, at this moment, that the proposal to take the school, the choir, the ringers, and all the rest of the people, never had my willing consent. It is true, I gave way—the march of the times required it at my hands. And a pretty march they have made of it—the people, I mean; no, not the people, but Gray—a pretty march he has made of Isaac Watson and Mary Cope. And if I could have foreseen that this grand march of the times had required at my hands such—such conduct between Isaac Watson and Mary Cope, I would not have marched with the times."

The vicar had pressed his hand heavily on the table while he was speaking; he now removed it suddenly as he leaned back in his chair, and all the glasses seemed to tremble and shiver in a sympathizing sensitiveness with the vicar.

"I always said as I thought—that is, when I objected to Gray's proposal, I said, such people as the Lawsleigh people were much better at home on Dartmoor minding their own business. What business had they with the march of the times and the Exhibition? You see I was right—I *am* sometimes."

The ladies longed to escape from the room, but Charlie telegraphed to his wife to sit still.

"This is just what may be expected from such innovations, such turning of the world upside down. If the people had stayed quietly in Lawsleigh, as they ought to have done, and as they have done for centuries from generation to generation this would not have happened."

Charlie insisted upon refilling his wife's glass after her long journey, and prevailed upon Mrs. Harcourt to have a slice of sweet cake.

"Do you think that Isaac Watson would have dared to touch Mary Cope here on Dartmoor? Do you hear me speak, Charlie?"

"I am no judge of these matters," said Charlie; "though, to say the truth, she is a pretty, modest-looking young woman, and I do not marvel much at any one being tempted."

"Marvel! why what are you talking about? She is the gem of the whole village! Is that drunkard, Isaac Watson—for he is a drunkard!" continued Parson Hiull, now' that he gave full play to his anger, "is that disreputable drinking and smoking Isaac Watson to have the gem of the village?—to be allowed to marry Mary Cope? I say he shall *not!*"

"Perhaps he has no such intention," said Charlie.

"No such intention! Oh! he has intention enough," said the parson, in a sarcastic tone; "or how dares he to—to——"

"Even modest young women allow such liberties to handsome men occasionally," said Charlie; "and, as Isaac is handsome, I suppose Mary had not the heart to say no."

"Charlie, boy, don't talk nonsense," said the vicar, in a softened tone, as he bowed his head; "I am grieved."

And then, after a few moments of silence, he seemed to remember that he had rather allowed his anger to run away with his courtesy, for he turned to Mrs. Harcourt and said,

"Now you must prove that you are charitable enough to excuse my unpardonable anger in your presence, and tell me what you think of this wine; it is some——"

"Indeed I should regret as much as yourself," said Mrs. Harcourt, interrupting him with an attempt to soothe his ruffled feelings, "if that pretty-looking young woman should make a bad match, or rather, I mean, marry a bad man——"

"Well, I *do* confess I am grieved about this business; I had hoped that you, Charlie, would bring me comfort, for I don't wish to condemn Mary if I can help it; and, to confess the truth, Gray's letters for this last day or two have been great worries."

"But my dear sir," said Charlie, "you will of course see Mary Cope yourself, and give fair play to her own account of the thing. She says 'she could not help it.'"

"Fair play! Why, do you think I would condemn her unheard?"

"Oh! I don't mean that you have any wish to condemn her; but Gray is zealous, captious, and inexperienced, and sometimes, even in spite of his strong desire to do right, he does the very opposite."

"If I could only hear the exact truth," said the vicar—"I mean, without any of Gray's own opinions, such as he has given me in his letters, until I am so mystified, I can make neither head nor tail of the whole story."

"Then go to the young woman yourself," said Mrs. Hill.

"And would you have me credit her statement in opposition to Gray's?" said the parson.

"Oh! no; I do not know what Mr. Gray has said—at least, I know but little," said Mrs. Hill; "but the young woman distinctly said 'she had done nothing'—that is, nothing that could excite Mr. Gray's anger, if properly explained."

"Then why did she not explain?" said the parson.

"I conclude Mr. Gray would not listen to her," said Mrs. Harcourt.

"She has at least prevailed upon you ladies to listen," said Parson Hill, courteously.

"No, indeed; few could have said less than she. We have told you all we know, and we both feel sure that, though the young woman is under a cloud, it may be found eventually to possess a silver lining."

"Umph!" said the parson, as a smile flitted across his face, "I think Mary must have made a favourable impression upon you."

The ladies now left the room.

"Are you in league with the woman?—and ready to fight Mary's battles?" said the vicar, as he pushed the decanter to Charlie.

"My feelings are interested for the young woman," said Charlie, as he filled his glass, "and against Gray. She does not look like a guilty, but a sorrowful woman—my wife agrees with me; Mrs. Harcourt is of the same opinion."

"You all row in the same boat, said the vicar, in a pleasant tone; "I am glad to hear it. I am glad poor Mary has interested you all in her favour—and, Charlie, I will see Mary as soon as I can; she will tell the truth to me—indeed, she is a very truthful young woman. Gray is a good fellow, but, between ourselves, he is apt to be a little severe; and then, as you say, he has had no experience; and, though I am sure I give him credit for the desire to do right, I cannot shut my eyes to the fact that he often does very wrong. It may be so in this matter, for I cannot think Mary guilty of such wickedness. She has always been a most modest and well-behaved young woman. And also, Charlie, boy, I feel that it is not possible—point of fact, it is impossible—that Isaac Watson should dare to take such a liberty with my schoolmistress!" And the vicar refilled his class, pushed the decanter to Charlie, and leaned back in his chair with a complacent smile on his face.

"Oh! but, excuse me," said Charlie, "we must believe something. There could not be such a hubbub for nothing."

"Well, what then?—what part do you mean to credit?"

"Why, about the kiss. I am afraid I quite believe that."

"You believe that, sir!" said the vicar in a tone of astonishment "Now that, in my opinion, is the most unlikely thing of all. Why do you credit such nonsense?"

"Because it seems to be the only thing that probably did happen. And the young woman said 'she could not help it.' Of course she could not. You know that as well as I."

"Charlie! Charlie!" said the vicar shaking his head.

"And really, with a fair opportunity, I do not so much blame Isaac; because, with a fair opportunity, I should be very likely to—kiss her myself!"

"Pshaw!—nonsense, boy!" said the vicar, as he rose to lead the way to the drawing-room.

X

WHICH TREATS OF MARY COPE'S EARLY MORNING VISITOR, AND OF WHAT WAS SAID ON THAT OCCASION

AT six o'clock the next morning, after a good night's rest, considering the anxiety of her mind, Mary Cope opened her eyes, and was pleased to see what she called "the beautiful Lawsleigh sun" shining full into her room. She sprang out of bed, hastily rushed to the window, and opened it, and was in the act of fastening the casement back, when, to her surprise and delight, she saw Isaac Watson pacing up and down in front of her cottage.

"Oh, goodness me! Why, it is Isaac!" said she softly, as she withdrew from the window. It is almost unnecessary to add that Mary's toilette was made more rapidly than usual; and when she was able to descend and open the door, she had no hesitation in letting Isaac enter.

When the joy of their meeting again had a little subsided, Isaac confessed he felt very angry with Mr. Gray. He could not understand why Mary must be separated from her own party, and go with the ladies by express train.

"The whole village of Lawsleigh," to use Isaac's expression, "had gone to town by excursion train, in third-class carriages; and why then should Mary be taken from them on their return journey?"

Of course Isaac Watson had a right to resent such interference on Mr. Gray's part.

Mary opened her eyes very wide, when the astounding fact was made known to her, that she had travelled express! She thought an express-train, and the telegraph, much the same sort of thing; and that if one could carry a message, as she had been told, thousands of miles in a minute, the other would allow passengers to get in at one end, and just shoot them out at the other, without any more trouble! And on learning from Isaac that she had herself been in one of these very superior trains, she said with much *naïveté*,

"Then, Isaac, it is only smaller carriages they have in those trains—not so big as ours by many times over." By "ours," Mary meant third-class. "And then they are all armchairs and cushions, and no space to walk about, but like a very little room. 'Ours' are much more roomy, and pleasanter, and not so hot, and——"

"But then you went along the line much faster, Mary," said Isaac.

"Did I? I am sure I did not know it. Why, you see, Isaac, I was so unhappy, I really did not know what we were doing. It seemed all very slow to me, with nobody to speak to. I thought we never should get to Lawsleigh. I was very, very tired, and so I went off to bed directly. And when did you get home, Isaac? And how is the good widow?"

"Why, Mary, dear, I have not been to the smithy, for——"

"Not been to the smithy, Isaac!"

"No. I only reached Lawsleigh at half-past five. Many of our large party are not yet arrived; and I came here at once to see you—because you see Mr. Gray puts himself so between us, that I wanted to talk to you—besides wanting to see you," added he, kindly, as he pressed her hand. "For as you and I, Mary, have agreed to have each other"—he had ceased to call her Mistress Cope—"I do no see the right of any one to come between us!"

Mary was silent, and Isaac proceeded.

"You see, Mr. Gray says—for I have had a talk with him—he says the parson will not let you marry me!—and so that is the reason why I so much wanted to see you. Because you *have promised* me; and besides, even the parson has no right to stop you from doing as you like in a matter that makes your happiness for life!"

"But, Isaac," said Mary, gently, and turning very pale, "how can I go against Parson Hill?—why, I could never think of such a thing!—you know he is my only friend, and he is so kind and good; and if I offended him, I must lose the school—and—that would make me very unhappy indeed. But I quite made up my mind that, as you have given up going to the 'Packhorse,' it must be all right with Parson Hill, because what can he have to say?"

In the first moments of their happiness, when Isaac declared his love and Mary acknowledged hers, they had both referred to Parson Hill with great satisfaction, agreeing in opinion that, if Isaac would give up his constant visits to the 'Packhorse,' that kind Parson Hill would raise no objection to the marriage. But when they were so unceremoniously separated, and so systematically kept apart, each had opportunities for thinking over his or her position, and both had more doubts as to the smoothing of their future path—now that they met again—than they had had when they parted. In Mary it amounted to a dread of meeting with or seeing Parson Hill. In Isaac there arose the fear that Mary would be persuaded to break her word.

"Yes, Mary, I *have* given up the 'Packhorse,'" said Isaac, in a decided tone, "and I cannot see that the parson can now have any objection—only if he has, why, you know, I have your promise."

"Yes, you have," said Mary, looking up brightly; "and, Isaac, I am glad that I have promised you, for I am always happy when I think about it; and you know we could wait—wait till—till Parson Hill is willing to—willing to give his consent—eh, Isaac?"

But somehow Mary had an awakening doubt that Isaac would not like to wait! And often have I observed, in my walk through life, that in engagements of this nature the women, some of whom may have been restless in manner and eager for admiration before they were affianced—though this was not Mary's case—the women, when they are actually engaged, invariably settle down into a quiet and satisfied composure, that seems to express an inward happiness superior to any they have before known—a happiness that makes them equal to the suspense of waiting with exemplary patience, till fate shall order that such engagements shall terminate by marriage.

Not so the men. No sooner are they assured that they have gained the love of the woman they prefer, than they become irritated with the smallest thing that seems to rise up between themselves and the possession of the coveted object; and in too many instances they ungenerously upbraid the woman for the presence of obstacles she has neither been instrumental in raising nor had the power to overcome. Intuitively, as it seemed, Mary comprehended this anomaly. She was contented to wait—to wait until her great patron Parson Hill would give his consent. But what of Isaac?— would he? Isaac felt his heart sink as he heard her words. His nature was generous, and he sincerely loved Mary Cope; and though an ardent admirer of pretty women, he was not one who would marry for beauty only. Mary possessed qualities of sterling worth, and Isaac appreciated them. The more he recognized her value, and the more he prized her love, the more he dreaded that she should, by connivance of any kind, be turned against himself—a fact that he feared might sooner or later be brought to pass.

Isaac thought little of the vice of inebriety when he left Lawsleigh; he returned with a horror of it, and also with a keen consciousness of the many humiliating positions in which he must frequently have been seen, not only by the inhabitants of the village, but also by Mr. Gray, and even by the vicar himself! And another thing—he felt painfully conscious that his intention of giving up the "Packhorse" would not be credited!—and his regret was increased by the conviction that it would take many months, perhaps even years, to do away with the past and establish a character for soberness. He knew that his past misconduct might be brought up against him by any one who wished to prevent Mary from marrying him. And, after a pause, during which these thoughts flitted rapidly through his mind, he said,

"It is not about waiting that I mind so much—only the sooner we are married the less people can do to separate us—it is your word, Mary, your true word that you will not be turned against me—that is what I want."

"Turned against you!" said Mary, reproachfully. "Why, what do you mean, Isaac should never think of such a thing."

"Dear Mary, I know you are so good," said Isaac, with rare caution, avoiding any explanation of the thoughts that had agitated him. "And

I came here this morning, Mary—for I could not rest until I had seen you—to ask you to give me your word that you will be true to me? I think if you will promise me that, I can settle my mind a little more easily."

Mary looked up at him with a fearless but rather inquiring expression of countenance, and paused before she replied,

"I listened to you, Isaac, when you said you loved me, and I did not doubt your avowal, though I was almost ashamed to feel how much I could return that love. This is only three days ago—you did not appear to doubt me then—why do you doubt me now?"

"I do not doubt you; if you are left to yourself, I know you will keep your word. But if anyone should try—try to speak ill of me to you—which perhaps they might, Mary—you might change your mind, and think me unworthy, as I know I have been; but I will do better—for your sake I will be anything."

"For your own sake, Isaac," said Mary, with a shade of reproach in her tone. "You must have a right principle within to cause you to stand against temptation. I am nothing," added she, sorrowfully; "for if you only reform for my sake, your reformation will not be lasting."

"There!" said Isaac, starting up, "you doubt me—that is just what I expected!"

"If you doubt yourself, Isaac," said Mary, meekly, "how can you expect me to trust you?"

"I do not doubt my power to do anything I attempt in a right spirit. I have always been self-reliant—I am so still. But, Mary, I feel very humble, and sad-hearted, and unworthy of you; my past evil deeds are ever present with me, and then I fear they are also present with you. I am half-ashamed to ask you—come what may—to promise me faithfully that you will have me!—I feel as if I were taking an unfair advantage; and yet I feel my pulses stir within me, and my heart beat quicker, as I say you shall never repent—so help me God!" added he, fervently, as he raised his eyes upwards; "my anxiety about you fairly weighs me down," and he seated himself heavily, and disconsolately leaned his head on his hand.

"But, Isaac," and a very slight smile of contentment seemed to play about Mary's mouth, as she said, "I suppose you are not any worse now than you were three days ago? You told me then of your past life, and I only honoured you the more for your straightforward honesty; you promised amendment, and I—I quite believe you will act up to your promise."

She held out her hand timidly as she spoke, though she could not restrain the crimson blushes that covered her face.

"God bless you, dear Mary!" said Isaac, as he seized the little hand, and drew her nearer to him. "No, I am no worse; but I get so afraid that you will repent, and you see I cannot settle my mind to anything. Somehow, just at that time when I spoke to you in London, I was so happy; I did not think of the many things that might happen to part us; and with Mr. Gray making such a fuss, and keeping you from me, and threatening that the parson will not let us marry, why, fairly I am more done up than I could have supposed from anything—and—and—and so, Mary, perhaps you will excuse me, and understand that only your promise can comfort me."

"I do not mean to change my mind, Isaac; and we both know how good the parson is, so I shall just think of that, and not care about Mr. Gray; and if you were to do the same, Isaac, I do think you would be happier."

Undoubtedly Isaac was much comforted by Mary's eloquence, and walked home a much happier man. And the interview terminated to their mutual satisfaction, and without any disagreeable interruption at the finale.

XI

HOW THE BELLS OF LAWSLEIGH RING FORTH A MERRY PEAL, AND YET FAIL TO MAKE PARSON HILL GLAD

THE day after the return of the Lawsleigh people from the Exhibition, little knots were seen gathered together in different parts of the village, expatiating on the wonders of the "World's Fair," and on all the marvellous sights they had seen.

Mary gathered courage to go to the smithy; for now that she actually "kept company" with Isaac, she felt a degree of shyness in going there that was new to her. Nevertheless she determined to go, for said she to herself:

"If I do not go people will talk about that, and perhaps only the sooner find out about Isaac and me."

The Widow Simpson was enjoying the calm summer's evening, according to her wont, in the shed at the front; but Isaac was not there.

"Mistress Cope! And you be come back all safe! I be pleased to see you. Tell I, be it a weary way to London?—and what be the Bishion (Exhibition) like to?"

"The journey was rather long," said Mary; "it took us all the livelong day to get to London, and then it was quite late at night, and so until we awoke in the morning we could not tell a bit what London was like. But my goodness, widow, why, it would take a long, long life to tell what London is like! Such sights as we have seen! such places as we have been to!—I mean Crystal Palaces, all made of glass, widow!—and such queer live animals—or I suppose have once been alive—in the gardens!"

"My! Mistress Cope, but it be wonderful!"

"Wonderful! I think so, indeed! And the fountains outside, and the great Egyptians inside!'

"Egyptians, Mistress Cope? What, then, be Pharaoh there, and all his host?"

"I should think there is everything there that you can ever have known about. And pictures, and naked people, like those in the Exhibition!"

"Naked, Mistress Cope? Can you be meaning stark naked people?"

"Well, widow, they are not alive, but they are very queer things to look at; and especially when Isaac was with me, it was most awkward, and I always wanted to get away."

"It be a shame, it sim to I, as they Londoners must let dead folk go naked!" said the widow.

"Oh! but then they never have been really alive, you know; they are made of marble, and, widow, you would think some of them could speak," said Mary, with a little awe, "but they cannot!"

"Isaac be almost fagged up," said the Widow; "he be fast asleep, he was so dead a-tired."

"No doubt he requires rest, widow," said Mary, as she went into the cottage for a chair, and so managed to hide her blushes at the mention of Isaac's name.

"Now, widow, look here," continued Mary, as she opened a parcel and displayed her treasures, "these needles were made in the Exhibition—do look at them."

"They be uncommon fine."

"Oh! they are wonderful!" said Mary, enthusiastically. "And look at this wool, two colours together! Did ever you see the like? It is most marvellous! I have brought it for you, on purpose that you may knit yourself some nice warm muffatees, such as you wear in the winter; and here are the knitting-needles, just the right size."

"Why, bless thee, Mistress Cope! And just to think as you should go all the way to London town, and to the Bishion, and then think on I! Massy me, I be most mazed!"

"Think of you! why, to be sure! Did you think when I was in London I should forget dear old Lawsleigh? Oh, no, widow, I thought a great deal about it, I can tell you,"—and Mary looked round the shed as she thought of her engagement with Isaac,—"and about you also—and Isaac and I talked about you—for of course I thought of you sitting here so nice, and still, and quiet. And did you like your nice new shawl that Isaac told me to choose for you? He was so pleased to buy one for you!"

"Maybe the lad be kind hearted; and I sim he do love his granny. Though he be such un a big un, he have always loved his granny just as when he was a little one!"

And then the old woman took a good look at Mary; and after she had silently made up her mind, she said:

"And you sim to me, Mistress Cope, to be that hearty pleased. For why be you so glad?"

Mary could not hide her happiness; it shone in her eye, rippled over her mouth; was heard in her tongue; and the old woman's penetration observed these signs. But she was far enough from suspecting the real cause of such joy. She took up the wool, and, after examining it, she said,

"This be amazing curious yarn! Two fresh colours all in one!—it be amazing, surely!"

"Yes," said Mary, "that is the beauty of it, and when you knit with it the effect is admirable."

"It be kind of you, Mistress Cope, to bring I this here wool, and it be kind of the lad to buy me a nice new shawl. But there be a table as the lad bringed home, so heavy, and with a box on the top, that be no use to I, and no use to nobody, but to stand in the way. The lad put it near by the window; will you go and look at it, Mistress Cope? It be a queer table, with queer legs."

Mary went into the cottage at the widow's request, and there, under the window, to her great astonishment, stood a sewing machine. Her exclamation of surprise and delight caused the old woman to lay down her knitting, and go into the cottage to see what was the matter.

"It is a sewing-machine!" said Mary, as she took off the lid, which the old woman had supposed was a box, and displayed the machinery underneath.

The glad sound of Mary's voice caused more intruders than one, for hasty steps were heard descending the stairs, and Isaac abruptly entered the room.

"Oh! Isaac, what a beautiful thing!" said Mary, as her eyes filled with tears of joy.

For she thought of his goodness to her in buying so expensive a present, and was half ashamed to feel how much this proved his love.

"Not half good enough or handsome enough for the one who, I hope, will accept it from me and use it to her own satisfaction," said Isaac.

"I never can thank you enough," said Mary eagerly, as she offered him her hand.

Isaac did not refuse the proffered hand, and, what was still more strange to the old woman, Mary did not turn aside from Isaac's proffered caress.

But, as it is not the custom, even on primitive Dartmoor, for great big men and pretty little women to be "billing and cooing" in the presence of their grandmothers, so these signs of attachment between the two young people seemed to be at once understood by the old woman, for she said in a tone of glad surprise,

"Why, children, be ye a-going to wed?"

"Mother, she is to be my wife," said Isaac, proudly presenting Mary to the old woman; "yes, it is true; she has promised to have me—have you not, Mary?"

"Perhaps the widow would not like you to marry me?" said Mary evasively.

"Not like! Mistress Cope, I be cruel glad, I be!"

And the widow kissed Mary, and stretched out her aged arms to touch the head of each as she said,

"May the Lord in heaven bless ye both, and make you good and happy!"

Isaac had stooped his tall person, for he intuitively comprehended that the widow would give them a blessing; and, as he arose from his humble position, he put his arms round her waist and hugged her close in his arms, kissing her tenderly, and whispering close in her ear,

"No more 'Packhorse,' mother, no more cider; you shall never again have to grieve for me, I promise you."

"God bless thee, lad!—ay, and he will bless thee, and help thee to keep thy word. And I be pleased, I be pleased, though, mayhap, I canna help to cry."

And as Isaac placed her in a chair, and turned away to hide the powerful emotion that stirred within him, Mary and the Widow Simpson took the opportunity to wipe away their tears; for, as Mary said as she kissed the old woman,

"You see, widow, I am very pleased, and very happy, but somehow— somehow I cannot help the tears coming."

"And you be a-going to wed the lad Isaac, Mistress Cope? I be most mazed!" said the widow.

"I must confess I have promised him," said Mary.

"Heyday! lassie, and what hast thee been a-promising?" said James Marvel who overheard Mary's words as he entered the cottage.

"Her has a-promised to wed the lad, and I be most mazed about she," said the widow.

"Oh—h!" said James, making a grimace, "then you be a-meaning to forbid the banns, widdy—be that it?"

"No, no," said the widow, hastily; "I have gived them my blessing, Mister Marvel, and that be it."

"Why, gude save us, Isaac, lad!" said James, looking at the sewing-machine; "I have a seed a thing like to that at the Bishion—doesna it cost a power of money, eh, lad?"

"Hark to it," said the widow, as Mary began to move the treadles. "I be a-thinking on a spinning-jenny, as I have a-heard tell of in my young days. Be this a spinning-jenny, Mistress Cope?"

"It is a beautiful sewing-machine," said Mary, enthusiastically. "I never heard a spinning-jenny, and I do not know what it is like."

The little party at the smithy was soon made larger by the addition of some other of the villagers, who had been in London, and who now came to tell the widow of all the wonders they had seen, and to compare their experience with Isaac's. As fast as the neighbours entered the cottage, the Widow Simpson informed them that "Isaac and Mistress Cope was a-keeping company," and the news seemed to give universal satisfaction. Some of the ringers were present, and they whispered to each other that it would only be fair to Isaac—who was himself such a capital ringer—if they were to just rush to the belfry and strike up a peal in honour of his engagement with Mary Cope.

"Just the very same," said one, "as us did when the passon told us as Master Charlie was a-going to wed his missus as he has a-got now."

"The very same, lad," said another; "come along."

They got the keys of the church from the old woman, who was as much pleased with the idea as they themselves; and calling together the remainder of their companions as they went down the street, eventually reached the belfry, and sent forth a peal from the old church tower, such as the inhabitants of the quiet village of Lawsleigh were only accustomed to hear on grand occasions.

"My!—why for be the lads a-ringing like to that?" said one.

"Coz why?—us be all comed safe back to Lawsleigh," said another.

"They be a-finding out if the bells be all right," said another; "coz the ringers was all gone to London town, and mayhap they bells might go to sleep."

But when by degrees the real cause became known, congratulations in a simple though hearty and friendly way were not wanting at the smithy cottage. It is true that there were some who shook their heads and said,

"Mistress Cope marry Isaac Watson! Why, and what be she a-thinking on? Cannot her see with her two eyes as Peter Barker be always a-wolloping Hannah, poor thing! And will Mistress Cope, and she such a little one, like to be wolloped by that there big Isaac Watson? My! her be fond!"

And at a part of the village that has been especially introduced to the reader, the dialogue ran thus—"Mistress Cope!—Molly Cope you be meaning—and she with she's face all spoiled; least-ways, it was spoiled when I seed she—be she a-patched up? Mayhap they big sores be not gone yet—be they?"

"She's face is not spoiled now, widdy," said old Jacob Smerdon, whose journey to London had not caused any reform in his habits, and who, unlike Isaac, had not given up his visits to the "Packhorse."

"Oh-h! she's face be bettered again, and she be a-going to wed Isaac Watson; and if Isaac comes to gie it to she same as Peter Barker does to Hannah, will her like that? Done you think, Mister Jacob?"

The spite and angry feeling of the Widow Mason towards Mary Cope was not reciprocated by Jacob Smerdon, and he did not reply. Jacob was a kind-hearted old man, and rejoiced in the prospect of Isaac's happiness. He knew that Isaac had promised never to visit the "Packhorse" again; but he was too wise to anger the widow still more by informing her of Isaac's resolution.

Meanwhile, Mary had not seen either Parson Hill or Mr. Gray. The latter, like all who had returned to Lawsleigh by the excursion train, found rest especially necessary; and he did not leave his bed until obliged to dress for dinner at the vicarage, whither he had been invited by his hospitable vicar.

And Parson Hill himself had been prevented from seeing Mary as he had intended, and from hearing her own account of the reports which had reached him to her disadvantage, by the arrival unexpectedly of a large party of friends for a long day on the moor. Such an influx of visitors was by no means unusual, but Parson Hill felt they had never arrived less opportunely.

Mary, with a beating heart, had called at the vicarage before going to the smithy, wishing, yet dreading, to see Parson Hill. But, as we have said, he was engaged, and Mary came away with her desire ungratified, but with a large portion of dread diminished, for, in a group of ladies on the lawn, she saw her late companions in the train, Mrs. Harcourt and Mrs. Hill, who both came forward and spoke to her, and their kind manners and their kind inquiries set her heart at rest, for she thought,

"If these two ladies are so kind, I do not think Parson Hill can be meaning to blame me much."

And not feeling to deserve the blame that had been so unsparingly heaped upon her, Mary felt happier than she had done since the unlucky moment of Mr. Gray's intrusion upon that "little minute," as Mary called it, when "it" happened, that she could neither foresee nor prevent. And so Mary felt herself quite at liberty to enjoy the evening at the smithy cottage, with all its attendant honours of good wishes from so many of the villagers, bells ringing and, though last, not least, Isaac's splendid gift of the sewing machine.

And the dinner at the vicarage went on much as all dinners do. But the conversation was suddenly stopped in its even flow by the bursting forth of a joyous peal from the old church tower.

"Heyday!—what is all this for?" said the vicar, putting down his knife and fork, and gazing round inquiringly.

No one could reply. One of the domestics was sent to the housekeeper to inquire if she knew why the bells were ringing. But the man returned as he went, without any solution to the enigma.

"Strange!" said the worthy vicar, looking perplexed.

"The men ought not to ring without asking your permission," said Mr. Gray.

"Oh! they know their duty," said the parson; "they know the times and seasons when the Church commands the bells to be rung; and as they always do ring on those occasions, I am sure they are welcome to ring on any other, without the trouble of asking my permission."

"But they ought not to think it a trouble to ask you; and, besides, it is their duty," said Mr. Gray.

"Perhaps they are ringing for joy at their return home," said Charlie.

"It may be so," said the vicar.

The bells ceased their joyous strain, and the incident was forgotten. But later in the evening, when the assembled party were sitting rapt in motionless silence, listening to Mrs. Harcourt's magnificent playing of one of Mendelssohn's "Lieder ohne Worte," a servant entered and spoke to Parson Hill in a low voice. He said,

"The bells have been rung, sir, because Isaac Watson and Mistress Cope are engaged to be married. There has been a large party at the smithy cottage, sir; all the villagers have been to congratulate them; James Marvel is just come in."

The good vicar leaned back in his chair, and for a few moments covered his face with his hands.

When Mrs. Harcourt left the piano, amid the compliments of her friends, she missed Parson Hill's voice; but this did not prevent her from observing that he looked paler than usual, and absent in mind.

"What is the matter with the vicar?" said Mrs. Harcourt to her friend Mrs. Hill.

"He has discovered the meaning of the joyous peal," said Mrs Hill.

"It might be joyless instead of joyful," said Mrs. Harcourt.

"Isaac Watson and our pretty travelling companion are actually engaged, notwithstanding all Mr. Gray's care; and, as Isaac is head of the belfry, in compliment to him, the ringers gave him a right merry peal."

"Poor Parson Hill!" said Mrs. Harcourt.

XII

WHICH TREATS OF THREE WIDOWS

WHEN the last of the carriages drove away from the hospitable Vicarage of Lawsleigh, and stillness seemed to occupy the house, in opposition to the Babel of tongues that had been so recently heard, Parson Hill led the way to his library, followed by Mr. Gray.

"Well, Gray, this is indeed a sad affair," said the vicar.

"I was afraid it would turn out so," said Mr. Gray. "And I cannot see how we can expect it to be otherwise, after that young woman's most shameful deceit."

The vicar was silent.

"I wrote you word, Mary Cope told me most distinctly on one evening that she and Isaac Watson were not engaged, and not going to be married; and on the next I saw Isaac with his arm round her neck kissing her."

"Bless me!—bless me!" said the vicar, shaking his head.

"Oh, she must be very bad to permit such a thing," said Mr. Gray, angrily; while Parson Hill moved uneasily in his chair, without making a reply. But after a few moments' silence, and perhaps feeling it incumbent on him to say something, he said,

"And now they seem to take things into their own hands—ringing the bells, and engaging themselves without saying a word to anybody! I cannot think what has come to the place! Lawsleigh used to be the most quiet village on the moor, and its people the most obedient; and now, here is Isaac Watson, the drunkard, going to marry Mary Cope, the school-mistress. A pretty thing, indeed!"

"Perhaps we can prevent the marriage," said Mr. Gray.

"They are both of age. You may be sure that sinner, Isaac Watson, knows that well enough; and you may also be very sure that he will instil that fact into that simpleton, Mary Cope—for she is a simpleton, and worse than a simpleton, for having anything to do with such a worthless character as Isaac. I cannot think what the young woman can be thinking of. If I could save her from the consequences of her own folly—if she would listen to me—let me save her"—the vicar paused, and leaned his head on his hand. "Poor thing! Can we save her, Gray, from becoming the wife of a sot!"

"If they are both of age, I fear we have but little chance; and yet, though the young woman was so deceitful with me, she might listen to you—at all events, it would be well worth an effort, both from you and from me, to try to save her," said Mr. Gray.

"You see, Gray, I shall always feel sure, if they had not gone to London, this could not have happened. As I have said before, such innovations do no good; and here we have under our very noses proof of much harm done."

"I don't agree with you there. I think these two, Isaac Watson and Mary Cope, were very intimate—indeed, a great deal too intimate—before they left Lawsleigh."

"Too intimate! But we will not discuss that now," said the parson, regretting that he had mentioned the journey to town. "And it is getting late," added he, as he put his hand to his brow. "I am detaining you from the repose that I am sure you must require after all you have undergone in London. Perhaps you will see me in the morning?"

"Yes, I will—for the sooner we come to some conclusion—that is——"

"You see, Gray, we are both tired to-night," said the vicar, with an attempt at a smile. "You with so much sight-seeing in London, and I with the pleasure of receiving so many dear old friends." And as he went with Mr. Gray to the hall-door, he added—"How magnificently Mrs. Harcourt plays!—does she not? That is music!"

"You are a better judge than I," said Mr. Gray, as he shook the vicar's hand, and went away.

"Umph! It is my positive belief that Gray would not know John Bull's 'God save the Queen,' from Mendelssohn's finest work. Well, well, some men are born without—without—but never mind that. She is a charming woman. She *can* play. I know a great many who can *not*—who make many attempts, and think they shine. I wish they would just listen to Mrs. Harcourt for one ten minutes! If that did not cause them to comprehend their own inferiority, nothing upon earth would. Conceited things!—females—ladies, I mean."

And in spite of the vicar's sorrow for the sad entanglement of his favourite schoolmistress, Mary Cope, with that sinner Isaac Watson, he laughed aloud at his own complimentary speeches to ladies.

On this same evening, while the vicar and Mr. Gray were conversing in the library, Charlie entered his wife's dressing-room, and said,

"It is my opinion that those two lovers will beat the governor and the curate all to nothing."

"I don't understand you, Charlie," said Mrs. Hill. "What have they done?"

"I have not any information to communicate, of particular acts done or committed by them," said Charlie, laughing; "but I learn that they have taken the very wise precaution to make their engagement known to the whole parish. And as Gray is considered by the parish an interloper, and as not belonging to it; and as the governor, since Gray's arrival, is become pretty nearly a cipher in it, it stands to reason that the parish will have the best of it, and probably insist upon marrying the poor things—just as it insisted on ringing the bells in their honour—and just for the sake of opposing themselves to Gray. By themselves I mean the people in the parish—and just because the parson is of no use at all—eh! Kate? What do you say to this?"

"You mystify me," said Mrs. Hill, quietly.

"That is not difficult," said Charlie.

"But what is the use of making such long speeches, and mystifying me? If you have any thing to tell me—tell me—if not——"

"Cut your stick! Very well, I will go," said Charlie, as he walked away; and then, turning ere he reached the door, he added, "But have you nothing to tell me about your charming friend?"

"Oh! Charlie, dear, that is delightful!" said Mrs. Hill enthusiastically; "beyond all doubt that will be a match!"

"I thought so," said Charlie, as he closed the door and re-entered the room. "An excellent match!" added he impressively; "the very match of all others upon which I have long set my heart—in point of fact, Kate, if anything could have made me more in a hurry to marry than I really was, this thought would have done it—I mean the thought that the governor would not propose to Mrs. Harcourt because he had a son living at home of a—a proper age to marry. And so you see, Kate, barring the love I had and have for you—which overtopped all other loves ever known in the world—I had a longing that the dear old governor should make his dear old self comfortable for the rest of his amiable and valuable life, and so marry Mrs. Harcourt, for the sake of making her comfortable for the remainder of her very elegant—very intellectual—and very excellent life; to say nothing of her music! which just touches the blessed old governor in the right place, and makes his dear old face gleam all over with smiles, and—well, to tell you the truth, dear Kate, I forget all the rest—excepting only that I just married you, to take myself out of the way of the governor and Mrs. Harcourt—and—and I thought you would make me happy for life."

"Has Mr. Hill opened his mind to you?" said Mrs. Hill.

"Well, Kate, after my long and heartfelt speech about everybody's comfort in this comfortable world, I expected something a little more *recherché* than that; but since you have asked the question, I reply—Catch the governor opening his mind to any one, until he has first opened it well out to Mrs. Harcourt, and she in return has laid bare her 'inmost soul' to him. Sly old fellow, Kate, though I do worship him so hugely, for he is worth it! But to my certain knowledge he has had Mrs. Harcourt in his appropriating eye for the last twelve months!"

"Twelve months, Charlie! then why do not they marry? I suppose there is no such obstacle to the union of Parson Hill with Mrs. Harcourt, as there is between poor Mary Cope and her handsome lover," said Mrs. Hill laughing.

"Oh! now you are indeed sentimental," said Charlie; "but honestly, I cannot accuse the parson of inebriety; and as an equal piece of honesty, I now add, I know no ill of the widow, nor do I know of any obstacle to their blessed union. And if the parson chose to call his own banns for three Sundays in Lawsleigh Church, joining the hand some widow's name with his revered own, I declare, again honestly, I would not forbid the banns."

"Charlie, Charlie, don't be so absurd!" said Mrs. Hill, as she again could not restrain her mirth.

"There you go again, Kate—never contented with my sentiments!" said Charlie, as he leaned his back against a wardrobe and put his hands in his pockets. "But now, Kate, I must say—and by way of looking the transaction fully in the face—I must say that, for a woman of a certain age, the Widow Harcourt has points that I appreciate and approve; and I do not hesitate to acknowledge that, even in his mature age, the governor has excellent taste. She is still good-looking, or rather one can see she has been handsome. She is always lady-like and well-bred—to say nothing of possessing a fund of information unusual with her sex. She is frequently witty in conversation, and this without overstepping the bounds we men think necessary to hedge round female propriety—she is an intellectual and charming woman, and I just wish her joy of the governor!"

"I agree with all you say, Charlie dear, but you have forgotten or overlooked the best point of all. She is so warm-hearted!"

"Warm-hearted, Kate! but we men conclude that of all women, widows especially. Just imagine a cold-hearted woman!—an unheard-of anomaly! My dear Kate, the men would feel themselves justified in throwing stones at her as she attempted to take her daily walks. And a cold-hearted widow would be utterly impossible; widows are always——"

"Why do you say 'widow?'" said Mrs. Hill, interrupting. "Can you not say 'Mrs. Harcourt?'"

"Widow is a title common to all women who have lost their husbands. I only give her the title to which she has a right. And by way of enlightening you on this subject, I may as well tell you that there are two well-known widows in Lawsleigh—the Widow Simpson, a good widow, and a lone woman; and the Widow Mason, a bad widow, and also a lone woman. You perceive, Kate, all widows are lone women. The Widow Harcourt is a lone woman, and she has as much right to the title of 'widow' as either of these I have mentioned, or even as the beautiful and unfortunate Widow Capet."

"Charlie," said Mrs. Hill, in a voice of consternation, "pray do not recall such horrible scenes!"

"What a vivid imagination you have, Kate! And so you really do remember all about poor Marie Antoinette? Now, between ourselves, I expected you to put the question, '*Who* is the Widow Capet?' But I was just going to add, and will still keep my intention, even at the risk of giving your fine nervous system a shock, that the Widow Capet lived and died a lone woman! Widows, as a rule, are only lone women as long as they are let alone; and therefore your charming friend, the Widow Harcourt, will, in all probability, soon lose all claim to her present title; for you will see, Kate, the dear old governor will not 'let her alone,' and then she will cease to be a lone woman!"

Mrs. Hill was by this time laughing almost convulsively, as she leaned back in her chair; but, rallying a little, she said:

"Do go, Charlie dear, I really cannot bear any more nonsense to-night—you quite take my breath away."

"And so that is all the thanks I get!" said Charlie, as he prepared to obey his wife's wish. But ere he reached the door, a gentle tap was heard. "Here is another visitor," said he, as he opened the door and allowed Mrs. Harcourt to enter. "Talk of the angels and they flap their wings!" said Charlie, as he closed the door, and left the two ladies together.

"Widows have many privileges," said Charlie, when he returned to his wife's apartment; "and I hope the Widow Harcourt has made good use of her privilege of entrée into my wife's dressing-room. "One A.M., as I am a living sinner," continued he, as he stood winding up his watch. "What could she have to say, Kate?"

"She says there is nothing between her and Mr. Hill."

"Who said there was? I am very sure I never suspected the governor—and more, I am sure I never had such a thought of the lady!"

"Thought of what, Charlie?" said Mrs. Hill, yawning.

"Nay, Kate," said Charlie, laughing, "you look up in my face and tell me there is nothing between——"

"Oh! Charlie, I am really too tired for any more nonsense," said Mrs. Hill, interrupting him; "but dear Mrs. Harcourt says there is no engagement between her and Mr. Hill."

"Humbug! If there is not now, there will be. She knows that; all women are by nature endowed with the gift of—not second sight, but—foresight, widows especially. And this particular Widow Harcourt most plainly foresees that the governor will ask her to have him, although, like a woman and a widow, she cannot help humbugging her own sex! Well, Kate, you must have given the Widow Harcourt all your smiles, for you give me nothing but yawns. But while we are on this subject, it strikes me that Lawsleigh is a highly-favoured place, inasmuch as it contains at this present time three widows! A bad one—we always give precedence to the worst; a good one—good people always come off second best; and a charming one—charming people always attract, and it is their own fault if they do not accept what is placed before them."

"I cannot quite understand her," said. Mrs. Hill.

"The governor can, but she has humbugged you."

"She only denies the fact of any engagement."

"She keeps you in the dark, until it suits her widowship to throw light upon the subject. Oh! Shakspeare! he says, 'Put out the light, and then——'"

XIII

SUNRISE AT LAWSLEIGH

AND the sun arose over the village of Lawsleigh in the same old-fashioned way. Thousands of years had he gilded the tops of the Tors on Dartmoor—thousands of years had he marched on the same untiring round. A famous "mill-horse" is the sun. He is never weary—a steady-going one, too, for he never changes his pace; and if he does sometimes conceal his bright face under a cloud, and thus sadden the hearts of his worshippers, there are also occasions when he rises, as it were, with a halo round his head, and at such times he sheds light, life, and glory upon the hearts of all.

And this was one of those exceptional risings, when he heralded his approach by gorgeous hues, and sent the stars to bed in a pitiless way, almost as if he were jealous of them; for he must see how they shine, and sparkle, and scintillate, and run along the blue arch of heaven—it may be on a visit to each other—and attract the notice of many more eyes than those of the well-known sage,

> Through his star-glass peeping love;

and this knowledge may call forth jealous feelings on the part of His Majesty the Sun.

But on this especial morning he seemed to have some great work to perform; and no doubt there was a loud fanfaron of trumpets heard by the angels as his kingship approached the Tors of Dartmoor, for, as I have said, he came in all his splendour, and the Tors, from the distance at which I had the pleasure of seeing them, might have been supposed to be laughing for joy.

At the Vicarage Mrs. Harcourt opened her eyes just as the sun touched the top of Sharpitor.

"Dear me! the sun has risen," said she, as she sprang out of bed, and threw open the window.

She wrapped herself in a dressing gown, and seated herself to enjoy the spectacle.

The sun came steadily on—if slowly, he seemed to make good his progress; he seemed, too, to be in the humour to make the whole moor look bright and beautiful. No pen can describe the charm of his gradual march forward; but few, if any, pencils depict so wild and magnificent a scene.

Mrs. Harcourt was an admirer of fine scenery, and she gazed upon the splendid view, as it gradually opened to her, with the eye of an artist, and the appreciation of an intellectual mind. Soon all nature began to stir, but Mrs. Harcourt still kept at her post. She saw the "early birds" gathering up the worms; she heard the voice of "proud chanticleer" answering from homestead to homestead, and the distant lowing of the kine coming to be milked; she saw the curling smoke rising up from a cottage here and there, and heard the tread of the labourers going to their work. She watched the bright sun still steadily pursuing his course, and gilding all things that it pleased him to touch, and she smiled. A sunny smile rippled from the corners of her pretty mouth up to her handsome eyes. She pushed away the luxuriant hair that, bursting from its slight confinement, fell over her face, and obscured her vision, and she said to herself,

"I declare the sight of this glittering sun, and this exquisite moor scenery, and the noise of these homely sounds, quite gladden my heart."

She sat apparently enjoying the scene for some time, then, suddenly turning, her eye rested on a table near, upon which lay letters.

"Ah! I remember," said she—"I put the letters in my pocket because I had not time to read them when they were delivered; and really, when I came to bed, I was too tired. I know what they are about—the same eternally wearing subject. One from Sophia, and one from 'dear Carry.' Ah! I did not see this was from Carry, or I am sure I should not have waited so patiently to know what it contained," and she opened the letter.

Mrs. Harcourt seemed to read with much inward satisfaction, until she came near the end; then her countenance changed, and she looked sad. When she had finished, she sighed deeply, and seated herself, leaning her elbow on the table and her head on her hand. The part of the letter that caused this change in Mrs. Harcourt, we will transcribe for the benefit of our readers.

"And so you really are going on a visit to Lawsleigh!—I rejoice at this, it will be a very agreeable change for you. And for me—I have, ever since I knew of your intention, been weaving the most charming romance, building my castles in the air, and saying to myself at least a hundred times a day, 'How thankful I am that my dear friend has so good a chance of—of a good husband, a charming home, and a peaceful, happy life.' I implore you, do not throw away such treasures, do not let the mournful past intrude upon your chance of a pleasant future. But write as soon as—as you can tell me I am a true prophetess, and as much sooner as you please."

After a short time spent in thought, Mrs. Harcourt opened a second letter.

"My dear, darling Mary," so the letter began, "and how do you get on?—I quite expected to have heard from you before this. I long to know how you were received, though I feel sure most warmly. I am very much engaged this morning, but I cannot help telling you how impatient I am to hear from you; and I beg of you, my dear Mary, not to keep me one moment in ignorance of your future happiness, which I cannot but feel sure is already in your own hands. You know I have but one wish—to see you placed once more in a home of your own, and in that position of life to which, both by birth and education, you have a claim.—With much love, I am your fond sister,

SOPHIA."

But we have said as much of Mrs. Harcourt at this time as our space will admit.

Now the worthy vicar of Lawsleigh rested in an apartment looking westward; consequently he did not see the sights that have been described, and he therefore remained asleep for a full hour later. When he awoke, he felt heavy-hearted and unhappy—an unusual feeling with Parson Hill.

"What is the matter" said he to himself. "Ah! I remember—it is all owing to that abominable Exhibition, and taking the villagers from Lawsleigh to London. What business had they there?—Dartmoor born—men, women, and children, careering off to a 'World's Fair!' I always did object, and I am very glad I did. I never could see that any good was to be gained by such people going to such a place. I was right—I am sometimes!"

And then, after a pause, and referring to Mary Cope, he said,

"I am sure I cannot tell how to save the young woman; and what horrible dreams I have had—Isaac and Mary both as drunk as fiddlers; Gray dancing a hornpipe, or Spanish fandango—much the same sort of thing, I suppose—and Mrs. Harcourt looking on, with a pipe in her mouth. One cannot help laughing at the absurdity of dreams! But even that last perversion of the *bienséance's* of life, and of Mrs. Harcourt in particular, must have been conjured up in my distempered brain by Gray's parting blessing;" and after again pausing for a few minutes, he added in an impatient tone, "I *do* really believe that man has no more soul for music than a pig!—and such music!"

Mary Cope opened her eyes when the sun had made good his entrance into her sleeping-room.

"It is a bright morning, I see," said she, drowsily; and then rousing herself, she added, "Why, how I have been sleeping!—goodness me!—but 1 must stir myself. Ah! now that is because I am so happy—so very happy, and so I have almost slept myself away."

Mary forgot that the fatigues and anxieties of the many days previously to her return to Lawsleigh had prevented sleep; and now that her mind was restored to its former contentment, the body would indemnify itself for its past exhaustion, and re-establish its customary energies by a double portion of "Nature's sweet restorer."

While making her toilette, her mind still clung to the events of the past week, and the probabilities of the next day or two. She no longer dreaded to meet the good vicar of Lawsleigh; she relied on his well-known desire to create all the happiness in his power, and she thought with pride on Isaac's promise to refrain from visiting the "Packhorse," and of her own joy in informing the parson of this unexpected resolution on Isaac's part.

Isaac Watson was one of those who saw the sun make his earliest approach to Dartmoor—who saw him on the tops of the Tors, picking out first one, then another, from the darkness, and giving to each a crown of light.

And Isaac Watson arose and went to his shed; so that if, among the sounds Mrs. Harcourt was conscious of hearing, she had also heard the strokes of Isaac's heavy hammer as he occasionally used it, there would not have been much to marvel at.

"I am a changed man," said he as he worked away, "and I pray that I may be strengthened in my wish to throw off all that is disgraceful, and in the future live a more healthful life and be a better Christian. Somehow I feel sadly downhearted. Mr. Gray is not the most kind of parsons; he is so hard upon the past—as if I could undo it," continued he with a little sneer. "I can alter my conduct, I can blot out the bad past by the better present if he will let me, but I cannot have the past thrown at me. Some men seem to think the past never dies nor does it in one sense," added he, mournfully, "but if a man cannot have the hope of becoming a decent member of society, I say it is very discouraging! And it is a marvellous thing that the very best of men give the least encouragement! They seem to take for granted, because one's career has not been perfect, that it can never amend. Ah! well," sighed Isaac, "that is because they themselves were born good; or—no, I mean they must always have led lives of peace and goodness. But if it had ever happened to such men—to have—well, I mean to have been accidentally drunk and disorderly, they would know how ashamed a man feels, and how glad he would be to reform, and how grateful for the notice of good men. Whereas, they do not believe it possible that a man can reform! And this hardness of belief on their part tends to prevent reformation! I am sure of it," added he as he worked the harder. "A man wants hope and the countenance of good men, but these are the very men who keep him down, though they do not know it. No, they mean to do right, and so, more is the pity that it turns out wrong. Here is the good Parson Hill; it is my belief he will not hear a word I have to say; and I am almost out of my wits with the thought that he will not let Mary have me. I know I shall not be able to stand any nonsense. If the parson will only take me and Mary by the hand, and believe that we will never go to the 'Packhorse' again—that is, I mean I will never go—not she, poor thing, God bless her!—then—then I feel I can do anything—anything! I will alter the old house—the dear old Smithy Cottage—I will build a new room out there by the garden, and a bedroom over, and I will——"

But here we leave Isaac to his twinges of remorse for the past, and his small hope of happiness in the future.

XIV

WHAT PARSON HILL SAID
TO MARY COPE

I WENT to the school and received her pupils in the usual manner. She kept up the ordinary routine as if she had not been absent from Lawsleigh one day. She was somewhat surprised, as the morning proceeded, to find she had the work all to herself; neither Parson Hill nor Mr. Gray appeared to assist her. But just at twelve o'clock, as she was in the act of dismissing the last of the children, she saw the vicar within a few paces of the door.

"Good morning, Mary," said he as he entered, "and so you are safe back from London?"

"Yes, sir; thank you, sir," said Mary as she met him with a beaming smile, "I never had such a treat in my life, and I am so much obliged to you."

Whether the parson wanted to put Mary at her ease, or whether he was staving off the disagreeable moment as long as possible, does not much signify. Certain it is, he asked her many questions about her visit to town, drew from her what she had seen, and where she had been. All of which Mary narrated in her customary simple way, but with more joyousness of manner, and with a countenance more intelligently expressive, than he remembered to have seen before.

The fact was, the happiness of Mary's heart shone like a halo over all she said and did; but at length Parson Hill suddenly introduced the subject that had all along been uppermost in his own mind by saying,

"What is all this about you and Isaac Watson?"

Mary blushed a very charming blush, conscious that there was "a something" that gave her a great deal of pleasure, but that somehow or other was difficult of explanation to a third person.

Mary therefore cast down her eyes and remained silent.

"Well, Mary, what *is* all this about you and Isaac Watson?"

Mary heard the change of tone in Mr. Hill's voice as he repeated the question, and her happiness seemed to flee from her in an instant. She turned very pale, and still she did not speak.

"I am told—but mind, Mary," and now the vicar's tones again became kind—"I do not believe it!"

Poor Parson Hill!—he must have forgotten the peal from the church tower of only the preceding evening.

"I do not—I can not think so ill of you. Now, Mary, listen to me. I am told you are going to be married to Isaac Watson—is it true?"

"Yes, sir," said Mary, in a low voice, and not daring to raise her eyes.

"To Isaac Watson the drunkard!" said the Parson, in an angry tone.

"Oh! sir, he is not a drunkard!" said Mary hastily.

"Not a drunkard! Do I hear aright? Is Mary Cope, the schoolmistress of the village of Lawsleigh, able to say with truth—with truth, Mary—that Isaac Watson is not a drunkard!"

And, after a pause of a minute or two, for Mary did not reply, he added,

"Why, you have seen him come reeling down the village street hundreds of times, and you only just escaped having your own brains knocked out by his heavy hammer in one of his drunken fits! And you know if he, and such as he, did not pollute this quiet village with their presence, that the Widow Mason might seek something else to do, for the 'Packhorse' would not pay for its stabling."

Mary now began to wipe away her tears.

"And that reprobate, Isaac Watson, is not a drunkard! What is he, then?—can you tell me that?"

"Oh! sir," said Mary, between her sobs, "he has promised never to go to the 'Packhorse' again."

And feeling that this asseveration must at once disarm the vicar's anger, she ventured to raise her eyes to his.

"Promised!—promised!—and you believe him!"

"Yes, sir—certainly, sir," said Mary, now with some return of her customary calmness; for she did not suppose that even the vicar himself would doubt Isaac's word.

"Why, you foolish young woman, he has only promised that to secure you!"

Mary did not quite understand what Mr. Hill meant, and wisely remained silent.

"I tell you he has made you a promise he has no intention of keeping!"

"Oh! sir, I am sure he will keep his word," said Mary, impressively.

"You seem suddenly to have found a very sturdy opinion of your own," said the vicar, with the authority of one whose counsel had hitherto been undisputed; "this comes of your going to London—I never did approve of it, and, now I see the results, I heartily wish I had never consented to so foolish a freak."

Mary, who thought the going to the Exhibition was as much Parson Hill's doing as Mr. Gray's, was again at a loss to understand his meaning, and remained silent.

"I tell you this drunkard, Isaac, has made you this promise to gain his own ends—to gain his own ends—do you understand me?"

"Why, sir," said Mary, thus forcibly appealed to, "I do not myself see what he has to gain—but perhaps sir, you know better than I—only——"

"You foolish little thing, you do not see what he has to gain!"

"No, sir," said Mary, simply; "to be sure," added she, as if to shew the parson her innermost thoughts, "I have a few bits of furniture, but that is nothing—nothing at all, sir, to compare with what Isaac has got—if not in furniture," said she, as she thought of the poorly furnished Smithy Cottage, or rather, poor according to her preconceived ideas—"in trade, and in houses, and in——"

"Oh—h—h!—so then you are going to marry him for his wealth?"

"For what, sir?" said Mary, meekly

"Why, for his houses, and his lands, his high position in the village, and his—his flattering tongue!"

"No, sir, I never thought about these things."

"Mary! Mary!" said the parson, in a tone of compassion, for he thought she did not speak the truth. "Then why, pray, do you enumerate them to me with such an air of grandeur, if they have never entered into your calculations?"

"Indeed, sir, I beg your pardon," said Mary, modestly, but earnestly, as an expression of pain flitted across her face. "I understood you to say—Isaac had promised me not to go to the "Packhorse," that he might by our marriage gain what I possess; that is, you see, sir, my books and furniture; and so, sir, I wanted to show to you that that could hardly be the case, because he is so much better off than I; but I assure you, sir, I never thought of these things when Isaac first spoke to me."

"Umph! but you seem now to awake to the fact that you will have the best of the bargain if you marry this reprobate!"

Again Mary cast down her eyes, and did not reply—in her "heart of hearts" she had awoke to that fact, and this very conversation with Parson Hill had helped to convince her she had "the best of the bargain," ay and much the best of the bargain! And as Isaac's handsome face and manly form rose unbidden to her mind's eye, her face glowed with the brightness of her hopes, and she remained silent.

"Why, child, if you had nothing in the world, not even your furniture, he would promise to you; this reprobate would *promise* you anything, just to gain you for his own purpose!"

"Would he, sir!" said she, smiling and blushing brightly, but without the most remote idea that the parson meant her to understand Isaac's "promise" would not be kept.

"You silly young woman!" said the vicar, angrily, "cannot you understand—all the man wants is yourself!"

Mary's smile did not fade, and Parson Hill now, losing all patience, added, still more sharply,

"And I almost feel inclined to think, by your looks, that you *would* give yourself to him, and still think you had the best of the bargain!"

A woman has no idea of her own value; at least, in a case of this sort, where she is very young, and has been properly nurtured. Mary turned away. Thought is rapid, and Mary felt in an instant how very much Isaac must love her. Even Parson Hill, who was so clever and knew everything, even he said, "All Isaac wanted was herself!" She had nothing of value to place against his comparative wealth and position. It is true, she had "the school" and a certain rank in the village. But as Isaac's wife, with a home of her own, and Isaac to protect her, how greatly would her circumstances be improved? And what had she to bestow in return?—Clearly nothing. And again she acknowledged to herself "she had much the best of the bargain."

But somehow the knowledge of all this brought the blood into her cheeks, and Mary turned away—turned away to hide her happiness from Parson Hill!

"And so you do then absolute intend to give yourself to this scapegrace, upon his promise not to go to the 'Packhorse'—a *very* credulous young woman, upon my word!"

The parson's tone was now bitter as well as angry, and a slight sort of fear seemed suddenly to invade Mary's happy frame of mind.

"Why, you will not have been married one month," resumed the parson, "no—not a week!— before he will resume his old habits, and treat you, in his drunken fits, as Peter Barker treats his wife Hannah!—And pray what do you think of that, Mistress Cope?"

Mary turned round with a face of horror! The good man was touched by this mute evidence of feeling. He forgot his anger in an instant, and only remembered he came to try to save her.

"Give him up, Mary," said he, in an altered tone; "give him up, he is not worthy of you. I will forget that you have had this foolish fancy; I will protect you from the village gossips—ay, from all the world, Mary; only you see you must give up this bad man."

"Indeed, sir, he is not bad," said Mary, as she stood now pale and trembling in the presence of Parson Hill. "He has not been lately, I should say; I do not mean to deny that he has been wrong many times, and so caused a great deal of anxiety and sorrow to his friends; but then you see, sir, if he gives up the 'Packhorse,' there is nothing else to complain of; and I know he will give it up—I *know* he will!" said she, for she spoke according to her own convictions. But the parson shook his head wearily, and Mary continued:

"And I thought, sir, you would be so glad! Indeed, sir," added she, eagerly, "half my own pleasure was in thinking of your satisfaction and of the good Widow Simpson's happiness."

"Oh, Mary, Mary!" said the parson, as he passed his hand over his brow, "you know you are only talking nonsense—stupid nonsense!"

Mary could not longer restrain her tears; she felt she only spoke the truth, but she felt also that Parson Hill doubted her.

Her tears again softened the parson, in spite of his want of faith in her asseverations, and he said kindly,

"Give him up, Mary. I tell you I will forgive all this. You can rely upon me. You know I will do as I say. I will never reproach you, or allow any other, if you will only break off this very foolish engagement."

Mary did not reply.

"Do you hear me, Mary? I want you to promise me to give up this vagabond, Isaac Watson."

"What, break my promise, sir! I cannot do that!"

"Then you will have to resign the school—and——"

"Resign the school, sir!" said Mary, in much consternation. "Oh, no! no! I hope not, sir."

"But you must do one thing or the other. On one side you have Isaac Watson, his great wealth, and his absurd promise"—and the parson's voice had a sneering tone—"which he will break before you have been married a week, and you will be a wretched woman for life. On the other, you have the school"—here the parson paused as if to give due weight to his words—"my friendship and protection, the support and encouragement of all good people, and the chance of making an honourable marriage in the future! Now, Mary," continued the parson, as he arose to depart, "think the matter over, and remember no one shall ever dare to upbraid you with this temporary act of foolishness. I will protect you. God bless you, Mary!" said he kindly, as he extended his hand, "and help you to form a right resolution, and abide by it, or act up to it. Good morning."

And Parson Hill went away.

XV

OF PARSON HILL'S OPINION
OF MRS. HARCOURT

AND in the evening of this same day Mrs. Hill and Mrs. Harcourt were strolling together in the grounds at the Vicarage. When they reached the entrance gate they stood watching the setting sun.

"He arose so magnificently this morning!" said Mrs. Harcourt "I never saw the moor in such a flood of light, or the scenery to my mind so charming—and now the sun is setting behind that great bank of clouds!"

"But that need not make you sad, dear. I hear, by the tone of your voice, some chord has been struck that has for the time being arrested the flow of your spirits. Of what are you thinking?"

"Of nothing worth mentioning—only his rising so gorgeously on this day and setting so darkly, seem to me like life—which opens amid flowers and song, and companionship and love, and closes in darkness and solitude, loneliness and the grave!"

And then, as a smile broke over her features, she added, in a brighter tone,

"Now I must laugh at my own sentimentality."

"But why do you harbour thoughts of 'loneliness'—you whose future looks so bright!" said Mrs. Hill.

"Surely you are not serious," said Mrs. Harcourt.

"Indeed I am. I have longed to congratulate you upon the—upon—I suppose, though it is scarcely etiquette to make one's congratulations before the engagement is announced?"

"Now what *can* you mean?" said Mrs. Harcourt, as she suddenly stood still and turned to face her friend.

"Has my brusquerie offended you?—pray excuse me," said Mrs. Hill, offering her hand.

"No, no, I am not offended," said Mrs. Harcourt, as she placed her hand in that of her friend. "But I must ask you to explain yourself."

"I congratulate you most heartily on a forthcoming most auspicious event, and I am ready at any minute to kneel and kiss the hand of—the Queen of Dartmoor!"

Mrs. Hill suited her action to her words, and was in the act of kissing her friend's hand, when Mr. Hill and Charlie came suddenly in sight.

The vicar stopped for a second or two, with a look of surprise, raised his hat, and then went on. Charlie turned to his wife, and said,

"I told you so—I told you so—'Queen of Dartmoor.'"

Mrs. Harcourt had turned away, and did not hear this, and Charlie followed the vicar.

"You are making extensive alterations here," said Charlie, coming upon the vicar in a particular part of his grounds, where many shrubs had been lifted, and where several men were at work.

"Ah, yes, Charlie, boy, it is a suggestion of Mrs.——"

But the vicar turned to give some directions to the men, and did not complete the sentence. Some little time elapsed before he again spoke to Charlie, and then he said:

"She has such perfect taste—and besides, I always did think this part of the shrubbery much too crowded."

"That yew is the most graceful tree of its kind I ever remember to have seen," said Charlie, as he stepped back to take a better view.

"The bole is laid open by removing these shrubs. You see the growth has been stopped on this side, and by great good luck the tree has grown marvellously elegant and graceful. By having been so crowded up, we might rather have expected deformity than beauty."

"Perhaps we did not expect either," said Charlie.

"I confess I had not noticed this tree for a long time. Sometimes I—I do neglect my grounds, and thus I feel the more grateful for this kind suggestion."

"Has she ordered it to be cut down?" said Charlie, with a mischievous smile.

The vicar stopped in his directions to his work-men, and turned to Charlie with an air of surprise. After a little pause he finished giving his orders, and joined Charlie, who stood at some little distance from the spot, evidently taking in the points.

"The shrubs have certainly injured the tree," said Charlie.

"That is of no importance, happily," said the vicar.

"No importance? Why, I thought you valued that tree?"

"So I do. But I value it in its present state—in its present position; and I shall value it ten times more when I have finished my present undertaking."

The vicar took from his pocket a small field-glass, and taking Charlie's arm, and retracing his steps to the yew-tree, he placed the glass in Charlie's hand, and asked him to describe what he saw. Charlie looked for a second or two, and then exclaimed, with a start of surprise:

"What! Barstock?"

"Yes. And look to the right."

"Ah! there is Prince's Town, and the Dartmoor Prisons, just nestling down like a large white bird."

Charlie returned the glass, and the vicar again took his arm, and they continued their walk in the shrubberies.

"We were lounging about that part of the grounds soon after she came," said the vicar, "and even at that time she pointed out the fact of the shrubs doing a serious injury to the tree. She has so quick an eye for nature."

"She!" thought Charlie; but he was wisely silent.

"And she also said the removal of the huge shrubs from the thicket opposite the yew would give a charming vista, and lay open Prince Town. And so it has proved. She is generally right."

"We have seen that view thousands of times from the field at the back of the shrubbery," said Charlie.

"True, Charlie, boy; but we never thought of opening that vista, and having the view from the bole of the tree! Women are so—oh! no, not all women; but she is remarkably quicksighted!"

"So quicksighted! or so far-sighted! or perhaps so observing!" said Charlie.

"All three," said the vicar.

After dinner, Parson Hill and Charlie again strolled out into the lawns and shrubberies, enjoying their cigars in the open air. And in due course of time they again came upon the yew-tree.

"Now, Charlie, suppose we seat ourselves," said the vicar.

There were now four elegant chairs, made of galvanised iron wire, placed under the arch formed by the boughs of the yew-tree.

The setting sun lighted up the distant parts of the moor, and the panorama was one of great extent and great beauty. There was still a sufficiency of rarity in the atmosphere to see distinctly the nearer part of the view, but the lengthened shadows added greatly to the charm. Charlie silently enjoyed the scene, puffing away at his cigar.

The vicar silently enjoyed Charlie's satisfaction.

"She was right, you see," said he, at last, quite unconscious that he had not mentioned any name.

"Was she?" said Charlie, with shameful imperturbability.

The vicar took his cigar from his mouth, and looked at Charlie for a second or two without speaking; then resumed his employment, as he said in a very gentle tone,

"I thought you liked her, Charlie boy."

"Did you?" said Charlie. "I cannot answer your 'thought' in a satisfactory manner, for I do not know the 'she' to whom you allude."

"Not know Mrs. Harcourt?" said the vicar.

"Ah—of course I know 'she,'" said Charlie, laughing, "but as you did not mention any name, how was I to single out the particular 'she' to whom you alluded?"

"Perhaps I was thinking of her," said Parson Hill, quietly; "I daresay I was—I often do—I admire her—indeed she is a very charming woman, don't you think so, Charlie?"

"I do," said Charlie.

"Ah, well," and now the parson seemed intent on being communicative, for he spoke with more energy than usual as he added, "she has an eye for nature—a very fine eye for scenery—and she revels in our moorland beauties."

"This is of course the same 'she,'" thought Charlie, but he did not interrupt Parson Hill.

"When she discovered the state of the yew tree, that is, that the branches grew so gracefully—'almost like the train of a peacock'—those were her very words, Charlie!—and in my own memory I have called it the peacock tree ever since—it is such an—such an original idea—she is full of original ideas!"

"Very enjoyable," said Charlie.

"Very," said the vicar heartily; "there is a great charm in originality—and, as you say, Charlie, she is very original."

"*You* said that," thought Charlie, but he did not reply.

"Ah!—I was telling you—she early discovered the state of the tree—she was enthusiastic in her admiration of the elegance and grace of the drooping branches—more like the growth of a cedar than a yew—and then she descanted on the advantage of removing the shrubs. Those that were close to the tree were of no use, and were doing a serious injury—those on the other side of the path only helped to block up a magnificent view. She was right."

The two gentlemen were silent for a minute or two; then the parson resumed—

"A wide expanse of moor, Charlie!"

"Yes, a wide expanse," said Charlie, with a smile, "and a goodly number of Tors."

"To be sure," said the vicar in a pleasant voice; "she is like me in her appreciation of this kind of scenery. I delight in the hoary Tors; in all weathers, in all seasons, at all hours of the day or night, there is a wondrous magnificence about them, that fills the mind not only with a sense of beauty, but with some degree of awe."

Charlie was scarcely prepared for so much enthusiasm on the part of Parson Hill. He arose, and, throwing away the end of his cigar, stepped back to take note of the yew-tree.

"You see, Charlie boy," said the vicar, joining him, "by placing chairs—under the arch made to our very hands—we have a comfortable arbour, and an exquisite view."

"So we have," said Charlie.

"All her own idea, I do assure you,' said the parson.

"Clever," said Charlie.

"Indeed, yes," said the parson, approvingly "You see she is a woman who thinks."

"*And* observes," said Charlie.

"And observes," said the vicar, in a tone of satisfaction "Some women— I may say rather—but few women 'observe' to such a purpose; and how few 'think,' Charlie? Many talk but that is a very different thing. Talk may be all very well, and I may say it is in her for she talks well. But some women do talk such stuff—"

"Perhaps they do," said Charlie, carelessly.

"Perhaps!—nonsense Charlie, we know it. I hear them—and so must you—I hear them, but I let them run on."

"Yes, run on with their 'stuff'—it would be a pity to stop them—we may infer they enjoy it."

"Of course they do: gabble, gabble, gabble. She never does that—I think it such a comfort."

"A very great comfort," said Charlie; "in point of fact, if you were to have a woman who 'gabbled,' you would be tempted to give up the vicarage to her sole use!"

The vicar stopped in his walk, looked steadily at Charlie with his eyebrows raised, and an expression of surprise or astonishment overspreading his features, and then slowly resuming his walk, he said,

"I do not quite see what you mean, Charlie. As my guest, I should certainly allow any lady to 'gabble' as much as she pleased, and I would endure with stoical firmness all the 'gabble' she chose to inflict upon me. But then I would carefully exclude the lady from the list of my guests in the future."

"Who is the lady?"

"Who!—why—I only put a case—"

But we left the two ladies on the lawn.

They had walked to a terrace that overlooked the road which skirted the vicarage grounds.

"How do you do, Isaac?" said Mrs. Hill.

Isaac raised his cap as he replied to Mrs. Hill's salutation, and, after a few kind words from the ladies, continued his walk.

"He is going to see the pretty schoolmistress," said Mrs. Harcourt.

"Parson Hill thinks she will give him up," said Mrs. Hill.

"Will she?" said Mrs. Harcourt, in a defiant tone. "He will not make me agree with him."

"I fear he takes a wrong view of the case."

"They are sure, Isaac and she, to be constant and true," said Mrs. Harcourt, laughing, "because people make such a fuss about them. The having had their wooing so unceremoniously abridged is enough to anger them both against all the world, and give them wonderfully good opinions of each other; and, besides all this, he is a handsome specimen of a well-to-do villager, and she is the simplest-minded and at the same time the most intellectual-looking young woman of her class that I have seen for many a long year. Oh! trust me, and my foresight, they will make a match of it, and I for one say 'God's benison be on them!'"

"You forget he is a great smoker, and such a dreadful drunkard!"

"Curiously enough, in spite of all I have heard, I do not credit that!"

"You amuse me so," said Mrs. Hill, "you never believe anything against a favourite."

"I never saw the man till now, so he cannot well be a favourite; but his manner and appearance are marvellously in his favour. He looks one full in the face when he speaks, sign of a steadfast mind. If he makes a promise, he will keep it. Such is my opinion of Isaac Watson!"

"Ah, you always take the part of those who are in trouble. But I am afraid he is a thoroughly unstable man, and if not absolutely unprincipled, at least one whose well-known propensity causes much unhappiness to his friends. Even Charlie shakes his head when I venture to hope for the best!"

"Man is rarely charitable to his fellow man, but love is a great purifier; his evil courses may be amended by his love for a pure, innocent-hearted woman, and see—he has stopped at the School Cottage," said Mrs. Harcourt.

XVI

MARY COPE'S VERSION TO ISAAC WATSON OF PARSON HILL'S CONVERSATION WITH HER

AND now we will follow Isaac Watson, who walked on at a moderate pace, rather as if he were eschewing some great thought than going to see his sweetheart.

Isaac's mind was full of the future, and of what he hoped to make that future. In the morning, when the sun rose, he had been desponding, the memory of his past life came before him in vivid hues, and although he had been made joyous on the announcement of his engagement both by the congratulations of friends and the presence of Mary Cope, his conscience did not always sleep, and on this particular morning it had been particularly troublesome.

Isaac worked hard all day, and during his work he listened to the flow of his grandmother's happiness; so that it seemed as if the bodily exercise to which he himself was subjected, and the garrulity of the Widow Simpson combined, gradually put to flight his sombre thoughts, and as evening drew near his spirits rose, and his expectation of seeing Mary Cope brought the smile to his lip once more. As he had been very desponding, so now in this reaction he felt very glad. He pictured Mary's welcoming smile, her joyous laugh, her charming simplicity, and her pretty surprise when he should produce another present he had brought from London—even a duet for soprano and bass—no other than Jackson's—of Exeter—"Love in thine Eyes," which, with several others of a like kind, he had picked up at old music stalls in his many walks about town.

He slackened his pace and trod with a lighter step as he approached Mary's cottage; these were not demonstrations of Isaac's well-known shyness; he was no longer to be called "shy," but he was very tender and gentle even in his thoughts of Mary, and he would not startle her by too hasty or too loud an approach if he could help it. As Mrs. Harcourt had said, "love is a great purifier," and it has a marvellous power in awakening dormant faculties. Isaac had always been unselfish and kind-hearted from nature and habit, now he was more—he was heroic; he would not advance his own joy one hair's breadth by a moment of uneasiness to Mary. He valued her composed and self-reliant manner, and he inwardly vowed that no act of his should ever disturb her serenity or embitter her peace. And Isaac repressed the joyous bounding of his heart and kept his steps in check, so that at length he knocked at Mary's door so gently, that, if she had not been watching for him, he must have knocked again ere he had been admitted.

Mary did not attempt to hide the joy she felt when she opened the door; and we are bound to add that the meeting was in all respects such as two lovers might reasonably expect and feel fully satisfied with—Isaac, that he had enjoyed his privilege; and Mary, that, in spite of her coyness, she was nothing loth. But such meetings do not absorb any great length of time, and the two were soon seated side by side, Mary's hand still retained by Isaac.

"I cannot tell you how glad I am you are come," said Mary, as she raised her eyes to Isaac, who fondly pressed her hand, but did not interrupt her speech.

In the first place, he liked to look at Mary and listen to her sweet voice; and in the second, he had quite enough to do to keep his throbbing heart in order, that seemed by the bounds it made at its own gladness as if it would "cry aloud" in its happiness, for he knew by instinct it would "tremble on his tongue," and so, as I have said, he simply pressed her hand, and remained silent.

"I wanted you so much, Isaac," and now Mary's tones became a little sad, "for Parson Hill has spoken to me."

Isaac was aroused from his quiet dream in an instant; he clutched the hand he held firmly, and with the other round her waist drew her nearer to him as he anxiously said,

"The parson has spoken to you!—he is a good and a kind man, Mary."

"Yes," said Mary, turning away her head, "he was kind this morning—"

Isaac did not like the appearance of things. He felt there must be something unpleasant to come, or Mary would not hesitate; but even this suspense, for the moment, seemed better than some dreadful reality and Isaac made no effort to encourage Mary's communication.

"I don't quite know how to tell you all that he said, Isaac, and yet I suppose I ought."

"You know best, Mary," said he, in a low voice; "it concerns me, I suppose?"

"Yes is, it concerns *us*," said Mary, blushing.

"He says he will not let you have me?—is that it?" said Isaac, in a voice that he intended to repress into tones of gentleness, but which strangely blurted out the words with a kind of spasmodic force.

"Oh, no!" said Mary, looking up brightly, and now speaking joyously, "indeed he said no such thing," for she felt that even Parson Hill had no power to prevent her marrying whom she pleased.

With a loud sigh of relief, Isaac once more pressed the little hand that he had never relinquished, and tightened his grasp on Mary as he said, in loud cheery tones,

"Thank God!—thank God! my dear Mary, I can bear anything else with comparative patience."

Mary looked with astonishment on Isaac's emotion, and then, as she met his eye, suddenly felt a strange bashfulness creep over her, which for the moment paralyzed her thoughts and the expression of them.

"I can bear anything else, Mary—anything but the loss of you," said he, fondly; "and perhaps I can advise you—can I?"

"Perhaps you can," said Mary, as soon as she found her tongue; "and so I had better try to tell you all that was said."

Mary seemed to have overcome that little bit of sadness that evidently came uncalled for at the recollection of Parson Hill. There was a something very satisfactory in Isaac's presence, and Mary now spoke in a confiding and straightforward manner, that completely put Isaac at his ease; and so, in this comfortable mood on both sides, Mary began her tale.

"I told the parson you had promised never to go to the 'Packhorse,'" said she, proudly.

Isaac only bowed his head and smiled.

"You see, he asked if it was true—I mean about you and me," said Mary, blushing.

Isaac pressed her hand, but did not speak.

"But he thinks you will not keep your word."

"What!—about that 'Packhorse?'" said Isaac, with scorn.

"Yes."

Mary did not like to proceed with her story; and Isaac remained silent. For the space of half a minute there was a little air of dissatisfaction visible on both faces. At length Mary resumed,

"I told him you would keep your promise—I knew you would."

No one who had seen Mary then, or heard the tone of her voice, could have doubted her perfect belief in her asseveration; though, if she had been asked upon what she rested it, it would have been found simply on Isaac's word.

"Did that content the parson?" asked Isaac, despondingly.

"No," said Mary, shaking her head; "he said

I had got a will of my own," and she raised her eyes, as if she would read what Isaac thought of so much temerity.

But as Mary did not explain what this will of her own had to do with the parson's want of faith, Isaac simply said, "Did he?" and then, as Mary hesitated, he asked, "What makes the parson think I will not keep my word?—why should I promise voluntarily if I wish to break my promise?"

"Why, he says you only do it 'to gain your own ends,'" said Mary, innocently.

But innocently though she spoke, she was greatly surprised at the effect of her words. Isaac's whole face became a burning red up to the very roots of his hair.

"The dastardly liar!" said he, impetuously; and he dropped the little hand he had so long retained, and clenched his fist.

"Isaac!" said Mary, staring at him with wide open eyes.

"Oh! I beg your pardon, my dear, but I could not bear to hear such things said to you," said Isaac, apologetically.

"No, they were not pleasant; and I told him it was not true," said Mary, so simply and guilelessly as to turn away Isaac's anger, and cause him to laugh a hearty laugh. Then he seized hold of Mary, and indemnified himself for the parson's speech by a slight caress, again keeping one arm round her waist, and with the other retaining her hand. "There, now you are pleased again. I am glad of that, because, though I tried hard to convince the parson you had nothing to gain, he did not believe me."

"Did not he?" said Isaac, again laughing, and pressing Mary tightly to him; for now it was his turn to feel he had *everything* to gain.

"I do not much wonder at the parson's unbelief," thought he, as he inwardly chuckled over the mightiness of his prize; and if his satisfaction was visible in his face, he took care not to commit himself by a single word.

"Why, I told him I was quite ashamed, when I thought about things, which of course I did not at first, for then I was only thinking of you," said she, blushing; "but when I did begin to think, I knew I had only my little bit of furniture, which of course is not worth any man trying to gain," and now Mary laughed at the ridiculousness of the supposition.

"Did he say anything more?" said Isaac.

"He said I was going to have you for your wealth and position—he did, Isaac. But though I told him he was wrong, I saw he did not believe me. But, Isaac, I hope you do?—for I never even thought about anything you had, until the parson said you wanted me for what you could get, and that set me off thinking."

"To be sure, and very naturally," said Isaac with a smile. "And we will not care much for the parson's unbelief, while we can so truly rely on each other."

"But I wish he would believe us," said Mary.

"So do I," said Isaac. "And we must contrive to convince him that we both say what we mean, and that we both mean well."

Mary's face became so beaming and joyous at this turn in the conversation, that Isaac forgot to be angry with the vicar, and they remained for a short time silent.

XVII

IN WHICH ISAAC WATSON TAKES HIMSELF OFF, AND LEAVES MARY COPE TO DO AS SHE PLEASES

"And so the vicar thinks I want to get your nice furniture, does he?" said Isaac looking round contentedly. "Why, Mary, there is no denying that I always did admire it very much; but then I admire you more!"

"Oh! and that is just what Parson Hill said at last."

"That I admire you, and value you much more than I either admire or value your furniture! Very true, Mary, so I do. I hope that pleased him?"

"No. He seemed more angry than ever. I cannot tell why," said Mary, artlessly, replying to Isaac's look of inquiry, and then resuming: "But he said I seemed to think I had the best of the bargain; and indeed I never thought about it."

"Of course not," said Isaac, kindly.

"And you—why if I had nothing in the world, not even my furniture, *you* would promise—promise me anything just to gain your own ends."

Isaac sprang from the sofa as he clenched his fists, and almost shouted,

"The dastardly parson! It is a lie! I say it is a lie!"

Mary's astonishment exhibited itself by suddenly rising and clasping her hands entreatingly together.

"Isaac!—Isaac!" said she, and yet she did not venture to go near him. "Isaac, what makes you so angry?"

Isaac neither saw nor heard her; he paced up and down the small apartment with hasty strides, heaping epithets of reproach on Parson Hill.

This continued for a minute or two. At first it was quite incomprehensible to Mary, and as she stood there silent and unnoticed, she could not restrain a loud outburst of emotion.

At this moment she arrested Isaac's attention, and he was at once recalled to himself. With all his tender gentleness returned, he took her by the arm, weeping as she was, for she did not remove her kerchief from her face, and once more placed her by his side on the sofa.

"Mary, dear Mary, I am ashamed of myself," said Isaac.

And we may say of him, if he was impulsive and unrestrained under anger, he was always ready to express his contrition, for this was the second time in this short conversation that he had used the same words.

Mary heard, but did not comprehend him, and, after a short silence, Isaac added,

"But now, Mary dear, did the parson say anything more?"

Mary had suffered so much by repeating the conversation between Parson Hill and herself, that she felt a very justifiable reluctance to say more at this time. But upon Isaac making it clear to her it had now become a necessity that he should be told all, Mary finished her communications by acknowledging that, though Parson Hill had not taken the matter in his own hands, or hinted that he would not permit her to marry Isaac, he had advised her to "give him up." He had placed before her in a strong light the advantage of retaining himself for a friend, the schoolmistress-ship of Lawsleigh, her present position in the village, and—Mary did not say a superior marriage, as Mr. Hill had said—but an honourable future; while, on the other hand, he had painted as strongly that she had only Isaac's word for the change he averred had taken place; and that the probabilities were more in favour of his return to his former habits after marriage than otherwise; for that the habit of inebriety was rarely, if ever, conquered!

She did not even fail to allow to Isaac that when she thought of his near neighbour, Peter, and his treatment of his poor wife, her courage sometimes failed her. She could not, at all times, keep off feelings of despondency; and though, with charming simplicity, she said, almost in the same breath, "that she never *could* believe Isaac would do such things," nevertheless, it was clear to him that the parson had jarred the strings of Mary's happy reliance on his future good conduct, and awakened, at times, doubt in her mind as to the propriety of placing herself in his power.

We ought to have said before this that, during the pauses of the conversation, Isaac's conscience not unfrequently recalled to view his past ill-spent life, and strongly placed it in juxtaposition with the well-known purity and quietness of Mary's. He felt that, though he would be everything to her that the heart of woman could desire, she might not unreasonably have strong doubts of his future career and not only doubt herself but allow those doubts to become certainties by the support they had in the opinion of others.

These thoughts, recurring as they did at every trip and turn of the conversation as Mary's simplicity and gentleness unfolded themselves to him, at length gained so much strength as to make him feel almost ashamed of taking advantage of his present position with her. He had felt all along that, if Parson Hill had advised Mary to make him—Isaac—prove that he was reclaimed before he married her, he would cheerfully have abided by the parson's decision and manfully have borne— with outward patience, at least—the check that would thus have been placed on his own wishes. If Parson Hill would take him by the hand, and give him a trial, Isaac felt equal to the emergency. But if, on the contrary, Parson Hill should exert his power to prevent Mary exercising her own free will, then he felt that bitter and angry thoughts or deeds would arouse him to defend himself, and rescue her from the parson's control.

Isaac would rise against oppression, but he gave way when he met with freedom of action, generosity of spirit, and kindness of heart. And so, when he at length found that, though Parson Hill had strongly advised Mary "to give him up," he had yet left her free to act as she pleased, and had even allowed her time to think over the circumstances of the case, so as to be enabled to decide equally free from a too strongly-exerted power on the part of the parson, or a too easy-yielding to the dictates of her own heart, Isaac's better nature came into play. He felt consoled that so good a man as Mr. Hill had thought it right that Mary should judge for herself in a matter that would be to her of vital importance for the rest of her life.

And now it was that Isaac felt the power of his position at this moment with Mary Cope. He looked at her, and instinctively as it were, felt that she would credit all he said, and that he could prevail upon her to have him in spite of Parson Hill's advice or the example of Peter Barker's conduct to Hannah. But, as we have said before, Isaac respected and esteemed Mary Cope as much as he loved her and he magnanimously said to himself:

"As the parson has done, so will I do. Mary shall have time to think over her position. I will never have it on my conscience that I have persuaded her to have me, and thereby caused her to lose, as I now very clearly see she must, the post of schoolmistress and the notice and protection of Parson Hill."

And having thus, by slow degrees, eventually arrived at this decision, he turned to Mary and said:

"The parson is right, Mary."

Mary only looked at Isaac, for she had no clue to his thoughts.

"The parson is right, you see," said Isaac, now manfully preparing for victory over himself. "You see he has left you free to think over your position—to choose, as it were, for the rest of your life the one or the other. It is clear, if you keep your word to me, you will lose both the school and the parson. And so, Mary, it is right you should have time to think, so as—so as to choose wisely, or—or, at least, by acting for yourself give no occasion for blame to anyone else in the matter."

"It would indeed be very hard to give up the school, Isaac," said Mary, for she did not understand all he meant to convey. "But do you think the parson would really take it away from me? Why, there is no one here who could attend to it! And he has always been so kind, I cannot quite feel that he would never speak to me, or come to see me. And, besides, Isaac, when you keep your promise so well, and when he sees it!"

"That is in the future," said Isaac, solemnly, "and you have to do with the present."

"Yes, it is in the future, of course; but you said, when we began to talk, that perhaps you could advise me—do so now, Isaac—tell me, what shall I do?"

There was such simplicity in Mary's manner, and such perfect openness in the expression of her countenance, Isaac saw at once she did not comprehend her choice lay between the school and himself. She seemed rather to infer from Parson Hill's well-known kindness, as well as from the difficulty there would be in finding another mistress, that she might marry Isaac and still retain the school. And so she did not foresee that Isaac was the last person to whom she should apply in such an emergency. The strong love he had for her, and her utter absence of suspicion at the power she thus placed in his hands, made him ready to advise her on the instant to accept him, and set the world at defiance.

But Isaac would not have been the generous-hearted man we have attempted to portray if he had given way to the unworthy thought. Once more he rose to meet the occasion, and said,

"This is just the only thing that I cannot advise about." Isaac paused, and Mary looked serious. "You see, I am pointed out to you as a bad man, and——"

"Oh! Isaac," said Mary, interrupting him. "Why, I should never believe that you were bad, even if you told me so yourself!"

Isaac was gradually acquiring some little knowledge of the devotion and self-sacrifice of women when they love. He would not have been a lover if he had not rejoiced in the faith Mary had in his promises, evinced by that impulsive outburst; but he knew he must not take advantage of it.

"No, Mary. It is a great satisfaction and happiness to me to know at least that you do believe me."

Isaac's emotion made him pause, the better to hide it; and Mary said wonderingly,

"Of course I believe you."

"But you should remember, for your own sake, that, sometimes people do not keep their promises, though——"

"And you, Isaac, to say such a thing!" said Mary, starting up in dismay; "and you would not keep your promise!"

"I did not say that," said Isaac, in a low voice; but he made no effort to replace Mary by his side. "It is due to myself to say I mean to keep my word, so help me God!" said Isaac, solemnly. "But Mary, the parson means you to understand that perhaps I shall not; and you ought to take time to think over what he has said to you—he is a good man, Mary, and means well; and then, Mary," said Isaac, his courage rising with his desire to be just with Mary, and to allow her time to be just to herself, "you ought to think how miserable and wretched you would be; for marriage is 'for better, for worse,' and in some cases it turns out all worse and no better—miserable, I mean, if I did not keep my word."

Mary was silent, from the intensity of her astonishment and dismay.

"And so," continued Isaac, as he rose to go, "the parson is right; you ought to think well over the matter, and choose between the two."

After a little pause, he added,

"I feel, Mary, very like one whose life is blighted by his own actions, and as I cannot in conscience say a good word for myself, except that I mean to keep my word, why, you see, Mary, you will have to decide for yourself whether you will accept the bad man and his promise to amend, or whether you will hold by the school and the parson."

Poor Isaac!—he spoke bitterly—he had not foreseen he should be so relentless to himself, or that the circumstances would require it. Mary could not understand him. He extended his hand as he uttered a very gentle,

"Good-bye, Mary."

But she was weeping, and trying to hide her emotion by covering her face with her hands.

Isaac turned to go, and once more said, "Good-bye, Mary."

He stood a second or two stroking his cap round and round; but Mary did not speak. And when at length she had courage to look at him, he was lifting the latch of the door, and leaving her thus alone and unsupported to decide on the most important event of her life.

Isaac's courage almost forsook him as he witnessed her mute despair. He knew she had but two friends in the whole world, and they had both turned aside in this her great extremity, and left her to decide for herself.

Parson Hill had thought it right that Mary should judge for herself. Isaac Watson thought the same. When he stepped forth and closed the door behind him, he knew he had done right. And though he felt sad-hearted and unhappy, he also felt a comfort in looking back upon his own magnanimity.

XVIII

WHICH TREATS OF THE DEEDS
OF PETER BARKER

It was just at this time that the village of Lawsleigh was awakened from its customary quiet, and steady flowing on in the even tenor of its way, by an event that struck horror into the simple minds of its inhabitants.

Peter Barker had returned from one of his visits to the "Packhorse" in his habitual state of intoxication and, as we may say, to the credit of the moor people generally, they were gradually inclining themselves to better things than wasting their time by smoking and drinking at the "Packhorse," so Peter Barker's conduct, as it was always more brutal under excitement than that of others who committed themselves, in a like way, was also more execrated by lookers-on.

On this occasion the man had made himself obnoxious to the women as he passed their cottages by applying disagreeable epithets to each, as they attended to the tiny round of their accustomed duties inside and out of their homes.

One woman was cleaning her windows, and throwing water upon the panes. Peter made an unbecoming remark, and the woman dashed a large basin of water in his face. Other instances, as he continued to walk through the village, occurred of women resenting in a fierce way some dastardly or disgusting speech made by him as he passed. And each time that Peter received the reward of his own behaviour, he grew more and more angry, and more and more intent upon wreaking his vengeance on some one.

He was pursued to his own door by several women, each armed with something to protect herself or her friends from his *grossièreté* and all talking loudly. The Widow Simpson was startled by the noise, and one of the women went to tell her of Peter's unseemly coarseness as he passed their doors. When Peter at length entered his home, the women pushed against his door, and would not let him close it. They knew instinctively that Hannah would be his victim, and they courageously followed him home with a view to protect her from his fury. Because, though Peter was the aggressor, it was plain that they had greatly augmented his naturally vile temper by their reprisals; and they knew also, from well-known experience, that until he had slept off his inebriety, and was thus partially restored to a right mind, he would not fail of having his revenge upon any unprotected person; but more than all others, this vindictive temper would expend itself on his wife.

"Hannah, poor thing, her be not there," said the Widow Simpson.

The women were glad to hear she was absent, and inquired if the old woman knew where she was to be found, because these kind-hearted creatures would take care to let her know in what state her husband was, and thus prevent any collision between them, or brutal treatment of Hannah by Peter, if possible.

"She be to the Vickridge," said the widow. "There be company, and Hannah have a-give she's help."

"Then, widdy, her won't be back afore the night?"

"No, no; Hannah be a deft-handed creature, and maybe her won't come back afore the ten or the eleven o'clock."

"Then us will leave Peter to hisself, and let him pull down the cottage in his surliness."

And after a little more talk, and a certainty that Peter had sought some place of rest, which they, poor things, concluded was his bed, the women returned to their own homes.

This took place on the very night Isaac had his interview with Mary Cope. The Widow Simpson told him on his return home all she knew; and Isaac's contemplation of his own position was none the brighter for the knowledge of Peter's state. He foresaw that, unless Mary and he were actually married, every occurrence of this sort would lessen his chance of so desirable an event ever taking place. He felt very keenly that, as he had to a certain extent been Peter's companion in many a debauch at the "Packhorse," so now Peter's deeds in all their vileness would also to a certain extent cast a shadow over himself. He recalled the old proverb, "You cannot touch pitch without defiling your fingers," and with a heavy sigh he acknowledged that the past years of his life had been deeply sullied by fits of intemperance, that had left a stain upon his name and character hard to remove, and that had also made indelible impressions on the minds of lookers-on, which no after-conduct could erase.

"I must bear it," said he to himself, as he tried to hide these upbraiding thoughts from the widow, and to appear cheerful in her presence. He lighted his pipe, and took his accustomed corner in the cottage; while the widow went to and fro as she attended to her home duties, and with the loquaciousness of age, congratulated herself and Isaac on his engagement with Mary Cope.

And so passed the evening at the Widow Simpson's cottage; while poor Mary Cope, almost beside herself at the strange and unexpected position in which she found herself so suddenly placed, at length retired to rest, more restless than ever. She hoped she should forget her troubles in sleep, but no such thing happened. Mary passed a wakeful night, tossing from this side to that, without making up her mind to anything.

"I cannot think what Isaac could mean," she repeated to herself, over and over again. "How am I to judge more than I have done?—I thought Isaac loved me—I did so believe all he said. And I thought he meant what he said about never going to that 'Packhorse' again; and now he actually tells me people sometimes break their promises; as if I ever thought of such a thing as that he would break his promise. Oh! Isaac, Isaac! And he even said again he meant to keep his promise. Then why does he leave me to choose?—and why cannot he advise me?—next to Parson Hill himself I am sure I should take Isaac's advice."

And then Mary recollected the substance of Parson Hill's advice, and she felt she did not wish to follow that, and then she turned again to Isaac in her thoughts, and said,

"If Isaac had advised me to have him, why, of course I should, because I should feel so sure he would tell me for the best; and then—why, then, all my trouble would be over, and I should be so happy, for I know what it is to be happy with Isaac Watson by my side!"

Poor Mary! She had yet to learn what was meant by trouble, for her life had been comparatively free from such a burden.

But the morning came at last. The little birds began their "tweet, tweet," the sun came slowly up from his rest, sounds of a stirring world broke upon the air, succeeded by the loud rumble of waggons rolling along, and the hoarse voices of the drivers rising above the sound.

"But," said Mary Cope, as she at length attempted to rise, "I did not hear Peter's voice—it is the most harsh and disagreeable of them all," and she went and opened the casement, and, looking out, continued her remarks, "He is not there; John Pike, and Abraham, and Joe Gadge I can see, but no Peter Barker. Now, that is odd; for though the man is so bad, and does drink so much cider, I never knew the waggons go to the quarries without him." And Mary began to make her morning toilette.

At the school Mary expected to meet Parson Hill. She went in fear and trembling. And Parson Hill had intended to see Mary, but another proverb now illustrates the position of Mary Cope and the vicar. "L'homme propose, mais Dieu dispose." And the parson did not go to the school. Mary feared to meet Parson Hill's eye, or to listen to a word he had to say; but she knew she must go through such an ordeal, and yet she had not in her own mind determined how to answer the queries she knew she might expect from him.

Mary's mind was so full of her own trouble she did not observe how few of the village children made their appearance that morning.

She went on mechanically with her round of duties, just attending to the present moment with her eyes and fingers from habit, and allowing her mind to absent itself in Isaac Watson's favour; still marvelling at the strange turn events had taken in their interview the night previously, and scarcely daring to look into the future for a satisfactory end to all these changes.

And the morning was more than half over, and Mary continued most disconsolately to perform her duties, until her attention was arrested by the sound of many voices approaching the school. In a second or two the door was opened, and there seemed to Mary to be a very uproarious Babel of voices, one of which said,

"Her was to the Vickridge till eleven. And, Mistress Cope, here you be a-sitting so awful still, as it sim to I, and so white like"—as the paleness of Mary's face attracted her attention—"just the same, to my mind, as if nobody wasna a-killed—that be *murdered*, I means!"

"Murdered!" said Mary, shrinking back with a face of horror. "Murdered, did you say? Who is murdered?"

By this time the schoolroom—usually so sacred a place from the intrusion of village gossips—was filled with Mary's absent scholars and their mothers, women of all ages; and one of whom, standing near to Mary, replied in harsh, unfeminine tones—

"Why, poor Hannah Barker. Peter has a-knocked she's brains out! Her be found laying with she's head again the bed postesses!—and pools and pools of blood! My! I say that comes of having a drunken husband! My!"

And the woman stared at Mary, and came so close to her, while she flourished her arms about in her excitement that Mary had no difficulty in recognising the virago face of Jane Sands, neither did this woman's presence tend to soften the news she brought.

And now Mary knew why she had not seen Parson Hill; for amidst the confused hubbub that followed, and the disturbance of all order in the school, Mary ascertained that as Peter did not make his appearance to join the waggoners going off to the quarry, one went to his cottage, as he had often done, for the purpose of arousing him. The man had no difficulty entering, for the door was unfastened, and even the window-shutter not closed; and after calling many times without getting a response, he went upstairs, where, to his horror and amazement, he saw the lifeless corpse of Hannah Barker extended on the floor.

The poor woman, from the appearance of her attire, seemed to have met her fate immediately on her return home. She had not attempted to disrobe, more than to take off her bonnet and shawl, which lay on a table near.

In the bed lay Peter, with his face turned to the wall, as if to avoid the sight of the ghastly object so near to him; his heavy carter's whip was by his side. The man called to him, but he spoke not, though he did not attempt to hide that he was awake. When questioned as to who had committed so awful a crime, he invariably replied he did not know.

He did not attempt to escape. When the proper authorities were at length aroused to a sense of the duties they were called upon to fulfil, and he was told he must submit himself to the power of the law, he submitted at once, only protesting his innocence. When the strange proximity of the whip was pointed out to him, and the clotted blood and locks of hair on the butt end shewn to him, he said he knew nothing about it.

The women who had followed him to his home reminded him of his surliness and *grossièreté* to them, but he denied even this. And if, therefore, his own word went for anything, there could be no doubt but that Peter was innocent of all the evil of which he was accused.

These are some few of the things that are so appalling in the life of a drunkard. During his inebriety he is to a certain extent unconscious of his words and actions. A drunkard walks through the world, for the time being, indifferent to his immorality and profaneness. He knows he has been drunk by the presence of certain racking headaches, and other uncomfortable sensations. This is all he knows. He even has the temerity to think himself hardly used when he is told he did this and that, and, in all probability, denies the fact.

And, as a rule, the man is not molested; people know he has been drunk, that he has shocked the moral and orderly class of society by his language and appearance; but they know also that during his state of inebriety he has not been accountable for his words and actions, and they leave him alone, as one too bad to mend.

But when, as in Peter's case, some great crime has been committed, and the law is compelled to step in and take its course, then the minds of lookers-on are for the time being awakened to the dreadful evils of drunkenness, and the consequent sins. Then they see this particular vice in all its naked enormity. For the time being they think it the worst of evils, and for a certain period they try to arrest its course. They are severe with offenders; they administer punishment, as far as the law allows; and, in their horror at the enormity of the crime it has produced, see no chastisement sufficiently severe, and allow of no toleration to one who is known to be a drunkard.

And thus Isaac Watson had not overrated the consequences to himself of Peter's drunkenness. Before he was made aware that any crime had been the result of this state of inebriety, he had convinced himself that, let Mary's decision be as it might, the judgment of all would be against him. Few, he knew, would give him credit for a desire to reform; fewer still would approve of his marriage with Mary Cope.

Parson Hill had already shown, by his advice to Mary, what he thought of Isaac's promises; and though Isaac, in his heart, acknowledged the justice of the parson's opinion—for had he not often promised to himself to reform, and had he not always broken his promise?—yet he felt both angry and ashamed of the fact.

And then, again, Isaac had always been on such good terms with the parson; must that, too, cease?—must he lose everything? He felt that even the village of Lawsleigh, that he loved so well, would be dreary enough to him without a kind word from the parson. How could he go to the belfry, if he were not friendly with the parson? How could he lead the choir without the parson's approving look? How lead the game at fives, played against the church tower in sight of the vicar as he strolled on his own lawn, and who, accustomed now and then to join the players, and throw a ball with the best, would now turn his back and avoid them, because Isaac was there? How win a cricket match without the parson on his side to bowl?—for his bowling was worth that of three men.

These things seemed heavy enough to Isaac to bear, and he, like Mary, lay moodily awake; and wondering when the sun would rise again, and light up the world.

But as the night waned, and the morning dawned, Isaac fell into a doze, from which he was rudely aroused by an unusual clamour in the cottage below, as of many voices all talking together.

"What can be the matter?" said he, as he sprang out of bed. In a short time he was able to leave his room, and on descending and entering his shed, the concourse of people assembled, and the noise and bustle of the crowd, told that some very unusual event had occurred.

When Isaac learned the truth—that Peter Barker had actually committed murder in his fit of drunkenness—he felt, in addition to the horror with which such a crime inspired him, that his own fate was sealed.

He felt that now Mary Cope was lost to him for ever! Peter's sin somehow seemed to shadow very darkly over him. He shuddered as he remembered it was only by a mere accident—and even then he injured another person, and one now very dear to him—that he, too, had not committed a like crime; and though at the period to which Isaac alluded he knew he had been sober, yet to commit murder, whether in a fit of passion or during a fit of intoxication, would still leave the crime the same. In his despondency he even fancied he saw the neighbours pointing at him, and prognosticating that "sorrows never come single;" and that, as one murder had been committed, another might soon follow; for what was Isaac Watson but a drunkard?

"Conscience," we are told, "makes cowards of us all." But this is only true of the guilty. Isaac's conscience, at this period of his life, did not leave him many happy moments. And though he knew and confessed himself to be guilty in the matter of too much cider, he silently registered a vow that he would never lower himself again through the effects of any stimulating drink. Conscience in this instance, made Isaac brave; brave to bear the jeers of his boon companions; brave to meet the eye of the parson, until he had, by his good conduct won him back for a friend; brave, even to lose Mary Cope, for a time, until he could convince her of his reformation.

XIX

WHY PARSON HILL'S CARRIAGE WAS NOT OVERTURNED

As will readily be understood, the whole village of Lawsleigh was thrown into great consternation by the sad event of Hannah's death. The unfortunate man, her husband, was taken before Parson Hill, who was the nearest magistrate, and who, to use his own words, never felt the duties of office so great a burden.

On one side here was a man past the prime of life, known to have lived in debauchery and low habits, known to have been merciless to his wife, and habitually quarrelsome even with his boon companions, placed at the stern bar of justice, to render an account of his deeds; a man whom Parson Hill had known for the better half of his life, whom he had often tried to conciliate with kind words, and to soften and humanise by little unexpected kindnesses; a man, reckless, it is true, and dissipated, but yet a man with a soul to save—a man in all respects in the eyes of his Maker, equal with all others, or rather standing an equal chance with all others for the proffered mercies of the Saviour; and as such, the good parson's efforts, as a clergyman to save him from the consequences of his wickedness had been many and great.

But, on the other side, as a magistrate seated in judgment over the events narrated to him, he could but act by the laws of the land he had sworn to administer; and much as the clashing duties of the priest and the judge jarred against each other, he knew that, for the time being, the latter must be paramount. He therefore committed Peter for trial at the next assizes on a charge of manslaughter!

None were surprised when they heard, almost immediately after Peter was sent away, that Parson Hill was suffering from severe headaches, and that he had other symptoms of indisposition. Mr. Gray intreated him to try a change of air. Mr. and Mrs. Charles Hill begged him to go with them to Paul Tavey. And at length the whole party at the Vicarage—for Mrs. Harcourt went also—took their departure. And once again the parish was left entirely in the hands of Mr. Gray.

In a few instances a change for the better took place in some of the most disreputable of the inhabitants of Lawsleigh after the committal of Peter. Parson Hill, from the bench, had spoken in strong terms of the demoralizing brawls at the "Packhorse," and had said that for the next offence the Widow Mason should lose her license. He added, also, that it was anything but a respectable house, and he greatly regretted that it stood within the boundaries of the parish of Lawsleigh.

The Widow Mason, therefore, took this as a hint to keep good hours, and only allow her house to be used by weary travellers passing to and fro, or, if by the inhabitants of Lawsleigh, in great moderation. She made her appearance at church with less absolute finery about her person, and, above all other things, she kept her slanderous tongue quiet. She did more than this—she made speeches to Mr. Gray, whom she waylaid in his walks about the parish, and so mourned over the "harshness" of the words used by Parson Hill against her at the time of the committal of Peter, and so set forth her own innocence in glowing colours as to awaken an interest for herself and her sorrows—in the form of a hope that she would amend— in the mind of that excellent gentleman.

Mary Cope continued her daily attendance at the school without her customary attention. Mary had never spoken to Isaac since that memorable night when he had so unexpectedly left her a prey to her own position; mistress and arbitratrix of it. Isaac's magnanimity had never been understood by Mary. She felt as if he had deserted her; and if events had so turned out that Parson Hill had remained at home, and had therefore followed up his intention of asking Mary for her decision for or against Isaac, undoubtedly in her present desponding mood—as she fancied, left to stand alone by him who ought to have been her most powerful support—she would have gone over to the parson, and left Isaac to reap bitter fruit from his great self-denial. And in that case, as all true lovers will see, she would have broken her own heart, as a proper punishment for her great temerity!

But Parson Hill had left his home. Fortunately also for Mary's present peace of mind, Mr. Gray had determined not to interfere in the matter between Isaac and her. He thought Mary too certainly guilty of deceitful conduct in London, to come out free from blot or speck if that conduct were rigidly examined into by Parson Hill, as Mr. Gray had no doubt it would be before Mary gained his consent for her marriage.

In the present state of Lawsleigh, with all the horror of Hannah's recent death and funeral, and Peter's committal to prison, Mr. Gray did not expect to find the parish otherwise than quiet and orderly; and as for love-making between Mary and Isaac, they might be as foolish as they pleased on that score, for one thing was certain, they could not marry without his assistance.

And so Mr. Gray "rested on his oars." He rested on his oars, and yet he was always brave in what he conceived to be his duty.

Most young men require experience, so did Mr. Gray. And if he was a little too confident in his own opinion and a little too eager to alter the existing state of things, it was in the former case a want of experience, in the latter, a conviction that he was rectifying abuses. Such a man, while "resting on his oars," may chance to regret even that short cessation from labour.

Parson Hill read Mr. Gray right; and with his usual charity made allowance in his own mind, for what to some appeared eccentricities, and to other's sheer ignorance. The latter was much oftener the case than the former. For the moor was a place peculiar in itself and only those educated for such a position could be charged with the moral obligation of understanding it, and the duty of acting upon that knowledge.

"I have been young and inexperienced myself," said Parson Hill. "I know that *now*—*then* I was the most egregious ass that ever brayed! It is true I thought myself a very Solon!—I made a mistake, as many better people have done in their day. If Gray's ideas of himself run the same course shall I blame him? Let him alone—let him alone, say I, he will mend with years. He desires with all his heart and soul to do right—to help me—to better the parish, or the people in it—to introduce improvements—new blood, as it is called in these days," commented the parson, elevating his eyebrows; "and to benefit the moor generally. He is self-denying, hard-working, zealous, charitable, and kind-hearted—I say, God speed him!"

And so, as we have said, Mr. Gray rested on his oars, and did not interfere with Mary; and though she, poor thing, was lonely and unhappy, she did not complain. Indeed, she had no companion—since the departure of Susan Picard—and contented herself with her daily routine of duties, and a quiet walk when she could get it on the open moor, away from the village and its inhabitants.

But Sunday came, and Mary, like others well brought up, went to church. Parson Hill came from Paul Tavey to assist Mr. Gray in the duties of the day. And now Mary felt her fate was sealed; undoubtedly the parson would see her between the services, and, as she called it, "bring her to book."

Parson Hill intoned the service, as usual, and the choir sang; but it was remarked Mary Cope's voice was very uncertain in power and sad in tone, and Isaac Watson's spasmodic and tremulous.

Mr. Gray preached, and he took the opportunity thus presented to him, to read the congregation a homily on their quarrels and bickerings; on their sins and follies; on their inattention at church; on the love of pleasure; on their ignorance; on their ingratitude to their superiors; on their self-conceit; and wound up his discourse by asserting that the evils he had enumerated were each and all as bad as the sin of drunkenness which had been the cause of the greatest crime known in the world, even murder, for which "Cain became a wanderer on the face of the earth!" And if they persisted in their bad courses and disregarded his warning how did they know that they might not all become murderers?

And the congregation separated, silent and awe-stricken! humbled in manner and sad at heart. To do them but justice they were astonished at the number and magnitude of their own crimes! They were alarmed at their position; but in their simplicity they did not know how they had suddenly become so wicked, or what to do to amend!

Mary Cope sat in her cottage between the services, awaiting in fear and trembling the visit of Parson Hill. But the parson—who lunched with Mr. Gray—was too much occupied by parish details, upon which the latter desired his vicar's opinion or advice, to have time to see Mary Cope, though it was certainly his intention to do so, and he was vexed to find his interview with her must stand over for another day.

In the afternoon the services were reversed. Mr. Gray read prayers, Parson Hill preached. His text was, "Brethren, love one another;" and he expatiated on the comfort and value of love. Apart from that love which surpasses all other, the love of God to man, he spoke of domestic affection—and Isaac Watson's heartfelt sigh was startlingly loud—and neighbourly kindness. Of love as the great purifier from selfishness, as the preventer of quarrels, as the greatest human blessing that could be bestowed upon creatures like ourselves—binding heart to heart—walking together hand in hand from the cradle to the grave "Love," said he, "in the words of a poet,

Love makes all things to be glad.

In suffering it is our comforter; it doubles our joy; it knits all human hearts together in one large pulse, that throbs from one end of the world to the other with like desires and hopes.

"Go, my friends," said he, in conclusion; "sorrows are sent to us by an Almighty hand but, in the words of Scripture I bid you 'comfort one another,' 'love one another,' and verily you will all meet your reward."

The different effect in the village caused by these two sermons can scarcely be told. The simple inhabitants all went to their homes comforted. Many a hearty blessing followed the parson's carriage as he was seen driving down the street to Paul Tavey.

"Isaac, lad—the passon has got a heart," said the Widow Simpson as Isaac and herself were walking from church.

"Ay, mother," said Isaac.

"There be Mistress Cope a-coming, don't thee mind I," said the old woman, attempting to draw away her arm from Isaac, "go to she, lad."

"Nay, mother, I shall not leave you," said Isaac, detaining her, and compelling her still to lean on his arm.

"Leastways us could wait for she," said the widow, standing still.

Mary and Isaac equally dreaded to meet, but from different causes. He feared that the sad event which followed so quickly upon their last conversation would bias her mind against him. She, ashamed to thrust herself as it were into the notice of a man who had—to express her own thoughts—"cast her off."

But they were compelled to meet nevertheless; for Isaac could not, in the face of the neighbours leaving the sacred edifice at the same time as himself and his mother, thus publicly go counter to her will, even if he had wished—and that too on the subject of Mary Cope, whom he so anxiously wished to preserve from the gossip of the curious. And so Isaac and his mother stood in the broad walk leading up to the church until they were joined by Mary Cope, who placed herself by the side of the old Woman, and they all three walked on together.

When they stepped from the churchyard into the main street, they heard the sound of wheels. Mary felt instinctively that it was Parson Hill's carriage. She did not dare to raise her eyes; she walked moodily on a few paces, and then was startled by a loud exclamation from Isaac, as he dropped the old woman's arm and rushed forward. Mary looked up in amazement. The carriage had turned the corner out of her sight, and Isaac, with a prayer of thankfulness on his lips, returned and resumed his place by his mother's side.

The facts were these: When Parson Hill saw the trio walking so cosily together he turned as the carriage passed them, and gazed upon Mary with a look of anger and dissatisfaction. As she was unaware of this, and did not raise her head, Parson Hill still kept his eye upon her, hoping that, when she did look up, he should be able to impress upon her how great was his annoyance. But all this time, and while the parson's attention was given to Mary Cope, his horses trotted gently on, and when they came to the corner of the street, took it so sharply, that only more by good luck than good management was the parson saved from an upset.

It was at the critical moment of danger that Isaac's exclamation came impulsively from his lips. This escape let loose his tongue, and opened his heart; he began to speak of the parson's sermon as so like the parson himself, who had a kind word and a kind feeling for everyone. Indeed, he was in the middle of a long speech, expatiating on all the well-known goodnesses of the parson, when they came to the turn that led by different routes to the two cottages—the school cottage, and the smithy cottage.

XX

ON TWO EVENTS THAT DISTURB THE REPOSE OF THE VILLAGE OF LAWSLEIGH

Mary Cope stopped, but the old woman took her by the arm, as she said,

"Don't thee go a-sitting by thee selfs—come along with Isaac and I."

Mary's reply rose in words to her throat, but there they stuck fast, and she looked down and blushed.

"It be fine and moonshiny at the night, and Isaac will walk home with thee—come."

"Would you come and have tea with me?" said Mary, for, thought she to herself then Isaac need not come if he does not wish.

"Ay, wench, ay," said the old woman, "and thank thee kindly."

And she hastily seized Isaac's arm, and began to walk towards the school cottage.

But, excepting the garrulity of the old woman, who seemed intent on expressing her happiness in being invited to drink tea with Mary Cope, no one spoke. Mary was silent from a fear that Isaac would leave his mother at her cottage door, and turn away home. And Isaac from a doubt as to whether Mary would admit him. They were both prevented acting for themselves by the old woman, who did not withdraw her arm from Isaac's protection until she was safe in the cottage. And when there, and seated in Mary's easy-chair, she began to give her orders as if the cottage were her own, though, to say the truth, it was only done with a kind desire to relieve the two young people from an embarrassment that could not be hidden even from her simple and untutored mind,

"Mistress Cope, sit thee down. Isaac, lad, shut to the door, and then come and take away my hood."

Isaac did as he was told. He took the black camlet hood, lined and quilted, and of a curious fashion, as compared with these days, and began to look round for a peg to hang it on.

"The lad doesna know this cottage so well as his own," said the old woman.

It was evident Isaac's shyness had returned; he found a place for the hood after some little search, and then he stood looking on without attempting to seat himself.

"I must stir up my fire," said Mary, jumping up eagerly.

But Isaac had now found something to do. He seized the poker before Mary could touch it, and so effectually stirred the fire, as to all but upset the kettle, which was standing partly on the hob, and partly on the fire. But this was quite enough—once more his tongue was unloosed, and Isaac spoke.

"I am very clumsy and stupid," said he, alluding to the toppling of the kettle, and, as he righted it, he added, "I cannot think why I am so stupid, and—" and the fire had another hearty good poke; but Mary interrupted him by saying:

"You stupid!—why, Isaac, you are the most clever and——"

But Mary turned her back suddenly upon Isaac, and began to talk to the old woman; her bonnet was slipping back as she stooped, and Isaac lifted it off her head, ostensibly to prevent it falling on the floor. Mary raised her eyes accidentally, and met his look full upon her—that look was quite enough. Isaac Watson felt that Mary Cope was not changed.

"I do think she has made up her mind to have me," said Isaac to himself, as he made great search for another peg or hook upon which to hang the bonnet.

"I do not think he can have deserted me," said Mary to herself, as she redoubled her attentions to the old woman, in the vain hope of hiding her satisfaction at the turn affairs were taking. "The kettle boils, I see," said Mary, aloud.

"And where is the clome (china), Mary?" said Isaac, in the very same glad tones she remembered so well.

For the moment she was too happy to speak. She walked hastily across the little room, and opened a corner cupboard, where in all its purity stood Mary Cope's clome.

"Not those—oh! no, not those!" said Mary, as Isaac began to take down the cups and saucers she had in daily use.

"You can reach to the top shelf, that is the good of being so tall, and there is the clome that I shall use this day."

And Mary even adopted the Devonshire word "clome" in her gladness of heart; though, we must admit that, as a rule, she did not use the patois of the moor. And we must pardon her pride in her china; for she was proud of it, and never attempted to hide that she was so. Nothing like it had ever been seen in the village of Lawsleigh—a perfect set of real Nankin, brought from China by Mary's grandfather. It was doubted if even the vicarage could produce a set like it. And so Isaac handed down the quaint teapot, the tea-caddy, the cream jug with a lid, the tiny cups and saucers, and the sugar basin. And now the old woman, peering with her aged eyes into all this finery, begged she might be made useful; and Mary gave her a soft napkin wherewith to dust the precious service, while she, as she called it, "whipped up the cream-jug and just ran over to Farmer Smithson for some cream," that thick Devonshire cream, the pride of the county!

And then, when the tea was made, and they were cosily seated enjoying the fresh butter and delicious bread, Mary wished, "she had known beforehand that she was to be so happy, and have such nice company, for then she would have had some hot cakes just ready."

But both the old woman and Isaac thought everything Mary had was perfect, and everything she did or said the same; and, as they contrived to make her very well aware of their thoughts, Mary would have been ungrateful if she had not felt happy—at least, for the time being.

At length they began to discuss the parson's sermon; by some strange internal agreement they did not mention Mr. Gray's, but "Parson Hill's discourse they would never forget to the end of their days."

"I be a-thinking as it be love as makes us all so happy," said the old woman; "the passon be right most times."

"Yes," said Isaac, fervently, "humanly speaking, love is the great purifier from the natural evil in our hearts. I know nothing more powerful in arresting a man's progress through the paths of vice than an honest love for a pure-hearted and gentle woman. The contrast of her angel-like innocence with his own demoniacal sins and follies shews him very plainly the great gulf that lies between them, awakens him to the enormity of his own wickedness, and attracts him to her as the reward of his amendment."

Isaac looked at Mary, who blushed a bright and happy blush.

"But," resumed he, "the parson meant to inculcate the virtue of charity—love to one's neighbour."

"Ay, lad, it be so; the passon meaned us all to love one another—and so us does," said the widow, looking at Mary; and then, turning to Isaac, she added, "But, I tell thee, lad, I be a-going down to my grave with peace. Now as I be sure thee hast got a good wife, or, leastways, as thee be a-going to wed, let alone the love as the passon meaned, I be glad as thee loves Mistress Cope, and as she loves thee, lad."

She took hold of Mary's hand as she spoke, and pressed it between her own as she added,

"He hath ever been a gude son to I, and he will make thee a gude husband."

Mary cast down her eyes, but did not, reply.

When they had finished tea, and Mary began to remove the china on to a back table, Isaac made himself useful in attempting to help her. It was during their turns up and down the little room that they contrived to get a better understanding with each other.

"Do you wish me to go away?" said Isaac, softly, when they were at a distance from the old woman.

"To go!—oh! no."

"Poor dear old mother does not understand—you see she thinks we are——"

"I am sure, Isaac, I do not understand," said Mary, with a little burst of petulance; "if you wish to go, of course you must."

By this time the old woman had wisely laid her head back in Mary's comfortable chair, and covered her head and face with her apron. In the fear of disturbing her, we suppose, Isaac and Mary now conversed in whispers, apart from the tea-table.

"Mary, dear, you are too good to say anything just to make me unhappy—just to pride yourself upon me, as many would—why, then do you say, 'if *I* wish to go?'"

"Why?—you have left me all this long time," and Mary turned pale at the remembrance of her own sufferings; "I thought perhaps you wished to go away——"

"I dare not come, Mary," interrupted Isaac. "I could not blame you if you did withdraw your promise. I know I am not worthy of you, although I will try every day to make myself more so. I know that the horrible event which has very justly filled the whole village with dread, must operate against me in a mind so pure and gentle as yours. I know everybody, except poor mother, will warn you to avoid me—will laud you for giving me up. I know you have nothing to gain; and I have life, honour, a good name, and a blessed future hanging by a thread. I dare not come, Mary. My stake was too heavy. I dreaded to know that I had lost you. I have borne with the suspense, cruel though it has been. I will still bear it, if you will, rather than hear myself cast off from all future hope."

"But you never mean to go to that 'Packhorse' again, Isaac?—you will keep that promise to me?"

"I will keep it, Mary, as sure as there is a God in Heaven," said Isaac, fervently, "and by his help."

"Massy me!—and where be I to?" said the old woman, as she pulled back her muslin apron, and stared round the cottage.

Mary and Isaac were by her side in a moment. And for the remainder of the widow's visit she busied herself in examining, with Mary's help, all the articles of furniture that she was unaccustomed to see. When she had sufficiently gratified her curiosity, she said,

"Isaac, lad, I can go back by my own self—my old bones will ache if I stop out when the sun be gone down."

I need hardly add that Isaac would not suffer his mother to go by herself; and Mary Cope was once more left alone.

We must pass rapidly over this part of our story. On the following Sunday, Parson Hill again drove into the village of Lawsleigh for the purpose of assisting Mr. Gray in the duties of the day. The criticism on the respective sermons of the vicar and the curate may be told in a few words.

"Well, widdy," said old Jacob Smerdon "so that young one be at us again. I be minded as him has a-tooked a new text, and preached the very same sermon."

"I be minded to the same, Jacob," said the old woman; "all about murdererses and drunkardses, and liarses, and thievesses and gossipses and every bad thing!"

"I be fair ill-tempered with he," said Jacob.

"It be cruel unbecoming of he," said the widow.

"But the cheery passon, widdy there be a man!" and Jacob gave his thigh a hearty slap to enforce the strength of his opinion.

"Ay, Jacob, him be the man; and let alone the whole earth to find another such!"

"Him tooked the very same text, widdy!" said Jacob, tapping loudly with his stick on the floor.

"The very same, Jacob," said the widow. "Brethrenses, love one another."

"But much differenter words in the sermon, widdy," said Jacob; "forbye they meaned the very same. Him be a most mazing passon, widdy."

"Him be so comforting-like—a comforting to us heartses as likes to love one anothers. Jacob, I loves the passon."

"Ay, widdy, so does I; and God bless the passon!" said Jacob, with another heavy blow upon his own flesh.

And a third Sunday came round, and the same events occurred. Mr. Gray preached in the morning, and denounced vengeance on all who persisted in their wickedness; at the same time that he accused his congregation of living in the habitual commission of heinous sins. While Parson Hill still took the same text, "Love ye one another."

Again the village gossips descanted on the two sermons and the two preachers. And it was clearly to be seen in that little community that they did love each other more and more; that they loved to do little neighbourly acts, and to encourage among themselves kind neighbourly ways, because the parson taught them these things so gently.

It was in the midst of the talk on the subject of the two parsons that the news came about Peter Barker. He had been tried for manslaughter and convicted on circumstantial evidence. He was committed to prison for two years, to the horror and grief of the inhabitants of Lawsleigh. It cast a gloom over the whole parish; people, when they met, shook their heads, and spoke in whispers; they were shocked at Peter's fate, and ashamed of the disgrace to the village. They wished the parson would come home; they did not think they should feel safe from harm until he did.

One morning, however a very bright morning, soon after this consternation through the parish, the bells of Lawsleigh burst out into a merry peal, and the people rushed to their doors.

"Be the passon a-come back?" said one.

"Us doesna know," said others.

"Be the young lads a-larning theyselves to ring?" questioned some.

"Can't say," was the reply.

There was a good deal of talk all up and down the village, everybody wondering, and everybody listening to the sweet sound of the Lawsleigh bells. And in process of time the mystery was solved—"Isaac Watson had married Mary Cope!"

It was on that morning Mr. Gray repented that, even for a short time, he had "rested on his oars." For the last fortnight Isaac had slept every night in a neighbouring parish, thus fulfilling the letter of the law, "for the fifteen days last passed," and then he procured a license. Mr. Gray could not refuse to marry them; they were both of full age, or the license could not have been granted. And they were married! But many blamed Isaac. They thought he ought not to have taken advantage of the vicar's absence, for one thing, and that he ought to have had his "banns called," for another!

By the inhabitants of Lawsleigh, to be married by license was looked upon as a piece of pride in Isaac, for the custom of Lawsleigh, from time immemorial, had been to be married by banns. It was not pride, however; it was because Isaac knew, if he allowed banns to be published, they would be forbidden. But a license, properly obtained, would secure his prize.

XXI

WHICH TREATS OF ENLARGING THE SMITHY COTTAGE

At the end of this week Parson Hill returned. By this time Mary felt so happy in her new home, and Isaac so thankful to have her, that all we can say is, they were both contented with their bargain.

There had been a little difficulty at first as to which house they should live in for the future. Mary feeling sure that there was plenty of room in her cottage for the good widow; and, besides, being more roomy, it possessed advantages not to be found in the smithy cottage, inasmuch as it was fitted up with grates—things unknown amongst the dwellers on the moor, because the natural fuel of the locality, turf, is easily procured, and coal is difficult to obtain, and expensive. Turf is burnt upon the hearth, rendering the modern grate unnecessary.

"And then," said Mary, "as the school cottage belongs to the school, it seems but proper that the schoolmistress should dwell there."

Some people have a strange faculty for casting away care. Mary had been distinctly told by Parson Hill that she must choose between Isaac and the school. And though this announcement troubled her greatly when it was originally made, day by day it faded from her mind, until at length it was forgotten.

Up to the time of her marriage, or, rather, of her complete understanding with Isaac, she had occasionally cheered herself by the recollection that now "she should keep the school;" but after her wedding-day was fixed, and after that ceremony had taken place, by a strange perversity she forgot that the gain of Isaac for her husband must be weighed against the loss of the school.

Isaac, as he was more experienced than Mary, saw more clearly into the probabilities of the future. He did not disturb her happy frame of mind by suppositions of what that future might produce; but he foresaw too surely that as soon as the parson returned she would lose her employment.

Mary had continued to attend the school just as usual, and in a perfectly contented frame of mind. But when the news of the vicar's return spread through the village, she felt a strange unusual awe creep over her at the thought of meeting him. She had never seen him, except during the services of the church, since the day that he had so entreated her to "give him up." But Mary had not "given him up." A new light seemed suddenly to break upon her, and she asked herself, "Oh, why did I leave my own cottage?" She had left the cottage belonging to the school at Isaac's request, for in his own mind he thought, "when she is married she has no right to it," and she had gone on her wedding-day to reside at the smithy. At the time this seemed a simple arrangement, hardly worthy of remark, because so unimportant in itself; it was more convenient, and Mary saw no objection. But the expected sound of the parson's voice made Mary reflect more on her present position than she had hitherto done, and now she blamed herself for her want of foresight; it appeared to her that "by having left the cottage appropriated to the schoolmistress she had virtually given up the school."

Mary did not, however, impart her troublous thoughts to Isaac. She was a shade less cheerful, and two shades more thoughtful, and Isaac did not require to be told what was passing in her mind. And on the Saturday evening, when two carriages passed the smithy, containing Parson Hill, and the party from Paul Tavey, Isaac put aside his own work, and calling Mary to him, opened out to her a plan for their future comfort, that so arrested her attention for the time being, and occupied her mind afterwards, as completely to extinguish for that night the care that had been corroding her thoughts.

"You see, my dear," said Isaac, "I have always known this old house would never do for you. You require more comforts, and you shall have them. We who are born and brought up on the moor, as we have never known anything better than humble dwellings, moderately stored with furniture, and turf fires blazing on the naked hearth—because, my dear, the turf is handy on the moor, and the smithy has a right to gather—so we never require or desire anything better. But you are different; you come from the South o' Devon, where the climate is genial, and luxury abounds. And I have been thinking of building a couple of rooms, or so——"

"Isaac, how kind of you!" said Mary.

"And I have a plan in my head, upon which I should like your opinion."

"It is so good of you to be always thinking of me," said Mary, gratefully.

"I must first build a new shed out there in the garden. You see I cannot get on without a shed; and the front shed *must* open into the back, as it does now, because there my men are at work; so all this part," continued he, pointing out to her comprehension the shed or workshops used by Isaac and his men when at work, "must be removed. We must build two nice rooms where the sheds now stand, and then place the sheds, on other side, still abutting on the house."

"What a great deal of trouble you will have," said Mary, as she looked round the shed in which they were standing, and saw the numerous tools lying about; and as she opened the door of the inner shop or shed, she exclaimed—

"Why, Isaac, you can never move all this great lot of things—such great heavy things—and——'"

"At first I thought of building the rooms outside the sheds, just there in the garden."

"Yes; that would be very pretty; and so have a window to look all down the street."

"To be sure," said Isaac, heartily; "I never thought of that; and as you say, my dear, that would be very pretty; and the little garden might grow up to the window."

"Yes, it might; and the sweet mignonette and the nice violets might grow under the window."

"But, Mary," said Isaac, looking a shade more serious, "you see, if I build the new rooms there, and have the sheds standing as they are, the old house and the new will be apart from each other."

"Yes—but that is nothing; because you can have a door open into the shed on the other side, the very same as it does on this."

"But I only mean to build two rooms. One on the ground floor, warm and comfortable for you, and one over for a bedroom for us."

"Yes; but why, then, is there a difficulty more on the one side than the other?"

Two difficulties presented themselves to Isaac's mind, only one of which he mentioned to Mary.

"Why, if I build on to the old house, the same stairs will do; and, of course, much less work in the walls. If I build here, I must have a better and a more substantial wall than this," indicating the outside wall of the shed, which was only composed of large stones loosely fastened together.

He did not say, I should not like to leave the good old mother all alone, as it were, in a house by herself; for so it would seem, he thought, if the rooms were so separated.

"Then there could not be the window to look down the street, Isaac; neither the sweet smell of flowers coming in with the air."

"We cannot have everything," said Isaac, philosophically, and hoping to turn Mary's mind to see that the other was the better of the two plans.

"Shall we ask mother," said Mary, "which she will like best?"

"No," said Isaac, as he occupied himself by looking up and examining the roof of his shed; and left Mary to digest the monosyllable as well as she could.

"No?" said she, inquiringly. "Why not, Isaac? Mother likes to give her opinion and I like her to have it, and I thought you did also."

Isaac had now found an occupation in measuring the length and width of his shed by his own paces, and remained silent.

"Isaac, dear, don't you like mother to have her opinion?"

"Certainly I do."

"Then, tell me, why don't you like me to ask her about this?"

"You may ask her, if you wish," said Isaac, who had now brought Mary's curiosity to the right point, and therefore condescended further to add, "Mother is very unselfish, Mary, and of my own accord I should not ask her, because I know beforehand she will decide against herself."

Mary's perceptions were not very clear on that Saturday evening. She certainly could not see what the widow would have to resign by having the old house made larger, and thus more comfortable.

"Well, Isaac, I cannot see what there is to give up," said Mary, a little pettishly; for it is astonishing how prosperity beguiles us into wilfulness; and Mary was not proof against the, to her, prosperity of the last week.

"Well, my dear, I thought I would just ask if you would like to have me build two rooms for you; and we need not settle all in a breath exactly how and where they shall be. I agree to build them—you agree to occupy them; and there we will wait a bit, and see how things turn out."

This judicious speech on Isaac's part quieted Mary in an instant. By some intuitive feeling she understood he did not wish for any more discussion just then on the subject; and she also saw there was something in Isaac's mind connected with the Widow Simpson that would cause him to build close to the old house if possible. But she was so occupied with her own happy position of the past week, and with the hope of retaining it in the future, she could not see the lonely position of the old woman.

As Mary had had permission from Isaac to bring the old woman's wisdom into the conferences on the subject of the addition to the cottage, she lost no time in apprising her of the anticipated change.

"It be like to you and like to Isaac," said the widow.

"You will like it, mother," said Mary, not comprehending what the old woman meant.

"Blessings on thee!" said the widow, heartily. "I say it be like to both on ye—like to Isaac, and like to you—to be a-thinking on I. I said to myself, mayhap Mary will coax the lad to go and live in she's pretty cottage; but you both on you think of I, and I be so glad as I shall not have to live all by my own self, and thanks to you, my dear!"

"Why, mother, we should never think of leaving you!" said Mary. "Don't you remember when I thought my cottage—that is, you know, mother it is as good as my own," added she, with a little pride, "for it is on purpose for the schoolmistress, as I am. And when we thought it would be better to live there, we meant to take you with us."

"Ay, ay, but I sim I knowed betterer," said the old woman. "I knowed I was not the schoolmistress of Lawsleigh,"—and she laughed heartily at the drollness of the idea—"and mayhap the passon might tell I to get out of that!"

"Then we should have gone out also," said Mary, as an undefined fear crept through her. "But you see, mother, if Isaac builds two rooms, we can all three be together so nicely; and my furniture and books and things can be brought here."

XXII

HOW MARY WATSON WENT TO MEET PARSON HILL AT THE VILLAGE SCHOOL, AND OF WHAT BEFELL HER BY THE WAY

BEFORE the close of the conversation related in the last chapter, the old woman had made Mary comprehend that the nearer the new rooms were built to the old ones, the better she should like them; and then Mary gradually saw through Isaac's meaning, without anything more definite being said by him.

When this clearly dawned upon her perceptive faculties, she blamed herself for having argued the matter with him, because she thought it might appear to be taking a selfish part against the old woman. Mary was free from errors of this nature, and Isaac had a just understanding of her real character, and a thorough appreciation of it. This prevented any dangerous misunderstanding from arising between them on that point.

On the Sunday Isaac was a good deal occupied with the bells and the choir, and the duties of the day—as was Mary, also, with the school and the choir. Mary had passed the day happily, for Parson Hill had neither perceptibly slighted her nor bestowed his notice upon her. Her spirits rose with her contentment, and she now almost longed for the interview she had a short time previously so greatly dreaded.

On the Monday morning the inmates of the smithy were up with the lark, and at their early breakfast Isaac's contemplated improvement was the topic of conversation. Mary gave her opinion unasked in a most decided tone, that it would be better to build the two rooms close to the old cottage, and not on the other side of the shed. And then Isaac became playfully ungenerous, and pointed out that she would not have a charming window, to take in at one view the whole length of the village street, the rustic bridge over the brooklet, and the church tower on the hill. That she could have no mignonette or violets, because the window must look west. And to crown the whole of the discomforts of placing the rooms close to the house, there could not be a door into the new shed, because there must be a chimney somewhere!

At first Mary was fairly taken aback by all this wicked persiflage, and began to think she had even misunderstood his former intention; but Isaac, who—deep fellow as he was!—could read every expression of Mary's face in an instant, took himself up without more ado, and comforted her by his ardent praise of her proposal.

"But, Mary dear, it is like you to say we will have the new rooms join to the old house; for, to tell you the truth, I should not like to be sleeping in a grand room over the way, as it would seem to me, and leaving my good mother in the old house all by herself. It is so comfortable to feel we shall be all together; and I am sure, my dear, I am very grateful that you have such a kindly feeling on the subject."

"And where be ye to have the chimney put to?" said the old woman.

"Well, mother, we will find a place; 'where there is a will there is a way,' and it is clear where there is a grate there must be a chimney. And then, Mary, all your nice furniture, that the good parson thought I coveted so," said Isaac, with a wicked smile, that poor innocent Mary did not in the least comprehend—"your furniture, my dear, can be moved into the two new rooms, and we shall be as happy as kings and queens can ever be!"

And when the time came for Mary to set off to the school, Isaac had entirely talked away her casual fear of losing it, by occupying and delighting her mind with his suggested improvements at the smithy.

And now, instead of desponding with the fear of dismissal, she seemed perfectly assured of retaining the school; and instead of setting forth at a slow pace, and with a heavy heart, she was ready a few minutes earlier than usual, and felt as if she could fly on the wings of the wind to meet Parson Hill, and once more apply herself heart and soul to the well-known duties of her beloved school.

"He will not like me to come away from the school-cottage," said she to herself, as she bounded along. "I know the parson likes that cottage, and thinks it so pretty and so suitable for a schoolmistress; and so it is. And I am sure I have often been quite delighted with the way in which he would point out to me the windmill on the top of the very distant hill, only seen like a white speck on a clear day, just as we can see Moorgarten Spire when the sun shines on it, though it is ever so far off. But then it is white." And here she paused a little, for she had brought up Moorgarten Spire as a simile, and had to go back in her mind, and recall the parson's speeches; and when she had found the place from whence she had diverged, she continued her talk to herself. "And the farmstead in the hollow, and the group of thorn in the parson's own glebe, and the Tors everywhere around. Oh! but he is a kind man, is the parson! and so clever—that is, I mean, talks so beautifully, makes one understand so many things; and I cannot think how I can have the heart to tell him I shall move my furniture to the smithy; for he gave me a good many things—that nice couch—there is not another in the whole village—and my work-table, and my pretty, pretty book-shelves, and oh! so many nice books—indeed, he is always giving me presents of one kind or other. No; I cannot tell him today about my furniture; I have not the heart. I must wait—yes, wait—until the new rooms at the smithy are nearly ready; and then he will come and see them his own self, and maybe say to me, in his kind voice—'so, Mary, you will have to remove all your nice furniture down here, or——'"

But Mary's happy thoughts were put a stop to for the time being, by one of the servants from the vicarage, who said—

"He was going to the smithy on purpose to see her."

Mary's first idea was that she was late, and she said innocently, as the man stood fumbling in his pockets.

"Is the parson at the school? Has he sent for me?"

"I don't know, Mistress Cope," said the man, ignoring Mary's claim to a change of name. "The passon be at his breakfast, and he sent you this here note."

The man turned sharply on his heel as soon as he had delivered the note, and set off in a sort of jog-trot home again; while Mary unceremoniously opened the note as she stood, and read——

"Mary Watson,—your services are no longer required at the village school of Lawsleigh. You will——"

Poor Mary! the earth seemed suddenly to turn round with her, large tears fell heavily on the paper, which she hastily crumpled in her hand, and turning round attempted to walk home.

At first her limbs trembled so, she could hardly put one foot before another; and to add to her trouble she met almost immediately Jane Sands, who stopped at some little distance from Mary as she was slowly retracing her steps, and staring rudely at her, said—

"I thought ye was a ghost, Mistress Watson—you be so white as any of they ghosteses as be a-walking over the earth continually!"

Mary walked on, trying to look unconcerned, but she did not reply to the greeting of Jane Sands; she was too much absorbed in her own sorrows, and too eager to escape notice from everyone. Her silence however, angered the woman, and she continued—

"Umph! You be uncommon proud, you be; and you be a white-faced doll, that you be! And you has never gived I the penny as——"

But Mary made a great effort to quicken her pace, and get away from the rudeness of Jane; for though the note had only that instant been put into her hands, she thought all the village knew of her disgrace, and that consequently she might expect an insult from every person she met. Fortunately, at the turn of a corner, she lost the sound of Jane's harsh tones, and, feeling this a relief, she tried to walk faster, but her attitude was desponding and her eyes cast on the ground. Presently she heard heavy hasty steps approaching, and, dreading a foe in every sound, she raised her head, and saw, within a few paces of her, Isaac Watson, who advanced without speaking, and tenderly drawing her arm within his own, led her to the smithy.

Isaac had foreseen that Mary would not be received at the school, and he was therefore ready to meet her the moment she turned the corner into the main street. And then, under the shelter of the smithy roof, and with Isaac's protecting arm around her, Mary read and re-read the little note that blighted—as she thought—her happiness forever. Its purport was to dismiss her from the school as mistress of it, and to desire her to remove her furniture within three days "from the cottage that was intended solely for the use of the schoolmistress of the village of Lawsleigh."

XXIII

IN WHICH ISAAC WATSON GOES TO THE VICARAGE

Mr. Gray made no mention to Parson Hill of Isaac's marriage until Sunday evening. And then, as a matter of course, it was decreed by the two gentlemen that Mary must be dismissed from the school on the following morning. Few things in his whole life had affected Parson Hill more than this marriage. To use his own words, "the very announcement of it made him feel ten years older," as if a sudden blight had fallen upon him. He became silent and reserved in his own family circle. Neither Charlie's ready wit nor Mrs. Harcourt's fine music seemed to have power to draw him from the absorption of his own thoughts. He never mentioned either Mary or Isaac, and thus his visitors were unaware that the two people in whom they were all three much interested were actually married.

But on the Tuesday, when Mrs. Hill was making her toilette for dinner, Charlie suddenly entered the room.

"You may go, Jones," said Mrs. Hill to her maid; and as soon as the door was closed, she turned to Charlie, and said, "something strange will surely happen when you are ready before me!"

"Something strange is happening. I am uncomfortable, disturbed in mind, and really I do not know whether to tell the governor or not! I hate spoiling sport, but then I cannot endure deceit!" and Charlie began to pace the room impatiently.

"What is it?" said Mrs. Hill, suspending the finishing touches to her toilette in her anxiety.

"Why that great big bear, Isaac Watson, is carrying off the furniture that belongs to the pretty schoolmistress—taking it away from the school cottage! I forgot to tell you last night, for that charming widow Harcourt takes up so much of your time I am left in the shade."

"A very happy shade for you; but do go on."

"Why, last night, I saw symptoms of a moonlight flitting at Mary Cope's cottage."

Mrs. Hill made no remark, though Charlie paused sufficiently long.

"Now, if that young woman is stealing away in the dark, she is not worthy of the kiss I have always intended to give to her on a fitting occasion."

"Are you then going to speak to Mr. Hill?"

"Nay, Kate, I want your opinion. The governor is unusually moody, I can hardly get 'a rise' out of him; therefore I do not wish to add to the weight of care he seems so burdened with just at this time. And yet I cannot take the young woman's part, for it is clearly wrong to steal away her goods in that way. If she wants to marry Isaac, as I suppose she does, why, then marry him openly; take away her goods the same, and, in spite of the governor's objection to the marriage, I would not mind standing treat. But to anger the dear old governor, whose opposition to their blessed union is all on the side of goodness—to anger him by such dirty work as moonlight flittings, to confess the truth, angers me too."

"Perhaps you are misinformed."

"Wisest of your sex! I saw with my own eyes what I have ventured to assert."

"I do not believe it," said Mrs. Hill, turning away and attending to the finishing of her toilette.

"Very well; I have done," said Charlie as he moved towards the door.

"Do not go away, Charlie; let us come to some understanding as to what will be the best to do."

Charlie turned round, and hesitated, standing with the door open.

"Now, Charlie, dear, do not go; I want you."

"When you venture to call a man a liar I wonder how you can open your mouth the next minute to ask a favour from him," said Charlie, still standing with the door open.

"I did not use such language!" said Mrs. Hill, surprised at the accusation.

"You said you did not believe me."

"I do not believe that Mary Cope is stealing away from her cottage," said Mrs. Hill, pettishly; "do not mistake me so, Charlie—nay, indeed, you understood well enough what I meant."

"I know, you might as well speak good English as bad," said Charlie, laughing, as he closed the door, and once more leaned his back against the wardrobe; "and I can tell you I would not have believed it of Mary, if I had not seen it."

"Mrs. Harcourt and I both remarked that Mary Cope looked very pretty on Sunday; she had on such a becoming bonnet, and——"

"Well," said Charlie, impatiently, "what has a bonnet to do with a moonlight flitting?"

"Do you think it possible they are already married?"

"Married! no; why, they could not marry without having their banns called, or going to the governor for a license—the former would be forbidden, the latter refused."

"Then you think she is first taking her goods safely away, and then going to another church to be married?"

"Indeed I do not know what she means to do first, I do not know any of her meanings from first to last; I do not know the meaning of Isaac walking off with the goods by moonlight. I tell you I am uncomfortable— there will be a row—and," said Charlie, as a little tap at the door arrested his attention, and then, speaking in a low key, he added, "I heartily wish the Widow Harcourt was safely married to the governor, and then she would not have time to break in upon——"

But, by this time, he had opened the door, and, putting out his hand to Mrs. Harcourt, he said,

"Come, come, come in—did you think we wanted your opinion? Now, tell me honestly—did you?"

"I can give it, if you ask me," said she, laughing.

She was then taken into their counsels, and she, like Mrs. Hill, did not believe any evil of Mary. Her opinion was to say nothing to Mr. Hill on the matter of the removal of the goods, unless he himself introduced the subject.

"In multitude of counsel there is wisdom," said Charlie, as he opened the door, and the party descended to dinner.

During dinner a message was brought to Parson Hill, to the purport that Isaac Watson had called again, and the vicar was reminded in an undertone by his old servant, George, that this was the third time.

"Isaac Watson!" said the parson, in an angry tone; "tell him I am engaged."

After a little time the man returned with,

"Isaac's duty to his honour, and when would Parson Hill please to see him!"

"Never!" said the angry parson, motioning the man away.

Charlie, however, unnoticed by Mr. Hill, quietly left the table, and went to Isaac.

"Well, Isaac, what is the matter?" said Charlie.

And Isaac very soon told Charlie all the circumstances of the marriage, and also explained to him what had before seemed difficult to understand in the removal of Mary's goods. And further, Isaac made known his present business with the vicar, viz., that there were some book-shelves at the cottage that Mary claimed as her own, alleging that Parson Hill had given them to her; and Isaac wished to know if the shelves were a present to Mary individually, or only to the schoolmistress for the time being.

"Are they fixtures, Isaac?"

"No, sir, they are strung together with cords, and hung up."

"Then if Mistress Watson—tell her I wish her much happiness—if she has any liking for the shelves I advise you to take them."

"What did the parson mean, do you think, Master Charlie, when he had the shelves made?"

"He meant them for Mary—that is, for Mistress Watson—she is very pretty, Isaac—of course he did."

"But I do not wish to anger the parson."

"Oh! he is—he is eating his dinner; I will tell him I have advised you to take them. Good-bye, Isaac. I shall come and see your wife, and drink her health; and I do now heartily wish you both much happiness—tell her so, will you."

And Isaac went away with a blessing on his lips for that kind-hearted Master Charlie; and removed the book-shelves with a clear conscience. And Charlie returned to the dining-room.

XXIV

WHICH TREATS OF PARSON HILL'S
OPINION OF ISAAC WATSON

WHEN the ladies retired, Parson Hill attacked Charlie immediately with,

"And so you must needs go and speak to that drunkard, Isaac Watson! I think you would have behaved better if you had kept your seat at the table."

"So do I, sir—to the company present."

"Umph!—I cannot think you improved by marriage, Charlie. Your wife ruins you—I would not let a woman ruin me—of course I mean in manner, in bearing."

Charlie thought of "the governor's" fate, if he should marry Mrs. Harcourt, and tried hard to refrain from a smile.

"Marriage improves most people," resumed the vicar; "why do you make yourself an exception?"

"Perhaps marriage may improve Isaac," said Charlie, as if thinking aloud; "I hope *he* will not turn out an exception to the general rule."

"Umph!" said the parson again; and then, after a little pause, he added with a sneer, "it will improve the late schoolmistress of Lawsleigh un-doubt-ed-ly."

"I declare, I thought she was making a moonlight 'flit,' as the people say, when I saw Isaac carrying away her goods last night."

"I wish you could find some other subject wherewith to entertain me. Do you think it a matter of congratulation that the best schoolmistress in the—in—in the world," said he at last, and raising his voice in his anger, "should neglect her duties and marry a drunkard?"

"No, sir, I think it wrong in schoolmistresses generally to neglect their duties; and very wrong in any one of the sisterhood to marry a drunkard.

But I thought you always had hopes that Isaac would turn out well at last—that he would, in fact, give up tobacco and cider, and perhaps take 'the pledge.' And as he has so fairly pledged himself within this last week," continued Charlie, alluding to Isaac's marriage, "who knows but that he may go on with the good work, and take a total abstinence pledge after all."

"He was seen coming out of the 'Packhorse' last night, reeling drunk!—he and that other drunkard, Jacob Smerdon."

Charlie now wisely held his peace.

"When I am next on the bench, I mean to speak of that woman's house and practices, and get her license taken away, as I forewarned her," said Parson Hill.

"Which is the woman you mean to unlicense—Isaac, Jacob, or the 'Packhorse!'" said Charlie.

It was now the vicar's turn to be silent.

"You see, the bad Widow Mason at the 'Packhorse' supplies wayfaring men, and she is the only bad widow in the parish; and I do not myself see what the parish will gain if we exchange her for a worse."

Charlie paused, but the vicar did not reply.

"Wayfaring men must be supplied, or they will die in severe weather as they cross the moor."

The vicar rested his head on his hand, and did not speak.

"The 'Packhorse' may be a bad sign; but what can be the use of changing it for a better, unless indeed there is any good in making the sign more attractive? As for Isaac and Jacob having been seen coming out, I must admit it is very disgraceful of the patriarchs."

"Well, Charlie, you seem to take things very easily, but I can tell you I am thoroughly unhappy. Here is a young woman, modest, good-looking, well educated for her station, and able to get her own living in a respectable way; and she suddenly turns round, casts to the dogs all her good qualities, and gives herself up to a reprobate!—to one who, though young in years—I do not think the man is more than five or six-and-twenty—is old in iniquity. Nay, Charlie," for he had made an ineffectual

attempt to interrupt Mr. Hill, "you have had your say, let me have mine.
If Isaac were, as I had once too foolishly hoped he might sooner or later
become, a changed man, I would be the first to bless his union with Mary
Cope. But his conduct for the last month or two has been execrable, past
all bearing! Gray tells me he took infinite pains and trouble with the man
during my absence in town, calling frequently at the smithy cottage, and
trying to conciliate him; and it is a well known fact, Charlie," said the
vicar, his anger rising with his subject, "that Isaac Watson went oftener to
the 'Packhorse' at that time than he had ever before been known to do!
What do you think of that?"

Charlie remained silent.

"Of course you know," resumed Parson Hill, "it was in a drunken fit
he so disfigured Mary's face for the time being! One morning, when
I was riding across the moor to Paul Tavey, Gray stopped the bells. He
afterwards told me the men were *all* drunk! But that sly Isaac came to me
on the evening of the same day apparently sober," continued he, shaking
his head, "and I hastily concluded Gray had been mistaken; whereas, *now*
I feel sure he was right. I myself saw him come out of the school cottage
reeling drunk when that silly little milliner was staying with Mary; and
last night—only last night, Charlie—Gray saw him come reeling out of
the 'Packhorse.' These are only a small number of the iniquities that can
be proved against Isaac," added the vicar, unconsciously exaggerating the
truth in his anger. "And now pray what would you have, Charlie!"

"I would have Isaac a better man."

"A better man, indeed—indeed," said the vicar, with a lugubrious shake
of the head; "now I told that foolish young woman that he only wanted
to marry her for his own ends, but I could not drive it into her! I told her
he would break his word—for he had actually sworn never to enter the
'Packhorse' again!—break his word in a week—and you see my words are
true, and more than true, for they have not been married a week—this
is Tuesday, and Gray married them last Wednesday. Now, Charlie, if you
have any respect for my word, I ask—can you have any respect for Isaac
Watson?"

"I have the greatest respect for you, sir," said Charlie, "and the greatest reliance on your word, but the puzzle to me is, that Isaac never appears bad! See him where you will, speak to him on any subject, and he is a respectable, sensible, just, and intelligent man, always greatly ashamed of his weakness for cider and tobacco, and yet, somehow, contriving, even with this failing, to keep his place in my heart, and, until now, I thought he did in yours."

"Alas! yes, you are right, Charlie. There has ever been about the man a something that has seemed to keep him still respectable, even though it was patent to all that he sinned vilely."

"I never saw him in a state of inebriety."

"And, strangely enough, Charlie, nor have I, excepting on those occasions I mentioned; but, though I have not seen him, I have heard him go singing down the street, and of course I have known but too well what was the matter. And sometimes, Charlie, boy, my conscience has reproached me that perhaps I have felt too sure of Isaac's reformation, though he still continued to sin, and so looked upon him with a kindly eye. For, with all my efforts to save poor Peter Barker, I could not look upon him as I did upon Isaac, and I too often turned from him cast down, dispirited, and hopeless of success."

"He was not a man of the same stamp," said Charlie; "and I am sure, my dear father, you ought to be comforted now with the recollection of your own great goodness to so thorough a reprobate as Peter! Your great forbearance and——"

"Ah! Charlie, it may seem well to you to try to comfort me, but I feel as if I were beyond such a luxury. I tried to conciliate Peter, hoping to gain power over him, and lead him on gradually to better things. But now that his sin has so surely found him out, I reproach myself that I was not more stern towards him—more active in trying to put down the bad house that sheltered him in his evil hours and encouraged him in his wickedness; for there can be no doubt that the 'Packhorse' and the Widow Mason are at the root of these evils."

"I cannot see, in these days of 'Temperance Leagues,' and other institutions for the amendment of the conduct of certain classes," said

Charlie—"I cannot see why we are to be bored with cider-shops! You, I suppose, can take away the Widow Mason's license; but can you prevent another cider-shop from being opened?"

"If the widow transgresses the law, she forfeits her license; but there is often a difficulty in proving the actions of such people. And then one crime so causes another, one almost shrinks from the responsibility; so many lies are told, so many swear falsely. You see, Charlie, boy, all the bad would swear for the widow that black was white. Your very good friend, Isaac Watson, taking up her cause, with his clever tongue and respectable appearance, backed by his bosom friend, old Jacob Smerdon, would—would—"

"Certainly very much astonish me if he were to attempt to swear that black was white for the sake of the Widow Mason! No, no, Isaac is not so bad as that!"

"Well! Well!" resumed the vicar, "the good do not like being mixed up in such cases—they do not like to be called forward to prove that such a disorderly scene was enacted when Parson So-and-so requested they would look into this and that. Stop, Charlie,"—for he again attempted to interrupt the vicar—"I am not going to shrink from my bounden duty because it is beset with difficulties; trust me, I will have the 'Packhorse' razed from the ground, and—and——"

"And the Widow Mason burned in effigy on the ruins thereof!" said Charlie.

Tea was announced at this moment; the conversation was interrupted, and the gentlemen proceeded to the drawing-room.

XXV

HOW ISAAC WATSON BROKE HIS WORD, WENT TO THE "PACKHORSE," AND CAME BACK MUCH THE WORSE FOR HIS VISIT THERE

By degrees Isaac set himself to remove Mary's goods from the school-cottage to the smithy. Unfortunately he was not able to do this without help. He applied to one or two of the neighbours for the little assistance he required, but without success. Only old Jacob Smerdon could spare time to Isaac on the two nights pointed out to him by the vicar's note for the removal of the furniture from the school-cottage.

Jacob had promised to meet Isaac and Mary at the cottage at a given hour on Monday evening—the day Mary received the note. But after they had occupied some time in packing up, ready for removal, a large number of things, as Jacob did not make his appearance, Isaac told Mary he would go and see after him. For the space of an hour, and more, Mary waited at the cottage for Isaac and Jacob, her mind anxious, it is true, for their coming, but not suspicious of evil.

She had been to the door to and fro, thus looking out for them, during the gathering together of her belongings, and they did not appear. But at length, on the stillness of the night air, she heard their voices. To her horror and dismay she heard the sounds of drunkenness, and almost sinking on the floor as she stood, she covered her face with her hands, and silently awaited their approach. They stopped at the cottage, but Mary did not move. She heard a confused sort of talking, words feebly uttered, and incomprehensible to her, and still she remained in the same attitude.

"Mary! Mary!" said Isaac's voice.

She tried to answer him, but her tongue refused her utterance.

"Mary! Mary! come here!"

Thus appealed to, and by the voice she loved, the spell was broken, and she rushed to the door. Her disgust and panic were not lessened by the sight of Jacob leaning for support against the wall of the cottage.

"Mary dear!" continued Isaac, "I must take Jacob home. You see—he was not at his own cottage—he was at the 'Packhorse,' and he cannot reach his own door without my help. Shall you mind waiting till I come back?"

"Oh, no!" said Mary, cheerfully, as she retreated from the nauseous smell of cider; for now that she saw Isaac was sober, her spirits and her hopes revived.

"I will not be longer than I can help, Mary, and I am so sorry to leave you by yourself," said Isaac.

"Do not think of me," said she, kindly; her thankfulness and gratitude, in that Isaac had not broken his word, made her feel equal to any emergency.

In little more than ten minutes Isaac returned. He caressed Mary very gently and kindly, and expressed his regret at the untoward circumstances that kept them so long about their work; and then he added that he would remove as much so he could without help that night, for fortunately the moon was bright, and on the morrow Jacob would have recovered from his night's intemperance, and be able to keep his word.

And Isaac and Mary worked on together in the little cottage, completing the arrangements it was necessary to make for the removal of the goods.

At first Mary thought Isaac unusually silent; then she thought his face had a stern expression she had never before observed; soon she felt herself again uncomfortable, from a disagreeable whiff of the scent of cider every now and then.

She concluded she must "somehow have got it in her head" when she was so disgusted by Jacob. But afterwards, and most reluctantly, she became painfully convinced Isaac had broken his word: kept it to the letter, since he was not in the same state as Jacob, but broken it in spirit, for he had certainly had cider in his absence. She could not go near to him, and doubt.

His silence and sternness were now accounted for—Isaac was reproaching himself with his shameful weakness, and did not dare to excuse himself to her.

"I will not say one word," said she to herself, as she hopelessly clasped her hands together, and watched him as he worked. I will never reproach him; but I—I will pray to God to shorten my life, and take me away from evils I feel I have not the courage to face."

She thought of Parson Hill's warning words. She shuddered at the recollection of the fate of Hannah Barker. And when their arrangements were at length finished, Mary loaded herself with as many light articles as she could carry, and Isaac took such larger things as were portable in the hands of one person.

Once arrived at the smithy cottage, Mary remained there; but Isaac went backwards and forwards till a late, or, rather, early hour in the morning, occupying himself by doing work that could have been done in one fourth of the time, if he had had help.

But Isaac had learned at the "Packhorse" that evening, that neither he nor Mary need look for anything but vituperation and sarcasm from his late boon companions. It was known, even so soon, that Mary was dismissed from the school; and the villagers, surmising that the newly married pair were cast aside by the parson, would not fail to show them all the ill-will and spite that had been formerly engendered by Isaac's prosperity and Mary's exclusiveness.

Then they who had been jealous of the great favour shown by the parson to Isaac, now rejoiced heartily in his downfall. They who envied his talents and learning, gratified themselves with the idea "that now Isaac would get no more fine books from the passon."

Several men amongst the ringers thought they could ring quite as well without Isaac as with him. And now that he had not the parson for a "standby," to use their own words, "they would stand by theirs and just kick he out."

The men of the choir thought there was no necessity that Isaac should be set over them. They had voices enough; and they knew music well enough without him. There was young Bill Sawyer had brought heaps of beautiful Church music from London; and he had a famous voice, which, if well practised in the choir, would be sure to turn out as good, if not even better, than Isaac's.

By degrees, as Isaac waited in the "Packhorse" for Jacob, he gathered this information from the many ill-natured tongues that were nightly harboured there, and that seemed to take a cruel pleasure in talking at him.

Isaac was repeatedly asked to join his old companions, and not set himself up for a great man, just because he had married Mistress Cope.

"She as was 'once upon a time' the schoolmistress of Lawsleigh," added they jeeringly.

Isaac did not reply to their jeers, nor indeed to any attack made upon himself. But when the Widow Mason stealthily filled and refilled the pewter pint from which Jacob was drinking, he told her—"That Jacob had promised to help him; that he was come to fetch him; and, indeed, had been waiting there a long time; and that he could not afford to lose his time."

"Hark ye to he!" shouted the widow. "Him be a fine friend to a poor widdy. First he takes his self away—coz why? him has a-gotten Molly Cope to his wife. And, pray, how be she's face, Mister Isaac? And then he comes here a-wanting to take away the cheery company as always comes to I the nights. Cannot he keep his precious self away, and let alone them gentlemans as likes the good old 'Packhorse' and I?" said she, bridling and looking round. "And him durst not to his life to touch a drop of cider—coz why? hissen's wife, Molly, would claw him's beard for he! Oh!—oh!—my!"

The men laughed long and loud at the widow's unseemly speeches, which were many and rude, and of the fashion of the specimen just given; but certainly not worth recording here. Isaac bore them all without reply, and only making an occasional effort to get Jacob away. At length, fancying the case hopeless, and that Jacob would not stir till the time had gone by in which he would be useful, and feeling very anxious about poor Mary, he arose to go away, saying to Jacob,

"I am sorry I cannot wait longer, but——"

"I will come—I will come," said Jacob, just as the widow had stealthily filled another pint.

"You must not leave your cider, Mister Jacob," said she.

"I have supped it up, widdy, and I be a-going," said he, rising unsteadily.

"Why, here be the cup full, Jacob," said the widow, as she showed it to him.

"Never mind that, Jacob," said Isaac, too glad to have the hope of getting him away; and in his eagerness forgetting his caution, "the widow has just refilled the cup—I saw her."

By this time the men were near the door.

"Oh!—oh!—you seed it, did you?—then take it with you," and the angry woman attempted to dash the cider in his face.

Isaac saw her intention. The widow then stepped back. Isaac seeing the woman withdraw, and thinking that now was his time, hastily pushed Jacob out, and attempted to escape from any further violence on her part; but he was too late.

In his agitation he had pushed Jacob, who had already had a good deal of cider, with too much force, and he fell over the door-sill and out into the street; while Isaac, dodging from the woman's uplifted arm, stumbled over the prostrate body of Jacob, as the contents of the cider-cup were dashed in his face, and thus blinded his eyes for the moment and saturated his clothes; which latter retained the scent of the cider for some time afterwards.

As the men lay sprawling in the street for a second or two, and at the open door of the "Packhorse," almost unable to help themselves from the nature of their fall, Mr. Gray passed by on the opposite side of the street. It was a bright moonlit night, and the curate stood waiting until the two men arose from their recumbent position, and then he recognised Jacob Smerdon and Isaac Watson, and saw them walk unsteadily on, Jacob leaning on Isaac's arm.

VOLUME III

WHICH TREATS OF PARSON HILL'S WEAKNESS

"My dear Kate, a word with you," said the vicar to Mrs. Hill, as she was leaving the breakfast-room.

"Quite at your service, most gracious sir," said she.

"I must attend the archdeacon's visitation at ―― to-morrow. On such occasions I make it a practice to dine with my reverend brethren; I see them so seldom, and am so little in their world, that, when these periodical meetings occur, I make the most of them. Therefore, for one day, I must commit my house, and my visitor, Mrs. Harcourt, to your care."

"I will do my best in your absence; but we shall all be sorry to lose you even for so short a time."

"Ah! you are very good; and I am sure you will fill my place admirably; and of course do, in all things, as if you were in your own house, as, my dear Kate, I can assure you you always are when you are under my roof."

"Thank you—thank you; I do feel most comfortably at home," said Mrs. Hill.

"I am glad of it—such is my earnest wish. And, Kate, if the day be fine, as it promises, I will ride to Colnhampstead, and then, perhaps, you and Mrs. Harcourt would like a gallop—eh?"

"Certainly—that is, I can answer for myself."

"And I can answer for Mrs. Harcourt," said the vicar; "she is fond of a good scamper across the moor; she rides well, and the grey mare just suits her."

And the next morning, by half-past eight o'clock—for the archdeacon's visitation was at eleven—the horses came round. Sir Harry and Grey Bessie for the vicar and Mrs. Harcourt, Duchess and Butterfly for Charlie and Mrs. Hill.

When the party were within sight of Colnhampstead, Mrs. Harcourt said,

"But why are we obliged to leave you here and return to Lawsleigh? There is morning service, of course, before 'the charge;' why may we not go to church?"

"Why, indeed?" said the vicar. "I had not thought of that; but there will be no difficulty, the horses can be left at the 'Crown,' Marvel will take care of them."

"Then will you like to stay for the service?" said Mrs. Harcourt to Mrs. Hill.

"Very much. I commend you for the proposal. I suppose the people will not be amused with our hats and habits, will they?"

"There will be plenty of hats, and plenty of habits; to keep you in countenance," said Charlie.

"But all the very reverend and very venerable gentlemen, including myself," said the vicar, "will have something else to do than to ascertain whether you wear hats or habits, or come without either!"

When the service was over, the congregation, as well as the party from the moor, remained to hear the Archdeacon's charge. All the world is aware of the eloquence of the Venerable the Archdeacon of —— and of his sound church principles. And that particular world, that listened so attentively to this particular charge, went away highly gratified, and fully contented. For the capacious and venerable edifice was crowded from one end to the other. There was a very full attendance of the clergy, and the laity were all eager to see and hear the new Archdeacon.

And as had been before agreed upon, the vicar remained to dine with the clergy, and the ladies and Charlie mounted their horses, and turned their heads homeward. And the party eventually reached Lawsleigh Vicarage, and, as Charlie said, "finished the day as well as they could."

They expected Mr. Hill would return about nine P.M., and Mrs. Hill ordered coffee to be ready immediately on his arrival. But instead of the vicar, came only James Marvel and Sir Harry. There was a letter for Mrs. Hill, which we will take the liberty of perusing first, for there was a second for Mrs. Harcourt enclosed in Mrs. Hill's.

"MY DEAR KATE,—I am almost ashamed to confess my weakness, but you are gracious and charitable, and will probably make some allowance for the temptations to which 'boys,' both old and young, are subjected. I have always had a goodly store of 'weaknesses,' and every now and then, and at the most unexpected times, and in the most unlooked-for places, they 'crop up,' and make me shew myself to the world in all my natural—eh!—deformity. This is one of those extraordinary 'times,' for my own house is full of visitors, and yet I leave them to do as they please, or as they best can, and accept a 'visit' myself from my Archdeacon! And even you, merciful and compassionate as I know you to be, even you will think the Rectory at Colnhampstead, the residence of my friend the Archdeacon, a strange 'place' for any of my 'weaknesses' to come to a head, and overrule me to my great delight!—ahem! But—in your own mind—keep the Archdeacon out of the scrape—he has no 'weaknesses,'—at least none—like mine.

"And then, dear Kate, next Thursday, the 29th, is 'the ladies' day' at Teign-ton-pont! Ah! you smile, do you? Have you not greatly desired to make one at those very charming county meetings, ever since you became 'one' of the county? You shall do so. That is, if you will allow me to direct your movements. But the fact is, that the match between the Plymouth Garrisons and Teign-ton-pont comes off on Thursday. The Teign-ton-pont-ers had depended a good deal on the 'Great Western,' but unfortunately he is laid up with a sprained ankle. Well, some half-dozen fellows here actually laid violent hands on me! In spite of my 'cloth,'—as Gray would say—or even in spite of the Venerable the Archdeacon's 'carved' roof—it is magnificent, tell Charlie—tried very hard to secure me in the place of the 'Great Western!' Mark that, Kate, 'in the place of!' that is to say, *not* a place in the Great Western, but in the place of the 'Great Western.' And I can assure you, my dear Kate, that the Teign-ton-pont-ers have 'a great loss' in the 'Great Western,' and that 'he' will be very poorly replaced by me, for I have already agreed to stand in his place. I have a weakness—it is in vain to try to hide it. I confess, therefore, that the idea was delightful to my ambitious mind!

"And then, Kate, I communed with myself—and, said I—'Can I conscientiously leave the dear old Teign-ton-pont-ers in their dilemma at this present moment, to be heartily beaten by that first-rate Plymouth Garrison, and *not* raise a finger to help them! Perish the thought! And then, to cheer me up, I suppose, for I had some misgivings about 'my cloth,' they told me, in strict confidence, that the very sight of my old-fashioned figure, and the widely-spread prestige of my 'bowling,' would so inspirit the Teign-ton-pont-ers, as to make them worth ten times over what they are at this moment—hampered as they are by the stoppage of 'the Great Western,' a great loss to the shareholders!—and so depress the minds of the gallant Garrison, as to make them feel themselves suddenly cut off from laurels they had predetermined to win. These two effects of my presence virtually give the palm to the Teign-ton-pont-ers; and as they have 'the palm,' it is not unreasonable to hope that they will win 'the laurels.'"

"Upon the purest principles of philanthropy, therefore, I go to this match; and I may add that I shall *not* be disappointed if the ladies—for once in a way—turn aside from 'red,' and bet on 'black' as most likely to win. Tell Charlie—though by-the-bye he ought to know all about it—to see that our hampers are well stored, to let us have plenty of champagne, fruit too in plenty, and of the choicest in my preserves. George must attend you. I shall send posters (four) to-morrow; Marvel has my orders on that head. But to you, my dear Kate, I say, do not be late. Four posters, even though accustomed to these roads, must have their time; it is a long distance, a wearisome way for the poor dumb creatures, but then again I suppose, if they were not doing that, they would do something else—why, therefore, should I waste my pity? To-morrow, Tuesday, the archdeacon proposes to drive me to Buckleigh. We shall call at 'the Court,' on Mr. Tremelly. He has a great deal of property in Lawsleigh and the neighbourhood. From thence we go on to my dear old friend the vicar of Ashbystead, and lunch with him, returning here, D.V. for dinner. I am very glad, dear Kate, to have the opportunity of calling both at Buckleigh and Ashbystead, for they are so distant from my moorland home as to be almost shut out from me for ever, although the dear masters of these locales will never lose their places in my heart and memory. I go to Teign-ton-pont on Wednesday. The match always begins the day before, and is concluded on the ladies' day. Bright eyes, shine your brightest! I have not attended a match for many years, though I have continued my subscription; for between ourselves, my dear Kate, the world has been gradually growing so good, that I had some doubts whether they—'the players'—would not think it a matter of conscience 'to bowl me off ground,' instead of allowing me to have the pleasure of 'bowling out' my adversaries! And again, my dear Kate, here on this moor I play cricket with the villagers of Lawsleigh, and any friends with me at the time. But I have, for many years, determined not to play cricket matches. 'There is no rule without an exception.' To play this match proves my rule; it is the exception to my ordinary conduct. You will be satisfied with my very clear case. If Gray only knew what a martyr I am to the non-indulgence of my weakness for cricket or any other manly English game, I do think even he would look with a tender eye on this my exceptional game. I must say a word of apology to Mrs. Harcourt, and, relying on your well-known amiability, my dear Kate, to pardon my absence at this particular time, believe me, &c.

"WILLIAM HILL."

And now we will look over Mrs. Harcourt's shoulder, and read what the vicar says to her.

"DEAR MRS. HARCOURT,—

"What will you say to so ungallant a host? But it is of little use to ask a question that cannot be answered; and so that cannot be what I meant to say. The fact is, I have been led into 'a match,' quite unintentionally on my own part, and, between ourselves, I am a little ashamed of my weakness—if weakness it can be called—that takes delight in all manly English sports and sees no harm in them. For, by one of those strange anomalies in human nature, and, in spite of my sense of shame, the anticipation of this 'match' seems to gild all my thoughts and actions for the time being with a sort of halo that is pleasurable to me. And so, if you cannot pardon the 'weakness,' you will not throw a cloud over the halo—will you? Another query—clearly that cannot be what I meant to say. Have you ever been to Teign-ton-pont?—never! Of course never. Moorgarten was at too great a distance—then you know nothing about it, and care less. Excuse me—that is *not* what you mean to say. All ladies who know anything of Devon, or of the society there, wish to go to a 'Ladies' day at Teign-ton-pont. You will go on Thursday, the 29th, with Mrs. Hill and Charlie—you see I lay my commands upon you. You will look your best—ah!—that certainly is *not* what I meant to say—for you always look so well, it would be impossible to look better. Do not spare my conservatory; flowers of the choicest are yours for the cutting. I wish I was at Lawsleigh to cut them for you. No!—that is *not* what I meant to say—because I cannot be one of the 'eleven' and yet be one with you. There is a limit to our pleasures on this earth; the 'eleven' and my 'weakness' for the time being separate me from you. The 'laurels,' when they are won—that is, if I have any hand in the winning— shall be laid at your feet. Now—I am wondering if that is what I meant to say? I thought when I took up my pen, that I meant to say something—perhaps I did. But it is late. Marvel and Sir Harry wait; and if I had anything to say, I have not time now. You will meet me at Teign-ton-pont, and the 'match' will undoubtedly be won either by 'us' or the Garrison. If you think the word 'us' requires explanation, explain it to your own satisfaction, and I shall be perfectly satisfied. I think I shall make up my mind that you quite forgive my rudeness in leaving you—my conscience has enough to bear at this moment, and if you do not pardon me, my remorse must stand over for some future occasion. Is that what I meant to say? Good night—good night—sleep well—rise well—be well—look well—and believe that

"I am yours, &c., &c.,

"WILLIAM HILL.

"Did I mean to write that?"

II

IN WHICH PARSON HILL MAKES A SPEECH

AND the Thursday came. The weather was all that could be desired; the attendance full.

If Parson Hill had been a vain man, he might have been a little annoyed that the party from the moor did not arrive earlier on the ground—the more so as he had forewarned them of the long distance and the bad roads, and expressed a wish that they should not be late. But he was far too much absorbed in the game to notice their absence. Teign-ton-pont had met their match! One of the gallant —— was as clever at "bowling" as the parson himself; and the good "bowlers" and the capital "bats" on *both* sides, made the battle a hard one to win.

Mrs. Hill and Mrs. Harcourt had not been many minutes on the ground, when a cheer proclaimed that the match was won. And the parson hurried from the field to tell the latter the "laurels" were hers, as he had promised. For Teign-ton-pont had beaten the Garrison.

And now the "elevens" came in by ones and twos and threes, and the ladies clustered together in groups, or promenaded on the green turf, until the announcement of dinner. The president on this occasion was not Sir Walter Pellew of Laccomb, nor Mr. Dunro of Hunsdon, nor Lord Chenstone, nor dear—and, at that time, well known—Henry Mayler. The president may have been a stranger to many, but he was evidently well-known to Parson Hill. The president, when dinner was announced, led the way with Mrs. Hill; Parson Hill followed with Mrs. Harcourt, and soon the large dining-room was full, and the company busy with the good things set before them.

After dinner the usual toasts were given and responded to, and last of all—as is the custom—the president gave, "The Ladies." I am not able to say that, by any pre-arrangement, Parson Hill rose to reply to this toast. It is certain that he did so.

"Ladies and Gentlemen,—Many years have passed since last I had the honour and the pleasure of standing in your presence. The snows of many winters have added a lustre to my crown; and with years come experience. I am, as you know, a country parson, living on Dartmoor; but neither my locality nor my cloth ever deters me from the heart-felt pleasure of returning thanks for the ladies. In my early life, fate sent me wandering from my native land. In all the cities of Europe—in sunny Constantinople, in quaint Nuremberg, in ancient Prague—I have returned thanks for the ladies. In the Valley of Chamouny, in the Vale of Tempe, and in our own beautiful dove-dale, I have returned thanks for the ladies. On Ehrenbreitstein, on the Righi, on the Rock of Gibraltar, on the Great St. Bernard, and on Mount Parnassus, I have returned thanks for the ladies. On the beautiful lakes of our own country, on Killarny, on Como, on the Lagunes of Venice, on the Bay of Naples, and on the Golden Horn, I have returned thanks for the ladies. On Snowdon, on Ben Lawers, on the Jura, on the Pyrenees, on the Alps, and on the Apennines, I have given thanks for the ladies. But never have I returned thanks for the ladies with more hearty good-will than on the present occasion. (Prolonged applause.) Never have I seen brighter eyes, never more lovely forms, never more charming faces, than meet my gaze at the present moment; and never was my heart more glad in returning thanks for the ladies than at the present time. (Loud cheers.) Ladies," and here the parson paused and looked round, "ladies, we, the Teign-ton-ponters, have this day met a gallant opponent, a fair foe in a fair fight, an honourable company of honourable gentlemen; and if the chances of the game went against them, it was not for want of skill, or want of any of those qualities that together make up the cricketer and the gentleman. We, the Teign-ton-ponters, had hard work to beat them. (Loud and prolonged cheers.) They are no sluggards at their work; they are as gallant a set of gentlemen as it has ever been our good fortune to meet, but, as I said, hard to conquer. Ladies, bright eyes, are dangerous weapons—yours are very bright (cheers); smiles are very encouraging—yours are more, they wound while they beckon. (Cheers.) Men who are glorious in fight, have warm hearts for the ladies; men who are hard to conquer by their fellow-men, succumb to the power of the ladies; men who are gallant, and noble, and true, are always true to the ladies. Such are the glorious—(Cheers.) Ladies, I have the honour to return thanks in your name, &c., &c," and Parson Hill seated himself amid a storm of applause.

And then according to the custom of the meeting, the ladies retired. On these occasions the gentlemen do not remain long at their wine. The festivities of the day always conclude with a dance.

III

IN WHICH PARSON HILL
MEETS MANY OLD FRIENDS

On the re-appearance of the gentlemen after dinner, Parson Hill was accosted by a young lady,

"Mr. Hill!—Mr. Hill!" clapping her hands, "I am so glad to see you!"

"I also am glad that I have the power to gladden you," said the parson, lifting his hat high from his head.

"It is such a long time since I have seen you."

"Is it indeed you have had no loss; but mine has been great. And you really look so young, and fresh, and charming—pray, were you 'out' when I was here last?"

"Why, I am not 'out' now—what nonsense you talk! Do not you know me?"

"The knowledge is on your side—all that I know is that you are a very fascinating young lady; if you are not 'out,' the gentlemen have a great loss; and, in my opinion, you ought to come 'out' immediately. Is that nonsense?"

"I am afraid mamma would think 'yes;' but I would so like to come 'out,' but mamma says——"

"Suppose you take my arm," said Parson Hill, suiting the action to the word; "and then we can and a very cozy talk."

"Yes we can," said the lady, taking his arm. "And I did so beg of mamma to let me come today—you see, there was a doubt, because the carriage was so full; but I offered to sit anywhere, or stand, or——"

"I am quite sure you were most amiable."

"And now I am so glad, because you are here."

"And I also am glad, as I said before; and certainly your presence adds to my gladness."

"Oh! You are so funny—you are just as funny as ever. I knew you would be, as soon as ever I saw you. But mamma says I am not to 'come out' until——"

Here the lady stopped, and with a pretty blush looked up at Parson Hill. He stooped his ear to a level with her face, and said,

"Until?"

"It is a secret," said she.

These words appeared to satisfy the parson, for he started to his full height in a moment, as he said,

"I always consider it dangerous to listen to secrets from young ladies. So pray do not tell me!"

"Oh! don't be so stiff," said she, as she tugged at his arm to make him unbend from his erect position. "Why, I daresay you know all about it."

"You 'daresay' more than I dare."

"Why, has not mamma told you? Because, though it is such a secret, and we are all told not to talk about it, and all that, yet we know mamma tells everybody. She does——"

"And has not told me! Then, of course, I am highly offended. And, most agreeable young lady, if you will take the trouble to understand my uncomfortable position, I think your kind heart will pity me. I do not know your mamma. I do not know you; and I do not know the secret. Now, what do you say to that?"

"Not know me!" said the lady, pulling his arm, and quite ignoring the other two parts of the parson's speech. "Why, I am Lucy! Look at me. Now, don't you see I am Lucy?"

"I see you are very charming."

"Oh, yes! That is just as you used to talk. But you have not been to our house for a very long time. But then, I of course, I know you just as ever. Why, we used to be such good friends."

"And she looked appealingly at him.

"And I hope we are now," said the parson, stopping in his walk, and looking down upon the lady's upturned face.

"Oh, yes? That is, I am sure I am," said she.

"And I am sure I am."

"There is mamma—look! and Isabel, and——"

And the parson and his companion turned to greet some ladies, who were evidently well known to both.

"And so you are the mamma to this charming Lucy?" said Mr. Hill, as he shook hands with the lady.

"I saw her seize hold of you as soon as you left the dining-room," said Mrs. Campbell.

"Pardon me. She is my prisoner," said the parson.

And then the two parties joined, and recommenced their promenade. But this arrangement was not a pleasant one to Lucy. And when, in the pauses of the conversation, Parson Hill turned to speak to her, she said,

"I wish mamma would go away—do not you?"

Parson Hill looked so extremely shocked at this speech, that for the moment the young lady was disconcerted; but rallying almost immediately, she pulled his arm, and said,

"I know you do not mean it."

"Indeed I do," said Parson Hill, *sotto voce*.

And he turned to continue his conversation with Mrs. Campbell.

"I do not believe you," said Lucy, when she could arrest his attention. "You are only making fun, as you always do."

"Remember, I am a parson."

But as, in gatherings of this sort, everybody knows everybody, it follows that everybody must speak to everybody; and thus it happened that Mrs. Campbell was greeted by another party, and Parson Hill was then set free to give all his attention to Lucy.

"There! I am so glad she is gone! Let us get away from the crowd."

"Miss Lucy Campbell, do you wish to distress the nerves of your aged friend?"

"Aged, indeed! Why, you are not at all old! You are just the very same as ever; and I am so glad! But why do you call me 'miss?' Don't you remember you always called me 'your dear little Lucy.'"

"Did I indeed! What could I have been thinking of, to take such a liberty with you!"

"Why, I liked it very much. And now I am going to ask you something—something that I want you to do. I have quite set my heart on it."

The parson stopped, and looked down upon the lady.

"Now, you need not make such a face, because I shall not believe you. We all want it so much."

"Not believe me! Am I in my senses?"

"Yes you are. And they made me promise to ask you, as soon as ever they saw you. There was such a clapping of hands in our carriage when Isabel spied you amongst the cricketers! Mamma was quite ashamed!"

"She might well be ashamed!—young ladies clapping their hands at the cricketers! But you say 'they' made you promise to ask me this something. Why did not 'they' ask me themselves?"

"Two or three of them said it would not do for them; but I could do it very well. And I was very glad to have to find you out, and ask you to walk with me, and all that!"

"Umph!" said the parson; and then he began to wonder within himself what the lady had set her heart upon, and who were the fair ones whom Lucy designated by "they."

"Will you have the kindness to tell me the names of those ladies who sent you to me? I hope they are not intended to be kept secret?"

"Oh! dear no! There was Isabel, and Charlotte Pitt, and Louisa and Jane Hammond, and a great many more, all the rest of us. Of course you know us all?"

"Do I?" said the parson.

"Now do not pretend such nonsense—of course you do! We want to have a day on the moor. We want you to ask our mammas and all of us to come to Lawsleigh for a long, long day."

"Can you not come without being asked?"

"Why, yes; but that will not do at all—we want a real long day, all of us together. When we go without having been asked, we are only two or three; but all together, everybody for a long day—that is what we want."

"Had you not better stay all night?"

The lady was a little disconcerted by this, but again she rallied almost immediately, and said, with such frank *naiveté*, "I never thought of that!" that Parson Hill saw she would have no inclination to refuse such a request, if he made it in earnest.

"Now you expect me to give an answer, and fix the day at once, do you?"

"Of course I do. I expect you to say 'Yes,' and to fix an early day. They all expect it—and they all said you would say 'Yes' to me."

"And so I would," said the parson, "only as you are not out, and therefore cannot come——"

"Indeed I go to all such places!"

"Such places, indeed!" interrupted the parson.

"Yes, all such places. Mamma takes me to pic-nics and water-parties, and archery, and such like."

"And would she bring you to the moor?"

"She would be delighted! and so would papa—he is so fond of the moor—and Edward, and Herbert, and——"

"Oh!—oh!—oh!" said the parson, affecting to groan.

"Now do not make such a noise," said she, giving his arm a good pull. "You know you like us all very much."

"Do I?" said the parson, in a tone that expressed a doubt.

"Yes. That is, you used to do," and the lady seemed also to allow some doubt of something to creep into her mind, for she said, in an altered tone: "But if you do not want us to come, why," and then there was a little sigh, as if she inwardly resigned all thought of that charming day on the moor, that had been so vividly pictured by her own bright imagination, "why, I am sure *I* do not want to come; and they will not; and I shall go and tell them," and she drew her arm from Parson Hill, "that you are quite altered, and do not care for us one bit!"

"Oh! Lucy! Lucy! and are you then going to leave me?"

"Why, you do not want me; you are quite changed!"

"Then you have changed me!"

"I! What have I done?"

"Have you not told me that you—you, my dear little Lucy," and the parson turned up his eyes despairingly, "that you do not want to come?"

"Well, that is because you are so strange; but really, I *do* want to come very much!"

"Then why did you tell such a falsehood, Lucy?" said Parson Hill, as he once more replaced her arm within his own. "And to a parson, of all people in the world!"

"Don't talk nonsense! You know I *do* want to come and see you; and they all want to come; and I only said that because I was proud!"

"Then people who are proud are allowed to tell falsehoods, are they?"

"Oh! do not trouble me about that, but just go on with what we have been talking about."

"And you are sure you may come, though you are not out?"

"Yes, yes, of course, I go to all such places. But I have to wait a whole year after that is all over, about Isabel and Colonel Ramsden, and so I shall not be out for a long time yet; but that will make no difference."

"Who are those young ladies standing in a group to the right?"

"Why, all the very people!—all the Hammonds, and Charlotte Pitt, and the Stones, and all your old friends!"

"All my old friends? Then why do they not come and speak to me?"

"Why, I told you they sent me, because they said you would be sure to say 'yes,' if I asked you."

"Then if I take courage, and walk up to them, do you think they will speak to me?"

"They will be delighted," said the lady, eagerly; "and you will be sure to tell them we may have our day."

"No," said the parson, shaking his head.

"No!—oh!—do you really mean that?" said she, earnestly.

"I commission you, my dear little Lucy, to invite your young friends to Lawsleigh Vicarage for this day fortnight. And now let us turn off at this side walk, just to make our arrangements for the grand day—we must have something to amuse so many people—shall we have dominoes?"

"Dominoes!—good gracious!—why, we want to be out of doors all day!"

"Ah! then hockey is the game—only mind the bogs."

"Nonsense—only boys play hockey. We will have croquet."

"Croquet!" said the parson; "and, pray, what is croquet?"

"Why, do not you know croquet?—why, everybody knows croquet quite well; and it would be so nice on the moor."

"Is it a sweet cake?"

"I tell you, it is a game like hockey."

"Well, then, if it is like hockey, why will not hockey do?—because I do not know the one, and I am well versed in the other."

"Oh! nonsense, we shall never get on in this way—and, there—now do not you hear the band?"

"Ah! and as my dancing days are over, I am ashamed to have appropriated my little Lucy all this time, and so caused her to lose the first dance."

"I should not care if I had, because I am with you. But they are not dancing yet; do not you see the groups of ladies still standing about?— they will all be gone as soon as the first dance is called. And you will promise me that we shall all go to the moor this day fortnight?"

"Yes, I promise. But may I get up a cricket-match for the gentlemen, as well as hockey for the ladies? Remember, the party is yours—*you* are to be the queen of the day."

"Oh! delightful!—charming!—do you really mean it?"

"I really mean it."

"Oh! most surprising!—and how I do hope mamma will let me. Queen of the day!—beautiful!"

"Do you think she will refuse any request of mine?" said Parson Hill, with a serious face.

"Oh! no—I am sure she will not."

"Then we will have a cricket-match and hockey; and I'll ask the Garrison, and the Teign——"

"No!" said Lucy, in her naive surprise.

"Ah, you object to the presence of so many gentlemen?"

"No, no, no; I am out of my wits with joy—ask them all, everyone. The only mistake is, the hockey—we will have croquet; and do make them all come."

"Then does croquet mean people?"

"We will do *without* croquet," said she, vehemently; "so, now, do not trouble any more about that. But I assure you everybody knows and everybody plays the game of croquet."

"Game! Then if everybody plays, of course, as you say, we will have it—there is plenty of room on the moor."

By this time they were near to a group of ladies standing together conversing; and Lucy exclaimed,

"You are all to go with me to the moor; and all the Garrison; and all Teign-ton-pont, and mamma, and everybody—oh! I *am* so pleased!"

Parson Hill drew himself up to his full height, raised his hat high above his head, and stood silent; while Lucy volubly and delightedly explained the success of her application.

Charlie came up to claim his partner, for the first quadrille was forming; and Mr. Hill took the opportunity of saying to him,

"When you are at liberty from the dance, just make a list of those friends of ours who are here to-day."

And when Lucy was claimed for the dance, the vicar made arrangements with the Garrison and the Club to meet at Lawsleigh that day fortnight. It is almost unnecessary to add that all the mammas of all the young ladies gave a willing assent to Parson Hill's invitation.

IV

THE DOG WITH AN ILL NAME

THE sun had risen on Lawsleigh long before Isaac Watson gave up his walk to and fro between the school cottage and the smithy. And when at length he thought he had done as much as one unassisted man could do at one time, he prepared himself for a little rest, previously to the commencement of the toils of a new day. He went softly into his bedroom, afraid of disturbing Mary, if she were asleep: yet half-longing she might be awake, that he might tell her of the progress he had made; but, to all appearance, Mary slept.

"How tired she looks," said Isaac to himself; "and I do think the pillow is wetted with her tears—poor thing! she frets about losing the school." And with a heavy sigh at Mary's vexation, Isaac put his head on the pillow, and, worn out with toil and anxiety, closed his eyes in sleep.

As soon as the steady rise and fall of his respiration proved that he was oblivious of all worldly cares, Mary raised up her head, and, bending over, looked at him as she said to herself,

"I declare his face is as good and calm in its expression as if he had not broken his word. And how he has worked through this weary night!—that is, weary to me," continued she, for she had not slept, "because my heart is so full of trouble."

Mary now sat up in bed; the sun's rays streamed brightly in at the window. They were gradually creeping over the bed from the head downwards. Mary turned again to look at Isaac as he lay in all his unconscious manliness and strength; his head without any covering, except the dark curls that clustered so thickly over it, and on the crown of which the sun's beam rested, throwing, as it were, for a minute or two, a halo over him while sleeping.

"Ah! how I love him!" said Mary, as the tears unbidden rolled down her cheeks. "He looks so good; nay, he is so good—no one, not even Parson Hill can deny that. He is good; good to me and to his mother, and to everybody, except himself, and—well! I never! But the sun does make him look handsome," continued she, as she gazed upon him. "I might say blessed; yes, blessed with that light playing round his head! And yet here I sit crying my eyes out, because—oh! what shall I do?—what will become of me? And I do love him so!"

And with a passionate burst of weeping, stifling her sobs as best she could, for fear of awaking Isaac, Mary once more put her head on the pillow, and tried to sleep.

Vain attempt! The shock had been too great for her physical strength. She had not the power of forgetfulness—that great boon to the weary-hearted. Isaac had broken his word. This one idea haunted her. She did not attempt to find excuses for him in his fault, or for herself in having too easily credited his honeyed words, and too willingly placed herself in her present position. All she said, and thought, was—"Isaac has broken his word."

But the morrow came, or rather, in this case, the hour for rising, in spite of the wretchedness of the night. Isaac still slept.

There was, to Mary's thinking, something strange in the repose of the smithy cottage this morning, as distinguished from others; for in these few short days of her early married life, she had become so accustomed to the stirring sounds of a smith at work, while she was dressing, she could hardly understand or appreciate the silence of the present moments.

"I must hide my trouble from poor mother," said Mary. "Ay, from everybody; from him; and I wish I could forget it myself."

And she bathed her face and eyes with cold spring water.

"I must try to look just my own-self." And again she attempted to remove the traces of tears from her eyes. "And I must pray to God for strength to bear what His will imposes upon me."

And now Mary began to feel a little more calm, and a little better able to sustain her part, as she had suggested to herself, and she went down to breakfast.

"The lad be a-weary after a-working all night," said the widow to Mary, as she made her appearance downstairs.

"He does seem very tired, mother—dear Isaac," said Mary, recalling him to her mind's eye, as he lay with the sun's beams playing round his head.

"Ay, lass, him be worth thy trouble; for trouble I can see thee hast got a-losing of the school."

And so, fortunately for Mary, both the Widow Simpson and Isaac thought she fretted for the loss of the school; and Mary, ingenuous even in her thoughts, said to herself,

"And so I should have fretted for the school if I had not had some weightier burden on my mind," and she sighed heavily as she remembered Parson Hill's words, "that in less than a month—ay, she would not have been married a week before Isaac would go to the 'Packhorse' again."

But, at length, Isaac made his appearance, and, in his hearty way, acknowledged "he had been very lazy that morning; he could not but feel ashamed at sleeping so long."

To a man accustomed to rise with the sun, it does appear "lazy" to remain in bed till eight A.M., whatever may have overruled the change of hour; and Isaac spoke, in the simplicity of his heart, the actual feeling of the moment. But now Mary's thoughts took a bitter turn, for she said to herself,

"If he had only that to feel ashamed of, how proud I should be of him—but I see now, I am not to be proud and happy, and think I have the handsomest and best husband in the world, though I did think so yesterday, and all my sorrow for the loss of the school—and it was real and great—could not take away the proud happiness about my heart."

And yet, though she suffered such thoughts to destroy her peace of mind—for she felt perfectly assured that Isaac had been drinking at the 'Packhorse'—yet, by a strange sort of perversity, she never turned her eyes upon him without being charmed with his frank and ardent manner, eager to anticipate her lightest wish, and always putting his hand to any kind of help either she or the good Widow Simpson required.

But Isaac went on with his daily work, and Mary tried to stow out of the way as many of her newly arrived treasures as she could. For, about ten o'clock, the bright morning had suddenly clouded over, and a heavy shower fell, and, as Isaac had not been particular in placing the goods under cover—indeed he had not space for them—they were in danger of being a good deal defaced.

While Mary and the old woman busied themselves by carrying into the cottage such articles as they could lift, Isaac set off to the nearest farm to borrow a tarpaulin. He failed in his first attempt, but, not suspecting his neighbour of incivility, he was hastily going off to another, when the farmer himself appeared and prevented him by saying,

"Isaac, thee would get a tarpauler down there to the Vickridge—eh! Isaac?—haw, haw, haw! The passon may be would lend thee one—eh! Isaac? Ax the passon to lend thee a cover for thy wife's fine bonnet—the passon be uncommon kind to thee, lad!"

The man continued his jeers, but Isaac now turned away home. Never in his life had he felt more angry. To think that the very man who, only one short week ago, would have been proud and pleased to do him any kindness, should now not only refuse his neighbourly assistance in a time of difficulty, but should actually insult him, first with the loss of the parson's favour, and then with the manner in which his wife chose to dress. But he did not reply to the man's abuse, only this conduct from one neighbour influenced Isaac not to ask from another what might a second time produce jeers at his change of position, instead of lending him the required help.

And so Isaac then gave his assistance to the two women, and removed the heavier articles under cover, which had filled up his shed, so as to preclude the possibility of receiving even one horse for its shoes, to say nothing of the teams crossing the moor that might at any moment require his attention.

About twelve the rain ceased, and the sun shone again, but the appearance of the clouds driving heavily before the wind seemed to threaten more wet ere the day was over.

"Mary, dear," said Isaac, as he fetched his hat, "I'll just go to the cottage while it holds up, and take Jem with me"—one of his men at work in the back shop—"and remove the drawers while the sun shines. You see, my dear, we packed them in fine weather, and did not forecast for storms, so now I will be off and get them in dry, if I can."

And so Isaac set off, attended by Jem; and together they managed to bring home the drawers before another shower prevented their going again to the cottage; and when that valued piece of furniture was safe, Isaac came in with a face radiant with good-humour, contentment, and love, and, rushing up to Mary, exhibited to her delighted eyes a large bouquet of choice flowers.

"Goodness me, Isaac!—what lovely flowers! Where did you get them?"

"Guess!" said the delighted Isaac, holding them high up, out of her reach.

"It be the passon, lad!—the cheery passon!" said the widow. "I knowed him was only making believe to be hard on you; the passon has a-got a kind heart; him be the man as have sended them posies!"

"Nay, nay, mother," said Isaac, "it is not the parson," as, with a heavy sigh, he gave the flowers to Mary, and stooping, kissed her tenderly. "When I passed the vicarage garden, Mary, the two ladies were there—Master Charlie's wife, and the other lady—and they stopped me, and asked how you were—and they asked for you, mother—and I gave them many thanks for the nice basket of fruit that James Marvel brought you from the vicar. And when I was returning, there they were again at the garden wall. And they called to me, and said they had gathered those flowers for you, Mary, and they hoped you would like them. So kind of them, my dear, was it not?"

"Oh! yes, Isaac, they are very kind, they are two such nice ladies, you cannot think how kind they were to me on my journey from town. They seemed to think—though they did not say so—to think that I was innocent of the things Mr. Gray had told them about me; and so I was, you know!"

"Quite innocent, Mary. And I like those ladies, my dear, as much as you do. They are very pleasant in their manner to me at all times; for in my walks to and fro to your cottage, before we married, I have often chanced to see them, and they had always the same kind, smiling, and encouraging manner; so that I could lift up my head and speak to them heartily! And I used to walk away happy, my dear, and say to myself, 'I feel as if those ladies thought well of me!' And to my dying hour," said Isaac, after a little pause, "I shall be grateful to those ladies for their treatment of you—for thinking you innocent until you could be proved guilty. 'Give a dog an ill name,' says the proverb. And I am myself a living proof of the truth of that saying For I fear the ill name that I have given to myself by my former deeds,"—oh! why did Mary think at this moment of Isaac's broken promise?—"will be a long time ere it leaves me, though I am now an altered man, for which I devoutly thank my Maker!"

And as, in his kind and tender way, he turned to caress Mary, she hid her face upon his shoulder.

V

IN WHICH ISAAC WATSON ENJOYS HIS PIPE, AND TASTES COFFEE FOR THE FIRST TIME

THE troubles at the smithy seemed to increase instead of lessen. The goods from the cottage were all removed in the given time, but there was great difficulty in finding room for them. Most of the cottages on that part of Dartmoor were built of stone, but the smithy cottage erected, by Isaac's forefathers, was of granite, and though so small and poor in comparison with less remote dwellings, was a model of sturdiness and strength. The one large room on the ground floor ran from back to front, and opened at the side into Isaac's shed. The two rooms above—that is, the space of the large room divided into two for bed-rooms—with some small offices on the ground floor, together made all the accommodation there was.

These three rooms were better filled with furniture than any other in the village, excepting only the school-cottage, which, as we have said, was fitted up with a certain degree of luxury for Mary's use.

Until Isaac could build additional rooms, it was very inconvenient to bring in many articles, and almost impossible to find room for them. For a day or two all kinds of annoyances accrued from this influx of heavy material, that could not by any amount of art be pressed into a small compass; and, to add to their troubles, the weather continued wet, and had become cold. Isaac's shed was full of packages, and men, bringing their horses to be shod, grumbled that both themselves and their horses must stand in the rain. It was plain something must be done. Isaac had wasted many hours of valuable time in trying to engage masons to commence at once the addition he contemplated making to his cottage, and had failed. Mary behaved well. She did not complain that the goods were getting wetted or defaced, or that they were inconveniently placed, so that the articles they contained were useless to her; she saw Isaac did all he could. And in her present state of mind, she would not have cared much if all her valued furniture had been set fire to in the middle of the moor, and burnt to ashes, so long as Isaac had only been true to his word, and never entered that "Packhorse" again.

A great sorrow absorbs the mind, and takes away our desire for earthly grandeur and earthly possessions; and Mary's grief at Isaac's succumbing to temptation was very great and very absorbing.

In the course of day or two, when the wind was less boisterous, and the rain had somewhat ceased, Isaac set about building a temporary shed of wood, that should be weather-proof, behind the cottage, and in a corner of the garden. It is true it was very inconvenient to have a shed there, and it is also true that, in the limited space at his command, he could never place it conveniently, and then there must be some destruction of garden produce; so that, all things considered, the influx of Mary's wealth seemed to impoverish Isaac rather than to enrich him; but if he did now and then heave a deep sigh over his work, and now and then shake his head, as he destroyed in the garden more than he had at first anticipated, he did not add to Mary's troubles by telling her of his own.

It was of first-rate importance to stow somewhere out of the way the many packages that encumbered his shed, for they prevented the men and horses from having their customary shelter in stormy weather. When Isaac set to work, he did not let the grass grow under his feet, and so, to use his own words, "he knocked up the shed, roughly enough, in no time," and then carried in as much as he could without more help,—promising to himself to complete his work early on the morrow, with the assistance of one of his men—but he managed to clear a good space in his own shed. It was late at night before he had finished, for the showers came on occasionally, and proved a great hindrance; but he gave up work at length and entered the cottage, saying, in his hearty tones,

"My dear, was I not fortunate? I had got all the best of the things safe before the last shower came, and now the place is snug and tight, and they cannot take any harm."

"But you seem so wet, Isaac," said Mary, gently.

"That is nothing, my dear," said he.

And he gave himself a shake, and sprinkled Mary all over with the wet from his clothes; but as he did not see the effect of his own action, Mary said nothing.

"The nice fire is very comfortable, my dear," said he, as he seated himself on the settle in the corner. "I shall soon be dry now I have taken off my waistcoat; and I think it so kind of you, my dear, to sit up all by yourself, and it is so very late."

And Isaac looked at the large clock that was ticking loudly, and pointing out the hour.

"Why, you have been working so hard, Isaac, and I am sure I am always very glad to sit up for you; and I made you some nice coffee—at least, *I* think it nice," said Mary, correcting herself. "I thought perhaps you would like it with your pipe," added she, timidly, for she could not forget his taste for cider.

"It smells very nice, my dear," said Isaac, who was not accustomed to anything but tea; but this coffee had been brought from the school-cottage amongst Mary's stores.

She poured out a cup, and put milk and sugar in Isaac's reach; and when he had tasted it, he declared there never was anything in the world that could be nicer.

"Why, Mary dear, cider is nothing to it!" said Isaac.

"I am glad you like it better than cider," said she, feeling her heart bound as if she now saw some light through the darkness that appeared to envelope her.

"Better! why, there is no comparison; it is most delicious, and so warm and comforting after being so wet. Thank thee, my dear Mary, and God bless thee!" added he, softly, as he placed his hand on her head.

"You know, Isaac, all the gentlemen at the vicarage have coffee when they smoke—never cider," said Mary, in sweet low tones, that fell pleasurably on Isaac's ear.

"Indeed, my dear! They know what is good!" said he, shaking his head and laughing.

"Why, many a time I have seen them with their pipes and cigars on the lawn, all among the flowers, and the men-servants handing them coffee, and little tiny tables set about here and there, and some gentlemen walking about, and some sitting down, and all talking and laughing together so happily, and perhaps some ladies at the drawing-room windows, and some gentlemen standing talking with them."

"Well really, my dear, that must have been a very attractive sort of scene. I know that beautiful vicarage lawn well," said Isaac, trying to stifle a sigh; "and I am sure the gentlemen must enjoy their pipes and their cigars there, all among the flowers, and the handsome ladies looking at them and talking to them. And then this coffee! Mary, I hope the gentlemen like their coffee as well as I do mine."

And Isaac drank off a large cup of coffee as if it had been a pint of cider.

"You see, Isaac, I often used to go to the vicarage summer evenings— perhaps between eight and nine o'clock—to fetch some books, or anything else Parson Hill had given me; and so then it was I used to see the gentlemen have pipes and coffee on the lawn."

"Yes, my dear, he was always a kind man, was the parson, and always trying to do good. He has lent me a great many books in my time. I am very grateful to him."

And Isaac sighed heavily as he thought of the loss he had in the parson's notice.

"And I could make you coffee any time you like, Isaac," said Mary, inwardly hoping Isaac would say—"Always, instead of cider;" but he only said—"To be sure, my dear;" and replacing his pipe in his mouth puffed quietly; while Mary turned away her face to hide her disappointment, and a silence fell upon them for the space of a minute or two. At length Isaac spoke.

"Is that the coffee kettle standing there on the turf?"

"It is the coffee-pot, Isaac."

"Oh! ay. I see it is quite a different shape from the tea-kettle. And so that is the coffee-pot?—and I am sure it has made some very nice coffee for me to-night. And I *do* like coffee," added he, kindly, for her silence had not escaped his notice. "And I hope to live to bless the day that first made us man and wife. And this day also, Mary, that you first made for me such delicious coffee."

And then Isaac took his pipe from his mouth, and put his arm round Mary and drew her nearer to him, for he saw the tear trembling in her eye, though he had no thought of the great sorrow that saddened all Mary's thoughts; and said in a gentle tone, as if he wished to comfort her,

"And, my dear, in spite of our present annoyances, we must bear up with courage. It is a long lane that has no turn."

Mary cast down her eyes, and did not speak. Whenever Isaac referred hopefully to their future career, she recalled his broken vow. But he, fancying her mind was running on the loss of the school, and her goods still in such jeopardy, said,

"And, my dear, we must have patience. I will get everything right for you as soon as I can. And I do not think the furniture will suffer any harm in the long run; for when the new rooms are built, I will polish up the tables and chairs, and get them all in order before they are put into use."

"Oh! I am sure you are always most kind, Isaac," said Mary, as the tear overflowed its boundary, and rolled down her cheek; for she understood that he had misread her silence.

"And I had need be ashamed if I was not kind, Mary. And, my dear, never in my life have I relished my pipe as I do to-night. It is all the coffee—most delicious it is."

And Isaac tossed off another large cup of the wonderful beverage at a mouthful.

Mary's heart again swelled with hope, and Isaac said,

"I declare, Mary, I might be a king!—that is, for my enjoyment of my pipe, and the coffee, and with you, my dear—God bless you!—by my side!"

And he pressed her tenderly to his heart.

Isaac forgot that the toil he had undergone made rest enjoyable and refreshment welcome; and though we by no means wish to do away with the propriety of Mary's forethought in providing the coffee, we feel it is just an even chance that, if it had been produced under less favourable auspices, it might not have been so highly relished.

VI

WHICH TREATS OF THE OLD SIMPSONSES BIBLE

THE Widow Simpson had always been what was called on the moor a "deft-handed" woman, that is, clever with her needle, or at knitting, or at household work. We might describe her as a thorough housewife, without an atom of the so-called "book-learning" that distinguished Isaac from his contemporaries.

Until Isaac grew up to manhood, she used no book but the Bible. Indeed books of any kind were great rarities on the moor. And even when Isaac was able to offer to her amusing or instructive books, they were no pleasure to her. Works on religious subjects she preferred; but curiously enough she always told Isaac she was no wiser at the end than she was at the beginning.

When Mary's store of books was added to Isaac's, the old woman was greatly astonished at their number, the beauty of the binding of some, the number of "picters" in others.

Parson Hill always sent Mary the "Leisure Hour," and these numbers were afterwards bound. The "Family Friend" was a luxury Mary had hitherto been able to allow herself, because, as she said to the widow,

"It is so useful; there are so many good patterns, and the stories are so pretty."

And now the widow seemed in a fair way to become learned in her old age. She repeatedly put aside her knitting to look at the "many picters in Mary's books." And when Mary explained the meaning of the "picter," her astonishment was very great. In her childhood she had never heard half so many wonderful tales as Mary told her now. For with great good-nature,

Mary would sit by the old woman, and, without reading the whole story aloud, give a synopsis of the principal events, that very much gratified her hearer. Then the old woman told Mary that

"Isaac's books be that hard as I could never make nothing out of them. And yet, Mary, the lad has a-tried to find a book as I should like."

"I am sure he would, mother; he is so kind."

"There be the old Simpsonses Bible, Mary dear. I have a-readed in that ever since I was but a little one."

"Yes, mother. This, I suppose," said Mary pointing to one on the side table, a quarto edition in two volumes, and an excellent print, "that I see you use every day?"

"Oh, no! That be the one Isaac gived I."

Mary, on examining the book, saw that she had spoken without reflexion. It had been published by the "Society for Promoting Christian Knowledge," long since the Widow Simpson was a girl.

"Us must have the large old Simpsonses Bible bringed down off the shelf, Mary."

But it was beyond Mary's reach, and, moreover, very heavy, and Isaac was called in to assist.

"And now, lad, as thee has got the book down, I must have the lines put in, about thee and Mary."

Mary did not understand; but she quickly fetched pen and ink; and then, under the records of former generations, she saw Isaac write, in his bold, clear, and clerkly hand:

"Isaac Watson married Mary Cope, &c., &c.

And after the little scene that followed the writing of the lines was over—Isaac gently caressing Mary, and the old woman giving them her blessing—Mary took the opportunity of examining "the large old Simpsonses Bible," and confessed to herself she had never, except only in church, seen one of such a size and beauty as this. It was bound in white calf, but not ornamented. The simple initials I.S. were on the cover. But in the midst of her admiration at the large size of the book, at its clear type, and its excellent state of preservation, she was not much surprised to hear that the old woman did not like the Bible Isaac had given her half so well.

"No, mother dear, it is not so large nor so handsome," said Mary; "but then it is more comfortable to use every day, and saves this large one for years and years to come."

"Ay, lass; but I never think of saving the Bible. Coz why, Mary, Bibles always lasts peoples lives, and the lives of their children."

"Yes; such a magnificent Bible as this would of course last many gene rations, and especially with this strong leather cover to slip on and off."

"But, Mary, why for do they call Adamses and Eveses breeches 'aprons' in this new Bible?"

"I do not know what you mean, mother," said Mary.

"Why, Mary dear, in the 'large old Simpsonses Bible,' the first man, that be Adam, and the first woman, that be Eve, the mother of all the living creatures," continued the old woman to Mary's mute astonishment, "when they seed as they was naked they made theirselves 'breeches' to cover theirselves, as was but right."

"Oh, no, mother," said Mary; "you have forgotten. I can show you the passage," and she turned to open the large Bible.

"And in that 'large old Simpsonses Bible' they have a-got 'breeches,' I knows," said the old woman, in a positive tone.

Mary, if she had spoken, would have said she never was so "taken aback" in her life! She actually rubbed her eyes, as if the fault, if fault it was, lay there. Then she compared the two editions, and understood what had before seemed strange in the old woman's query.

Isaac entered the room at this moment, and the old woman explained to him—"Mary be quite so much 'stonished as I be to that there new Bible."

Isaac turned with a smile to Mary, for he comprehended at once that her wonder would be at the old edition, and that she was only familiar with the new. And Mary confessed,

"I never have seen a Bible with that passage printed otherwise than, 'They took fig leaves and sewed them together and made themselves aprons.'"

And if Isaac had not been a little more reflective than his two companions, and if he had not had a clearer understanding of how the precious book was at length "done into English," Mary might have thought that "the old Simpsonses" were queer people, for even their "large old Simpsonses Bible" was totally different from all other Bibles.

But while we relate some of the incidents occurring in Mary's married life, we must not forget that our second "heroine"—if she deserves that title—is not yet married, and that we must advance her history in some degree.

"And so you two will sit and stitch in a morning in spite of all my arguments to the contrary," said Parson Hill, coming up to the open drawing-room window where Mrs. Harcourt and Mrs. Hill sat at work.

"Indeed we are not wedded to our work," said Mrs. Hill.

"I am heartily glad to hear it; I should not approve of such a strange wedding," said he.

"You would like Mrs. Harcourt to be better 'wedded,' and to have a better 'wedding'" said Mrs. Hill, laughing mischievously.

"I should like her to be better mated, if you mean that," said Mr. Hill; "the song says, 'for men must work'—why then should a woman be 'wedded' to work?"

And then, without waiting for an answer to his question, he turned to Mrs. Harcourt, and said,

"Will you not come out and breathe this fine air? I declare I feel as lonely as—as the man in the moon when the earth is enveloped in fog, and he sees and feels himself the only living soul; and as, at such times, he cannot wile away his time by looking down upon us, so I——"

"You want your playfellow in point of fact," said Mrs. Hill.

"I desire companionship."

Mrs. Harcourt left the room.

"I know you do, and it will be your own fault if you are left without it," said she, playfully.

"Will not Mrs. Harcourt come out?"

"Yes; she is gone for her hat and mantle—at least, I interpret her absence thus favourably for you."

"And you—are you too intent on those stitches to give them up for——"

"I am waiting till Charlie comes from the stables. I am afraid I must ask you to excuse me. Charlie says Sir Aston has a bad cough, and——"

"There is always something the matter with Charlie's horses. They are too highly fed."

"Oh! no—that cannot be; Duchess never ails anything."

"Ah! she wishes to prove herself an exception to the rest of her sex."

At this moment Mrs. Harcourt entered the room, equipped for walking.

"Then you will take pity on my loneliness?" said Parson Hill to Mrs. Harcourt, and they went out together.

Soon afterwards, Charlie entered the drawing-room.

"How is Sir Aston?" said Mrs. Hill.

"He will do very well, I daresay," said Charlie; "at all events, a little exercise will do him good. At what hour will you ride?"

"We must ask Mrs. Harcourt."

"That is the vicar's business," said Charlie.

"They are walking together," said she.

"Look, look, Kate!" said Charlie.

Mrs. Hill turned her eyes upon the lawn, and saw Mrs. Harcourt with a magnificent magnolia in her hand, and Mr. Hill standing by her side gathering a second.

"Now, do look, Kate! And so we see he will gather his splendid flowers for her, and yet he has hitherto treasured them like gold—nay, I do think that miser never valued gold more than he values those flowers."

"They are so very rare in this locality, and he has taken such pains to give them warmth and shelter."

"Look, look, Kate!"

The vicar held the last gathered flower over Mrs. Harcourt's hat, and stood bending down and talking to her.

"Yes, Charlie, yes; it must come to something—they cannot go on in that way and mean nothing."

"Does she still try to throw dust in your eyes?"

"No, no; I cannot accuse her of a wish to mystify. She is too retiring, and, I should say, does not give enough encouragement to Mr. Hill. She always looks as if she did not believe his compliments."

"Oh! Kate, Kate, do not try to cram me in that way. Fancy the governor wanting encouragement at his time of life!"

"Well, Charlie, what else can it be? Surely he has had ample time to propose!"

"He has surely given her his most devoted admiration and attention; and why he does not, or has not proposed, is a mystery to me. But look again, Kate."

Mrs. Harcourt had taken off her hat, and was placing a magnolia in it. When she replaced the hat, the vicar slightly altered the fall of the flower, and then they again walked on together.

"I never knew him so slow at settling anything," said Charlie; "and yet I can see no room to doubt what the end will be, unless the widow is coquetting, and already prepared to say 'No,' when he makes his speech."

"She is no coquette, I am sure," said Mrs. Hill.

"Humph! I will not say as much for any woman."

"You are rude, Charlie."

"Sorry for it, my dear; truth is not always palatable."

VII

WHICH TREATS OF THE FATE AWAITING THE LAWSLEIGH ELEVEN, AND OF THE DESPAIR OF MASTER CHARLIE

BUT the day for the fête was approaching. The weather was now fine; and as in out-of-door amusements the weather is of the first importance, so the present agreeable change was pleasant to all.

A few days before the great event, Charlie joined his wife on the lawn at Lawsleigh Vicarage, and drawing her arm within his own, said,

"Oh! Kitty, Kitty."

Mrs. Hill looked up smilingly, but did not speak.

"Kitty, Kitty, my darling," said Charlie, pressing her hand, and looking down upon her.

"I do not like to be called Kitty," said she.

"Well, then, Katy—will that please you?"

"No; I do not like Katy."

"Sheer nonsense!" said Charlie, impatiently.

"Ah! no, Charlie—it is a very sensible dislike of mine."

"I have often heard of a 'foolish' dislike to this or that, never of a sensible one—so pray explain."

"You only call me Kitty or Katy when you have something unpleasant to say, or when you are uncomfortable in some way, and so trying to hide your discomfort from me."

"Most clever Kate!—you are a 'cheese'—indeed, you are a first-rate 'cheese.' You have hit the right nail on the head."

"Ah! I knew you were full of care—open your heart, and let me know the worst."

"The dear old governor!"

Mrs. Hill looked up wonderingly.

"The door old governor is in a terrible scrape."

"Scrape, Charlie?"

"Scrape, Kate."

"Then do tell me what about? When he set off for a ride with Mrs. Harcourt, about half an hour ago, he looked happy enough."

"He is always happy when he is with her; but I assure you he is in a fix."

"If you would but tell me, Charlie?"

"I am here on purpose to tell you. It is about this gathering at Lawsleigh."

"What, the party on the 15th? How can that be any annoyance to Mr. Hill? There is nothing he more enjoys than a large influx of his personal friends."

"He will not like to be well 'thrashed;' and that will be his fate on Thursday."

Mrs. Hill looked at Charlie inquiringly.

"Isaac for a 'bat,' and the governor for a 'ball,' and the Lawsleigh eleven stand a fair chance of beating all comers. But just fancy the dear old governor without Isaac—I cannot bear the thought."

"Then why cannot Isaac come?—I thought Mr. Hill and Mr. Gray had arranged that all the villagers should have a share of the enjoyment."

"Yes, that is one of the governor's old-fashioned ways. He never has any really grand fête without regaling the whole village. Bells ringing, flags flying, choir singing, everybody happy. And there again, Kate, the bells! Isaac is such a famous ringer! Bless my heart, my care is heavier than I thought! I am in despair."

And Charlie seated himself disconsolately on a garden chair.

"But how can Mr. Hill ask the whole village, and not ask Isaac and his wife?"

"His wife! What! that wicked schoolmistress, who preferred a husband to the governor's friendship! Kitty, Kitty, that will never do."

"But do you mean to say, Charlie, that Mr. Hill can or will ask all the people in the village, and omit only those two—Isaac, the handsome smith, and Mary, his pretty wife?"

"I think the handsome smith and the pretty wife would soon be ordered out of the governor's presence if they were to show their 'pretty' 'handsome' faces on his lawn! But they are too discreet for that."

"Oh, Charlie! Mr. Hill will never be at enmity with his parishioners— he will live in peace with all."

"'Mr. Hill' will not encourage self-willed schoolmistresses—it is all against the parson's province to allow such people to have wills of their own; and then he had been so particularly kind, and gracious, and encouraging to this particular schoolmistress, that he ought to feel the more angry, though I am not prepared to say that he does. Neither, Kate, will he encourage clever-tongued drunkards in their expertness in carrying off said self-willed schoolmistresses; and to ask Isaac and Mary here so soon after they had been known 'to fly in the parson's face,' would be doing both."

"This is terrible, Charlie!"

"It is terrible, and I may well be in trouble and come to you for sympathy and comfort. Kitty, Kitty, I tell you the Lawsleigh eleven will be 'batted out' and 'bowled over' like ninepins!"

"I do not mean terrible on that head, Charlie."

"But I do. And pray on what other head would you have the governor beaten?"

"I do not want Mr. Hill to be beaten; but I am thinking of Isaac and Mary, Charlie; poor things, it seems to me so cruel to leave them out of the fête."

"Why, I am sure the governor will be just as unhappy as Isaac and Mary, though from a very different cause. He must as a principle stand aloof from them at present, but I know it grieves him to do so. But what must be, must. They have——"

"But, Charlie dear, they had a right to marry if they wished."

"Ah, my dear Kate, do not run away with the wrong end of the rope. We know they had a right to marry; but Mary was wrong to marry in the governor's absence for one thing, and to marry a man of such a character as Isaac's for another. The dear old governor is not unreasonable, Kate; and if Isaac had taken his flattering tongue to the vicar, and asked permission to marry Mary, after he had proved himself reformed, I am sure the governor would have given him the chance. But Isaac has been wrong through all the business. He is usually very straightforward, and thoroughly to be depended upon; but in this case the governor has been hoodwinked—whether intentionally or not, I cannot say. Certain it is, he thought Isaac was making love to that pretty milliner girl who came on a visit to Mary a few months ago, and all the while he was, as the villagers say, 'a-keeping company with Mistress Cope.'"

"I declare, Charlie, I am quite unhappy about Isaac and Mary, and Mr. Hill and you, dear!"

"Your unhappiness does you credit, my love!" said Charlie, as he put his arm round his wife's waist and drew her closer to him. And then he resumed,

"Isaac has always been such an open-hearted, honest fellow; he has always had so many good qualities as a set-off to his one well-known vice, that when he marries in this foolish way, one feels fairly lifted off the hinges! If he had gone to the governor in his manly honesty and stated his case—if he had asked the governor to fix a time for his probation or reformation—if he had asked the governor to give him 'the hope'—only 'the hope,' that his own continued good conduct should secure to him the hand of Mary Cope, the dear old governor would have been a firm friend and judicious adviser to both! I cannot understand that upright Isaac Watson condescending to steal his wife as he has done!"

"Perhaps he did not like to wait a long, long time, as Mr. Hill might have required him to do."

"I can quite appreciate and agree with your remark, my love."

"But now, Charlie, dear, I cannot see how Mr. Hill can avoid asking Isaac and Mary when he asks the whole village of Lawsleigh—of course they must be included in that wholesale invitation; and then, of course, they would come——"

"Ah! you fancy the governor sends cards round, do you?

> The Vicar of Lawsleigh desires to see on his lawns the villagers of Lawsleigh, on Thursday, 15th inst., at II o'clock A.M.

And I agree with you, Kate—the march of the times requires it of him; and I wonder Gray has not pointed it out to him. He may have done so, and the cards may have been sent. And, in that case, Isaac and Mary may consider themselves among the fortunate invited, and may fortunately come, and, more fortunately still, save the governor and his eleven from the disgrace of an unfortunate defeat. But I am afraid the governor is not yet sufficiently initiated into 'the march of the times' to have adopted so very excellent a plan, for I have heard nothing of it; and then these two excellent people—big Isaac, the handsome, and small Mary, the pretty—must content themselves on the day of the fête with neglect from the parson, their own humble roof for shelter, and their own mutual reproaches at their own mutual loss."

"Charlie, I cannot bear the thought!"

"Nor can I, Kate. The Lawsleigh eleven to be beaten in the dear old governor's old age goes to my very heart!"

"I do not care about your Lawsleigh eleven; they may all be beaten to a mummy for——"

"Kate! Kate!—beat the governor to a mummy? You would find it rather difficult."

"I care about Isaac and Mary, Charlie."

"This comes of 'keeping company' and making love! The vicar will say it comes of Exhibitions, and so, to a certain extent, it does, for what was only in embryo here, developed itself into a fine butterfly there. And, Kate, talking of exhibitions, a pretty exhibition of their prowess the Lawsleigh eleven will make! Oh! dear—oh! dear!"

"I cannot see how Mr. Hill can go on living in enmity, Charlie."

"He never does that; and if big Isaac will keep himself sober, the governor will look them up some time or other."

"Of course Isaac will keep sober, Charlie!"

"I see no 'of course' in the matter," said Charlie, shaking his head.

"Do you not think I could manage to walk to the village, and so tell them I shall expect to see them?"

"Do not put your pretty finger in so exceptionable a pie!"

"Well, then, Mrs. Harcourt: now if she made a favour of it to Mr. Hill?"

Charlie did not reply.

"What do you think, Charlie? Shall I set Mrs. Harcourt to plead for Isaac and Mary?"

"I have heard of 'setting a thief to catch a thief,' but I never heard of setting a handsome widow to plead to her own admirer for a disagreeable drunkard!"

"You will run Isaac down so."

"Kitty! Kitty! I wish I could run him up with a clear conscience. And then that wife of his! Dear me!—dear me!"

"Nay, Charlie, do not say a word against her!"

"The dear old governor's groans this morning were enough to melt a heart of stone."

"Groans, Charlie?"

"At last, in his despair, he turned his kind eyes on me for a moment. I was sitting in the library, pretending to read the *Times*, but, in reality, watching him at his desk, and listening to his half-stifled sighs and occasionally audible groans; and when he turned to me I looked up, quite accidentally, of course, and said, 'Can I help you?—can I do anything?'

"'Ah! Charlie, boy, I must be off—will you just see to this business' —pointing to some papers on his desk—'and get them posted to-day?' leaving me to finish his work, for off he went like a shot."

"Yes; and what had you to do?"

"Six or seven advertisements, Kitty, for as many different newspapers, making inquiries for a trained and intelligent village schoolmistress."

"Oh! poor Mary!"

"She is offered a cottage and a liberal salary. Now these things try a kind-hearted old man like the governor, and fairly, Kate, I myself cannot stand it—it positively 'tries' me, too."

"But cannot we all three together—you, and I, and Mrs. Harcourt—bring this terrible affair round?"

"If we could make it 'all square' I should be contented."

"Oh! we must manage it somehow."

"Sensible woman, do not become a—a——"

"Well, Charlie, dear, can we do anything?"

"No."

VIII

HOW ISAAC AND MARY SPENT THE DAY OF THE FETE AT THE SMITHY COTTAGE

On the occasion of a fête at Lawsleigh Vicarage, Mr. Hill generally strolled down the village street and invited the people himself. If a match were to be played, the men were drawn a week or so before the day; for there were twenty-five members of the Lawsleigh Cricket Club, and from these the eleven were taken. But now the vicar deputed Mr. Gray to go round the village, announce the day, ask the people, and make the necessary arrangements.

Charlie was right—the vicar was troubled. It was a custom at these times for the choir to sing glees and madrigals, while the company feasted.

But no Isaac, and no Mary!—then where were the glees and madrigals? The vicar might well be troubled. He was troubled that Isaac and Mary must be absent; but, then, he was also troubled for the cause that separated him from them, for he could not think Mary had acted prudently. He was troubled for the loss of Isaac's bat; troubled for the loss of Mary's voice; troubled that he could not and must not notice them; troubled that Mary would, in all probability, be wretchedly unhappy for the rest of her life, after her short dream of faith in Isaac was over. In short, the vicar was in a very unusual frame of mind; he was troubled with the anticipation of the fête, which formerly would have been a great pleasure. He foresaw clearly enough the Lawsleigh men would have no chance with the Garrison or the Teign-ton-pont Club.

But the day arrived; the sun shone; the air was balmy; the preparations were all completed; the tents erected; flags flying, and even the bells ringing. And now I must admit, no orders had been given about the bells. This was very unusual; but then it was an unusual fête, at an unusual time; the people brought together in an unusual way. But as it happened several of the cricketers who had not been drawn for the match were also ringers, and they taking for granted that the bells must ring, as customary at such times, went to the smithy cottage, as a matter of course, for the keys of the belfry. And then Isaac, who had been troubled and unhappy ever since the fête was announced, "saw his way clearly," as he said to himself. He determined to do what he considered to be his duty. He went off immediately with the ringers, and the Lawsleigh bells pealed forth. There was always a difference in the ringing if Isaac was in the belfry; and his presence there that morning was known to the vicar as soon as the bells were raised. He happened to be sauntering on the lawn with Mrs. Harcourt. She had addressed some unimportant question to him. Instead of replying, he turned to leave her, as he said, "Excuse, me," and walked into the house.

Charlie saw him.

"There, Kate," said he, "the governor hears the bells; he knows Isaac is ringing, though he *is* cut off from the pleasure of the day! Now the dear old governor can appreciate such conduct. Some people would say—I will not mention Gray, Kate—but some people would say, 'the man is only doing his duty.' Ah! they have cold hearts, Kate; not that I wish to say a word against a man for doing his duty, as 'England expects every man;' but I say human nature is human nature; and the man whose nature will allow him to put out a helping hand and try to make a pleasure-party go off well, the sight of which gives him and his pretty wife nothing but pain, such a man's nature is a noble nature! And the dear old governor feels at this moment that Isaac is a noble fellow, and——"

"Oh! Charlie, perhaps he will send for them."

"Bosh, Kate."

The carriages began to arrive; the games commenced; to Miss Lucy Campbell's delight, there was croquet for those who wished. The villagers came in their best attire, old and young, pretty and plain.

Now the arrival of this day had been a great care to Isaac. He wished so much to comfort and support Mary through the disgrace of this neglect from Parson Hill; but as Mary said nothing, he also remained passive until some occasion should warrant a remark. He went to the belfry three or four times during the day, as was customary on such contingencies; but each time he felt himself more unpleasantly situated. The men had discovered that instead of going with them to the vicarage for refreshment, he always stopped at the smithy cottage. They saw also that Mary was not at the fête. Then the men began to jeer Isaac, and ask why his wife did not go with the women to see the fun—was she too grand?

And so the day was a long and a weary one to Isaac. To do him but justice, he had no spite or ill-feeling towards Parson Hill. He recognised the propriety of the parson's neglect, until he himself could prove that he deserved better treatment. If he had spoken with Mary at all, he would have pointed out to her that, for the present, they must be contented to try to do well, and wait patiently for the result—wait until his own continued good conduct should convince the parson of his reformation. Once or twice he thought of trying to make a friend of Mr. Charles Hill, and of making an effort to convince him that the change in himself was real, and that he would be steadfast. But he could not see that any good to him and to Mary would accrue from this; convincing Master Charlie was not convincing the vicar.

The Widow Simpson was one of the very few who did not go to fêtes of any kind. Isaac went off to the belfry as usual, and both he and Mary were very cheerful in her presence; the widow had therefore no suspicion of the neglect and disgrace from which they were both suffering.

"Ma-ary, Ma-ary," said the old woman, "come here."

The widow was seated in the porch with her knitting, and the gay company were passing by to the fête.

Numbers of carriages drawn by four horses—for the hills were many and steep,—beautiful pony carriages driven by handsome ladies, a groom at the head of each pony to cheer and assist the pretty creatures at their work over such terrible roads. Gay cavaliers on horseback passed, and after resting their eyes for a short time on the picturesque old smithy, on the old woman in her quaint attire, and on Mary standing by her side, two or three turned their horses' heads and galloped back again.

Mary did not notice them; she was telling the names of the visitors to the old woman.

"That is the Vicar of Ashbystead and his lady. Parson Hill and he are very old friends; he it was who got me the post of schoolmistress here— Mr Talbot wrote to him for me," and, then, feeling she was treading on dangerous ground, she added, a little hastily, "You see, mother, the Vicar of Ashbystead always drives grey horses; and he is like Parson Hill, a very kind gentleman and very much beloved; and so is his lady also. And, oh! mother, that is the archdeacon in the funny hat, there, in the next carriage."

"Ma-ary, dear, how skilled you be; and how does thee know the deacon?"

"The archdeacon, mother—why, I was confirmed at Ashbystead and Archdeacon D—was there; he was amongst the company that went to the vicarage for luncheon; and the bishop was there, mother—I saw him— the Bishop of E——"

"Ma-ary, my dear, I be most mazed. What heaps of quality folk you have a-seed, surely. And the bishop be so big as the Queen, eh, Ma-ary?"

"I do not know, mother; but he is a little man, and——"

"Ma-ary, look, look!"

And now the cavaliers who had been seen galloping back, were again approaching, preceding Major Dashwood's drag, drawn by four horses, and full of ladies and gentlemen. It stopped at the smithy.

"Ma-ary, they be a-wanting shoes to the horses," said the old woman, as she stood up and curtseyed.

"Dame, can you tell us the way to the Vicarage?"

"Yes, sir," said the old woman; "I be sure the lad can do it—he be skilled in them things."

She thought they had stopped for Isaac to give them some help. And he who had asked the way, had only asked for an excuse to say something— he did not hear the old woman's reply, for he had busied himself by pointing out to the newly arrived party the beauty of the situation, &c., &c.

Meanwhile the ladies and gentlemen in the drag were standing up, and every face was turned towards the smithy.

"What a wonderful granite cottage! It must have been built ages ago!—how picturesquely placed!—what a view of magnificent Tors, rising one above another!—what old casemented windows!—what a shed for a blacksmith, standing so closely to the side of the cottage!—what a simple-looking village girl!—and what a dear darling old woman!"

Some voices in the drag objected to the last epithet, but the lady who had applied it maintained that it was correct, and that the old woman standing curtsying there was the veriest "darling" of an old woman she had ever seen in her life.

"That is 'a darling' of a young one," said a gentleman's voice.

"Goody, can you tell fortunes" said a lady.

"What be the quality a-saying, Ma-ary?"

"No, madam. Mother does not tell fortunes," said Mary, blushing.

"Can you eat sugar-plums? Here, dame, hold out your apron."

"Hold out your apron, mother," said Mary.

"And yours, pretty maiden," said a gentleman.

Mary blushed again, but she did as she was told. And such a glittering shower was tossed into her apron by the inmates of the drag—little bunches of gold and silver paper twisted up—she did not understand them at all. Mary and the old woman curtsied and thanked the ladies, and the widow found little sweet cakes in her apron.

Major Dashwood turned to a gentleman riding by the side of the drag, and said:

"Why, the little puss wears a ring!—a plain gold ring!"

"Oh! nonsense!—she cannot be married," said a lady. "Why, she does not look more than sixteen!"

The face was so simple and innocent, cares had not yet prematurely stamped it with wisdom.

"Are you married?" said Major Dashwood.

"Yes, sir," said Mary, curtsying.

"Good; and where, then, is your husband?"

"The lad be a-ringing, please your honour," said the old woman; "but I mind as the horses be a-wanting shoes, and the peal be most out."

The gentlemen did not understand. Mary explained "that the old woman thought they had stopped to have their horses' shoes attended to by Isaac." This made both gentlemen and ladies laugh heartily; and then Mary was told "that they would stop on their return on purpose for 'the smith' to see that the shoes were all right."

"The lad will be sure to wait your honour's pleasure," said the old woman, curtsying.

"Who is 'the lad?'" said a lady.

"My husband, madam—Isaac Watson," said Mary.

The ladies laughed at the idea of a boy and girl being married at so early an age; they imagined Isaac Watson, "the lad," as boyish-looking as Mary was girlish.

"We will call again," said Major Dashwood.

For by this time the drag and the attendant gentlemen on horseback had stopped the way, and there was a large number of carriages, &c., waiting to move on.

> Crabbed age and youth
> Cannot live together—
> Youth is full of pleasure,
> Age is full of care,

sang the gentlemen in the drag, as Major Dashwood turned round the corner to the vicarage. But in this instance it was

> Green contented age and
> Simple modest youth
> Living happily and cosily together.

When Isaac returned from the belfry this scene was related to him, and the old woman said:

"I told his honour as you would be a-ready to tend he."

Mary shewed her gold and silver treasures, and Isaac told her they were "crackers," probably with mottoes.

"Come, Mary, dear, let us try our luck," said he.

The old woman was startled by the noise, and astonished at the result.

"And be that there sugar-plum made in that crack? Massy me!—but it be queer times us lives in!"

When the thin roll of paper was spread open the motto was,

       Love laughs at locksmiths,

which Mary thought a wonderful idea.

On the return in the evening, true to his word, Major Dashwood stopped at the smithy. Mary and the old woman were in the cottage; Isaac stood at the entrance of the shed.

"We want the 'smith,' if you please," said Major Dashwood.

"I am the 'smith,' sir," said Isaac, doffing his cap—"what can I do to help you?"

"You!" said Major Dashwood, in such a tone of surprise as to astonish Isaac, and make him raise his eyes inquiringly.

The drag was full of ladies and gentlemen, as it had been when it passed in the morning, and quite a cavalcade of gentlemen on horseback came up at the same time.

"Are you then the husband of that pretty young girl we saw this morning?" said a lady.

"I am proud to acknowledge, madam, that I have a very pretty young wife," said Isaac, raising his cap to the lady.

"Have you been married long?"

"Only about a month, madam."

"A month! Then she is your bride?"

But while Isaac's attention was engaged with the lady, Major Dashwood had time to discover that "the lad," whom he had expected to see a hobbledehoy of sixteen or seventeen, was a full-grown, burly-looking, and handsome man, of nearer thirty than sixteen; and, moreover, one who would not be likely to stand any nonsense. He had asked for a "smith," but there was nothing for a smith to do.

"What can I do, sir?—something wrong about the horses?"

"Oh, no! no!" said Major Dashwood. "I asked for you, that we might have permission to enter your cottage. My wife, and her friends, took such a fancy to your pretty bride as they passed this morning, they wanted to see her again."

But the ladies were actually alighting from the drag; and then they stood talking to Isaac, and asking questions about the scenery.

And the ladies found Isaac so handsome, so courteous, and so intelligent, so little like "the lad" they had expected to see, that he became as great a wonder to them on that far-off and uncivilized Dartmoor, as his wife or mother had been when they passed in the morning.

The ladies entered the cottage for a minute or two; but as there was no room for the gentlemen, they stood outside the window, and looked in, and joined in the conversation occasionally.

The sun was near the horizon, and the ladies followed Isaac to look at the view. He pointed out now this Tor, now that, as seen from the entrance to his shed.

The scene was totally different from the brilliant one of the morning; in some respects it was even more beautiful, for the presence of deep shadow enhances the radiance and splendour of light.

And while Isaac bestowed his courtesies on the ladies, Mary and the old woman came forth to talk to the gentlemen. And then Isaac stood back and held his hat high over his head—Mary thought he was imitating Parson Hill; but Isaac was habitually punctilious and polite—while the gentlemen handed the ladies into the drag.

"Here, Goody, have some sweet cake," said one.

And the widow again held out her apron. "The bride must have a bouquet," said a gentleman.

"Mr. Smith—for I do not know your name—" said Mrs. Dashwood, "where is your bride?—she shall have our flowers."

"My name is Isaac Watson, madam. Mary, my dear, come here."

And Mary once more held out her apron, and all the handsome bouquets that had been put together with such pride for that day's fête were thrown to Mary, as if she had been one of those queens of song accustomed to such oblations.

But no. She was only queen of the smith's heart; and her kingdom was the smithy cottage.

"A cheer for the smith and his bride!" said the gentlemen.

And then uprose the hearty cheer that only English lungs can give; and the cavalcade moved on—Isaac bowing, Mary and the old woman curtsying as long as they were in sight.

And when the scene was over, Isaac clasped Mary in his arms, and declared he never had been so proud and so happy in all his life.

"I declare at this minute I am as happy as a king, even though I am in such sad disgrace with our kind old friend—for he was a friend, Mary—Parson Hill."

And Charlie was right. Parson Hill and the Lawsleigh eleven were ignominiously beaten.

IX

OF THE WICKEDNESS OF THE
SEWING-MACHINE

As soon as the smithy cottage was divested of as much of Mary's furniture as could be stowed away in the temporary shed, Mary set herself steadily to work. The sewing-machine was brought into use, to the old woman's manifest astonishment. She could not find out how it could do so many stitches in so short a time, all so neat and regular; for she still prided herself on her very neat sewing, and was therefore a good judge of such work. She watched Mary, and saw the quantity done in half an hour; this excited her wonder and awe; her intellect seemed powerless to comprehend that so much could be done in so short a lapse of time, and by one woman!

"Her canna be a witch," said the widow to herself, as she gazed at Mary in mute amazement. "But sometimes I be almost feared! Her be a nice young meeden. I be a-wishing her wouldna go a-working in that way. It be as if her had a-gotten the 'old one' to help she!"

And the old woman's awe, combined with her ignorance, was gradually communicated to others, until at length the sewing-machine was talked about in the village as something uncanny. Little by little the position of Isaac and Mary altered in the village of Lawsleigh—almost imperceptibly at first, but still surely. On Sunday, when they went to church, they did not receive the friendly nods and greetings to which they had been accustomed. Isaac, in his attempts to get a tarpaulin and afterwards help of different kinds, as well as masons to build his new rooms, had gradually learned that the people of Lawsleigh were more pleased to jeer and ridicule than to aid him in his present position. The loss of Parson Hill's countenance and protection was quite enough. The bad now had Isaac somewhat more in their power. The timid did not wish to be mixed up in such quarrels, and so kept aloof; while the strong said,

"Us will see what that great big Isaac be a-made on. Him hath a-been reading the passon's books; him havena gotten no books from the passon now!"

Mary had been as great an object of jealousy to the women as Isaac to the men. To some—for example, Jane Sands—she had given offence by her treatment of the children in the school, which treatment, however just, was not understood by their mothers. These women were as glad of Mary's change of position with Parson Hill as the men were at Isaac's. Such is human nature! Rejoicing in the downfall of a fellow-creature, whether deserved or not, and ready to return imaginary evils with real insults. But at the close of the day Isaac said to himself,

"The Sunday is over at last!—what a weary day! How unlike a Sunday! It has been such a long, long day. How ill the men behaved in the belfry-putting every peal wrong—hunting out of compass. But what is the use of thinking—"

And, resuming the subject soon afterwards,

"As for the choir, I really thought they would not let Mary get up to her place. I managed to push into mine—but she, poor thing! she has not my strength. Now, I wonder what they all mean? It seems as if they meant to get me out of the bells and out of the singing!—Well, well, I must take it quietly. And next Sunday, Mary and I must mind and go in good time, and so secure our places early, and do away with this unpleasantness."

Isaac said nothing to Mary, hoping she did not take the conduct of the choir to heart. And Mary said nothing to Isaac for she thought it her duty to try to bear the evils of her position with patience, since undoubtedly she had brought them on herself. On the Monday the weather became fine and warm; there were cold showers on the Sunday, but now the temperature was higher, and the air balmy. In the afternoon, Mary asked Isaac to lift the sewing-machine into his shed, for said she,

"I perceive you are at quiet work to-day, Isaac; that great hammer is rather too much for me, if I am very near—"

"Yes, my dear, of course it is. I shall be obliged to use it before the afternoon is over, but I will delay it as long as I can, for your sake."

Mary was some time preparing work for the machine before she could use it. The old woman eyed it furtively every now and then, half afraid to remain seated on her stool so close to it.

At length Isaac was ready to use his hammer earlier than he had expected, and made some little apology to Mary for the noise he must necessarily make. But the widow told him it was music to her, and she liked to knit to the sound of it. And so, when Mary put her machine in motion, there were the three sounds chiming merrily together, as it seemed to her. For the old woman went on with the "click, click" of her knitting, Isaac with the "bump, bump" of his great hammer, and Mary with the rapid "tric-trac" of her machine.

Mary was silent, from the fact that her work required all her attention; Isaac, from a newly found faculty, that of building castles in the air as to the future happiness of himself and Mary; the old woman did not speak from absolute fright. She tried to conquer this feeling, because, said she to herself:

"The meeden be good, and the lad be good, and him gived the thing to she, so it canna be wrong. But I be most mazed, and I be a-thinking what be all the young meedens to do for work! Coz why, one of them can do so much as twenty; and be all the tother nineteen to stand idle?

> For Satan finds some mischief still,
> For idle hands to do.

The thing must be the work of the 'old one,' just to get the tother young meedens to stand idle, and then him will find some mischief for them. Poor things! I give them my prayers, poor things! I be all of a tremble with thinking about such things. It must be no good to have such a thing in the cottage; I will shut my eyes and not see it."

But while she sat thus, attempting to shut out evil from her sight, it appeared to her that by some strange chance Isaac's hammer and Mary's machine kept time together. She opened her eyes to look if they had approached nearer to each other. No. Isaac was at work with his back to Mary, and yet, somehow, the hammer and the machine seemed to understand each other. She once more closed her eyes to try and shut out from her sight and mind this dreadful companionship, but without effect. Bump, bump, bump, went Isaac's hammer; tric-trac, tric-trac, tric-trac, went Mary's machine. And then she suddenly remembered that

> Satan finds some mischief still,
> For idle hands to do.

And she started into active life, and began to knit at her topmost speed. What was her astonishment and terror to find that now her needles also kept time with the great hammer and the dreaded machine!

Knit, knit, knit, on she went, saying to herself, "Massy me! massy me!" She raised her eyes, and saw Mary looking calm and contented as an angel. She turned to Isaac, who no longer stood with his back to her and Mary, and his face was radiant with the joy in store for him and Mary in his aerial palaces.

"The 'old one' be making both of them happy, and if he should clutch hold of them before they finds out his tricks, what be I to do? I be that mazed, I——"

She sat still for a short time with her knitting lying on her lap, but was again aroused to exertion by the lines she had twice before repeated, "For Satan finds, &c.," and she resumed her knitting.

"I be a-knitting slow, and slow, and slow; and then mayhap I shall put the 'old one' out of his count, and break up the thread of the witchery," said she to herself.

She did so—tried to knit slowly—but to her horror and alarm found her needles were still keeping time with Isaac's hammer and Mary's machine.

"It must be she as done it; she must be a witch a helping of the 'old one' to clutch hold of the lad and me. I be fair mazed! I must call to the neighbours—I must give a big shout!" but, in attempting to make a noise, the poor old woman fell from her stool insensible.

Isaac, as may well be imagined, was by her side in an instant; and if the good old woman could have opened her eyes, and have known that her fall had had the effect of stopping both the big hammer and the bright machine, she might even have been contented to have been taken ill. But as it was, Isaac lifted her up tenderly, and carried her into the cottage, and placed her on Mary's couch, which, fortunately, had been left in the large room down-stairs.

"I will set off for a doctor, Mary," said Isaac; "shall I try to get some neighbour to come to you while I am away?"

All this time they were chafing the old woman's hands, and placing her in a comfortable position:

"It is warmth and comfort that old people want, Isaac, more than doctors and medicine. Suppose you get some blankets and pillows downstairs, and suppose we make up a good fire and give her something hot."

Independent of these being Mary's real feelings—for she had had some experience in such cases, by having nursed a great-aunt through an illness—she did not like the thought of Isaac going so far away from her. And Isaac, though he did not care a straw for the fatigue and trouble of walking across the moor, was nevertheless, glad to feel that he might remain at home.

In time, as Mary had foretold, the old woman revived. She did not seem to know what had occasioned her illness; she regretted being—what she called—a burden to Isaac and Mary, taking up their time. But it was evident to them both that her perceptions were none of the clearest. She was of a great age; Isaac had heard her say she vas married on her twentieth birthday; and then the record in the "old Simpsonses Bible" would prove her to be in her ninety-fifth year. But longevity was common on the moor, and her age was not an unusual one for dwellers there. She seemed scarcely to remember any recent event, for when she spoke—excepting to thank them for their kind nursing—it was with reference to some occurrence in her past life.

X

OF THE SUNDAY MORNING
AT LAWSLEIGH

As may well be understood, Mary's work with the sewing-machine was stopped for that day.

The machine was not replaced in the old woman's sight, and fortunately there was nothing to recall the late scene to her mind. In a day or two she seemed quite herself again, and Mary began to resume her enjoyment of the machine. But as the weather was less warm, and it was thought imprudent for the old woman to sit so long in Isaac's shed, Mary went on with her employment in the large room; and the widow, as she busied herself in household affairs, was not acted upon, for the time being, by the noise of the machine, the more especially as Isaac's hammer was not at work. But in the course of the morning, James Marvel looked in at the open widow, and said,

"Mistress Watson, and pray what be you about?"

"I am making some aprons for mother," said Mary, pleased with James Marvel's notice, and gratified by the exhibition of her skill.

"But, Mistress Watson," said James, knitting his brows, pushing his cap on one side, and his fingers through his hair, "do you mean to say as that there dumb critter can help you, or, leastways, do a stitch of this here fine work?"

"It be fair oncanny, James," said the widow, "been't it?" as she felt her terror revive.

"Oncanny, widdy!—I do not just see that, to this time—coz why? there be such heaps of these machines, as does everything; but, widdy, it be astonishing—to my mind it be wonderful astonishing!" and James leaned into the room as far as he could, to get a better sight of the curious invention.

"Come in, Mr. Marvel," said Mary.

"No, thank you," said James, drawing back in spite of his curiosity; "I must be off—it be a queer kind of chatterer, that critter there. Morning, Mistress Watson—morning, widdy."

As James walked down the village he was accosted by first one and then another, asking for news, to which James replied,

"I have a-comed from the smithy, and I havena a-heard no news."

"What be Isaac 'bout to the smithy?" said one.

"I havena seed Isaac; I just stopped at the window, and speaked to Mistress Watson; and, to my mind, that chattering critter be a queer one."

"What dost mean, lad—Isaac's wife?"

"No, no, that queer machine as the mistress does she's sewing with. The old widdy thinks it be oncanny, and I be blest if I don't most 'gree with she."

This was enough for the unlettered inhabitants of Lawsleigh, for James Marvel was a great authority. Their ignorance alone would lead them to invest such a machine with supernatural powers. No kind of machinery had been seen on the moor; the roughest kinds of farming implements were still in use. The old never left their homes to see the wonders of this age of science, as gradually new marvels were introduced; and the young, if they did occasionally go to the surrounding towns, were uninterested in what they did not comprehend; and for the most part, in their isolation from society, were too shy, and even too ignorant, to ask questions, and—if it were ever awakened—satisfy their curiosity.

And so the sewing machine began to be talked of in Lawsleigh as a something unlawful to possess and dangerous to use. The "wise men" and "wise women," who were known to inhabit remote parts of the moor, required no such assistance in their art. They could tell where the cow that had strayed from her pasture might be found. They could tell where the skin of the sheep that had been lost on such a night was hidden! And many other wonderful things were at their command, without the assistance of his "sable majesty." For all of which knowledge they were duly honoured, looked up to, and dreaded. None would dare to offend a "wise man" or a "wise woman," the consequences of such effrontery would be terrible. But here was a young woman setting herself up above everybody, and possessing a cursed machine, with which she could do any amount of mischief! Abraham Clark's colt died. Three days ago, it was as fine a colt as any on the moor!

"It must be she as have a done it!"

John Lear's cart broke down a-coming over the moor with coals for the parson; he had been told to fetch fifteen hundred at a time, but he brought eighteen hundred, "fifteen for the passon and three for himself," and his cart ran up against a piece of granite, and the wheel was wrenched off!

"It must be *she* as done it!"

Innumerable were the instances of witchcraft and diablerie assigned to Mary, and the talk in the village became daily more abusive. Isaac did not notice that at all sorts of odd times the men of the village would come by threes and fours, with stealthy steps, and peer in at the large window that looked into the street, and then creep as silently away. It was now October, and the widow and Mary no longer sat in the shed, but pursued their separate avocations in the one large room; and besides, as there was a certain amount of work that must be done by hand before the machine could be used, and also a certain amount of finishing after the machine had done its part, it followed that sometimes Mary did not use it for several consecutive days. And so the Sunday came round again, and as Isaac had promised himself to be at church early, the trio set off in very good time. It had been Isaac's custom to take his grandmother and place her in her pew before he went into the belfry to ring. She said "she liked to sit in the church and read her bible," and this she had done all the long summer. But after Isaac's marriage he went to the belfry at the proper time alone, and Mary and the old woman came at the time appointed for the assembling of the congregation. But on this day Isaac left the ringers to manage the bells as they pleased, for he had set his heart on securing his old seat in the choir without having to bandy words with his fellow-townsmen, and also on seeing Mary comfortably placed. And so they entered the church some minutes earlier than usual, and first took the old woman to her accustomed seat, and then turned to place themselves. What was their astonishment to find the seats appropriated to the choir quite full! All the old singers were there, and several new ones, who, Isaac knew—or suspected—had no business there. He went forward bravely to face the men who were trying to annoy him, and asked,

"Why they had not left room for him, and why Mary's place was filled up?"

"The passon said as I might come and sing," said one; and several voices speaking together assured Isaac that there were none there without the consent and approval of the vicar.

"Let us come away!" said Mary, gently, for the congregation began to assemble.

"You can ax the passon what you bees to do!" said another, in a jeering tone, to Isaac.

This struck a sensitive chord in his heart, and he feared, if he asked for an explanation from Parson Hill, that he should be no better off; for he thought it very improbable that the parson would see him. He looked kindly down upon Mary, and listened to her request to turn away from the choir.

And after a few moments of indecision—for though he knew these men had no right to usurp his place, he also knew that was not a time or locality to exert his prerogative—he granted her request, and they went and seated themselves by the old woman.

This harsh and unexpected treatment of Isaac and Mary by their neighbours did not prevent them from lifting up their voices in praise, and their hearts in prayer to their Maker. It is true, they both felt humbled and cast down; they both felt they had been unjustly deposed from an authority vested in them by the vicar himself. But it is in the season of our humility we turn more truly to our God for help, and Isaac and Mary "humbled themselves before the Lord."

When the service was over, Isaac had prepared himself to pass unrecognised, as it were, with his mother and wife, by those whom he had known from childhood. Some amongst the women said, "Morning, widdy, and how be you?" But the mass of the people passed the three unnoticed, or sneered at them, and muttered to each other as they walked on.

Isaac was prepared for this, but not for what followed. The Widow Mason was standing amid a group of men half-way down the broad walk that led to the church, and as Isaac and his wife and mother approached, she said aloud:

"It be she as have a-done it! Her has a-got a dumb 'critter' as can sew, and her be a witch! And her deserves burning with fire and brimstone, she do!" and she snapped her fingers in Mary's face.

"Hollo there!" said Isaac, sharply, and turning round upon the six or seven who were following them. Then, remembering in an instant that the day was Sunday, and the locale the churchyard, he felt he must not give cause of offence, or it might be the means of raising an unseemly brawl; he therefore moderated the tone of his voice, and said: "What is the matter, pray?"

"The matter, Isaac!" said one, apparently more friendly than the rest; "why, it be said in the village as you have a-gotten a witch for your wife!"

"A witch!" said Isaac, in a tone more of surprise than anger; "and who dares say such a falsehood!—I may say such an absurdity?"

"They have a-seed she and the 'critter' a-talking together," said the Widow Mason, in loud tones.

"Have seen who talking together?" said Isaac, now standing still, and facing his foes.

"Why, the 'critter' and Molly there," said the widow, pointing to Mary.

Isaac understood she meant some insult, but the sewing-machine was as far from his thoughts as the Tors are from heaven! After a little pause, he said:

"I know not what you mean, unless that you mean to tease Mary because she is my wife, or even to try to worry me because I have given up drinking cider."

Here he was interrupted by jeers and suppressed laughter, and he turned on his way home, as he said:

"At all events, it is very unneighbourly conduct."

"It be unneighbourly to hide a dumb 'critter' in your cottage as witches everybody!—that be unneighbourly!"

Isaac was about to reply, but at this instant Mr. Gray was seen coming out of the church, and the crowd separated, and went on their different routes, and he and his wife and mother went on towards the smithy.

Now, of the trio that had stood to be insulted in the churchyard of Lawsleigh, the old woman had the best comprehended what charge was made, and against whom. She did not say anything, she thought Isaac and Mary understood as well as herself. For every now and then, at intervals of time, the scene in the smithy, when the great hammer, the knitting-needles, and the machine made, in her imagination, so unmusical a trio, arose unbidden to her mind's eye. She did not remember falling down ill, she had glimpses of the scene as it had really occurred, and the locale was so correct, and she was so accustomed to sit there, that she sometimes thought it must have happened.

Fortunately that was the only time that the machine had been carried into the shed, and as she could not remember ever having seen it anywhere but in its corner in the large room, this circumstance left room for doubt, and she could not tell if she had had a dream, or if it had been a reality. She had heard James Marvel call it a "dumb critter," and, in her ignorance, she attached a meaning of witchcraft to the words. She had once said to herself, speaking of Mary, "Her canna be a witch; coz why?—her be good!" But when she heard her called "a witch" by others, she began to doubt her own judgment. And so, on this Sunday, slowly and sadly, Isaac and his wife and mother returned to the smithy,

XI

"ENGLAND EXPECTS THAT EVERY MAN THIS DAY SHALL DO HIS DUTY"

AND on the Monday Isaac's thoughts were still more gloomy than they had been in the previous week. He knew Parson Hill was too just to take from him either the choir or the bells as long as his own conduct was irreproachable. But, as regarded Mary's position in the choir, room for doubt had arisen in his mind. Isaac knew from good authority that advertisements were out in the different county papers, making inquiry for a schoolmistress for Lawsleigh—one with a good soprano voice and a knowledge of music, as she would be expected to lead the choir. Therefore it appeared to Isaac that, when the post of schoolmistress was taken away from Mary, she also lost her position in the choir. Isaac saw that Mary did not understand this, but, as he systematically avoided any subject that could give her pain, he did not enlighten her.

Mary was not exactly in so happy a frame of mind as when she first married, constantly recurring annoyances kept her always in dread of an undefined something. Her sadness was only heard in the tones of her voice, or guessed from her reticence, sitting apart apparently in deep thought, instead of chatting cosily on any, or all subjects, as she had been accustomed to do, for she was not of a complaining temper. And then, though Isaac knew it not, she had no confidence in his reformation. The smell from the cider thrown upon him by the Widow Mason had never entirely left his clothes. Isaac himself thought nothing of it, indeed, scarcely perceived it, but this occasional whiff of something sour, as Isaac passed and repassed, was a disagreeable reminder to Mary of the night at the school cottage, and it sometimes increased her sadness. And though Mary's confidence in Isaac's integrity was disturbed, she did not make herself still more unhappy by watching or setting spies upon him. He was often absent attending to his trade in the different cottages or farmhouses in and near Lawsleigh; she knew he had plenty of opportunities to go to the "Packhorse" unknown to her, and she had been told he could drink a large quantity of cider without producing any unpleasant effect. It is true he never had been actually inebriated in her presence since their marriage, he had never offended her sensitiveness so grossly, but she lived in the apprehension that even this last misfortune might happen.

Isaac, who felt so strong in his good faith—Isaac, who had lost all relish for the cider that was to take him into low company and away from Mary—Isaac, who longingly looked forward to the time when Parson Hill should again become his "friend"—Isaac had no conception of Mary's doubts. He had never told her of the Widow Mason's ill treatment of him when he went to fetch Jacob from the "Packhorse;" it was a principle with him to avoid all disagreeable subjects or discussions.

"Mary would not like to hear of such unseemly brawls—how should she, poor thing?"

And Isaac did not like to speak of them. The remembrance of the scenes at the "Packhorse" on that very evening had made Isaac silent and stern when he returned to Mary.

Isaac was indignant with himself that he had ever in his life condescended to sit under the roof of such a woman, or mix with such a low class of the uneducated on Dartmoor. Isaac was praying in his heart for strength to do away with the erring past, and for courage to go on in a more respectable and satisfactory course. And poor Mary misread these signs, and grew faint with the smell of cider. But now, at this period of her life, Mary said,

"I have not even the comfort of thinking I can trust to his word—that was very soon over, as Parson Hill told me it would. Only I *do* pray to God that he will not leave me here long, though I could be so happy," added she with a sigh; "but I know I cannot bear to see him become like Peter Barker."

And Mary shuddered as she recalled the horrible scene of Hannah Barker's death.

Isaac saw these fits of gloomy abstraction seize upon Mary at intervals. When he could afford the time, he would sit down by her side and turn the current of her thoughts into a happier channel. On one occasion Mary was searching for something that could not be found, and Isaac wanted to know if he could help her, or if she had lost anything of consequence.

"Yes; it is of great consequence, Isaac. It is my knitting gauge. I cannot think where I could have put it when I came from the school."

But Isaac interrupted her. The "school-cottage" was a painful subject, and should be mentioned but seldom, if at all.

"Never mind where you put it, Mary; tell me what it is like. Perhaps I can make you one."

"You make one! Oh I am sure you cannot!" said she, thoughtlessly.

Isaac only said,

"But perhaps you will explain to me what you want."

"Why, mother has a large piece of knitting for the centre of a counterpane; and I want to find needles of the same size as those she used."

"Yes; now show me your needles."

"Look, Isaac!"—and Mary took up a piece of knitting and some needles that were lying on the table—"This needle, when I put it into the stitch, is too small; this too large. Now, if I had my gauge, I could try the sizes of these two needles, and know the number of the intermediate size, and so send by the carrier for——"

"Send, my dear! I will get you what you want. I dare say I have the proper sized wire in store. I will look. Give me the two needles."

Isaac went into the shed, and soon returned with wire of the exact size, which he promised to fashion into knitting needles immediately.

"Is your gauge a piece of brass with holes in it?" said Isaac, as he worked away at the knitting needles.

"Yes, Isaac. I cannot think where I can have put it."

"Here it is, my dear," said Isaac, as he took it from a shelf in his shed, and tossed it to her. "I picked it up that wet night, when I was stowing away your furniture. I did not know what it was, and put it in my pocket, meaning to ask you about it, my dear; but that delicious coffee you made put it quite out of my head, more shame for me, my dear and the next morning, when I found it in my pocket, I put it on the shelf, and forgot all about it. You see, Mary, I have had so many things to think of."

And Isaac stifled a sigh.

But Isaac had quite sent away Mary's sadness.

"How glad I am to have my gauge! Thank you, Isaac. And what nice needles—just the very size, I do declare! Oh, mother, do look!—is he not clever!"

And once more Mary was the proud married woman—proud of her handsome husband, and proud of his great expertness. Although Isaac "laughed in his sleeve" at the idea of Mary thinking so much of her knitting needles.

"And now, Isaac, you just tell us," said Mary. "You see mother knitted this a long time ago;" and she unfolded a large piece of very fine knitting, yellow with age. "She did it for the centre of a counterpane; and then, you see, she had other work to do, and it did not get finished."

"It is a very large piece of work, Mary—astonishingly large, I should say."

"Yes; but it is most beautifully done, Isaac; and I was thinking of knitting a deep border, that would make it large enough for our bed. And so nice and cool for a summer quilt it would be—would it not?"

"Ay, Ma-ary, them coverlids be cool to summer times," said the old woman.

"It seems to me a very nice piece of work," said Isaac, "though I am no judge; and of course it would be useful."

"Yes; and was it not lucky I made mother turn it out? She had got it shut up in a large chest."

"It was lucky, indeed; how did you know she had such a piece of fine work? I am sure I did not," said Isaac.

"Why, I was showing mother my patterns, and choosing one for a centre, to make one all myself. Look, Isaac, here they are."

And Mary spread out her books of patterns.

"These are splendid!" said Isaac in astonishment. "You do not mean, Mary, that you can imitate these beautiful designs in knitting?"

"She be rare and skilled, Isaac, Ma-ary be. I have a-seed some as she has a-done, and it be 'stonishing grand, surely!"

"But, my dear, if you can do such wonderful devices as these, why do you not make the counterpane all new together? Mother's work cannot be done in patterns like these."

"No, lad, I didn't never see such hard things as them be. But I doed the letters; and them was thinked so much of in my young days, as Ma-ary's hard patterns be now."

"Letters?" said Isaac, in a tone of inquiry.

"There is a beautiful motto in this centre piece of mother's," said Mary; "no such things are ever seen now; and it is so beautiful—just help me to spread it out."

"It be about Nelson, lad," said the old woman; "in my young days us was most mazed about Nelson."

"About Nelson!" said Isaac, in a tone of wonder, as he helped to unfold the work.

"Ay, lad, about Nelson. Now, Ma-ary, I be a-going to take this corner, and you the tother, and let the lad read about Nelson."

And Mary and the old woman stepped back towards the window, holding the work by the two upper corners, so that as the two lower fell to the ground, the light at the back made the motto clear. And Isaac read aloud, "England expects that every man shall do his duty."

"Is it not beautiful?" said Mary, with enthusiasm. "Nothing of the kind to be seen now-a-days."

"Oh! most beautiful," said Isaac, rubbing his hands, and laughing gleefully. "Why, mother, how clever you are!"

"Clever!" said Mary; "indeed, it is very clever—do look how perfect every letter is; and such quaint letters too." And she waved the work backwards and forwards, looking down upon it admiringly.

"Mother, mother," said Isaac, rushing up to the old woman and caressing her, "it is the most splendid piece of work I ever saw in my life; and so appropriate, as you say, about Nelson, and cool in the summer. I am so pleased I cannot help laughing."

And Isaac laughed and danced about the cottage in the exuberance of his glee.

"Now, it would never do to lose this, Isaac, would it?" said Mary, in a tone of hopeful inquiry.

"Lose it" said Isaac, in a hearty tone, "why, it is worth untold gold. What Englishman would ever wish to forget Nelson? Mother, it does you honour and credit to give us a chance of remembering the old fellow." And then Isaac seized upon Mary and caressed her, as he said in a serious tone, but with a merry glitter in his eye, "And England does, even in our day, 'expect every man to do his duty,' and of course, my dear, I will do mine."

"Yes, Isaac; that was just what I said to mother—you always do your duty when you know it; and so, you see, it is the more valuable because it is so true. And then such a nice keepsake it is of dear mother's work."

"That be like you, Ma-ary, dear; and I be glad as I doed it in my young days. And it be all right for the lad, Ma-ary—coz why? Isaac always does his duty, and 'tends to everything."

"Well, to my mind, it is the most wonderful thing that this wonderful century has as yet produced," said Isaac, rubbing his hands with great glee.

"And lad, when I doed it, nobody thought nothing about it," said the old woman.

"Very strange," said Isaac; "why, I think very much of it."

"And so do I," said Mary; "and I shall knit a border to go all round—will it not be beautiful?"

"Why, there was not many folk in Lawsleigh as could tell they letters in my young days. Isaac Simpson—rest his saule—was a larned man. I knowed some things afore I was wed, and then Isaac larned I more—coz why? he would have I to read to he in the 'old Simpsonses Bible;' and the Lawsleigh folk said I be a larned woman to that time. But bless your pretty face, Ma-ary, they Lawsleigh folk couldna understand 'bout Nelson!"

"I am quite sure they did not understand," said Isaac, stroking his chin, as he smiled on his mother.

"And be you going to put something 'bout Nelson round the border, Ma-ary?"

"Why, I do not know," said Mary, thoughtfully; "what do you think, Isaac?"

"I think that, as it now stands, it cannot be surpassed," said Isaac, in a very cheery tone; "and I think it is quite enough about Nelson; and I also think one of Mary's beautiful patterns round it for a border will finish it off admirably, and make it a prize such as few possess."

"Such a wonderful thought," said Mary, "because the motto is so well known, and so good, and yet seldom or never used!"

"An excellent thought, my dear," said Isaac, "and admirably worked, though I do not pretend to be a judge."

"I can see you be pleased," said the widow, "and I do be proud of thee, lad—coz why?—thee does thy duty."

"To be sure I do, mother," said Isaac, again smiling.

"Eh, Mary? The lad, he does his duty, and does his work every day, and makes the cottage cheery with his noises—"

"Yes, mother, Isaac is very good."

Mary was so entranced with the wonderful counterpane, she quite forgot, for the time being, Isaac's breach of faith, and only remembered his good qualities.

"If I did not do my duty," said Isaac, again catching hold of Mary and caressing her, "I had need to be ashamed of myself. But never you think I shall be such a lazy laggard of a man—I am made of better stuff—and I will always do my duty, my dear, I promise you."

"Of course, Isaac," said Mary, gently disengaging herself from his embrace.

"I be that happy 'bout that coverlid," said the old woman, "as I be most mazed to feel so cheery, *I be*."

And Isaac went to work in his shed, with the smile still lingering on his face, and the glitter in his eye.

XII

"COMING EVENTS CAST
THEIR SHADOWS BEFORE"

"WHY does Mrs. Harcourt want to go away?" said Parson Hill to Mrs. Hill.

"She does not wish to go," said Mrs. Hill.

"Then why does she go?" said the parson.

"Nay I should say, ask her, not me!"

"I have asked her to stay longer, but she seems to think she must go."

"That is absurd," said Charlie.

"Very, for so sensible a woman, more absurd than—than one likes—" and the vicar walked hastily away in an unusually testy mood.

"What can be the matter now?" said Charlie, "and what can that charming widow be about to think of running away at this crisis in her fate!"

The sharp pattering of rain was heard upon the windows, and the vicar returned.

"Then you cannot tell me why Mrs. Harcourt wishes to go to town?"

"No, I cannot, she has not announced her intention to me," said Mrs. Hill.

"Do you know if she has any particular engagement?"

"I am afraid she is not engaged," said Mrs. Hill.

"Humph!" said the vicar, testily, "I thought as much."

"But then, if you think that an evil, it can easily be remedied," said Charlie.

"What is an evil?" said the vicar, abstractedly.

"That the Widow Harcourt is still a widow," said Charlie.

"Oh—h—" said the vicar, as if Charlie had given him a new idea; and then he drew himself up and said,

"If she must go to town, she must; of course I do not wish to stand in her way;" and he turned to leave the room.

"I do not see any 'must' in the case," said Charlie, crossing the vicar's path, and preventing him from making his escape. "If you were to ask her—if you were to propose to her—if you were to tell her you hope she will not go to town, perhaps you might succeed in preventing such a calamity," while Mrs. Hill turned aside to hide her smiles.

"She knows I do not want her to go; she knows I am delighted—or she ought to know—delighted to have her here; what can I say or do more?—Do you think, Charlie, I am going to put my private wishes in opposition to hers!"

"Oh, nothing of the sort; I quite think her private wishes and yours coincide."

"Do you look upon me, at my time of life, as a mass of selfishness!—who, because I enjoy the society of so charming and so intellectual a woman—because I delight myself in her amiability—in her—well—her—I mean I am not such a selfish dog as to—to wish her to stay here—here on Dartmoor, at the fag end of civilization, when she has London to go to—the finest capital in the world—all London to worship her—all the resources of London for the cultivation and enjoyment of her own charming mind—all the amusements of London, the refined amusements, to solace her when she pleases, or when she has nothing better to do. No, Charlie, I am not so selfish; and, I may add, I do not wonder that she wishes to return—the marvel would be if she did not."

"She really does not wish to go back!" said Mrs. Hill, impulsively.

The vicar stooped his head in the attitude of listening, and remained silent.

"She does not wish to go, I assure you," said Mrs. Hill.

"Nonsense, my dear Kate!" said the vicar; "or, pardon my rudeness, it is true ladies are sometimes difficult to comprehend, and I may have mistaken Mrs. Harcourt's meaning. I understood her to say she wished to go to town one day this week. Then, does she tell you she wishes to stay here, at the same time she asks me to send her there? If she does, it is acting unlike herself."

"Perhaps she is sensitive," said Charlie, "and thinks she is making a long visit."

"She is sensitive," said the vicar, "and did say something of that sort. I then asked her to lengthen her visit."

"She could not refuse that!" said Charlie.

"And why not? I tell you she does refuse!"

"Oh! she would not refuse you if you would only ask her in the right way."

The vicar was very obtuse; he did not understand the hint.

"She is shy—very shy," said Charlie.

"Charlie, boy! what on earth is there to be shy about?"

And the vicar turned to leave the room.

"Suppose you were to repeat your invitation; put it in a different form; she might accept."

"I do not think so, Charlie," said the vicar, again turning round; "and, besides, I am a man of few words."

"I shall be so sorry to lose her," said Mrs. Hill.

"You see, there is no denying the fact that London is the place for her; she will be appreciated!" said the vicar.

"Indeed, I think we all appreciate her here; if that is all, she need not go to London to be appreciated!"

"Ah! my dear Kate, I do not wonder at your eloquence. But—I cannot see that I can do anything more," added he, thoughtfully. "I have asked her to stay longer, and she gave me the impression that she thought she had been here long enough."

"Long enough! She has not been half long enough!" said Charlie, with energy.

The vicar smiled as he said,

"I really do not know how long she has been, and I told her so. I told her it appeared a very short time to me, and—and indeed I went so far as to say I should be very sorry to lose her."

Here the vicar paused, and looked his listeners in the face, turning first to one and then to the other.

"We shall all be sorry," said Charlie. "I dare it will make quite a revolution in doings if we lose Mrs. Harcourt!"

"I shall miss her so much, I think I must try and persuade her to stay a little longer," said Mrs. Hill.

"Yes, she must not go," said Charlie. "She ought by this time to know better than to play her cards so ill."

The vicar looked from one to another, and remained silent.

"If you would only propose to her," said Charlie; "that is, make proposals."

"Well, Charlie?" said the vicar, looking brightly up.

"You see it is all in your own hands—or you ought to see!"

"But I don't see, Charlie! What do you mean to propose to me to do?"

"No, no, I did not want to propose to you, but for you to propose to Mrs. Harcourt!"

"To stay longer?" said the vicar. "Ah! I have done that once. It will not be right to press her to remain here when she can be so much happier in London."

"I disagree with you entirely," said Charlie; "I feel sure she will be happy here, if you will let her."

There was a pause of a few seconds, and then the vicar said, in a tone of intense surprise:

"Charlie, what are you driving at? What queer idea have you got in your head?"

The vicar turned and left the room hastily, and Mr. and Mrs. Charles Hill were left looking at each other in silent astonishment. Charlie broke the spell.

"Then, Kate, he never did mean to marry her after all?"

"I am sure I cannot tell what he meant! What will Mrs. Harcourt think?"

"What a strange affair!" said Charlie, as he walked up and down the room. "Here was I pleasing myself with the idea that the dear old governor's old age would be made happy by the companionship of so charming a woman as Mrs. Harcourt, and all the time he is bent upon thinking her happiness lies in London!"

"It is abominably selfish, after all his attentions to her!"

"No, Kate, dear, he is not selfish;" and then Charlie became thoughtful. "If I knew what to do—but I do not," resumed he, "I would do it; for I confess, Kate, I am sorry to see this affair broken off thus."

"And now look, Charlie," said Mrs. Hill, as she pointed to the lawn.

The shower had passed, the sun shone; and Parson Hill and Mrs. Harcourt were walking together.

"Yes, Kate; and he smiles, and looks down upon her, and she looks up to him, and gives him the same sunny look. Oh, Kitty! Kitty!"

"Now do not call me 'Kitty' because you are vexed about this!"

XIII

WHAT WAS EXPECTED FROM MRS. HARCOURT

WHEN the post arrived at Lawsleigh Vicarage on this memorable morning, there were letters for Mrs. Harcourt, one of which we will take the liberty of perusing:—

"MY DEAR MARY,—

"I think I never have been more disappointed in my whole life than I am now by your letter. I cannot understand how it has happened that Mr. Hill has not proposed. Had you not better stay a little longer? I should seriously advise you not to give up your chance. I am sure you have a good chance, if you will seize it; but somehow or other you always seem to throw cold water upon all that is said on this subject. If you would but encourage, instead of 'snubbing,'—I daresay you 'snub' Mr. Hill,—that is just as you treated Barbarossa.

"Now, what is to become of you? Do you mean to say you can live upon a hundred and fifty pounds a year? The thing is simply absurd. You cannot, and you know you cannot; and that is an additional reason that you should remain yet longer at Lawsleigh Vicarage, and make something of the chance you still have of marrying Mr. Hill.

"If you were twenty years older—but you are not, and so that is settled. But if you were, you might sink your money, and so get eight or nine per cent., and then you would have an income of three or four hundred a year; but if you are not twenty years older, you cannot. And so I may put aside that plan for your benefit. And now, pray, how are you to live for the next twenty years, until you can sink your money advantageously? You have not given the subject a thought. I dare say not; but I have; and I can tell you, you cannot live—you will die!

"What do you think of this summing up? Does it please you? You have, at least, the consolation of knowing you have brought it on yourself by refusing to marry Mr. Hill, or, at least, by not encouraging him to propose I know—as well as if I had been present all the time—I know that is what you have done. You did the same with Barbarossa.

"Do you think I should ever have been married to Mr. Curtis, or be the happy wife I am, if I had kept him at 'arm's length,' and not allowed him to propose? I was wiser, I can tell you; and I am rewarded with a good husband, a fine-hearted, noble fellow, as generous as he is good; and I have a charming home, and every comfort, and, I may say, luxury. But, then, my manner is encouraging; yours—well, Mary, you really are too proud, and haughty, and hard to please. Barbarossa would have been as good as gold to you, if you would but have given him the smallest encouragement. You really do surprise me; and yet I should not say that; for nothing you do surprises me now. You annoy me. That, at least, is true.

"What is to become of you? I am sure I quite worry myself with thinking about you! And you, of all people in the world, to act in this way! Brought up as you have been, accustomed to every comfort, and every attention. And now I think of it, pray how did you ever manage to get married to Mr. Harcourt? You did not 'snub' him, I suppose, or he would have imitated the example of others, and left you to regret your behaviour when it was too late to amend it. It is a marvel to me, when I think of the matter, that you should ever, at any period of your life, have condescended to encourage a gentleman who admired you, and finally allowed him to marry you.

"You had had nine offers when you accepted Mr. Harcourt. I hope he, at least, felt proud of his conquest. I was contented to accept my first offer—dear Mr. Curtis! But some women love to count up the number of their adorers, and some can be satisfied with one. Now you need not purse up your lips, as I know you are doing at this moment, and tell me you never boasted of your conquests. I did not say you did. On the contrary, I think you were just as silly then as you are now. Love letters, and offers and that kind of thing, are always amusing to read; but you even grudged your sisters that little bit of fun, and were then as chary of giving us information on such subjects, as you are now of encouraging an eligible offer. We outwitted you then, and knew more than you suspected. I heartily wish some man would outwit you now, and make you marry him, and so give you a home. I only wish this for your own good; and so you need not be cross at that.

"However, here I am wasting my whole morning in writing to you; and wasting my time and my arguments, I know I am; for you always will have your own way, and so you must have it now. And a pretty way it is, and a pretty pass you have brought yourself to, with all your superior airs and graces! That is, I mean—'brought your pigs to a pretty market.'

"What do you think Mr. Curtis says—'Sophia, my love, I hope you are not giving Mary a jobation!' And what do you think was my reply? 'I am sure it is no use to leave it for you to do.' And then he said, 'Poor Mary, don't worry her, my dear!'

"Did you ever!—I worry you! Why, I should never think of such a thing! I know I am angry; and so would any sensible woman be in a like case. I cannot help being angry; it would be unreasonable to hope the contrary. And of course you must expect it—but then, you know, Mary, I am not 'a worry,' nobody can say that of me.

"You know this. I should have been most delighted if you had only accepted Mr. Hill, or made him propose, or done something. But when I look the matter clearly in the face, and remember that you have not accepted Mr. Hill or any one, or made him or any one else propose, and that, in point of fact, you have done in this affair as you have done in others, 'nothing,' I feel that you come back 'like a bad penny,' and I am accordingly annoyed.

"It is for your good I am so anxious. What will you do without a home of your own? I declare, talking of 'worry,' I worry myself with thinking what *is* to become of you. But I am wasting my whole morning, as I said before, and I really have not time to say half that I can say, and must when I see you. I am not sure that I should have written at all, I feel so cross with Mr. Hill, and you, and the whole thing; but Mr. Curtis asked me to write and, tell you, you should be welcome here when you come up from Devon. That is more than I can say. I cannot feel the least wish to receive you after your stupidity. Of course I shall be very glad to have you, and all that; but you do not deserve compassion, or welcome, after such unwelcome tidings. There. Good-bye! I wish I was not cross; but I am. Nevertheless you will come to us; the carriage shall meet you at Paddington, if you will let us know the day. And now, dear, excuse all my crossness, though you have brought it on yourself, and believe me to be

"Your loving sister,
"Sophia Curtis."

XIV

WHICH ACCOUNTS FOR THE ABSENCE OF A QUEEN ON DARTMOOR

THE up-train to London was on the point of starting from the station at N——, and Mrs. Hill and Charlie were standing at the door of a carriage in which Mrs. Harcourt was seated.

"And so this is the end of you," said Mrs. Hill; "I had hoped better things!"

Mrs. Harcourt's reply was lost to the world, for the train moved on, and Charlie and his wife were left standing on the platform.

"And so, after all the fuss, this is the end of the Widow Harcourt! I shall not easily recover from the disappointment of such a finale," said Charlie, when he and Mrs. Hill were again seated in their own carriage.

"Poor thing!" said Mrs. Hill. "I am so sorry to lose her."

"Sorry!—so am I—so is the governor! How grumpy he will be! I say, Kate, we shall not be able to stand Lawsleigh now the fascinating widow is gone; we must cut off home, and take the governor with us and cheer him up. Everything here will remind him of his loss; whereas, if he goes——"

"Nonsense, Charlie! 'Cutting off home,' indeed! Let Mr. Hill be reminded of his loss—the surest way to bring him to reason. And 'grumpy,' too, who cares if he is 'grumpy?' If there is any reason for his 'grumpiness' it is not your fault, or mine. Let him feel the misery he has brought upon himself."

"But, Kate, dear, the governor is not unhappy; by 'grumpy' I only mean——"

"Then I do not care what you mean, Charlie. Why did he not propose to Mrs. Harcourt? No one can give a sensible answer to so reasonable a question."

"Except the governor himself. I see now, Kate, he never had the most remote idea of marriage with any one. The idea has existed in our minds, not in his. We should blame ourselves for forming plans to which he could not consent. We never asked his permission to marry him to Mrs. Harcourt."

"There never was such a chance in this world, for an excellent, kind-hearted, and gentlemanly man, to be made happy by an elegant, true-hearted and lady-like woman. How he has thrown it away!" said Mrs. Hill.

"But he is happy," said Charlie; "he is of a happy nature."

"Then he ought not to be 'happy' without Mrs. Harcourt. I have no patience with him!" said Mrs. Hill.

"I perceive that, my dear; but then since you blame the dear old governor so much, has he deceived the widow?"

"Of course he has. Has he not deceived you and me?"

"We have deceived ourselves. Do you think the widow has deceived herself? I am sure that dear old governor would never mislead her even a hair's breadth. And then you say—'The governor threw away his chance.' And what has the widow done? Has not she thrown away her chance? Why did not she encourage him? He is shy!"

And Charlie laughed a pleasant laugh as he put his horses on.

"You men are the most cowardly creatures," said Mrs. Hill pettishly. "You always throw the blame upon us, whichever way the wind blows."

"But, Kate, we all acknowledge the widow was a 'charming woman.' Now, the governor knows the old song of that title; and he may have felt the advice there given to be good:

> *Don't* marry a 'charming woman,'
> If you are a sensible man.

Depend upon it, the governor was bent upon proving himself 'a sensible man.'"

"Why did he feel bound to make such a fuss with her, poor thing, if he did not mean to keep her for ever?"

"I have not inquired of him," said Charlie.

"I am so vexed!—I am really cross!" said Mrs. Hill.

"And so is the widow," said Charlie. "She tried to look very demure, and natural; and I must say her efforts did her credit."

"Everything she does, does her credit," said Mrs. Hill, interrupting.

"Except running away from the governor. She should have stood her ground. In my judgment, she had very good ground to stay. But then a man may err in his judgment on so nice a point; and you women are such strange creatures, and contrive to mislead us very often. Some time ago I remember describing to you the three widows who were then in the village of Lawsleigh—to wit, the buxom and bad Mason; the aged and good Simpson; the fascinating and handsome Harcourt. But of all the three, I find the bad has the most courage, the good the most faith, and the fascinating the most despondency."

"What a fuss you do make about widows, Charlie! And I don't like to hear Mrs. Harcourt called a widow. I wish you would not give her that title."

"My dear Kate, it is hers by right of her widowhood, in common with all womankind similarly situated. But I have something to say on the subject of widows, and so listen, Kate. The bad Widow Mason—I think I have before told you the bad always take precedence—this bad widow dashed a cup of cider in Isaac Watson's face! That was her greeting to him on his marriage. Amiable woman! you will say. Gray misled the governor by telling——"

"Misled the governor, Charlie!"

"Do not interrupt me, Kate, or you will lose the benefit of my learning. And so to return: Gray misled the governor—he told him Isaac and Jacob came rolling drunk out of the 'Packhorse'. It is true they rolled out, for Jacob, who was in a state of helplessness, fell down, and Isaac fell over him, and so they rolled out together, and Gray saw them; but Isaac was sober; he had not—to his credit I speak of it—touched a drop of cider in the Widow Mason's house that night; nor can I learn that he has ever been to the 'Packhorse' since his marriage, except that once, and that was to fetch Jacob away; nor has he ever been seen in a state of intoxication."

"Oh! then, Charlie, that will come all right."

"What will come right?—intoxication?—Jacob?—'Packhorse?'—Widow Mason?—or

"Charlie! Charlie! you know nothing vexes me like your pretending to misunderstand me."

"Do not accuse me wrongfully," said Charlie, with a smile; "if you will tell me to what 'that' you allude, perhaps I can agree with you in opinion."

"You know I mean marriage—Isaac's marriage with Mary."

"I know now, Kate; and I may confess to you, I *am* hopeful on the subject of that marriage. But I am on the subject of widows at this moment—let me say my say. To return once again to the bad Widow Mason: she flouts the power of the law to remove her, or to take away her licence. She has grown cunning, and cannot be caught in her transgressions; she grows more and more popular with a certain set, and plumes herself accordingly; she insults where she formerly cajoled; and if the governor do not bestir himself, she will win, for she will leave no stone unturned that will serve her purpose. And so, you see, the bad widow has the best chance of winning, because of her courage and slyness; for she turns up her eyes and bobs her curtsies to Gray, and thus keeps him in check; for he, too, like the governor, does not like to have to take away the bread from a lone woman."

"These parsons have such tender consciences. Their consciences may be unwilling to take away bread from any one—it would be more becoming to them to charge themselves with the blessing of giving bread," said Mrs. Hill.

"Kate, I never heard you so bitter in my life," said Charlie, "or so false to your real sentiments; for you know full well that the clergy, as a body, are men who are in the daily practice of charity; of charity in all its forms—in the giving of alms, in feeding the hungry, in clothing the naked—of that charity also that, as the apostle says, 'never faileth;' that charity that 'rejoiceth not in iniquity, but rejoiceth in the truth; beareth all things, believeth all things, hopeth all things, endureth all things.' You have made me eloquent, Kate; but indeed such harsh words from your lips took me by surprise. The fact is, you are smarting for the loss of your friend, and so cannot be reasonable."

"Parson Hill might have given dear Mrs. Harcourt bread for the rest of her life," said Mrs. Hill.

"True, my love," said Charlie, with returning good-humour; "if he had so willed. A man may do as he pleases with his own; and it seems the parson had no intention of giving bread to the handsome Widow Harcourt. But once again, to return—you interrupt me so, Kate, I shall never come to the end of my story. The next on my list of widows is the aged and good Widow Simpson. The governor says she is more than ninety—think of that—more than ninety! Now, she is a pattern to the rest of the world—a little old-fashioned pattern, that will never be surpassed by the newer-fashioned generations that will follow. She is quite sure everything is right; if it is not, it was intended to be; she is sure there is a God and a heaven to go to; she is sure she would never do any evil; she is sure others are like herself, pure in intention; she is one who steers clear of all scrapes, for if, with a desire to shake her faith in the goodness of others, she was suddenly, by some superior mind, inveigled into a sea of troubles, she would say, 'Him never didn't mean it;' and thus *she* would keep her faith, and *he* would have his trouble for his pains. There is nothing to be done with her but to leave her alone in her goodness. Faith is a mighty rock! And so you see, dear Kate, of these two, one wins by her bad deeds, the other by her good. I have managed to make them both win this time," and Charlie paused in his long speech.

"I suppose you are trying to amuse me," said Mrs. Hill, as she leaned back in the carriage.

"I suppose I am," said Charlie, as he again put his horses on. "Do you mean to say you are not amused? If so, I must try and get over the ground in 'double-quick' time—though that term is not one of the clearest in the world."

Mrs. Hill did not reply.

"Well, Kate, shall we gallop off home, or shall I finish my speech and wile away the time?"

"Oh! pray go on," said she.

"Now I come to the Widow Harcourt, and we can both testify that for the last two months she had been publicly wooed, publicly courted, by the governor. Why, then, does she privately run away? Answer me that, Kate."

Mrs. Hill remained silent.

"You may look as uncomfortable as you please, and remain as 'mum' as you please, but *I* say she had good ground to stand upon. And you say, or think, she ought to have 'stood her ground;' while she, more learned than either, felt it 'crumble' from under her very feet! There is no denying that, Kate!"

"You know nothing about it, Charlie," said Mrs. Hill, as she turned away her face and pulled down her veil.

"Do you, Kate?" said Charlie in a tone of surprise, as he tried to read the expression of his wife's countenance. "Has she then refused him?— and have you kept me in the dark?"

"Keep you in the dark!" said Mrs Hill, laughing; "I am not half clever enough for that."

"Oh! trust me to credit you! I know you to be quite as clever as your clever friend the Widow Harcourt, and you would 'hood-wink' any man, if you wished. And so now, Kate, out with it. Do you surmise that the widow refused the governor?"

"No; since you wish for the truth, he never proposed! After all those undeniable attentions!"

"Ah! unfortunately there is a difference between attentions and intentions," said Charlie, as he allowed his horses to walk slowly up the hill.

"The governor's 'attentions' to the lady were seen and misunderstood by the crowd around—his 'intentions' towards her were best known to himself, though the world thought itself very learned even on that head. Well, 'one man can take a horse to water, but fifty cannot make him drink.' And so the governor would not drink—I am sure he seemed sufficiently thirsty!"

"But what a foolish simile, Charlie! Why did Parson Hill praise her so, and admire everything she did, and listen to all she said so courteously?"

"I am not in the governor's secrets."

"But you must think he has behaved ill? I should if he had treated me so."

"You are a wife, my dear, and therefore would have a right to feel ill-used under such treatment."

"Nonsense, Charlie! You always pervert my meaning. You must think he has behaved ill to Mrs. Harcourt?"

"Pardon me, I have no such thought. I never heard the governor say he wished to marry; and I think he behaved extremely well to Mrs. Harcourt. You lose sight of the fact that she understood him. His conduct to her was the very perfection of the fine breeding and gentlemanly ease of the old school, which conveyed to most women that they were admired—to all, that they were appreciated. Old Harcourt was just such another as the governor; he had that same courtly manner. But, Kate, it strikes me now that the Widow Harcourt is a wise and strong-minded as well as an elegant and fascinating woman. She certainly understands the governor better than any other woman, and it is as certain that she was not misled by his attentions. Remember, Kate, she always said, 'There was nothing between them.' I quite give her credit now for having spoken the truth; but, 'lookers on,' who are said 'to see more of the game than they who play it,' seem for once to have been taken in."

"It is a great shame to have misled us all in this way," said Mrs. Hill.

"Nay, nay, Kate; we misled each other. I had somehow taken up the notion that if I had a home of my own, the dear old governor would look out for a mate. I knew how highly he appreciated Mrs. Harcourt, and I thought she was just the woman to make him happy. As I have before said, I married to get out of his way, and now I find I have made a mistake."

"In your marriage?"

"Ha, ha, Kate—you have me there. It was fortunate for me, my love, that my heart was already given, and my hopes of a happy future centred in a union with one who, I am glad to say, does make me happy. Perhaps the vista of my own future helped to blind me to the governor's present. I have been blind."

"Ever since I have known Mr. Hill, he has talked to me about Mrs. Harcourt; Mrs. Harcourt does so and so; Mrs. Harcourt does this and that. She seemed the one only woman in the world who was perfect in his eyes."

"True, Kate, so it seemed to me; but I am now convinced he never had a thought of marriage."

"It is very hard upon Mrs. Harcourt."

"No, no, Kate, I do not see that. She surely understood him from the very first. She is a first-rate specimen of that anomaly in the female sex, 'a strong-minded woman.' Such women are generally shunned and disliked, for they have no feminine foibles to counterbalance their strength of mind, and so to create an interest. But Mrs. Harcourt is the exception that proves the rule. And while I dub her strong I cannot deny that she is a very amiable and fascinating woman."

"What an uncomfortable drive I have had," said Mrs. Hill, as the carriage stopped at the Vicarage.

"Umph!" said Charlie, to himself, "that is not my fault. I thought I had talked nonsense enough to satisfy any woman; but the fact is, she is put out about the Widow Harcourt; and, for that matter, so am I, and so is the governor, and so is the widow herself! A sad ending to our joyous hopes!"

XV

OF THE ILLNESS OF PARSON HILL

THE incidents that occurred in the churchyard of Lawsleigh sunk deep in Isaac Watson's mind. As we have said, he had not comprehended the attack on the sewing-machine, nor did he know that the ignorant villagers had gifted it with strange powers. And also, though he understood that disagreeable things had been said of Mary, he had no clue to the real ill-will, no clue to the fact that she was credited with the wickedness of witchcraft, and execrated throughout the village as one who worked evil upon any one she pleased, by means of the "dumb critter."

Isaac himself was too enlightened to entertain ideas of this sort, as applied either to any piece of machinery, or to any person. Not so the inhabitants of Lawsleigh. It was to be regretted, in this instance, that Isaac's well-informed mind, and general intelligence of character, unfitted him from estimating their ignorance at its real value. It was this very ignorance that caused them to fear what they could not understand.

The reader must remember that still the "wise men" and "wise women" inhabit the more distant parts of Dartmoor. Still the illiterate villagers apply to these people in times of doubt and difficulty, in times of losses or misfortunes. And the "wise man" or "wise woman," upon the payment of a sum of money, casts the spell, and gives advice.

That they should invest the sewing-machine with a species of diablerie is not to be wondered at. But if Isaac did not know the extent of the evil that existed in Lawsleigh against Mary and the machine, he had seen enough of the jeers and spite of the people to feel that his position and Mary's would be very uncomfortable if this unneighbourly treatment could not be put an end to. He knew—or thought he knew—that it was the loss of the parson's favour that had so suddenly made all the villagers his enemies. If he had known how greatly he had excited their envy and jealousy in the days of his prosperity, he would not have marvelled at their malice now. But Isaac was too really free from such unamiable qualities in himself, to suspect them in others.

As we have seen, Isaac left his work and tried to lighten Mary's sadness. He made her knitting-needles, exactly the right size; he found the supposed-to-be lost gauge, he took an interest in the "knitted counterpane," all to make her forget the care that, for the time, seemed to be corroding her mind, and rendering her days unenjoyable. But when he had made his wife and his mother happy, when he returned to his shed, and to his own thoughts, "the glow" faded from Isaac's brow, and he looked well into the subject that gave him so much uneasiness.

And now Isaac determined that he would not lose either "the bells" or "the choir" without a struggle. Nothing but the parson's own orders should take them from him. He must see the parson. And Isaac sighed heavily; for, if the parson would not admit him, what could be done? He would see Master Charlie; he would state his case to Master Charlie, and pray him to get the vicar to grant him an audience.

"Master Charlie knows now," said Isaac to himself, "that I do not go to the 'Packhorse,' that I do not drink cider. I had a good talk with him a few days ago, when he came to see after the shoes of his handsome black mare, for he is very particular—as he ought to be—that his horses are well attended to. I could not say as much as I wished to him then, because there were so many standing outside the shed looking on, and listening to every word; but Master Charlie will befriend me if he can, and I must see after him."

The vicar was always just—Isaac relied much on that. He would not take away the bells except for some bad conduct, and that should never be. In like manner, through the well-known equity of Parson Hill, he trusted to retain the choir. With Mary the case was different; her post in the choir was lost with the school—there could be no use in struggling to bring back what could never again be hers!

"But she can sing—bless her heart!—as well as ever, and her voice fills the church, and rings round and round so as to make the parson look at her; and I dare say, at such times, he heartily wishes he had her back again to lead the choir, and to conduct the school, and to be a comfort to him in the parish—as of course she always was; being able—as she did—to tell him about the behaviour of the mothers as well as of the children. Well, Parson Hill just will not get another such schoolmistress, I can tell him. But then, good man, he knows that."

And now Isaac made up his mind. He would say nothing to Mary, but he would watch for an opportunity of speaking to Master Charlie, and so get the matter settled before another Sunday. He would not go to the vicarage; he would not give the smallest cause of offence to the vicar if he could help it; he would not do anything that might ever so slightly irritate him. He would "way-lay" Master Charlie, and open his mind to him. And, for the next day or two, Isaac watched here and there, and everywhere he could think of, for Master Charlie; but he only saw him once, and that was in a carriage, driving the ladies to the station, as he afterwards learned.

The week was almost gone, and Isaac began to think Master Charlie must be quite gone, for he never could set eyes upon him. And so the Sunday came and went, and it was only less disagreeable than the preceding, because the weather was stormy, and the congregation, on coming out of church, were glad to hasten to their own homes. But, if Isaac and his wife and mother had not been insulted, they had been shunned, for not one single person spoke a word of any kind to them.

Early in the week Isaac learned "that Master Charlie and his missus were gone to Paul Tavey!"

Here was an end to his gathering hopes! In the acuteness of his disappointment, Isaac even thought of Mr Gray as of one likely to befriend him. "The drowning man catching at the straw."

Towards the end of the week, James Marvel looked in at the open window as he was passing by, and said,

"Morning, widdy. And how be you?—and have you heard the news?"

"The news, James? And how be you? No, us havena heard the news."

"The passon be ill."

"The cheery passon, James? The passon ill! Massy me! but that be cruel bad news, James!"

"Bad news, widdy!—it be the worstest news as I have a-heard for many a-day!"

"And what for be the passon ill, James? Be he a-going to die? Massy me!"

"The passon be ill—coz why? All the nice young folk be goned away."

"Goned away?—what! all gone, James?"

"Ay, widdy; Master Charlie and his blithe young missus, and the tother lady as the passon was always a-walking and a-talking and a-riding with— they be all gone, widdy; and I be blest if the passon has a hold his head up ever since!"

"Deary me! So then, James, the cheery passon have a-got his trouble!"

"Ay, widdy, he have—and he will not have a doctor, widdy."

"Doctor! my, James!—be us to lose the cheery passon in us old ages, James?"

"No, no, I hopes not; I havena heard nothing to that sort, though they does say as him be mighty bad! And all the blithe young folk gone!"

"And why for don't they come back again, James?"

"They have a-sended. No, widdy—I means they be a-going to send to Master Charlie. Morning, widdy."

And James Marvel walked away to carry his news of the parson's illness to other cottages. And now Isaac reproached himself for a want of courage, which, after all, had only been an unwillingness to give any cause of offence to Parson Hill.

"I ought to have gone to the vicarage and asked for Master Charlie, only I was so chary of irritating the parson by seeming to presume upon former favours. And now Master Charlie is gone, and the good parson himself ill. There is still—Mr. Gray."

And Isaac sighed heavily.

"Well, well, we must get through another Sunday as best we can—and I have a journey to take on Monday. But after that, I must come to some better understanding, both with the parson and with the people in the village; we cannot live our lives in this fashion—poor Mary and I. It is clear we shall have no peace till things are put on a better footing."

"The vicar has sent a basket of vegetables for the widow," said a servant from the vicarage, breaking in upon Isaac's reverie.

The widow came forward and made inquiries as to the parson's illness. But the domestic replied, "That the parson said he was not ill; but everybody at the vicarage knew that he was ill, because he lay in bed very late in the morning, he ate no breakfast, no luncheon, no dinner, although he went through the ceremony of sitting down to that repast daily; that, excepting a cup of tea now and then, and a bit of dry toast, he had had nothing since Master Charlie and his missus went away a week ago. That they were all in a great anxiety at the vicarage, and were talking of writing to Master Charlie!"

This was sad news; but, when the messenger went away with the empty basket, Isaac said,

"God bless the dear and good Parson Hill, and restore him to health and happiness! He never forgets my dear old mother—God bless him!— though he thinks it right not to notice me."

XVI

THE STRANGE WARNING

ON the Monday following the news of the parson's illness, the inmates of the Smithy Cottage arose early, because Isaac was obliged to go to Exeter, where he had an appointment on business. But he told Mary "not to put herself out about the unneighbourly treatment they had met with. As soon as he returned, he would see Mr. Gray if he could not see the parson, and through him learn the vicar's pleasure as regarded the belfry and the choir."

"For," said he "Mary, though we have married, nobody, not even the parson, as I have said before, had a right to prevent us. And as he has always been lenient, even to those in the commission of daily sins, I cannot think he will be so very hard upon us now, if the matter is put fairly before him. I do not mean that Mr. Gray is the best mediator in the world, but, in the absence of Master Charlie, I have no choice. And then again, my dear, I do not think Mr. Gray will be unjust."

Mary shook her head at the mention of Mr. Gray, but she made no remark; and Isaac let this slight dissent pass without notice: he had made up his mind to try to make a friend of Mr. Gray.

"I may not be with you again till to-morrow night, Mary, or I may get my business over, so as to reach N—— by a morning train; and in that case, I shall be home early; and so keep up your spirits, my dear. No one can be very hard upon us, after they once see we only want to do our duty in our station, and live peaceably with all men."

But Isaac turned away to stifle a sigh, for he knew he had lost the friendship of Parson Hill by his own unseemly conduct before his marriage; and Isaac only knitted his brow the more sternly, and sighed the deeper, as he recalled his own wilfulness in going to the "Packhorse" during the time that Mr. Gray took such pains to convince him of his unworthy behaviour.

The morning was dull. All nature seemed drowsy.

"It seems unusually dark," said Mary, as she seated herself at breakfast.

"We are earlier than usual," said Isaac.

In a few seconds after they had assembled, one single loud clap of thunder, without any previous warning, for they had not seen the lightning, broke apparently over the cottage.

"Massy me, lad!—it be awful!" said the widow.

"What a terrible——"

A second report prevented Mary from finishing her speech. This was also one clap, not a roll, of thunder.

"Two of them!" said the widow. "It be the Lord God Almighty as——"

Another single loud clap of thunder again interrupted the old woman's speech; and then she took fast hold of the table with both hands, and with difficulty placed herself on her knees. Isaac and Mary followed her example, and she prayed aloud:

"The Lord also thundered in the heavens, and the Highest gave His voice—hailstones and coals of fire. Comest thou in anger, O Lord! To all three does thy warning voice speak. If we have sinned in Thy sight, O Lord! we humbly pray Thee, of Thy great goodness and mercy, to save us from the consequences of our sin! Three times have we heard Thy voice. Three times hast Thou warned us of the evil days fast coming to overwhelm us. Lord, we are Thine; do with us according to Thine own will. And if it please Thee to take us from this earth of sorrow, and trouble, and care, take us, O Lord, to thy blessed heaven. Not for our deservings, but for the sake of Thy dear son. Forgive us, O Lord; accept our submission. Hearken favourably to our prayer."

Not to trouble the reader with the Widow's Dartmoor dialect, I have judged it wiser to translate her prayer into readable English.

For a minute or two the trio still remained on their knees in silence, and with heads bowed down.

Then they arose, and attempted to resume the breakfast that had been so suddenly interrupted.

The old woman explained to one at least of her listeners "that this was not a common thunderstorm; for now the sun sent his bright beams in at the cottage window; and the breakfast apparatus, and the three seated, were in a blaze of light; that a single clap of thunder, coming unexpectedly, was always sent as a warning, or foreshadowing of evil to come; and as there had been three single, distinct reports, so there would be three 'evils,' or one great calamity, in which the three persons sitting together there would be involved."

Mary turned pale, and trembled perceptibly. She had always felt uncomfortable at the thought of Isaac going away even for a day, and now an undefined fear shot through her heart.

"Then I suppose, mother," said Isaac, "this bright sunshine means we shall all come safe out of our troubles, and be happy together?"

"I don't never know about the blessed sun, Isaac," said the old woman; "but I be learned in they single claps of thunder."

Mary's lips turned white with a curdling dread at her heart; but the old woman did not notice this, and continued,

"There was one comed when my pretty maiden was a-lying in she's bed, with the lad in she's arms, and I tooked the poor bit creature from she, coz why?—I knowed as her time was comed, and it was—she died!"

"Oh, mother! mother!" said Mary.

Isaac, perceiving her emotion, put his arm round her, and whispered he would explain all to her. And when the breakfast was over, he led her aside and said:

"I do not think it necessary to say anything to my mother, because, in the first place, she would not understand, and, in the second, she has already forgotten that such a thing has happened."

"Oh! Isaac! she remembers what happened when you were a boy!" said Mary, reproachfully.

"Yes, my dear, she can recall the events of her early life; but the passing incidents of the present day make no impression upon her. I assure you she has quite forgotten the three claps of thunder!"

"But, Isaac, even you must admit—though I know you will try to comfort me—but even you must admit it was very strange thunder!—so sudden, so loud, no rain!" said Mary.

Isaac pointed to the window-panes, which still showed signs of recent rain, and said:

"The shower was falling even while the sun shone! If we had taken the trouble to look we should have seen a rainbow, and then," said he, with a smile, "mother would have drawn a happy omen."

"But I never heard thunder like that, Isaac!" said Mary. "Such terrifically loud and distinct claps; and only three!"

"Then, if these reports had been more in number, you would have been less alarmed, should you?" said Isaac.

"I think it was odd to be three claps of thunder just over the heads of only three people! It seemed, as mother said, one for each of us!"

"Well, Mary, now I must say I did think you were wiser than to fall into such errors," said Isaac, with a little reproach in his tone. "But tell me, then, my dear," added he, in a more gentle tone, softened by her evident distress, "do you think we three were the only living creatures who heard that thunder? There was the whole village of Lawsleigh. What would the inhabitants say to your three single, loud, distinct claps?"—unconsciously Isaac spoke impatiently. "And then, Mary, there was the good vicar, quite alone, and ill; what idea did these three reports convey to him? I suppose even mother would say one would be enough for the parson, now that he is by himself!"

"I never thought of that!" said Mary, some of her terror subsiding. "But, at all events, Isaac, I never heard such thunder in all my whole life!"

"That may be, and I cannot explain all the causes to you now, Mary, because I must set off on my journey. The plain way to account for these three discharges, and no more, is that the balance between the electric clouds was restored."

Mary stared, evidently not comprehending. Then she said, with some degree of awe in her manner:

"But they broke just over our heads, Isaac, all three of them!"

"How many seconds of time do you think there were between the first discharge and the second?"

"Seconds of time!—seconds of time!—why, six or seven, perhaps more!" said Mary.

"And between the second and third?"

"More—more, Isaac; half a minute, at least."

"Then, Mary dear, assuming that the first discharge was immediately over this cottage, by your own shewing the second was a mile and three quarters off, and the third much more distant! Sound travels at the rate of a quarter of a mile in a second of time!"

"Isaac!" said Mary, almost breathless with surprise, for such knowledge had not fallen in her way, "why, how wonderful!—how very wonderful!—how can you know this, and know it for certain?"

"Mary, my dear," and Isaac spoke in a very serious and impressive manner, "will you believe me there is nothing in the thunder this morning but the natural consequence when two electric clouds meet?—I will show you my books on scientific subjects when I come back, and explain all to you."

The mention of books was enough to Mary. All her former confidence in Isaac's talented mind returned; she knew, in her own small experiences, that books were authorities she might safely rely upon, and she said in a glad voice,

"Oh! yes, dear Isaac, I do quite believe you. But how very clever you are!" And she gazed at him from head to foot with a proud and gratified look.

"Well, never mind my cleverness; only remember, you have no cause for fear. Mother has already forgotten all about it, so she will not return to the subject."

"And you, my treasure," said Isaac, solemnly, as he clasped her in his arms for a parting embrace, "do you keep your mind from superstition, and your heart free from anxiety, for I shall soon return."

And Isaac set off on his journey; but somehow even he could not shake off a feeling of sadness that was both discouraging and disheartening.

XVII

OF THE VISIT OF THE WIDOW MASON AND JANE SANDS TO THE SMITHY COTTAGE

AND Mary was alone. It seemed so to her now that Isaac was gone. She set herself to her daily work, however, and did not allow her mind to dwell on the thunder—Isaac had entirely dissipated her fears. The old woman went about the cottage as usual, attending to her morning duties, and accidentally set down on the sewing-machine a jug she had brought with her downstairs. In her failing, sight she had not perceived that this was the dreaded machine, and as her hands were full, she placed, as she thought, this jug on a table standing there. What was her astonishment to see it topple over, fall to the ground, and break in a thousand pieces. She had placed it on a corner of the box or case that covered up the machinery, and thus the jug, insecurely placed, fell. But she did not understand it had been her own fault, and amid her loud lamentations for the loss of the jug, she mingled many regrets that "the critter" had ever been brought into the house.

It was now that Mary discovered the old woman's terror at its supposed diablerie; and it was now that she had some clue to the words she had heard spoken a week or two ago in the churchyard. Mary's hair almost stood on end with fear, as she ascertained, bit by bit, that the old woman's opinion agreed with that of the Widow Mason, and of many others, in the supposition that Mary was a witch. Poor Mary! she had never heard of "the Lancashire witches," or she might have had some comfort under that title. She had only read of the witches of bygone ages, and knew that some had even been burned to death!

We cannot say that in these enlightened days Mary contemplated such a fate for herself; but she certainly did not feel easy under the title of "witch!" We have before intimated that Mary if she spoke but little, and sometimes did not appear to advantage, was, upon the whole, a sensible and rightly-judging young woman. On this day, during Isaac's absence, she particularly wished to use the machine; the positive attention she must give to it, to work well, would draw her from herself and her own melancholy thoughts, and the long and lonely hours would thus appear to pass away the quicker.

And now, though she had discovered the old woman's strange antipathy to the machine, she thought it would be wiser to try to conquer her prejudice by a daily use of it, than, by giving way, render Isaac's superb gift useless, and deprive herself of a great help in her sewing, as well as of a great amusement. Whether Mary acted in this instance with her usual judgment we leave to the decision of our readers. Certain it is, she set to work in her customary manner, and the old woman in due course of time took her knitting.

Mary did not notice the furtive looks of the widow as she now and then raised her eyes from her own employment to steal a glance at the dreaded "critter." Mary had purposely placed herself by the window that looked into the garden, in the hope that at that distance she should not only not give offence, but probably remain unseen and unheard; and thus placed, if her thoughts were at any time withdrawn from her work, they only fell back upon Isaac, his absence, his probable return, his steadfastness—for the moment she had forgotten his breach of faith—his kindliness and goodness, and her own great love for him. The widow and her timid terrors were soon far away from Mary's attention in the present moment, or her calculations in the future. But the widow, on the contrary, the faster the machine seemed to work, and the louder its tric-trac, the greater became her hidden fear. It is true she continued to knit, for still the same words haunted her—

> Satan finds some mischief still
> For idle hands to do;

and she certainly felt herself in greater danger when sitting idle, than when, with her knitting, she was keeping time with the machine. She made no visible demonstration of her agitation, beyond the movement of her lips in the verse she kept repeating over and over again, as if it were a charm to protect her from evil, and the furtive glances she occasionally gave to Mary.

It happened at this time that the Widow Mason, in her stroll round the village, retailing the news brought into the "Packhorse" by men crossing the moor, met Jane Sands opposite the smithy, who was returning from the school, where she had been summoned by Mr. Gray, on account of the continued ill-behaviour of her pet child Joe—"the cherubian Joe," as the vicar had called him. And here the two women stood for a gossip in the street, Jane telling the widow all that her poor boy had been doomed to endure in the hands of that "there coorit—rabbit him!" added she, as she clenched her fist.

They had not stood talking many minutes before they saw the Widow Simpson seated at the window, and they both simultaneously spoke of the unusual expression of her customarily very placid face. They saw her lips move, as if she were muttering to herself, and her eyes extend themselves, and stare, apparently, into vacancy, while her aged fingers plied her knitting-needles with a rapidity that, to the looker-on, seemed marvellous, but that to the old woman herself seemed to be a race she was running with the dreaded "critter," and the winning of which her excited imagination and real ignorance compelled her to attempt.

"Look to she!—look to she, Jenny, 'ooman!" said the Widow Mason.

"She be most mazed, to my thinking," said Jane.

"Most mazed!—that witch will kill she!—kill that poor old body! Here, Jenny, 'ooman, let us go up to the window."

The Widow Mason and her companion went close up to the cottage, and they stood gazing at the Widow Simpson sitting knitting, with every symptom of terror expressed on her countenance, close to the window; and at Mary, plying her skill so quietly, and so unconscious of intruders at the other window—for the windows were opposite each other, looking back and front.

"Us will speak to the widdy, Jenny," said the Widow Mason. And she accordingly placed her stout person close to the casement, and shouted out, "Open the window, widdy!"

The poor old woman, startled by an unusual and unexpected sound from her dream of horror, screamed aloud, as she dashed her knitting on the floor, and started to her feet.

"Open the window—open the window!" said the Widow Mason, trying to arrest her attention, and so far succeeding as to cause the old woman to turn and look at her. But she did not attempt to reply to the Widow Mason's request by opening the window.

Mary had left the machine, and was now standing by her side. She had no more inclination than the old woman to open the window; though, for that matter, she did not even know that the Widow Mason had dared to make such a request, since she was not one of the frequenters of the smithy cottage, nor one whom Mary ever willingly noticed.

The two women on the outside, seeing that the window was not opened to them, went round to the cottage door and let themselves in.

"I be glad you be come," said the Widow Simpson.

Her terror was so great, she was glad of any change. But if the old woman had been in her customary quiet state of mind, she would have been one of the last to welcome either the Widow Mason or Jane Sands.

"Mother!" said Mary, in a tone of surprise, "I am with you, why need you fear?"

The old woman was very pale, and trembled so as to require support. She leaned upon Mary, for she could not stand alone.

"Ma-ary, I was afeared as the 'old one' would take us;" and then she began to weep in a demented sort of way, as she turned to the two intruders and said, "May be as the Lord sended you to I to keep the 'old one' at a distance, as he shouldna touch I!"

For, in the confused state of her ideas, and in her personal dread of the machine, she had not lost her belief in a superior being, or her reliance on his power.

"The 'old one!' bless us and save us, Jenny, woman! The 'old one!' Hark to she, Jenny!" said the Widow Mason.

"Mother! mother!" said Mary, speaking with some asperity, as the ignorance of the old woman displayed itself to her.

"You be a dear, good old widdy!" said the Widow Mason, coaxingly. "May be as I can help ye?—tell I what be your trouble?"

"The 'old one' be come to us," said the old woman; "him be there!" and she pointed to the machine.

"Oh—h! Jenny, woman! hearken to that! There be the 'old one' a-seated hisself on that there table!"

"I have a-heard on it," said Jenny. "It be she"—pointing to Mary—"as have a-bringed him!"

"Ay, ay," said the old woman, not comprehending the drift of Jenny's speech, but understanding that she meant to point out the machine as belonging to Mary. "Us be clean in the hands of the 'old one!'"

"Mother!" again interrupted Mary, in great astonishment, and some anger, "what are you saying?"

"Allow she to tell the truth," said Jane Sands, menacing Mary with her clenched fist.

"Tell truth, Molly, and shame the devil, I have a-heard say," said the Widow Mason, laughing.

"It is only a sewing-machine," said Mary, to the women, for a strange sensation of helplessness was fast creeping over her, and, almost unconsciously, she tried to propitiate them. "It is only my sewing-machine, dear mother; there is no harm in it."

"No, Ma-ary, no," said the widow, kindly; "only I be most mazed, and I don't like to go near it!"

"Poor old widow! most mazed! Hearken to that, Jenny, woman; and it be like enough she be most mazed."

"Been't you 'shamed of yourself, mazing a quiet body that fashions?" said Jane Sands to Mary.

"You have no business here, Jane," said Mary, with some spirit. "Neither have you," said she, to the Widow Mason; "and I request you will both leave my cottage."

"Oh—h! you be mighty grand, you be!" said the Widow Mason; "but I be a-going to speak to this here old widow. Jenny, 'ooman, stop you there."

The old woman had not understood what had been said; she had been busy collecting her needles and wool, and knitting.

"Widdy, I comed to see how you be," said the Widow Mason, artfully taking advantage of the old woman's temporary loss of power.

"And I be very glad to see you, and thank you kindly, and sit you down. Ma-ary, the Widow Mason will stop and cheer us up a bit now, as Isaac be not here."

Mary said nothing. She turned away with a sinking heart to put away her work, and keep all her attention upon her enemies.

XVIII

OF THE MINERS AT THE SMITHY COTTAGE

"And where be that there big Isaac" said Jane Sands; "why for does he let his old mother be feared out of she's witses?"

"Isaac, Isaac," said Mary, hesitating to proclaim his absence.

But the old woman said,

"Isaac be gone to Exeter—he will come back to-morrow, and then us will be safe."

"Safe, mother—you are safe now," said Mary, though her voice faltered as she thought that Isaac could not be with them till the morrow, and that these women would not have dared to press their presence upon her if she could only have said, "Isaac will be here in a few minutes."

"Oh-h-h! him be a-gone to Exeter—umph!" said the Widow Mason, bridling and sneering, and inwardly glad to hear that Isaac was away, because this fact, combined with the old woman's weakness, gave her present power over Mary. "Him be a uncommon big man," and then, turning to Mary, she added in a sneering tone, "Do he take a drop of cider now and then—do he, spite of your white face?"

Mary's face might well be called white. She had always had an indistinct fear of Jane Sands, even while surrounded by the powerful protection of the vicar; and she was no stranger to the slights and scoffs of the Widow Mason towards herself. And now, therefore, to have these two women invade the privacy of her own cottage in Isaac's absence, and take part with Isaac's mother against herself, however wrongly, was enough to send the blood from her face, and to fill her mind with anticipated dread in the present, and to banish hope for the future. She felt the taunt conveyed by the widow's last words, perhaps even more than her uncomfortable position at that moment; for it so sadly confirmed her own strong suspicion that Isaac did drink cider, did go to the "Packhorse" occasionally, unknown to her, for she never could do away with the fact that there was at times a smell of cider about him—faint, it is true, but still there it was.

And so Mary stood silent and pale in the presence of her two most malicious foes. The Widow Simpson raised her head when she heard a hint given of Isaac's liking for cider, and the Widow Mason replied to her look of inquiry by saying,

"Ay, ay, widdy, Isaac likes his drop, there be no denying that—forbye, him be uncommon sly!—uncommon sly!" And she peered out of the corners of her eyes to see how her shafts struck and being satisfied that they had done their duty and made Mary wretched, she tried her skill upon something else. "Jenny, 'ooman, it be not fair to leave this here poor old widdy all by she's self, that there white-faced doll will poison she afore Isaac comes back, or, leastways, put she in that there worry with that 'critter,' as it been't safe to leave she, Jenny. I be minded to stop by she's side, and take care of she, poor thing. I say, widdy," continued she, arresting the old woman's attention, who had been quietly sitting resting her head on her hand, and not noticing what was said, "mayhap, widdy, it would be a comfort to you if I just stop and take care as the de'il doesna catch you?"

"Ay, ay," said the old woman, eagerly; and clutching hold of the widow Mason's clothes to prevent her from rising; "sit you still. It be a awful thing, widdy, to know as the wicked one, when he roameth the earth, can just shut hisself up in a thing like that," pointing to the machine.

"Ay, bless your heart, so it be," said the Widow Mason, taking one of the old woman's hands, and keeping her attention entirely upon herself. Then turning to Jane Sands, she continued, "And, Jenny, 'ooman, don't thee stop no longer. Go thy ways to the 'Packhorse,' and tell them as I be here, a-doing of my duty, and a-taking care of the good old Widdy Simpson from the demonses and the de'il hissen."

"Ay, and from that there witch, as would poison she," said Jane, clenching her fist at Mary, whose thoughts, upon the Widow Mason's mention of cider, had strayed away to Isaac, and who had been occupying herself in the back part of the cottage by gathering up the different pieces of her work, and who had not taken notice of the conversation going on. "And if so be as my Joe be a-comed from his work to his dinner, him shall just get the men all together, and they will gie you a good ducking in the swamp, you witch!" and with this blessing, Jane bounded out of the cottage.

Mary stood transfixed. It is needless to say she was now even more terrified than the poor old woman had been. She had heard and read of lawless deeds done by cruel men in remote districts. She knew these two women were more bitterly inclined towards her than any others. She saw herself in their power; that power unconsciously aided by the Widow Simpson's ignorance and terror. Isaac was absent; the parson was no longer her friend.

She had only one source from which to expect help in time of need. If her position were so lonely, and man so hard upon her, she had no helper but God. Inwardly she raised her heart to Him, and prayed Him to bestow His mighty protection and care upon her, deserted of all others. And though this short prayer comforted her for the time being, and gave her courage to stand and endure what might fall upon her, if He willed it, it did not take away the horrible dread of approaching evil, or the certain knowledge of the brutal treatment she was likely to receive at the hands of the miners on Dartmoor, if Jane Sands put her threat in execution.

As these thoughts filled her with terror and dismay, she continued to gather her work together, and at length turned to put away her sewing-machine. But the Widow Mason called out in loud discordant tones—

"Let he alone!—let he alone! Don't go for to raise the devil in my presence."

Mary held in her hands the box or cover that protected the machinery from dust; but the old woman said,

"Let she do it—let she. Coz why?" and she made the Widow Mason stoop while she whispered, "when she covers up the 'critter,' him be quiet. Him never makes no noise when he be covered up, only, if you touch he, him may break the 'clome' all to pieces." For she remembered the jug broken only that morning.

As the old woman ceased speaking, Mary put the cover over the machinery, and left the machine standing in its accustomed corner of the cottage, close to the window.

Mary seated herself at a distance from the old woman, and her companion the Widow Mason. She argued the matter silently, as to whether she should defend herself from the evil insinuated by this woman—for to speak to Isaac's mother on the subject she saw was useless—or whether she should let them have all the talk to themselves.

"She will only insult me the more if I do tell her I am innocent of any evil intention. It is not so much that she thinks me wicked, as that she rejoices in her own power to harm me, and has a keen pleasure in seeing me unhappy. I do not know what I have done," continued she, as the tears rose unbidden to her eyes. "And how I do wish Isaac had never left his home! And the parson! Oh! if he would only see me for one minute, I am sure he would never let that bad woman——"

But Mary's reverie was interrupted by a loud laugh from the Widow Mason, and the room seemed suddenly darkened; and as Mary looked up to ascertain the cause, she saw her in the act of opening the casement, and a crowd of rough-looking men standing outside, and completely blocking out the light from the window.

Hardly had Mary realized these facts, before the door of the cottage was opened rudely, and Jane Sands came in, saying, in harsh tones, as she rushed up to Mary,

"I have a-got they men. Here be my Joe; and Paul Read, and Jack Brag; and——"

But Mary heard no more. She staggered back, and, taking hold of the table-part of the machine, just preserved herself from falling.

Presently she recovered the powers of her mind sufficiently to understand what was passing before her eyes.

"Her be a witch—be her!" said one of the men at the window. "Us must burn she!"

"Yes; her be a witch—a right down bad witch!" screamed the Widow Mason. "Her have most mazed this poor old body. I be stopping by she's side to comfort she, poor thing!—been't I, widdy?"

"Yes, you be; and thank you kindly," said the old woman, looking wonderingly at the crowd of men.

"Where be she to? Be she a-standing there?" and the man pointed to Mary.

"Yes," said the Widow Mason. "Her have a tooked hold of the infarnel 'critter.' Coz why? it be him as be shut up there, as helps she to witch folk."

"Lor' bless you, widdy!—an 'infarnal critter!'"

"Oh! Paul, lad, her be a fine bad 'ooman, her be—a-going to poison this here poor old widdy!"

"Poison the old widdy! Then where be that there big Isaac as marries a white-faced witch, and allows she to poison his own mother?—where be him to?"

"Him be to Exeter, Paul," shouted Jane Sands.

"Them big men most times be big cowards," said Jack Brag, who was a little dirty-looking man.

"Hark ye, lads!" shouted Paul Reade—"hark to I! Her be a witch!—her have a-witched folk!—her be a-going to poison the good old widdy!—her have a-made the passon ill!—her have a-sended Isaac out of the way!—and her have a-got up this here row!"

"Let us swamp she!" shouted a loud voice.

"Let us have a bonfire and burn her," said another.

"I am not a witch," Mary attempted to say, as she clutched the table firmly; but, to her added horror and dismay, her voice had lost all sound; her lips moved—but this was all.

"Her be a-talking to the 'critter,'" said Jane Sands, who seemed to take a strange pleasure in watching Mary's terror, as it was increased by the circumstances that had so quickly surrounded her.

The men and boys now crowded into the cottage. Mary, pale and trembling, still kept her place by the machine. She was thankful to see that all kept at a respectful distance from herself, though they eyed her with looks first of curiosity, then of spite and ill-will.

"Well, widdy—and so you have a-gotten the de'il in your house?" said Joe Sands.

"I be a-feared so—it be a awful 'critter,' surely," said the Widow Simpson, as she stared upon the strangely intrusive crowd, without in the least comprehending the reason of the intrusion.

"It be feared you be for your life, widdy—eh?" said Jack Brag, as if he would convince himself of the truth of the Widow Mason's accusation.

"Yes, yes—I be feared," said the old woman, innocently supporting the Widow Mason against Mary.

"Be you feared of she, widdy?"

The man paused; but the old woman did not understand him. She had no fear of Mary—on the contrary, she was much attached to her. She did not comprehend the spite and malice of the people, or even know that Mary was in danger, if not of losing her life, at least, of very rough treatment, at the hands of cruel, hard, and ignorant men. She looked up inquiringly at the man, and did not speak. The man nodded to his companions, as much as to say,

"She be feared of she, but she be feared to tell us!"

And then he turned again to the widow, and said,

"Us be going to burn the 'critter,' widdy!"

"Burn it!" said the widow, starting up with singular energy. "And blessings on ye!—and blessings on ye!"

And she stretched out her arms and moved her hands, as if she would have given her blessing separately to each one of the many there, so heartily did she appreciate and approve the good action they were about to do.

"Mother, mother!" said Mary, with passionate emotion forcing out her voice, "don't be so foolish, mother—it cannot hurt you!"

"Hark to she!" said the Widow Mason, "a taking part with the de'il hisself!"

"Now, lads, don't be feared for this here row!" said Paul Reade, who was a tall, ill-looking man. "It be she as have a got up this here row, and she be a witch! Us will have a bonfire—eh, lads?"

A great shout arose at this proposal, and poor Mary put her arms round the box on the top of the sewing machine, to save herself from falling.

The crowd went out of the cottage to make preparations for the bonfire, and Jane Sands clapped her hands and rushed up to Mary as she said,

"I telled you so! I telled you so! They will burn the de'il with fire and brimstone, and stick you heels uppermost in the swamp!"

XIX

WHICH TREATS OF THE ESCAPE OF THE WITCH

MARY had looked on with the utmost sense of horror at her position; her tongue clove to the roof of her mouth. She saw men in the prime of life, filthy in appearance, with pipes in their mouths, unsteadily reeling about her cottage, touching all things that she valued, polluting with their fetid breath the very air she breathed, and looking more like demons than men. She heard the clamour of tongues outside, and she felt that the fate of the sewing-machine was sealed. She clung to it as if she could save it, or as if her strength could protect it from their fury; and yet, amid all her thoughts, she acknowledged to herself the uselessness of contention, the feebleness of her power.

"Lots of wood, lads; now lend a hand!" shouted Jack Brag; "come, come, us will pull down the shed."

"Look, Jack, there be another shed, a betterer than Isaac's lumbering shop, and it be made of betterer wood," said Jane Sands, pointing to the one so lately erected for the protection of Mary's furniture.

"What be that there shed for?" said one; "us will take a look inside."

The words were scarcely uttered before the staple was wrenched off, and the door opened.

Jane Sands was the first to gratify her curiosity, and see what the shed contained; and when she recognised many articles of Mary's furniture she had formerly seen at the school cottage, another implement of power seemed suddenly to come into her hands.

"Jack, lad, look you—these be she's bits of things, all covered up this fashions. My! it will burn well, lad, and save a mint of trouble."

"Ay, ay, Jenny, 'ooman," said the man, as he pulled out a chair, which in its delicacy and fashion—though only a common chair in ordinary use in other parts of England—struck him as something totally unlike what he had ever seen before. "It be a uncommon pratty chair, Jenny, 'ooman—it be most a pity to burn it," said the man.

"Why for does she have such chairs? Can't she sit she's self on stools like to other bodies quite so good as she?" said Jane.

"I tell you it be a pity," began the man.

But a rough and strong arm from behind seized the chair, as he said in loud, indignant tones,

"Pity!—pity!—what be you about, lad? Why, she have a-poisoned the old Widdy Simpson; witched poor Peter Barker for to kill his wife; witched the passon ill; raised the de'il in the village of Lawsleigh, as never had the de'il in it before; and she have a-got up this here row. What be you about?" added Paul Reade, for it was he who had seized the chair. "Us must burn all she's bits things, and swamp she!"

Poor Mary, who heard every word—for the reader will remember she was standing by the window looking into the garden, and the new shed was built close by—Mary thought, if that was her character in the village, she did not much wonder at the treatment she received now, or was likely to receive at the hands of these ignorant and cruel men. But she had not much time for reflection, for, to her amazement and horror, she heard the wood crackling in the front of the cottage, and knew that the men had begun already to put their hideous threats into execution. She saw the flames—through the opposite window—begin to rise; she saw her own furniture carried out, and piece by piece heaped on the pile; and what tended more than all to increase her regret, and add to the hopelessness of her position, she saw the good old Widow Simpson calmly looking on; and she heard the Widow Mason urge on the men to destroy as much as they could.

The old Widow Simpson, it is true, stood calmly looking on, but she did not see that the huge bonfire, which was every moment becoming brighter and increasing in size, was fed by Mary's furniture. All that she saw was the blaze that was to consume the "critter."

And now Mary began to think it might be better to try to escape, rather than to stand there quietly awaiting the approach of bad men to drag her to a horrible death! She looked round at the crowd on all sides of the cottage, and saw but little chance of success; but yet she determined to make the attempt. She thought within herself, "They will not hurt the poor old mother," and her eye fell sorrowfully upon her, as she saw her now sitting a little apart from the window, rocking herself to and fro, and the large and fat Widow Mason apparently trying to soothe and protect her. "Yes," resumed Mary, "I feel sure they will not harm the old woman; but they will burn the sewing-machine, and murder me if I stay—I must try to get out of the window."

She watched for an opportunity, for with the constant rush into the cottage of new-comers, all wishing "to get a good look to that there witch," she saw there would be some difficulty. After a few minutes of intense anxiety, she thought she perceived a favourable opportunity, and stealthily getting upon a chair, she mounted into the inner shelf, or window-sill, and there stood ready to jump into the garden. It was only about three feet, nothing of a height to terrify her; but at the corner of the shed, assisting the men and boys to purloin furniture, she saw Jane Sands, and she knew that to be seen by that woman making an attempt to get away, would only subject her to a stricter surveillance, and, in all probability, to greater miseries.

She drew back, therefore, still standing on the sill, and when Jane left the shed, loaded with fuel for the bonfire, she made a spring into the garden. She was too late. She had been seen by the Widow Mason, who immediately raised a hue and cry after her.

"Be that there witch to be let loose on all the world? Here, you, Jack Brag, go after she, and bring she back!"

Mary did not hear all that the Widow Mason said, she only knew her attempt at escape had been discovered, and she felt how quickly her enemies would follow, and how feeble were her own efforts in her own cause.

We have before had occasion to mention the natural spring of water flowing from a rock at the back of the cottage. The cliffs or rocks that extended in a sort of chain down the length, and at the back of the village, rose to the height of many feet above the dwellings generally. Just where the water burst forth, the cliff projected some four or five feet, leaving, at the back, a hollow or cave, dreary, damp, and dripping with moisture, the entrance to which was concealed by the branches of trees that drooped in wild disorder.

Mary heard the shout of voices as she dashed past the spring, with an intention of running down the village. She saw the men draw back from the window that had favoured her flight, where they had eagerly clustered on the first alarm, and she knew, almost by instinct, as it were, that she and her pursuers from different routes would meet at the garden gate. Irresolute for one second, she knew not what to do; but seeing the garden side of the cottage entirely deserted, and feeling satisfied that the men had seen her making for the village, and therefore were likely to pursue in that direction, like a hunted hare she doubled on her own footsteps, went past the spring of water once more, and hid herself in the hollow caused by the jutting out of the rock.

The men and boys rushed out of the smithy cottage, as she had foreseen, and ran some distance down the village street before they discovered they were on a false scent.

"Her goed these ways," said a boy.

"Her be a witch," said another. "Her have, maybe, ridden away atop on she's stick!"

"Witches can't never witch theyselves away from honest folks, never!" said Paul Reade, in a loud, stern voice "Witches be always catched, and witches be always swamped, or, eithermore, burned with fire and brimstone!"

"And shall us catch this here witch, Paul?" said a very little boy, with eager looks.

"Ay, lad, us shall be sure to catch she, though she have a-hided she's self; us must hunt the garden."

And they turned to do his bidding.

Mary heard the steps of the crowd approaching, as she stood trembling in her dripping and dreary hiding-place. She heard the oaths and foul words of the men, as they grumbled at the loss of their prey; and she shudderingly felt, if she were discovered, she had not made her case better by attempting to get away. Then she heard the loud coarse voice of Jane Sands saying,

"Us will find she, dead or 'live! Her be a witch, but us will find she. And if us finds she dead, or if us finds she 'live, us will stick she heels uppermost in the swamp. My!" and Jane laughed a fiendish laugh.

This woman, so dreaded by Mary, came nearer and nearer. Mary heard her voice louder and louder; and shiveringly she crept closer still to the damp wall, and went farther back in her disagreeable hiding-place.

She heard Jane stop at the spring, and drink, and continue her foul language to the boys, and add to her horrible threats against herself. She heard her dash the water in the faces of the men and boys, and laugh her demoniacal laugh at their annoyance. She heard her tell them to peer about into holes and corners, and look well for the witch.

"Coz why?" shouted she. "A witch can't put she's-self a-inside of a hazel-nut!"

And then Mary heard the trampling of many feet in the garden, and knew that the search had commenced in earnest. She concluded Jane Sands was heading the troop, who, to use Jane's words, were "to leave no stone unturned 'till they had found she, dead or 'live."

But no—Jane Sands stood by the spring, close to Mary's hidden retreat.

XX

WHICH TREATS OF CARRYING OFF THE CRITTER, AND FINDING THE WITCH ALIVE

BUT though apparently so many had gone from the work of destruction at the smithy cottage to pursue Mary, there were still plenty left to add fuel to the fire, and to get all things in readiness for the burning of the machine, and the carrying off of the supposed witch to Cranbourne Pool,'[1] and what they termed "duck" her—that is, plunge her into the swamp, and keep her there until she was exhausted; then bring her out, and let her recover. After her recovery, plunge her in a second time, and, on recovering from that, a third time.

With very little trouble, the men and boys managed to raise an excellent bonfire; and amid the cries of the crowd, Mary could discover that every now and then something better than usual had been thrown into the flames.

But at length a silence seemed on a sudden to fall on the numbers there; and Mary could not, from her hiding-place, tell what had caused it. Had help arrived? Her heart almost ceased to beat with the intensity of her attention to catch a new sound—a strange voice—a voice of authority. No!

She heard the murmur of the crowd begin again, and unconsciously she heaved a deep sigh—for up to this time she had scarcely dared to breathe. Jane Sands heard the sigh. But she restrained all movement on her own part, and stood listening, if by chance another sound would guide her to her prey.

The hubbub in the front of the cottage began again. The men and boys had evidently given up the search in the garden, and Mary hoped

Jane Sands had gone away with them. She had supposed Jane had been as active in the pursuit as the others, and did not know she still stood by the spring.

"The garden is so still and quiet," thought she. "I will just peep out, and see if there is any one near."

She began to put aside the branches which hung down from the cliff, and concealed the hollow at the back of the spring. But the first movements of her hand, by disturbing the foliage, aroused Jane's attention. The woman's eyes flashed with a fiendish pleasure, as she foresaw Mary was about to put herself in her power. But, like a cat, craftily pretending to sleep, the more easily to catch her victim, so Jane, by keeping perfectly still, lulled the alarm of the desolate Mary, in order, again like the cat, to start into active life at the critical moment, and seize her prey.

Mary moved noiselessly, as she supposed; but her enemy was on the alert. Mary removed branch by branch skilfully and quietly—she could now see into the garden.

Jane had foreseen that Mary would look well around ere she ventured forth; and, gloating over the fullness of her own power, she suffered her to enjoy these moments of hope—by keeping herself perfectly still and in the shade—that she might the more intensely feel her misery when caught in the very moment of fancying herself free.

Mary looked round and round—she saw no one. She heard the noise now increasing in the front of the cottage—now sullenly subsiding; she heard the crackling of the wood; she saw the lurid light of the great fire throwing its red hues on all things near, and she made up her mind. Breathlessly, with the twigs firmly clutched in her hand, she stood listening for the slightest sound that would betray the presence of anyone. All was still in that part of the premises; she concluded, therefore, she could cross the garden in safety and escape, unseen by the crowd in front of the cottage. She gently pulled aside the only branches that now concealed her in her retreat, and, disentangling herself from them, sprang hastily forward, and screamed aloud with redoubled terror as she felt herself caught in the strong arms of Jane Sands.

"And you be here, be you, a-giving us the trouble to run after you? Comfortable, eh?" added Jane, in a sneering tone, "comfortable in that there dark hole? My! you be fond of hiding youself, you be!"

Imprisoned as she now felt herself, Mary no longer resisted; she was already very faint and very weary. The future seemed so terrible—life itself, under the anticipations of that terrible future, of no value.

"If I could but die where I now stand," thought she.

"You-u—you-u put my boy Joe a-top on a stool in your school, did you?" And the woman held her fast with one strong arm, and lifted the other menacingly against her. "Then I be a-going to put you a-top on a stool in my school, I be." And she beckoned to the men in the distance to come to her aid. "Here be the witch," said Jane, as the men approached.

"Lor' bless us, Jenny, 'ooman, how skilled you be, surely—so you have a-found she, and 'live?"

"Come, come along with you," said one of the men, pulling Mary roughly by the arm; while Jane Sands walked by her side, and gratified her malevolence by her rudely taunting language.

"Would you gie I the penny as my boy Joe gived you to your school, when you had a-got a school?"

Then she stooped her tall person, and whispered,

"Gie I the penny, and may be I could get you off. Eh, Molly?"

Mary heard not this mockery. The shrinking sense of helplessness in the hands of Jane, followed by the shivering sensitiveness of degradation when churlishly pulled by the men, swallowed up all other feeling. She felt herself dragged along, and hurried round the corner of the garden in front of the cottage. The immense crowd, the enormous fire, the shouts that filled the air—of all this she was conscious in a dulled and crushed acceptation. She felt her brain grow confused, her respiration difficult, her sight gone. She knew no more.

But we must return to that part of our history when Mary—in her hiding-place—knew that the noise round the bonfire had abruptly ceased, and hoped that some powerful help had arrived. We must account for this cessation of amusement to the numbers assembled there, and apparently making so great a jollification of the destruction of property belonging to another.

The scene in the front of the cottage had been progressing unfavourably for Mary's property; and the fire was pronounced sufficiently large to burn the de'il himself!

Paul Reade, amid the shouts of the populace, entered the cottage to fetch the "critter."

"Where be the 'critter' a-hided?—can you tell?" said he, to the Widow Mason.

"There, Paul, lad, a-standing by the window."

"Where to do you mean, widow? It be the 'critter' as I be comed for."

"Eh, lad?—what be about, then? There—that there little table!" said she, pointing to the machine.

"That there bit on a table, widdy?" said the man in a loud voice of astonishment; "that bit of a thing to make such a big fuss!" added he, in a jeering tone, and pointing at it contemptuously.

Then he took hold of it with one finger and a thumb, and said,

"Come, pussy, pussy, pussy!" as if he thought it so small, so light, and of so little consequence, that he need not take any trouble to move it; but the table remained stationary. "Come, come," said the man, turning his back to it, and taking hold of it with both hands this time to draw it gently on.

The table did not move.

The man's mirth and jeers were suddenly stopped. The crowd of eager lookers-on through the window and in the cottage, all anxious to see the dreaded "critter" pitched into the flames, suddenly hushed their clamour, and sound and motion seemed abruptly suspended.

Paul Reade was not a man to be daunted by a trifle. He now turned round once more, and took a good look at the table; then he turned to look at the myriads of eyes—for alarm multiplies objects—extending themselves in a terrified stare as they watched him. Paul ascertained that "the table," as it seemed to him, was not fastened to the wall; he saw that it was small, and apparently lightly-made—how then could it be so sturdily immoveable? He had not seen the machinary under the box at the top, and thus had no clue to its real weight. It had been accredited with supernatural powers, and his untutored mind admitted to himself that "the dei'l" was stronger than man.

Paul Reade turned pale. The hitherto awed silence of the crowd now was broken by the sound of footsteps stealthily attempting to leave the cottage. Some walked away immediately to their own homes, with blanched faces and fear in their hearts, telling all who would listen to them that Paul Reade, who was known to be so tall and strong, could, not, with all his strength, move a tiny little bit of a table—'not so big as a three-legged table in ordinary use—because the de'il himself was shut up in a box at the top, and his huge cloven feet were under the table, plain to be seen by all men. It was during Paul Reade's unsuccessful attempt to move the machine, that Mary had so ardently hoped help had arrived.

"At it again, Paul!" shouted a voice from the outside of the window.

The speaker felt himself comparatively safe, and able to run away if anything occurred to warrant his doing so; but he had nevertheless a strong curiosity to see, as far as he could, how his neighbour would fare in his tussle with the "de'il."

"At it again, Paul!" shouted the man.

Paul eyed the machine steadily, but looked irresolute.

"Paul Reade, you be a big man—and Joe Sands, you be a big man," said the Widow Mason; "and then there be Jack Brag and his brother."

The men clustered together as the widow mentioned them by name, but stood listening.

"If so be as you four strong men was to just catch a hold of the 'critter' to the four corners, and so to put your biggest strengths, my belief as you four would be too many for the very 'de'il hissen!'"

The men looked at each other, but did not speak.

"And be you four big cowards" said the widow.

"Just you be quiet, widdy," said the voice from the window; "my belief as you four could beat the 'de'il' all to shivers! You be no cowards—no, no!"

"Us could but try," said Paul Reade.

And the men, flattered by the opinion of the looker-on at the window—to his great satisfaction—agreed to try their strength with the "critter." The men cleared away any obstacle standing near to the machine, and each placed himself at a corner.

"Now mind you be ready with your biggest strengths," said the voice at the window, "and I will gie the word. One-two-three!"

The four men exerted their utmost strength at the same moment, and up went the machine, unnaturally light this time. A sewing-machine can be lifted—according to its size—by the moderate strength of one man. But the concentrated efforts of four strong men, as they are needless, so they reduce its supposed weight to insignificance. But there was no insignificance here! Its very imponderability now, contrasted so forcibly with its enormous gravity but just before, that the four strong men trembled as they stood. They looked in each other's faces, and saw the blanched visage, awe-struck eye, and hair standing on end!

The man at the window shouted aloud, the people remaining outside of the cottage—for the inside had been cleared—cheered heartily, in anticipation of the approach of the "critter," and the four strong men, in spite of the fear curdling at their hearts, took courage, and moved away with the machine. A deafening shout arose from the assembled crowd, when the "awful critter" was seen outside the cottage door; and the shout was made much more jubilant as Jane Sands, with the "live witch," made her appearance from the garden at the same time.

[1] "This pool is, in fact, a great bog, which in winter is converted by the rains into a lake, of an oblong form, about 150 feet in length, and 80 in breadth. The water in it gushes from a bed of gravel, beneath a stratum of peat bog. Situated about the centre of Dartmooor, at a considerable elevation amongst the hills; twelve miles from Moreton Hampstead, eight from Tavistock, and six from Oakhampton."—*Moore's History of Devon.*

XXI

OF ISAAC WATSON'S RETURN HOME

WE have seen that Isaac set off early in the morning of the day in which the events last related occurred, to keep an appointment in Exeter. He had been unable, when he went away, to specify the exact time of his return, for although the means of travelling easily and speedily had been greatly facilitated by the opening of the railway to N——, yet as he could not foresee how long he might be detained in Exeter, he had given Mary to understand he probably should not be at home until the afternoon of the morrow.

But, contrary to his expectation, his business was over on the Monday, and he was enabled to take the last train to N——, arriving there, it is true, very late, after twelve o'clock at night. He had then ten miles to walk across the moor, but he thought it wiser not to start off at that hour, but to rest a short time, and still set off so early as to surprise Mary and his mother by knocking them up at half-past five in the morning.

It was a lovely morning. Isaac saw the moon just drop behind a light cloud, and the stars twinkling high up in the heavens. As he neared the moor, and saw the Tors gradually coming into view by the light of the moon—no longer hidden by a cloud—and throwing an oblique light on distant objects, his mind was attracted by the beauty of the scene, and home and Mary banished for a time.

Isaac, among his reading tastes, had picked up a slight knowledge of the stars, and in his walk across so large an open space as Dartmoor, had an opportunity of seeing to advantage such constellations as were then visible. His heart was light, for he had kept his word to Mary, and not touched cider in his absence. His mind was easy, for he had transacted the business he went upon greatly to his own satisfaction; and thus, as he stepped quickly on, he felt in the mood to enjoy the works of God; for, with a devoutly grateful heart, he acknowledged His great goodness and many mercies to himself, and prayed Him to watch over and ever protect Mary, his dear wife, and his mother and himself, from all future evil.

And so Isaac counted the stars. "Perseus and Auriga in the zenith," said he, "and the old bear coming up to windward. I wonder if Mary knows anything about the stars; she ought, considering she was the schoolmistress."

Here Isaac gave a little sigh, for he remembered she could no longer lay claim to that title, and that her deposition from the chair of office was a great grief to her. But this recollection faded from his mind; he turned again to contemplate the heavens.

"Aries, Taurus, Gemini, Cancer, and the head of Leo—it is indeed a night for brilliant stars; the nebulæ in Cancer very distinct. I must walk out with Mary in the winter evenings, and if she does not know the constellations, I will point them out to her. No one on Dartmoor who can read ought to be without some knowledge of the stars, because there is such an enormous space, without any interruption, of high buildings, or objects that ordinarily shut out the heavens from us."

And then his thoughts reverted to Mary, and he pictured her happiness on seeing him return so unexpectedly early.

"She cannot expect me at this time of the morning—that I am sure of;" and Isaac chuckled at the thought of her pretty surprise and pleasure. "I should not wonder if she makes me some nice coffee; and I shall be very glad of it, after my long walk. How bright Orion is! And how grandly Sirius scintillates!" And after contemplating the heavens for a few moments longer, he turned again to earth and to Mary. "I will build two nice rooms, dear Mary! I will make her so comfortable though it is such a pity that the parson casts us off—I must see him or Mr. Gray," and now Isaac sighed heavily. "However, I live in hopes of better days, though I have got such a bad name now, one would think it must wear out in time. 'It is a long lane that has no turn.' 'Rome was not built in a day;' and if Mary has not got the school, she has got a home of her own—bless her!—that I shall be proud to make better every day of her life."

And thus Isaac whiled away the time, and piloted himself by the stars, for the moon set in the first hour of his walk, and then the moor was in darkness. When day began to break he enjoyed the wonderful tints that heralded the approach of the sun, but he quickened his pace, for now he was near his home.

"They will be stirring before I get there, if I do not mind what I am about. Why, the sun rises at six, and I see he will soon be above ground. I had intended being earlier; I must have walked slow—but here I am!"

And he joyfully ran round the corner that led into the village street, and close by which stood the smithy.

Poor Isaac! If he reproached himself for having walked slowly, he found he had arrived too soon for his own peace of mind.

"What on earth is all this rubbish?" said he, as he saw the remains of the large bonfire that had been there the day before.

There was not light enough for him to distinguish objects clearly, but he saw there was an unusual heap before the door of the smithy, and almost blocking up the high road.

"I cannot think what can have been the matter. Let me see—it is October," said he, doubtfully—"it is not the fifth of November; and if it were, they have no business with a bonfire there, for I do declare it seems to me, in this uncertain light, as if there had been a bonfire, and a very large one!"

The sun rose on the other side of the house, so that Isaac was comparatively in darkness; but he went on, now moodily enough, and entered his shed. Strange marks of violence were visible to his experienced eye, even through the darkness. He was so struck by these unusual appearances that he went on, without turning into the cottage, through the back sheds into the garden; and there, by the light of the rising sun, he saw that the door of the shed he had so recently built had been carried off; the furniture, which he had left so nicely packed up, almost all gone, and what was left in strange disorder and confusion, many articles lying about defaced and broken.

"What on earth can have been the matter?" said he wonderingly, as he gazed around.

Then he saw that the casement looking into the garden stood open; and putting in his head he called out—"Mary!—Mary!" Then he said to himself—"They must be up, or the window would not be standing open."

He hastened to enter the cottage. The door stood ajar, and the large room bore the marks of the crowds who had trampled upon its clean floor yesterday. The furniture was in disarray, but though these things struck Isaac painfully, as indicative of some evil having happened, he was very far from imagining the truth.

Now he rushed up stairs, loudly calling "Mary!—Mary!" Alas! no voice replied to his summons. The bedroom that he and Mary occupied remained in the primitive neatness in which it had been prepared the day before. The bed had not been slept in. The room evidently had not been used on the past night.

A strange awe seemed to creep over Isaac, and the silence of the cottage was appalling. Isaac no longer called "Mary!" He mutely gathered one by one the proofs of her absence, and stood horror-stricken.

"Mother!" said he softly, as if he feared the sound of his own voice. And then, as it were, recovering himself, he laughed a hideous laugh, as he reeled out of the room into the next, saying, "She is with mother—of course she is! What a fool I am! Mother! mother!"

But his dismay and astonishment may be better imagined than portrayed, when he saw that room also in the same neatness in which it was customary to prepare it in the morning of the day; and when he understood at a glance that the bed had not been occupied for the night, and that neither his mother nor Mary was there, Isaac's knees knocked together, his muscles relaxed their tension; large drops of perspiration gathered on his brow, and rolled down his cheeks unheeded.

He had seated himself on the bed to save himself from falling, and now he perceived that the casement here also stood open. With difficulty he dragged himself to the window, the more easily to ascertain what had caused the confusion he had seen on his arrival at the smithy; and as he stood there gasping for breath, at the weight of these accumulated horrors, he saw distinctly now, now that the sun had risen sufficiently, the remains of a large bonfire. To his horror and indignation, he could not mistake the broken pieces of furniture that he recognised as Mary's, lying here and there among the rubbish; and—"Did he see aright?" thought he, as he gazed with eager eyes and compressed lips, his tall person leaning far out of the window—"Did he see aright?—did he see needles glittering in the light?—and reels of cotton, such as belonged to Mary's sewing-machine?"

As quickly as his consternation and terror would let him, Isaac turned and staggered downstairs; and as he passed through the large room, he saw the machine was not standing in its accustomed place; then he rushed out to examine the remains of the bonfire. Yes; he could no longer doubt—reels of cotton, scissors, needles glittering here and there in the sun, riveted his attention. In his despair, Isaac gave one long, loud moan. He gazed around—tossing his arms wildly—not knowing where to go, or what to do.

At length he saw in the distance a child coming from the village towards the smithy; and he knew her to be Phœbe Morris, taking a can of milk to a cottage in the lane.

He awaited her approach; but when the child saw who stood there, looking more like a mad than a sane man, she slackened her pace, and seemed afraid to come on.

XXII

HOW ISAAC WATSON LEARNED THAT THE WITCH AND HER FAMILIAR SPIRIT HAD BEEN BURNT; AND HOW MASTER CHARLIE FOUND ISAAC LYING IN HIS SHED, DRUNK AT SEVEN A.M.

"Come along, Phœbe, come along," said Isaac, impatiently.

But as the child still hesitated, he tried to soften the tones of his voice, for he felt conscious they were unusually loud and unsteady.

"Come, Phœbe, come—I am Isaac Watson—do you not know me?— poor child, how should she?" muttered he *sotto voce*, and then he added aloud, "I shall not hurt you."

Thus encouraged, the child walked on.

"Can you tell me what has been done here?" said Isaac.

"They made a big bonfire to burn she and the 'critter,'" said the child, looking terrified.

"To burn what?" roared Isaac, with startling energy.

"The 'critter,' as witches folk."

Isaac did not understand.

"What 'critter' do you mean?" said he.

"Why, they have a-telled I as there was the witch, and the witch's familiar; and as the witch have a-poisoned the old widdy, and so they have a-burned she."

"Child! child! do you know what you are saying?—will you drive me mad?" said Isaac, as he seized hold of Phœbe arm, and shook her roughly.

The child screamed with pain and fright. From a neighbouring cottage a woman peeped out. Seeing the child held thus by Isaac—for in his agony he knew not what he was doing—she rushed forward to rescue her.

"Isaac, Isaac Watson, been't you ashamed of yourself?" said she, liberating the child.

"Where is my wife, Kitty?—where is my wife?—where is my mother?" said Isaac, in the loud accents of despair.

But as Isaac's grasp on the arm of Phœbe Morris had—unconsciously to him—been very tight, he had left the marks of his fingers on the child's flesh, and the woman's attention and sympathy were both given to her, and she took no notice of his words. While Isaac, maddened with the strange appearance of things, and with the harrowing suspense, now seized hold of the woman, as he once more shouted out,

"Where is my wife?"

"Oh-h! Isaac, let I be!" screamed the woman.

"Hollo, there!" said the gruff and hoarse voice of a man who came hastily out of his cottage to his wife's assistance; "if so be as you havena got a wife of your own, you better let alone other folk's wifes."

"It be a shame on you, Isaac," said the woman, as she escaped from his grasp; "why for do you be a-hurting womens and childrens this fashions?"

"I do not want to hurt you," said Isaac.

"It be not my fault what they have a-done to she and to the old widdy, so you let alone I; and my man was to work to Bovy, so he, good man, hadna got nothing to do with the witch, neither the 'critter.'"

Isaac did not understand; he put his hands to his brow and stood silent.

"It be that 'critter' as have a-done the work," said the man; "us doesna like such queer things here to Dartmoor."

"But can you not tell me what has been done?" said Isaac, entreatingly; "and do tell me where is my poor mother?—where is my wife?" and the pathos in Isaac's voice touched the woman, for she raised the corner of her apron to her eye, as she said,

"Poor Isaac!"

But the man took hold of her, and said, "Come along, Kitty, come along," and they turned to re-enter the cottage.

At the door the woman called out,

"Come in here, Isaac, come in here and have some breakfast."

But Isaac heard not; he leaned against the wall of the smithy, and seemed almost unable to stand. After a few minutes he raised his head, and said,

"Ay! I must try to reach the vicarage—the parson will know what all this means; I am sure I do not, for I am almost out of my senses."

He turned into the shed with the intention of taking his hat; but the excitement and painful suspense of the last half hour had been too much for him—he fell all his length, and lay there unconscious of anything.

Presently, as the village awoke from its sleep, first one and then another passed by the smithy.

"Isaac lying there drunk! It be early in the morning for that!" said one.

"Ay, ay—dead drunk!" said another, as he passed the first speaker and went on to his work.

But as it happened, there was one strolling leisurely along on that early morning, his dark hair blown about by the breeze, his hands in his pockets, and the pleasant smile on his lip, proclaiming to the simple villagers the presence of "Master Charlie." He cheerfully whistled as he went the favourite air from the last new opera, and turned the corner of the street to pass by the smithy.

"Hollo!—who lies here?" said he, starting back as he saw Isaac lying in the shed.

"It be Isaac Watson, sir," said Phœbe Morris, now returning with her empty can.

"Isaac Watson!" said Charlie, in a voice of dismay.

But he went up to the still body lying there, and, looking at the pale face, he stooped down and began chafing Isaac's hands, while Phœbe Morris said,

"Please, sir, Isaac Watson be drunk! He have a-hurted my arm."

But Charlie heard her not, for he said, in a commanding voice,

"Run, child, run to the vicarage for brandy, and help—help—hollo!—run!—fly!"

And, as his tones became—unconsciously to himself—louder, he was heard by those in the nearest cottages, and two or three came hastily out.

"Run to the vicarage, good woman, and bring me brandy; Isaac will die!" said Charlie in his alarm, as he bolted out his words in hot haste.

He seated himself on the ground and took Isaac's head upon his knee, telling the standers-by to chafe his hands while he loosened his cravat. He placed his hand upon Isaac's heart—for he shewed no sign of life—his eyes were shut, his mouth and teeth rigidly closed!

"Bless me!—bless me!" said Charlie, as he redoubled his efforts to recall him from the sort of swoon in which he lay.

"Him have a-been most mazed about the poor old widdy and his wife," said the woman who had spoken to Isaac before he fell.

"And no wonder!" said Charlie.

But he did not know that the woman had left him in strange ignorance of what had really happened.

"Will they never bring the brandy?" said Charlie.

XXIII

WHICH TREATS OF "DUCHESS" AND HER RIDER

But we left Mary in the hands of rough men, with Jane Sands walking by her side. And as we have said, the people shouted:

"Let us gie the 'witch' a warming before us swamps she!" said Jane Sands.

"Ay, ay, Jenny 'ooman; us will set she a-top of the 'critter,' and——"

"And that be just where I think she ought for to sit," said Jane.

"Ay, Jenny, and let she have a lick of they flames; and after that us could carry she off and swamp she in Cranbourne Pool!"

"Hark ye, lads!" said Paul Reade in a loud voice, and the crowd hushed its clamour, and listened. "If you sticks she a-top of that," pointing to the machine, as he wiped the perspiration from his brow, "you won't never get she off again, my belief! That be a 'infarnal critter,' I can tell you."

And the man shrugged his shoulders and shook his head, as he remembered the extraordinary freaks—in his comprehension—that it had been guilty of.

"If you let she sit she's-self a-top of that 'critter,' my belief she will ride off clean away, and us couldna catch she again to swamp she."

A loud groan rose from the crowd.

"You hold she fast, Jack Brag, whiles us gets the 'critter' into the fire."

And the tallest and strongest from the crowd came forward, as they said, to help to pitch the 'critter' into the flames, when suddenly a man on horseback came full speed round the corner.

So little prepared were the horse and his rider for the enormous fire burning in front of the smithy, and so fast had been the gallop with which they had approached the bend in the road, unsuspicious of evil, that the noble animal rushed impetuously, as it appeared to the lookers-on, almost into the flames.

"Soho! Duchess, soho!" said her rider, drawing his rein tightly, as the beautiful creature reared with her fore feet over the fire! snorting, terrified, and restlessly moving her hind feet, without, for a second or two, attempting to turn away. Her rider kept his seat, even with his own head in reach of the forked tongues that played so luridly and venomously around.

"Duchess!—good Duchess!" said he, trying to turn her head from the fire, which, when he at length accomplished, she brought her fore feet heavily to the ground, and in her next movement stepped upon a burning brand! The animal plunged violently, snorting and trembling perceptibly, while her rider tried to soothe her with his voice.

"Him be Master Charlie!" said Jack Brag to Jane Sands.

The woman did not wait for another word; it was now her turn to run, and to try to get away from the scene of ruin, of which she had been the instigator. Mary heard the words; she saw the woman turn away; she knew the men no longer held her.

"Master Charlie!" her lips murmured, but no sound came forth; "save me, save me!" and she fell fainting and exhausted. Meanwhile Paul Reade and Joe Sands had gone to Master Charlie's assistance; and, holding his beautiful mare while her master dismounted, Charlie's first words were expressions of gratitude to the men for their timely interference.

"Thank you, Paul; thank you, Joe;" his first act to examine the legs and feet of the mare.

"Poor Duchess!—I hope she is not much hurt!—but what is the matter?"

The men's faces had a hard and sallow expression, and they did not answer his question.

"Isaac! Isaac!" shouted he, as he rushed up to the cottage. "And who is this poor creature?" added he, looking down upon Mary lying in a swoon—her hair hanging loosely, her clothes in disorder; he did not recognise her.

"Isaac Isaac!" again he shouted; and then, as Isaac did not reply, he turned to the men and said, "Where is Isaac?"

"Well, Master Charlie, it be all the 'critter' and she," said Paul Reade, in a deprecatory tone; but Charlie had again stooped to examine his mare's fore legs, and did not hear the words or notice the man's manner.

"I wish Isaac would come," said Charlie. "Isaac! Isaac!" and Charlie again walked up to the cottage window. "But what is all this about?" And now he turned to look at the fire, for his thoughts had been, for the few minutes in which he had been present at this scene, taken up with "Duchess," and the injury she might have received.

"And who is this?" continued he, as he stooped to look at Mary. "God of heaven! is this Isaac's wife! What have you been about?—why don't you help her?—help! help!" shouted he in at the cottage window.

He turned to ask for assistance from the great crowd that was there on his arrival; but all were gone. The fire blazed and crackled, and put out its feelers for more fuel; and in the distance he could see the late disturbers of the peace getting away from the scene of their wickedness by twos and threes as fast as they could. Charlie did not understand this. He rushed up to the cottage window, and once more called "Isaac!"—there he saw the poor old woman weeping and lamenting as if she were demented; and the fat widow Mason by her side—also weeping!—but hers were "crocodile tears."

Charlie took in at a glance the strangely disordered appearance of the interior of the cottage. But all that he could understand, as he looked around, was that something very wrong must have happened.

His own consternation, on riding as it were into the very midst of the flames, had subsided through his fear that the mare was injured; and this dread had absorbed his attention, and prevented him from realising, to a certain extent, the facts before his eyes! And though, before he reached the smithy, he had seen the light caused by the flames, and heard the uproar of the assembled people, he had not had the smallest suspicion of a riot. The village of Lawsleigh had always been one of the most peaceable on the moor.

Master Charlie had concluded the villagers were making merry. A cold shudder ran through his frame as the truth seemed to burst upon him, that this was not the scene of a merry-making. The downcast and guilty looks of the two men convinced him he had rightly surmised. These things Charlie understood in a second or two, though they take some time to write; and then he set himself to work to recover Mary from her faintness.

"Bring water," said he authoritatively to the Widow Mason; and he returned to Mary, and kneeling by her side, tenderly chafed her hands.

"You see, Master Charlie, she be a witch!"

"A witch!" shouted Charlie in such a voice of dismay as to make Duchess start, and keep the men fully employed in holding her, and trying to soothe her fears. "Give me the water, woman gently—she is beginning to revive!" said Charlie to the Widow Mason.

"She have a-poisoned the poor old Widdy Simpson," said Joe Sands, hesitatingly.

"She have a-raised the de'il in the village, Master Charlie," said Paul, sturdily.

"She have a-got up this here row," said Joe Sands.

"She and that there 'critter' have a-done all the mischief, surely," said Paul, his tones becoming louder.

Charlie heard every word. He took no notice of the men; their own words, intended to defend themselves, had convinced him of their desperate and lawless conduct.

When Mary began to revive, Charlie turned to the men, and said,

"Joe Sands, take Duchess to the vicarage—lead her carefully—and tell Marvel to send the carriage here immediately. Mind what I say," said Charlie, his tones unconsciously very stern. "The parson is ill. See Marvel; and tell him I want the carriage. And you, Joe, remain with the mare until I come. How is she now?" said Charlie to the Widow Mason, who was attending to Mary's recovery.

At this instant Paul Reade attempted to steal away unperceived by Charlie; but he was prevented from exercising his wish.

"Paul," said Charlie, "you seem to have been present at, even if you have not participated in, a great deal of evil. Suppose you finish your day with a good action? I may want your assistance."

The man stood sheepishly looking on.

Mary, when she recovered from her swoon, could not stand without assistance; but she was able to tell Charlie that Isaac was away, and that she did not expect him to return till the afternoon of the next day; that the people of the village had credited her sewing-machine with supernatural powers, and herself with witchcraft; and that but for his opportune arrival, the machine would have been destroyed, and she herself have suffered worse than death at the hands of these cruel men and women.

No words can paint the horror and consternation of the young man when Mary finished her slight description of the troubles of that day. Charlie eyed the large strong man standing there with looks of anger and contempt. And when the carriage arrived, he had Mary and the old Widow Simpson placed comfortably in it; for he saw, by the ruin and desolation around, and by the unprotected state of the two women, that it would be unsafe to leave them in their own cottage, unless Isaac were there to protect them. He had sent for the carriage on purpose, though neither Mary nor the widow knew this.

Charlie said but little; but his lips were firmly pressed together; and Mary told Isaac, when they met again, "that Master Charlie's face was so white and so stern, she was half afraid of him, only he spoke so kind to her."

XXIV

IN WHICH MASTER CHARLIE "TWITS" ISAAC WATSON

The good old vicar of Lawsleigh, Parson Hill, was ill in bed, and Charlie had ridden hastily over from Paul Tavey to inquire for him, which accounted for his very welcome presence on passing the smithy at the critical moment.

The Widow Simpson and Mary were placed under the care of the housekeeper immediately on their arrival at the vicarage, and treated with all due kindness. The sewing-machine was sent for. Mary had the gratification of receiving it uninjured. The loss in needles, scissors, &c., was trifling, and Mary told the housekeeper "that the sight of the machine in such good condition—only slightly defaced by the marks of dirty hands—more than anything else contributed to make her feel herself again."

The Widow Simpson was profuse in her "blessings" on the head of Master Charlie. She had never understood that Mary was in danger from the people until a minute or two before Charlie's arrival, when she accidentally saw her come round the corner of the cottage from the garden in the very rough hands of a miner. And though the reader may remember that the sewing-machine, in the hands of the four men, made its appearance on the scene of action simultaneously with Mary, the widow saw it not. All her thoughts were at once riveted on Mary, and the wicked Widow Mason prevented her from rushing excitedly out to help Mary, and try to save her.

"Ma-ary! Ma-ary!—they shall not hurt a hair of she's head!—oh—h— Ma-ary!"

When, therefore, on Charlie's arrival, Mary was saved, the widow's gratitude could not be restrained. She entirely forgot the dreaded "critter," with the obliviousness of age in the past, when strongly absorbed in the present moment; remembered nothing but that Mary was restored to her, and her fondling and caressing of Mary, while she heaped blessing after blessing on the head of Master Charlie, made even him feel doubly glad that he had arrived in time. An outburst of gratitude is precious to us all. With thankful hearts Mary and the Widow Simpson slept that night in peace and comfort, and when they arose in the morning they thought and talked of nothing else but of their rescue on the previous day by that kind Master Charlie, and of Isaac's expected return.

Not to keep our readers in unnecessary suspense, we may mention here that Master Charlie succeeded in recovering Isaac from the state of insensibility in which we left him, and that he too was brought to the vicarage by the kind-hearted young man. And, curiously enough, while Mary and the Widow Simpson were enjoying their breakfast in the housekeeper's room, and longing for Isaac's return, and counting the hours until he might reasonably be expected, Isaac himself, under the same roof, was in the dining-room with Master Charlie. And this same Master Charlie said:

"Come, Isaac, old fellow, your troubles are over now. Sit down, and get a hearty breakfast—hush, if you please—not a word!" and Charlie held up a prohibitory finger.

George came in at the same moment with hot cutlets, &c., &c., and when he left the room Charlie continued—

"Not for one second shall you see your wife or your mother until you have eaten a hearty breakfast. Come, sit down!" and he helped Isaac to all that was necessary, while he added: "They are very well—thank God!—as I told you; and after your long walk, and all else, which we will not talk about now, I insist upon you eating a good breakfast. Do you like coffee, Isaac?" said Charlie, with a merry twinkle of his eye, for Charlie had had a talk with Mary, all of which has yet to be recounted to the reader—"eh, Isaac?—will you have coffee?"

"Like coffee!—yes, God bless her! I do, Master Charlie!" said Isaac, recalling the wet night that Mary had made coffee for him, and, thinking of Mary, he said "God bless her!"

But Charlie said, "God bless her!—oh, Isaac! what nonsense!—why, coffee is 'it'—not 'her.'"

"It was Mary, Master Charlie, God bless her!" said Isaac, "that I meant."

"But you did not tell me, Isaac—how was I to see into your thoughts?" said Charlie, as he poured out the smoking coffee.

But while Isaac and Master Charlie are enjoying their morning meal, we wish to make known to our readers that, on the recovery of Mary and the Widow Simpson from the fatigues of the day, Charlie made a point of going to the housekeeper's room, and of gathering from Mary as much information as she could give on the subject of the riot. Mary only knew one of the men—Joe Sands. The miners generally were a lawless and very ignorant set of men. The very nature of their employment prevented them from being known to their neighbours, their work being fully as much at night as in the day. When they worked in the night, they were in bed all day; but the miners as a body of men kept well together and supported each other, although they were not well known to their immediate neighbours. But Charlie gathered enough from Mary, in addition to his own observation and knowledge when he arrived on the scene of action, to make him declare, in her presence,

"He would have the whole village either pounded into mince meat or roasted alive!"

He congratulated Mary on the evident reform in Isaac's habits. Mary looked up timidly, for she wondered in her own mind if Master Charlie knew of that night that Isaac went to the "Packhorse" to fetch Jacob! Charlie saw she was not quite at her ease, and he then said,

"Isaac told me the other day that he had never entered the 'Packhorse' but once since his marriage, and that was to fetch old Jacob Smerdon away. And also that he had never tasted cider or any other kind of fermented liquor since the night he had accidentally entered a gin palace in London. Is it so?"

"If Isaac says so, sir," said Mary, blushing, and not liking to hint at her own knowledge to the contrary.

"You see, Mary," said Charlie, "that Widow Mason is the most spiteful creature. I quite wondered to see her in your cottage this morning. I should never have suspected you of liking such a woman!"

"Indeed, sir, she never was in my house until this very day," said Mary, with energy; "and if Isaac had been at home, she would not have ventured to intrude upon me. She and Jane Sands came in without being invited."

"I will have them well 'pounded' with the rest of the village—eh, Mary!" and Charlie laughed. "But, as I was saying, that widow is the most spiteful creature the world ever saw; it was spite when she dashed the cider in Isaac's face, and all over his clothes!"

"Dashed cider in Isaac's face, sir!—why, when was that?"

"What! did not Isaac tell you? Why, on that night he went to fetch Jacob. She could not prevail upon Isaac to drink, and so she waxed wroth," said Charlie.

"Oh! that night, sir, when he went to fetch Jacob!"

Mary spoke in rather joyous tones.

"Yes, she threw the cider all over his clothes!"

"Oh—I am so pleased," said Mary, and then she repeated her words as she clasped her hands together, "I am so glad—I am so pleased!"

"What!" said Charlie, in some surprise, "pleased at your husband's discomfiture!"

"Oh-h—I do not mind that one bit—not one bit!" said Mary, joyously.

Charlie now fixed his eyes reprovingly on Mary, and stood in mute astonishment!—and he looked so like Parson Hill—at those times that he too reproved without speaking—that Mary was suddenly recalled to herself.

"You see, Master Charlie," deprecatingly, "I could smell the cider about Isaac, and so I thought—"

"Oh-h-h—you thought he had been drinking!"

Now Charlie's tone was reproachful, and Mary felt this: she did not reply.

"Did you accuse him of evil practices, then?" said Charlie—and his tone was not pleasant—"did you open your mouth wide?" added he, looking fixedly at Mary, "did you taunt him with breaking his word!"

"No, sir," said Mary, subdued as much by Charlie's manner as by his queries, which were painful to her. "It is true, I did think he had broken his word, but I kept my sorrow to myself, and did not remonstrate with him, and Isaac never knew that I had suspected him. And now, sir, that I know he did not break his word, I cannot help being glad!"

Mary finished her sentence in a tone of apology, for she was conscious she had allowed her delight in Isaac's innocence to be expressed enthusiastically. But Charlie folded his arms and leaned his back against the wall, as he stood for a minute or two thoughtfully looking at Mary, before he said,

"Have you had any other cause for suspicion of Isaac's breach of faith?"

"No, sir, never."

"He makes you a good husband?—eh?"

"Yes, sir—very—very indeed," said Mary, blushing and looking up brightly. "He is most kind both to mother and to me, and there never was but that one thing on my mind against Isaac and now that you tell me, sir, even that was an error, I cannot be happier, that is, I mean when he comes back."

And Mary heaved a sigh as she thought of the troubles of that day.

"And you make him a good wife?"

Again Charlie looked like Parson Hill, and Mary cast down her eyes, as the thought quickly obtruded itself that she should never again meet Parson Hill's kind eye bent approvingly upon her.

"I try, sir," said she, with a little sigh.

"And you take his pipe away, because you know the 'Total Abstinence Society' will not even allow smoking!"

"Will they not, sir?" said Mary, looking puzzled. "Then Isaac cannot belong to that, because he always has his pipe."

"Oh-h-h—he always has his pipe!—lucky dog!—and you give him water to drink?"

"No, sir—he never drinks water. Once, when he was very tired and wet"—and Mary heaved a sigh as she remembered that all the care he had taken on that wet night had been worse than useless, for her furniture had been destroyed in the riot that morning. "Once, when he was so wet and tired, I made some coffee for him, and he said he liked that better than cider!"

"Coffee!—well done!—why, if we do not mind what we are about, Dartmoor will become civilized in this 'fast' nineteenth century!

"He liked it very much, sir, and I was thinking—when I could send to N——, I would get more coffee, and so make it for him whenever he likes!"

"Yes, yes—yes, little woman, yes," said Charlie, stooping and patting Mary on the head, "let him have it by all means, and, take my word for it, with a pipe to smoke, coffee to drink, and you by his side, Isaac Watson will never again frequent 'The Old Packhorse!'"

Charlie left the room, and Mary raised her heart in prayer and thankfulness to her God for the great mercy vouchsafed to her in Isaac's reformation, as well as for her rescue from her foes on that morning.

And so Master Charlie "twitted" Isaac with his liking for coffee; but Isaac ate a hearty breakfast, and bore all Charlie's fun with his usual good-humour. And then Charlie said,

"Now, Isaac, as I have made a man of you once more, now you may go and see your wife."

XXV

OF THE SKILFUL "PHYSICIAN" WHOSE TREATMENT RESTORED PARSON HILL TO HEALTH

PARSON Hill was lying ill of quinsy!

The vicarage was situated in its own grounds, just at the entrance of the village, on the opposite side to the smithy. The shouting and noise of the late riot had not disturbed the parson. He quietly reposed in his bed, as far as his indisposition would allow him. He objected to medical attendance; to use his own words, "he always doctored himself."

When Charlie arrived at the vicarage on this day, Parson Hill could not speak. Such signs as could be understood he used, and, when these were valueless, he wrote his orders or his requests. But Mary and the old woman were accidentally brought to the vicarage, and in the course of the day they learned the nature of the malady from which Parson Hill was suffering. The Widow Simpson was reputed, in the village of Lawsleigh, to possess a knowledge of "simples," as she termed them, and their uses, which was highly valued. She did not go about the moor from one place to another boasting of her skill, and pretending to effect wonderful cures, but she could relieve pain in many instances, and comfort the patient until better help arrived in extreme cases.

In the "olden time," the ladies of England had a knowledge of pharmacy that sufficed on all ordinary occasions. When the ladies discarded this knowledge from their acquirements, it fell into the hands of "old women," —"dames," as they were called in villages. In our day, the numbers of educated gentlemen who practise medicine render an acquaintance with herbs almost unnecessary. Remote districts are reached by "the parish doctor" for the poor; and the rich do not now depend upon the skill of an unlearned old woman. To the rarely-seen "leech" of former days, the numerous gentlemen of the faculty of the present day offer a strong contrast. To the numbers of educated ladies in former times who exerted their skill in the hour of sickness, and applied their knowledge with favourable results, the old Widow Simpson, "standing alone in her glory" on Dartmoor, also offers a strong contrast.

To Charlie's anxious mind, the vicar appeared to be getting worse, and he entreated to be allowed to send for medical help. Parson Hill would not permit this, and Charlie left the room with a sad heart. The housekeeper followed Charlie, and told him that the "old woman" said "she could cure the parson!"

"And I dare say she can," said Charlie, in a tone of hope. "She will know of some simple remedy, to which I make no doubt my dear father will submit. At all events, I will see the 'old woman' at once."

The result was that the parson yielded. He wrote upon a slate—"Let her come, *she* can do no harm."

And the "old Widow Simpson" was installed sole mistress of the ante-room leading into that occupied by the sick man. Where there was illness the Widow Simpson made herself useful; she now set herself to work—under the parson's roof—with the same heartiness of manner and confidence in her own skill as she would have done in that of the poorest cottager. An application of hops was recommended by the old woman. Hops were always to be had at Lawsleigh Vicarage, for the parson brewed his own ale. The light-handed maidens that belonged to the vicar's establishment acted by the widow's orders. We are not going to describe the scene in Parson Hill's room, where the old woman's knowledge of a simple remedy in all probability saved his life. We shall only say that the hops were applied as directed to be; and, sooner than was anticipated, the quinsy came to a head and broke. The vicar was relieved, and in a fair way for recovery. But when all these troubles had passed away, and Charlie had once again the pleasure of a quiet talk with his wife, he said,

"It struck him as a curious thing that he should ride over the moor to see his father at that particular time; that he should reach the smithy only just in time to save the machine from being burnt, and Mary from a fate worse than death itself; that he should take Mary and the old woman to the vicarage to keep them in a place secure from harm until Isaac should return; and that in taking them, he took exactly the help that was wanted! Truly, he had been guided by the hand of God!"

XXVI

WHICH INTRODUCES TWO
NEW CHARACTERS

THE riot in the village of Lawsleigh caused more sorrow, and made a deeper impression on the inhabitants, than even the murder of poor Hannah Barker had done; so many were implicated in the former.

"Master Charlie" was indefatigable in searching out the ringleaders, and bringing them to justice. But as our space will not allow us to recount all the particulars of his zeal, or even the names of those who met with the punishment due to their misconduct, we must content ourselves with assuring our readers that Mary was fully satisfied with the decision of the magistrate before whom the men appeared; but of Isaac, we fear his heart, for the time being, was made of sterner stuff.

When the officers of justice went to the "Packhorse" to execute their orders, and seize the fat Widow Mason, she was nowhere to be found. Great search was made at the time in all her known haunts, but unsuccessfully. The little maid who attended to the customers at the "Packhorse," and assisted the widow in her daily work, said "that a great waggon drew up at the 'Packhorse,' and the widow knew the driver, and wanted to go with him, and see her relations; that the man agreed to take her; that she took her boxes and went, telling the maid she should return on the morrow."

But the morrow came, and many morrows, and the widow did not return. When the house came to be searched, she had taken off with her, besides her clothes, every article of value she possessed. The furniture, such as it was, was small in quantity, and poor in quality; and when the goods were sold, and the sign of the "Packhorse" taken down, there was not enough money raised to pay the girl's wages, and the expenses of the sale.

The landlord lost his rent, but he was a young man recently come into his property; and in his walk over his estate, with a view to its future improvement, the old "Packhorse" had been included in the survey, and he had said jocosely,

"The Widow Mason had saved him from the rudeness of desiring her to find another home, for that he had another use for the 'Old Packhorse.'"

This gentleman, Mr. Tremelly, of Buckleigh Court, and the son of a former friend of Parson Hill, came, with his uncle, Mr. Ladds, on a visit to Lawsleigh Vicarage soon after the riots we have mentioned, for the purpose of examining his estate on that part of the moor.

But we have omitted to state that Mary was reappointed schoolmistress of the village of Lawsleigh, and leader of the choir. Isaac still retained his post as head of the belfry, and none now dared dispute with him his old seat in the church at the head of the choir.

And now that the vicar and Isaac were once more on friendly terms, we need hardly add that Isaac's contemplated improvement at the smithy had been talked over with the Parson. And it happened, when the vicar and his two friends, Mr. Tremelly and Mr. Ladds, were traversing the parish, and looking over the property belonging to Mr. Tremelly, that, on arriving at the smithy cottage, Parson Hill spoke of Isaac's intended alterations.

It will be remembered that the smithy, and some small pieces of ground at the back, belonged to Isaac. And after a little conversation with him— for the gentleman had heard his history from the vicar—Mr. Tremelly observed,

"It strikes me that you are wrong to build two rooms to the old house. Material is plentiful, and while you are about it do the thing well. Build a new house."

"Build a new house!" exclaimed Isaac, in dismay, and shaking his head. "I am afraid that would be quite beyond my means. Besides, what should I do with the old one? We do not require really more than two rooms."

"Not at present," said Mr. Tremelly, *sotto voce*, to the vicar.

And Isaac continued—

"And then, you see, the old house is so good," and Isaac looked at it with an eye of pride, for it was decidedly the best in the village. "And—and," added he, hesitatingly, "I would not disturb my good mother."

"True, true, Isaac," said Mr. Tremelly, "the suggestion does you credit. But *you* must build for the next generation. Think of it—think of it."

And the gentlemen walked away, leaving Isaac in a state of doubt and uncertainty, unusual with him, as to what he ought to do, for the last words lingered on his ear, "You should build for the next generation."

Isaac's property abutted on that of Mr. Tremelly, and on examining the part immediately adjoining, the latter remarked,

"Isaac ought to build here—this position is better than where the cottage now stands, though that site was well chosen. He shall have a few acres here at a moderate price, contiguous to his own land."

"You seem to think Isaac will fall into your notions," said Parson Hill; "but he is like many a denizen of this moor, very sturdy in his opinions; and though certainly enlightened in an unusual degree, I fear not sufficiently so as to induce him to build for the next generation. His forefathers for several generations have occupied the same cottage he now uses. Granite is very enduring; and tradition says the Simpsons have been a hard-working, pains-taking, and orderly people, until the grandfather of this man took to the 'Packhorse,' and cast a blot upon their hitherto fair name. And Isaac, though so superior, has never changed his mode of life; every meal is taken in the same primitive simplicity as a hundred years ago, and he will not see the necessity for a new house and new ways."

"But I have two reasons to give as a proof that I am right: Isaac's little wife knows something better than the manners and customs of the moor; she will gradually introduce to his notice new forms and new ideas. While the old woman lives, I grant you, there can be no change; and also I grant it would be wrong to disturb her old age with refinements and luxuries unheard of here, and which she would neither appreciate nor understand—as, for instance, the sewing machine;" and then, digressing from the immediate subject, and laughing cheerily, he added, "And if she endows the sewing-machine with a power of devilry, what will she say when you and I can talk to each other by means of the electric telegraph—in your snug vicarage on the moor, I in Paris, or Constantinople, or any out-of-the-way place—in her idea of the matter? She will give up the ghost without more ado; and then, though I do not mean to be profane, and I greatly honour old age, then there will be one obstacle to the new house removed."

XXVII

COMING EVENTS CAST THEIR
SHADOWS BEFORE

"Your youth makes you sanguine," said Mr. Ladds; "I candidly confess I do not go with you; and I doubt whether Isaac, or even his wife, would appreciate a house such as you would like to see built."

"Yes, it is my youth—my glorious youth!" said Mr. Tremelly, enthusiastically, "that makes me talk for the future, build for the future—I trust not castles in the air—live for the future; and it is because Isaac is young that I feel I shall bring him over to my views. Sanguine you say I am—yes, one must be sanguine, one must march on—this is the age of wonders, of progress, I should rather say, such as no preceding century ever surpassed if, indeed, it was ever equalled;" and then, as he paused to take breath, for he had spoken with much rapidity and eagerness, he added, turning to the vicar, "but, my friend, to return to Isaac Watson— here is a backslider retracing his steps, suppose we give him a helping hand, and show him we appreciate his own efforts. I will let Isaac have the large piece of land adjoining his own at a merely nominal price, upon his promise to build a new house."

"You are very generous," said Parson Hill; "and I am sure Isaac will value your kindness, even if he refuses to build."

"It is rare, oh! so rare, to find one drunkard retrace his steps and come back to good conduct, that I confess I feel a great interest in Isaac's future career," said Mr. Ladds. And then he turned to the vicar, and said, "The fact is, the change from old customs must be very gradual on this moor. You know—by experience—better than most men living, that work as hard as you will, and improve, and improve, and try this and that, you know how little can possibly be done in these remote districts, I therefore shall not marvel if Isaac refuses to build; but I do marvel very much that, from having been a drunken and disorderly person, he is now apparently so worthy of your notice, and I give the man credit accordingly."

"Yes, as you say, and truly, change must be very gradual; and much as I have attempted, and sometimes with success, still much remains to do," said Parson Hill. "The earth and the people are always growing either better or worse. Here, on Dartmoor, until this last month or two, when Peter Barker set the example of ill-doing—here I had hoped we were getting better; but the recent, and very unpardonable, riots in Lawsleigh prove the contrary; and——"

"Oh! do not despond!" said Mr. Ladds, "for though the people ought to have known better than to make such a hubbub in the county, and do so much harm, still the Dartmoor of the present day is not the Dartmoor of fifty years ago." After a little pause, Mr. Ladds resumed—"And that fresh importation of yours, not much more than a year ago, had that no influence on Isaac? Do you think your pretty schoolmistress, whose fate you so lamented a few weeks since—do you think she was a cipher in his estimation from the very first hour he gazed upon her?"

"Undoubtedly his honest love for Mary has been one great means of his present reformation," said the vicar.

"I was here with my dear father," said Mr. Tremelly, "at the opening of your new schoolroom. And then I saw that Isaac Watson appreciated Mary Cope. But there was a much greater difference between them then than now. Isaac is already more polished from close contact with a more delicate and refined nature than his own."

"These things are pre-ordained," said Mr. Ladds. "The right person is sent at the right moment, and the change that our former efforts could not produce is made in an instant."

"True," said the vicar; "and Isaac and Mary are the right people in the right place; together they will be a great benefit to this village."

"For ages, as one may say," said Mr. Ladds, "this village of Lawsleigh has had no influential person resident among its people, but the solitary clergyman. And for those centuries of time, when civilization, which was creeping on in different parts of England, was debarred from entering on the moor, because the roads, for the vehicles then in use, were impracticable; for those ages the pastor, kind and good, and of habits almost as simple as his parishioners, was sufficient. In most cases he was farrier, doctor, lawyer, magistrate, farmer, squire, and parson—all in one."

"Right—right!" said Mr. Tremelly. "But, thank God! these times are not like those! Railways now come up to the very edge of the moor, the roads on the moor itself are infinitely better, though the hills are as lofty, the valleys as lowly as formerly, but the vales are not all swamps, nor the hills all inaccessible. They are both now made of use to man and beast. Bridges are built where formerly only a few lumbering and unsteady stones thrown into the bed of the river helped the weary traveller to get across. And soon, soon from the nostrils of the 'iron horse' will curl the smoke, as he gallantly rushes over the moor, and opens it to the 'wide, wide world.'"

"Your enthusiasm charms me!" said the vicar. "I feel as if I were growing young again, when I listen to your graphic sketch of the future."

"And when we have bridges, and roads, and trains, and letters, and books, and electric telegraphs, shall we not have man to people this sometime desert? Shall old customs, worn threadbare long ago, remain in use when new ones are better? Shall the parson do all the work now, as he has done in these remote districts, to his credit, be it said, so nobly and so well, for ages past? No. He shall only have his fair share. For, by the blessing of God, he shall have companions. And the villagers shall know other rulers—rulers to keep them in order, it is true, but by their own good example."

Mr. Tremelly paused, and turning round to contemplate the view from the top of the hill they had just ascended, he pointed out a clump of trees in the distance.

"Do you see that group on the edge of the moor?—say some five miles off?"

"Yes—Bankerton Fort," said the vicar.

"Just so; there I mean to build my moorland home."

"You!—you!" said the vicar, raising his hands enthusiastically.

"Even I. Through Bankerton Valley to Mary Tor, then a turn to the left, not much more than three miles from Lawsleigh Vicarage. What do you say to that?"

"That I never thought to see such a sight, or have so near a neighbour in my day," said the vicar.

"Yes, I mean to build a house there, and dwell in it for a part of every year."

"And then I shall have the honour of resigning the squireship of the moor into worthy hands," said the vicar.

"But now to return to Isaac," said Mr. Tremelly, "from whom, like a young and unbroken colt, I seem to have run away. He is one of this village—he lives now where his forefathers dwelt formerly—he is essentially one of the people—in the next generation he will be looked up to—now he is envied. But even the envious and jealous reform, or die out of the way, like better-behaved people; and their children will be taught better things than to be envious and jealous, and make better men and women, let us hope. Isaac will be one of that grand social link that unites the people with their rulers—himself one of the people, truly, but yet greatly superior to his contemporaries; his children will probably occupy a higher rank than he—for such material will creep on, will find its way upward. They will be well educated, for Isaac values learning; and now that I have given so full an opinion of Isaac, and prophesied so largely for his future, pray what can you tell us of his pretty wife?"

"That though modest and almost timid in character, she is thoroughly well-principled, very well read for her position, and altogether a clever little woman—in short, just the woman who—having great confidence in her husband's powers, as she has in Isaac's—can be easily moulded by such a man to be a blessing to her own family and to her neighbours."

"And as the next generation rises around her, and the cares, and enjoyments, and dignity of maternity increase upon her, will not she too improve in steadiness of purpose, in self-reliance, and in all the good that will arise from her superior position? Then I say, such people ought not to be left to dwell in a cottage without a solitary comfort of any kind around them. They are the pioneers of civilization for the village of Lawsleigh, and as such, should now in these early days become more civilized themselves."

"Isaac will build his new house, I foresee," said the vicar, laughing.

"To be sure he will. And if you please, we will again stop at the smithy as we pass, and see what impression my parting words made upon him."

"That he must build for the next generation."

XXVIII

IN WHICH ISAAC WATSON CONSENTS TO BUILD FOR THE NEXT GENERATION

AND Mr. Tremelly repeated his former suggestion to Isaac; and to the worthy vicar's astonishment, Isaac only shook his head and smiled. Isaac's character was essentially firm; and Parson Hill had expected a flat refusal on being further pressed. True, Isaac still said, "He did not see how it could be possible to do so much."

And though he readily acknowledged it would benefit future generations to have a good house ready built to their hands, he seemed to think that the old house, with a little addition, could be made to contain all that Mary and he could desire.

"Have you had your wife's opinion on this momentous subject," said Mr. Ladds, "eh, Isaac?"

"Why, no, sir. I have not seen Mary since you passed—she is at the school."

"Then tell us, Isaac," said the vicar, "which do you think she will prefer?"

"I am afraid I cannot help acknowledging that Mary has been brought up in a better house than the smithy cottage; and from such observations as I can at times make, she seems to have better ways for doing most things than I have been accustomed to see; and I know, if I ask her, she will prefer a new house."

"To be sure she will," replied Mr. Tremelly; "and she will be quite right, and you will be very glad to make her so happy, and to build one for her."

Isaac shook his head rather lugubriously this time, as he said, "No, sir; it is not in my power. And as I am not able to let her have a new house, I should carefully avoid such a subject with her."

"Not in your power!" said the vicar, laughing; "that we know to be nonsense, Isaac, for you are a rich man."

"For my present position, sir, thank God, I am," said Isaac, in humble and thankful tones.

"I do not wish you to change your position," said Mr. Tremelly; "nothing further from my thoughts. I only want you to build a new house, instead of adding two rooms to the old one; and tell me, why cannot this be done?"

"In the first place, sir, I have no land, or not enough—only the little bit attached to the smithy cottage; in the next, it would cost too much money; but the best reason of all is, that we do not require it."

"Not at present," said Mr. Tremelly, jocosely; "but come with me—come with me," added he, taking Isaac by the arm, for this conversation had taken place in the well-known shed, and they walked away together; while Mr. Hill explained to Mr. Ladds some of the circumstances of the late riot, and pointed out the locale.

Perhaps some twenty minutes had passed before Mr. Tremelly and Isaac returned; and then Parson Hill saw at once that Isaac would build "for the next generation." Mr. Tremelly looked very composed and quiet; but Isaac's manly features glowed with pleasure. It was as if the two had changed places, for now Isaac had all the enthusiasm, Mr. Tremelly all the repose. And he could afford to repose, for he had brought to bear a point upon which he had set his heart. And in Isaac had been stirred new hopes, new dreams, new ambitions, new modes of benefit to himself and his neighbours. All these glittered on his brow.

"And so you have conquered," said the vicar, as the three gentlemen walked away from the smithy cottage.

"Yes, I have made him promise to build a new house; and I have given my promise that he shall have a certain piece of ground—lying conveniently near to his own—that he shall have it mapped out, and legally transferred to him by a given day."

"These are indeed signs of progress," said the vicar.

"Yes; you will not have all the good work to yourself; hard as you have worked in this parish for the last—I forget how many years," added Mr. Tremelly, laughing; "but I have been accustomed to hear my father speak of the time when you and he were young men together, and I learned from him that the living of Lawsleigh was sinecure."

"What it was at that time you would hardly credit," said Mr. Ladds.

"Yes, I would; I tell you, I have heard my father say what Lawsleigh was when Mr. Hill was first inducted," and turning to the vicar, he continued, "you were then as I am now, young, sanguine, eager. If it shall please God to allow me to live as long, I shall look back with grateful thanks, if I can feel I have done in my day as much good as you in yours."

"Hush! Hush!" said the vicar, deprecatingly; "you know not what you say. When you have lived as long as I, and done as little," added he, with a sigh, "you will feel inclined to say, in the words of the patriarch, 'Few and evil have the days of the years of thy servant been.'"

"Nay, nay," said Mr. Tremelly, interrupting, "I cannot permit you to storm my position; you must excuse me if I say you should not despond over the idea that you have done so little."

"Remember," said the vicar, impressively, "it is youth that gilds the future; but age looks back on the past."

"True," said Mr. Ladds; "but in this instance I agree in the opinion that to those who knew Lawsleigh when you were inducted, and who see it now, the marvel is that you have been able to do so much."

"It appears little to me now," said the vicar humbly.

"Because it contrasts strongly with the outer world," said Mr. Ladds. "The waste places of the earth cannot be put on a par with modern improvements and civilization.—But Lawsleigh thirty years ago!—and Lawsleigh now!—come, come——"

"Well, well," said the vicar, with a smile, "and at all events I have a most excellent curate, he will meet you at dinner. Now Gray is young, sanguine, eager, and I have no doubt when he understands the people he will do very well."

"When he understands the people!—that my father said was one of your great gifts—it was the secret of your success," said Mr. Tremelly.

"But the time has arrived when the people must change," replied Mr. Ladds; "the next generation will not be like the ignorant unlettered boors of the past; their children are educating for the future; the march of the times invades their homes; and Gray, your worthy curate, is the very man to head the march, and carry the rising population with him! He was sent here just at the right time, for the right purpose!"

"He is a thoroughly good fellow," said the vicar, laughing, "but, to confess the truth, what between his crude ideas upon dress and propriety among these swamps, and his great zeal in trying to knock all old customs on the head, when he first became acquainted with the moor, I had well nigh resigned the living of Lawsleigh into his hands, and taken up my abode at Paul Tavey, for I hate worries, but I tried hard 'to hold my own,' and we understand each other better now."

"I am glad our morning's walk has turned out so well," said Mr. Tremelly.

"About Isaac's new house!—yes, indeed," replied the vicar, "but we may thank you for that. I confess to a great liking for Isaac Watson and his nice little wife."

"You picked him out from the crowd of ungifted ones," said Mr. Ladds, "and brought his gifts to light. Isaac is your own work, in his education, in his reformation. Had you been harsh and severe during the time of his intemperance, as I confess many might have thought it right to be, he would in all probability have hardened his mind against you, and have indulged himself 'to the top of his bent.' But he always retained a respect and admiration for you, which, coupled with your forbearance, I have no doubt often saved him from temptation."

"And then," said Mr. Tremelly, "my father steps in and builds you a magnificent schoolroom, and you transplant a pretty and intelligent woman from a large and luxurious city into the very heart of dull and dreary Dartmoor!"

"Those epithets are libellous," laughed the vicar; "look at the Tors——"

"And woman has her place even in this march of civilization," said Mr. Ladds, "but a modest, comely, and sensible young woman is a prize in deed at such an epoch."

"Then you mean to say that Mary is the right woman in the right place?" said the vicar.

"I have no doubt the handsome smith thinks so!" said Mr. Tremelly; and the gentlemen entered the vicarage.

XXIX

IN WHICH MARY IS NOT ALLOWED TO "JUMP OVER THE MOON"

WHEN Mary returned from the school, Isaac told her of the visit of the three gentlemen. And as he had made up his mind as to his future proceedings, he thought that now Mary might as well be brought to agree with him and he set himself to work to produce the desired result.

"Mr. Tremelly, the proprietor of the greater part of Lawsleigh—that gentleman you saw in the vicarage pew on Sunday my dear—"

"Yes, Isaac—"

"He objects to my building two rooms to the old smithy."

"He objects! why, Isaac!" said Mary, in a tone of surprise, and stopping in the act of untying her bonnet.

"I told him I had promised you to build them."

"Yes; but the smithy is your own, I suppose," said Mary, coming close up to Isaac.

"It is my own," and Isaac stooped and kissed the pretty anxious-looking face.

"Then why can you not build the two rooms?"

"I never said I could not."

"You say Mr. Tremelly objects; do you mean to be guided by his opinion?"

Mary stood with her bonnet in her hand, and Isaac saw her eager wistful look.

"Yes," said Isaac.

(Oh! Isaac, Isaac!—how can you take such pains to mystify your little wife—human nature!)

He saw an expression of disappointment sadden her features in an instant; he heard her stifle a sigh as she turned away to hang up her bonnet.

"You are sorry, my dear Mary?"

"I cannot deny that, Isaac," and she still kept her back to him, that he might not see how much annoyed she really was. "But then, Isaac," resumed she, "I am sure, when we have all three been preserved from so many horrors and miseries, I think I should indeed be wrong to be unhappy because you have changed your mind about the rooms."

And now, with an attempt at a smile, Mary turned round and offered her hand to Isaac. Isaac accepted it, and then would not relinquish his prize.

"You see, Mary dear, Mr. Tremelly advised me to build for the next generation." Isaac paused. But Mary's thoughts on the subject of the "next generation" were not yet awakened. "And he has been very kind to me, my dear," resumed Isaac, "he has given me a large piece of ground—that, that lies between the garden and the high road."

"All that immense piece of land, Isaac?"

"Yes; all that. And he wants me to build a new house there, and so leave the old smithy cottage untouched. It is so pretty as it is. It never ought to be altered, if we only come to think on the subject."

"Build—build a new house!" said Mary, slowly and dubiously; "you will not do that, Isaac?"

"Well, my dear, I shall be sorry if you object, because I like to please you;" and as Mary's face was still turned to him, and as the smile was becoming more radiant every moment, he gave her another kiss; "and to confess to you the honest truth, my dear, I have promised Mr. Tremelly to build there."

Isaac's arm was now round Mary, and he held her close to him, as she replied,

"To build a new—new house?"

"To build! Yes, my dear Mary, a new house."

"Why, Isaac, then that will be much better than two rooms."

"You think so, truly—truly, Mary?"

"Yes, to be sure, yes. How I shall like a new house, all your very own, Isaac!"

And Mary's eyes sparkled now.

"Then you won't fret much about the loss of the two rooms?"

"Fret, Isaac! what nonsense! Why, I am so happy, I could jump over the moon!"

"Do not thee do that, Ma-ary," said the old woman, shaking her head. "For though the moon doth look near to the earth at odd times, I never heard tell in all my days as anybody could touch it!"

"I will hold her fast, mother," said Isaac.

"Mother, I am so happy!" said Mary.

"Ay, wench, ay; and I be glad as you be happy. But don't thee go for to jump over the moon—don't thee try to, when the lad lets thee loose. If thee was to try, Ma-ary, and then tumble thyself down a-tother side of the moon, my belief us should never find thee again."

"Promise not to try, Mary," said Isaac, "or I shall still hold you fast."

And Mary hid her laughing face on Isaac's shoulder, and gave her promise; and Isaac set her at liberty.

In the course of conversation, when the gentlemen were at dinner at the vicarage, Mr. Gray said,

"I was in hopes you would raze the 'Packhorse' to the ground."

"That would be short-sighted, would it not?" said Mr. Tremelly.

"What! will you not do away with the 'Old Packhorse?'" continued Mr. Gray.

"I should rather like to let the old horse work on," said Mr. Tremelly, with a smile. "He has been a good servant in his day. When there were no roads for wheel-carriages, he traversed them; when there were no waggons, no coaches, no railways, he carried the people; when there were no postage-stamps, he carried the letters, paid and unpaid. It is true, he has grown old; but, for my part, I like old servants. New modes, new ideas, science, the arts, and civilization, if you will, but old servants, if you please. I like to make them comfortable in their old age; and as they have spent their youth in honourably doing their duty, so I should like to do my duty, and let them spend their old age happily, and unencumbered by cares."

"I confess I do not understand what you propose to do with the 'Old Packhorse,'" said Mr. Ladds.

"And if you and the vicar do not understand me, I shall not much wonder, seeing that it is time you two old servants of the public"—Mr. Ladds being also a clergyman—"were unencumbered by cares of any kind. Your mines have been pretty well worked, and good ore has been plentiful produced. But Mr. Gray is young; his mine is full of rich veins of ore, unworked, unused; he should join me in renewing the youth of the 'Old Packhorse'"

Mr. Gray smiled, but remained silent, for he did not understand Mr. Tremelly.

XXX

HOW MASTER CHARLIE AND JAMES MARVEL WENT IN OPPOSITION TO THE POWERS THAT BE

IN less than a year after the events just narrated, for it was in the month of September, 1863, a carriage stopped at the "old smithy," as it was now called, from which a gentleman alighted, and the carriage drove on.

"Well, Isaac, and how are you?" said Master Charlie—for it was he, and he shook Isaac's hand heartily; "and tell me of the good widow—the last report was not favourable."

"Thank you," said Isaac, "she has rallied quite beyond our hopes and even goes backwards and forwards to the 'New Smithy'"—as Isaac's new house was called—"several times a day."

Isaac and Mary, and a baby only a fortnight old, now lived in the new house. The Widow Simpson, by her own choice, remained in the "Old Smithy," and at night the little moor maiden, whose duty it was to attend upon Mary in her new home, slept at the "Old Smithy," to be near the Widow Simpson, if she at any time required care or assistance.

"My wife and boy are gone on to the Vicarage," said Charlie. "Mary is getting on well, I hear; and her boy is a fine specimen of the human race!"

"Yes, thank you, Master Charlie, Mary is doing very well; and for the boy," added Isaac, laughing, "my mother says 'the little one is a 'normous big one!'"

"Good old creature! I cannot stay to see her now; but I would not pass you, Isaac, and not shake you by the hand, and tell you how glad I am to see you so prosperous and so happy."

"You are very good," said Isaac, in a grateful tone. "The parson told me you would be sure to come before the month was out, and that your boy was to be christened here."

"Yes, we are come for that important event, and Mary is to bring her boy at the same time; is it not so arranged? Mine is to be called William Charles, after father and grandfather, who is also godfather. And how, pray, how do you call yours, Isaac?" continued Charlie, as a mischievous smile spread broadly over his face.

A slight touch of Isaac's former shyness seemed to come over him at this moment; it was a second or two before he replied.

"I do think one name quite enough—I confess it, Master Charlie; but Mary says the boy must be called Baldwin Isaac; and as Mr. Tremelly and the vicar say it is all right, I suppose it is."

"Of course it is. So then you have—like me—given the names of father, grandfather, and godfather. And would you have Mr. Tremelly come and offer himself to stand godfather, and then not give his name to the child? Isaac! Isaac! 'it most mazes I!'" said Charlie, laughing; and then, holding out his hand, he continued:

"Well, old fellow, we were boys together—and fortunately that was before you became such a 'sad dog,' and so you did not lead me into scrapes—but now we are men, and, by the blessing of God, our children shall play together, and gladden the hearts of their parents. Good-bye; my wife will come and see Mary as soon as she can; no doubt they mean to compare babies—my wife is very proud of hers!"

And Charlie walked away, with the glow of bright good-nature glittering on his handsome face.

Isaac's position was gradually altering, as Mr. Tremelly had foreseen. He employed more men now; for, since the Exhibition, he had turned his attention to the making of ingenious and safe locks, and had met with success beyond his hopes.

So Isaac had given up the great hammer, and turned the large room at the "Old Smithy" into a sort of work-shop for himself, where all the neater parts of his handicraft were done. And so still the old Widow

Simpson sat knitting by Isaac's side, exceping only at such times as she chose to "stretch her old legs a bit, and take another good look to that there big leetle 'un' as most mazed she!"

And when the christening took place, the old Widow Simpson, though she had not been able to get to church for the last few weeks, would not be left at home. She must stand near the font, to give her blessing to the little ones as soon as they were received into the Church.

When the several queries in the baptismal service were put by the officiating minister, Mr. Gray, the responses were made in the clear and manly voice of the vicar himself; and when was said, "Name this child" to Mrs. Hill's boy, the vicar replied, "William Charles;" and when the same was said to Mary's boy, Mr. Tremelly replied, "Baldwin Isaac;" and the two gentlemen took upon themselves the duties of "God-parents" to the children.

And the aged Widow Simpson, still following the custom of bygone times, stopped the infants as they were taken from the font, and, putting her hands first upon one and then on the other, distinctly gave a blessing.

When the service was over, and Isaac and his party turned to leave the church, he could not help inwardly noticing how vigorous, for her age, the good widow seemed. She appeared to have suddenly regained a strength she had not had for many months; and when this apparent re-juvenisation continued, Isaac at length told Mary of the great pleasure he had in watching the old woman step from one house to the other several times a day, and appear all the better for the exertion.

"Well, Isaac," said Mary, in her simplicity, "I always said to myself, if mother could only live till baby was born that then she might take up again; because you see the dear little fellow is more to her than her own child; for I have been told all grandmothers—and she is more, Isaac, she is a great-grandmother—'live again in their children's children.' And so you see it is quite true, for she seems to gather new life."

Isaac smiled at Mary's deduction, but he said,

"No doubt you are right, my dear, for it is plain she is in excellent health, and as happy as the day is long. Nothing but praises to God and thanks to Him for preserving her to see my boy and hold him in her arms, excepting my dear blessings on your head and on mine!"

"And I have such faith in the prayers and blessings of the aged and the good," said Mary.

"And so have I," said Isaac.

Only on the morrow after this conversation were Isaac and Mary startled at their dinner by the "little maid" running from the "Old Smithy" to say that "the widdy be tooked bad."

Mary put her infant in the cradle, and followed Isaac immediately. They found the old woman seated in a luxurious easy-chair, newly imported by Isaac, and a present to the widow on her ninety-sixth birthday—her eyes closed, her lips inaudibly muttering. They gave her a cordial which partially restored her, and she then asked to be carried to bed.

"Ma-ary—Ma-ary, blessings on thee, my lass, for a good kind heart! I be going to leave thee, Isaac, my lad."

She was at length placed comfortably in bed, but she was still alive to this world.

"That there—big—leetle un—" she gasped at intervals, and the child was fetched, but she was fast sinking.

She stretched out her hand and touched the little head; the word "blessing" was all that could be heard.

After a few minutes of repose, she said,

"Isaac, lad—the saule bell—to call the cheery passon."

"Ay, mother," said Isaac, as he saw her close her eyes and doze again.

Now, as it happened, in this eventful year, when some "old customs" still lingered on the moor, "the new curate," Mr. Gray, had worked hard, and with considerable success, to introduce "new customs," to do away with, what he called, the remnants of Popery, and establish such as are in use among the Protestants now.

What the Widow Simpson called "the saule bell" was no longer heard in Lawsleigh; and Isaac, with his heart full of sorrow at the sudden and very serious illness of his aged relative, and regret that the custom had not lingered to the end of her days, hastily walked to the vicarage for Parson

Hill, and he reasoned with himself as he went on his way—"If she sees the parson by her bed-side, she will think he came at the 'call of the bell.'"

And Isaac sent in his message, and the vicar sent out word he would be at the "Old Smithy" in a few minutes.

As Isaac returned over the vicarage lawn, he met Charlie, and the two young men exchanged a word or two; and Isaac explained that, instead of going to the belfry, as in years gone by he should have considered his duty, to call the parson by the sound of the bell, he had been to tell the vicar that the Widow Simpson was dying.

As Isaac ascended the stairs at the "Old Smithy," to his grandmother's dying bed, to his surprise and satisfaction the great tenor bell rang out that famous "clang, clang, clang," that the Widow Simpson, in the earlier chapters of this book, had described to Susan Picard as "calling the parson."

"Ay, ay, lad, they be a-calling the passon, God bless them!" said she, waking up as Isaac re-entered the room. She dozed again for an instant or two, and then said, "Tell I when the cheery passon comes, Ma-ary—coz why? I canna see, my eyesight be gone."

But yet she retained her other faculties, and was able to assure her kind relatives that she was free from pain, and to reply to the few queries put to her. But she repeated several times, as the very aged do, "that now that she had seen Isaac's son, and knew that the lad—as she called Isaac—was happy with Ma-ary by his side, she was content to die."

Now the vicar himself, as he too hastened to the dying bed of the widow, was startled by the clang, clang, clang, of that bell.

"Humph!—now that is Isaac—of course it is. No one else in this parish would dare to do such a thing without my permission. I really did think better of him—so intelligent and sensible a man should not, on any occasion, or for any one, go in opposition to the powers that be. I must make some excuse for him to Gray, for he will be very clamorous at this return to popery, after all the trouble he has taken to root up old customs from the face of the land. And yet I daresay Isaac saw that the old woman would not die contented if she did not hear 'the soul bell'—I must tell Gray."

By this time he had arrived at the "Old Smithy." What, then, was his astonishment to see Isaac kneeling by the bedside of his aged relative, and covering her hand with caresses, for still the bell pealed on. Though now it had changed to the solemn "boome, boome, boome," that the old woman had explained to Susan "called upon all good Christians to leave their daily work, and pray for peace to the dying soul."

In less than ten minutes after Mr. Hill's arrival, the old Widow Simpson spoke for the last time.

"Don't fret, Ma-ary—I be happy—and God Almighty—bless the passon, and all his family, and the lad—and—I hear they be chiming—chiming—"

These were her last words; but her imagination, or rather her knowledge, of what must follow had misled her. The bell still tolled the solemn toll for the dying—the call to prayer; and it was only when, by the little maid from the smithy, word was sent to the belfry that the widow was dead, that the chime broke out that was supposed to "Call us to thankfulness for our brother's or sister's deliverance."

"Strange again!" said the vicar to himself, as he walked homeward; "it is plain Isaac has no hand in this—who can have done it? There, now they chime—well, well, I am very glad, for the sake of the poor old woman, brought up in such customs."

"And so the old Widow Simpson is gone to her long home?" said Charlie, when he met the vicar at dinner.

"Yes, she went suddenly at last, as such aged ones often do; for they tell me she has been unusually strong and well since the christening—the last bright gleam from the dying light. But I cannot think who could dare to ring out the 'soul bell.'"

"I did," said Charlie.

"You! You could not ring the tenor without help!"

"No, and so I took Marvel with me. The vicar's son, and the vicar's servant, have dared to fly in the face of Gray!"

Parson Hill leaned back in his chair, and did not speak.

"I am heartily glad you did revive the old custom, Charlie, just for the old woman's sake," said Mrs. Hill.

Still the parson remained silent; but Mrs. Hill thought she saw him put his finger to the corners of his eyes before he resumed his dinner. When he spoke it was almost in a whisper.

"Charlie, boy! upon my word I cannot think what Gray will say!"

"Nor can I," said Charlie; "but if he should be so unreasonable as to speak to me on the subject, I am afraid I shall tell him that I would have rung that bell while the Widow Simpson lay dying, if it had cost Lawsleigh another riot!"

"Charlie!" said the vicar. "Why, the men are still at their hard labour, would you like to join them?"

"Joking apart, the exception proves the rule," said Charlie.

"And having proved your rule, change your subject!" said Mrs. Hill.

And the heavy boom of the "soul-bell" was never heard again at the village of Lawsleigh-on-the-Moor.

XXXI

OF THE HILLS AND THE DALE AND "THE OLD PACKHORSE"

EVENTUALLY the cottage that had borne so disreputable a character while belonging to the Widow Mason, became a dwelling of a large size. A house of call—as it had always been—for all wayfarers crossing the moor, where hot coffee and refreshment could be had for the men, and stabling and provender for their horses; from whence an omnibus went daily to and from the station at N——, for the convenience of Lawsleigh, and even of more distant villages, carrying passengers and parcels. The daily papers were to be had; there was also a reading-room, suitable for men of the class likely to congregate there; and it was a telegraph station, connected with Exeter, Plymouth, and the Dartmoor Prisons. The sign was a railway train, crowded with passengers, the name of the engine "The Old Packhorse!"

And so "The Old Packhorse" of the last century emerged young and gay from the ashes of the Widow Mason's cottage. And still he bears his burden cheerfully; still he brings comfort and joy to many, and, if sorrow to some, it is the lot of mortals; but, as Mr. Tremelly said to Mr. Gray, "We should never forget, or seek to put aside, 'The Old Packhorse,' the time-honoured servant of man!"

But we have neither time nor space to describe the gay doings at the opening of the new building, or the astonishment of the simple villagers of Lawsleigh. Tho vicar said, as he shook the Lord of the Manor by the hand:

"This day has exceeded my most sanguine hopes, for right good progress you have made in your present short reign!"

"And it is progress among the Tors and the Valleys," said Charlie; "the most difficult piece of civil engineering in the world!"

"I deny that," said Mr. Tremelly, "upon the principle that there can be no difficulties between friends and neighbours; for it is well known that the hills and the dales have never parted company since the world began!"

"But the hills always look down upon the dales" said Mrs. Hill, "notwithstanding their great friendship."

"I shall not bandy words with a lady," said Mr. Tremelly; "but this much I will say, in the presence of this august gathering, that my 'Parson Hill,'" patting the Vicar on the back, "is equal to any 'Parson Dale' that ever charmed a reading world!"

"Only he lives and dies in obscurity," said Charlie.

"Say, rather," said Mr. Tremelly, "he has not had the good fortune to be immortalized by the greatest writer of this or any other day!"

"We cannot have every thing, can we?" said Charlie, to the vicar.

"Send your shafts home into the very hearts of the 'Hills,' if you will!" said the vicar; "but pray allow the worthy 'Dale' to enjoy his well-deserved supremacy in peace!"

THE END